EVE

• • •

MORE DEADLY THAN THE MALE

• • •

JAMES HADLEY CHASE

INTRODUCTION BY GREGORY SHEPARD

STARK HOUSE

Stark House Press • Eureka California

EVE / MORE DEADLY THAN THE MALE

Published by Stark House Press
1315 H Street
Eureka, CA 95503, USA
griffinskye3@sbcglobal.net
www.starkhousepress.com

ISBN-13: 978-1-944520-40-3

Book design by Mark Shepard, SHEPGRAPHICS.COM

First Stark House Press Edition: August 2017

First Edition

EVE

Clive Thurston is living a lie. Having claimed a dying playwright's masterwork as his own, he is hailed as a brilliant, new author. Thurston is now living the good life in Hollywood. He has a house in the country, a manservant, a beautiful fiancée….then one night he meets Eve. Eve isn't beautiful at all, but she's got a way about her. Thurston is captivated, and in no time, he becomes obsessed. But as everybody knows, Eve is a prostitute, and his reputation around town begins to suffer. His fiancée has been patient, but she can take no more. Thurston is drinking too much, and making bad decisions.

But what he can't figure is why Eve keeps rejecting him. If he can only make Eve love him, maybe his own redemption is at hand…

MORE DEADLY THAN THE MALE

"George knew the exact moment when he fell in love with Cora Brant. At one moment Cora was just someone with whom he hoped to alleviate an hour of lonely boredom; at the next she was someone he was physically and mentally aware of in a most overpowering way. He had bought drinks, and he had been startled that she tackled a pint of beer. And when he looked more closely at her, he realized she was not immaculate in the accepted sense of the word. But George was not critical. Any woman was a novelty to him, and a girl like Cora Brant was far more than a novelty—she was an exciting experience."

George has been living in a gangster fantasy in which he is always the hero. Now he meets that world head on. George's troubles have only just begun…

THE SOFTEST WEAPON
By Gregory Shepard

James Hadley Chase dealt in desire and violence. In the noir tradition, he created characters driven by their desire for wealth and sex, who generally acted out their needs in the most expedient, self-destructive fashion. *Eve* and *More Deadly Than the Male* single out and examine the aspect of desire stripped of most of the violence, and present us with two of Chase's grimmest tales.

Eve is the story of a cad. Clive Thurston, who tells the story, is the first to admit it. In his own words:

"…because of my complete frankness, you may have come to the conclusion that I am an exceedingly unpleasant person. You may even have decided that I am unethical, dishonest, vain and worthless. These conclusions are not due to your insight and perception, they are due entirely to my own frankness."

Clive is frank all right. He admits that his entire success as a writer and playwright is due to the fact that he took credit for a dead man's play. Trouble is, he really doesn't have any talent as a writer, and guilt and insecurity have turned him into an arrogant monster. He eventually turns on everyone he knows, including his agent, and his fiancé, Carol, the only woman who really loves him.

Clive doesn't need any of them. Clive has all that he needs in Eve. Eve the prostitute. Eve the obsession. The beauty of his relationship with Eve is that she doesn't love him. She doesn't even like him. And she tells him so every chance she gets. Eve is in love with her husband, Jack. Jack—idolized Jack—who had enough of her self-obsessed ways, and left her. Which has left Eve as insecure as Clive. They are, in fact, the perfect match: two sociopaths feeding off each other's anger, insecurity and disdain.

Eve is a curious book for James Hadley Chase. He had already developed a misogynistic reputation in books like *No Orchids for Miss Blandish* and *The Dead Stay Dumb*. Now he pulls out the stops and really explores the core of a woman-hating man. Make no mistake, Clive Thurston is not a sympathetic narrator. You will find yourself despising him, hating him, and at times, you'll want someone to throw a good, solid punch at him. But there is something sad and pathetic to him as well. He wants to love. He wants the security and comfort of a relationship with Carol, the good girl in the book. But he just can't help himself—he is drawn even stronger to the bad girl, the woman who spurns him, the self-loathing prostitute.

He is drawn to his own destruction.

But, of course, Clive doesn't see it that way. Like any egotist, he wants what he wants when he wants it. And he uses every rationalization in the book to justify his actions. But Chase lets us see through him, to the coward underneath all the bravado. Some readers have found *Eve* too depressing. There is certainly that. Not everyone enjoys the tenets of noir fiction. But I might suggest that this is really the *ultimate* noir: the story of a loser whose downfall is painful to watch because it feels so real. Gil Brewer wrote many novels about men who become completely obsessed by younger women, end up committing a crime under their influence, and are left holding the bag at the end. These books allow the reader the safety of distance from the pathetic nature of the protagonist who is headed for hell.

Chase doesn't give you a crime in *Eve*. He just gives you the raw obsession. No "safety of distance" here. And he follows it right to the bitter end, to the ultimate, purging humiliation. This is what noir is really all about: the screwed getting more screwed.

You've been warned. There is no happy ending to this one. It would be interesting to know who or what inspired Chase to write *Eve*. Was he working on some private demons? Did some of the critical backlash to his first few novels make him feel like lashing out with a character who steals someone else's idea then beats himself up over it? After all, Chase had been accused of stealing ideas from authors like Raymond Chandler and William Faulkner. Maybe this was a way of dealing with his own resentment and anger at this backlash, with Eve representing his tormented muse. Or perhaps *Eve* demonstrates a bit of a self-flagellation on the part of the author.

It's an interesting thought.

And it's certainly easy to read a lot of personal issues into *Eve* because his very next novel explored this issue from another angle in the autobiographical, *More Deadly Than the Male*. This was the only book written under the Chase pseudonym of Ambrose Grant. (Of course, Chase itself is a pseudonym for the author's real name, René Lodge Brabazon Raymond, but for the sake of continuity, we will continue to refer here to the author as James Hadley Chase.) Both books were originally published in the mid-1940s, after Chase had been chastised by the courts for excessive violence in *Miss Callaghan Comes to Grief.*

Chase had exploded onto the literary scene with *No Orchids for Miss Blandish*, and followed this up with a variety of American gangster novels. *Eve,* set in Hollywood, is the first Chase book that takes place somewhere besides New York or Chicago. *More Deadly Than the Male* is the first Chase book to be actually set in the author's native England. The main character, George Fraser, is a gentle giant of a man who bolsters his shyness and fears with fantasies of being an American gangster. He entertains the woman who brings him his tea with tales of his criminal "exploits," which he pulls from the magazines he reads.

> "These stories which George recounted so glibly were the figments of his extraordinary imagination. He had never been to America, let alone seen a gangster; but, being an avid reader of the lurid American pulp magazines, and having seen every gangster film ever made, he had acquired a remarkable knowledge of American crime. The gunmen as depicted by such magazines as *Front-Page Detective* and *True Confessions* completely obsessed him."

George makes his living selling children's encyclopedias—but he's not very good at it. Fantasy meets reality head-on when he is given a new partner in the form of weasely Sydney Brant, whose abilities as a con-man make him perfect to sell door-to-door. One evening Sydney introduces George to his "sister" Cora, a fellow hustler, and it's love at first sight. Soon, George is involved in the very crimes he had only been daydreaming about before.

There really isn't another book in all of James Hadley Chase's output quite like *More Deadly Than the Male.* For an author who began his career writing about American gangsters, this one is exceedingly English. The action all takes place at the heart of London, and the only gangsters are the characters who exist in George's stories. And like Chase himself did before fame struck, the main character sells encyclopedias. The scenes of George canvassing the neighborhoods and trying to figure an angle to get his foot in the door have the ring of truth to them. You can almost imagine Chase himself —Walter Mitty-style—writing his first novel in his head as he made his door-to-door rounds.

But at the heart of this book there is also a very dangerous woman. Eve isn't dangerous except for the damage that her callousness inflicts on Clive's ego. Cora is dangerous in another sense. She knows exactly what she's doing as she manipulates George. In Cora, Chase creates a femme fatale to end all fatales. She represents, not a muse this time, but an anti-muse. Cora represents the Fear of Woman that is inherent in every painfully shy man. She isn't pretty, but she is striking. She doesn't dress well, but well enough for George. She doesn't even concern herself with personal hygiene, but her own particular womaness is a potent perfume that draws George toward her. She certainly isn't kind, but her cruelty is just what George needs to complement his own timidity.

As Chase puts it: "There was something about Cora which tortured George." And we certainly feel his pain. Inherent in his situation are both the promise, and the fear, of sex. Cora cuts him no slack either way.

Both Eve and Cora represent male fantasies, albeit negative ones. Eve is the unobtainable, and Cora the manipulative *and* the unobtainable. Both deal with the nature of obsession, and do so in a very noir way. *Eve* and *More Deadly Than the Male* are not the most violent books Chase ever wrote. Quite the opposite. But they are probably the darkest tales he ever penned. They are about the oldest battle of them all: the battle of the sexes. And the weapon this time…the softest weapon of them all.

—June 2017
Eureka, CA

EVE

. . .

JAMES HADLEY CHASE

CHAPTER ONE

Before I begin to tell you the story of my association with Eve, I must first tell you, as briefly as possible, something about myself and the events that led up to our first meeting.

Had it not been for the extraordinary change in my life at the time when I had resigned myself to the mediocre career as a shipping clerk, I would not have met Eve, and consequently, I would not have endured an experience which was ultimately responsible for spoiling my life.

Although it is now two years since last I saw Eve, I have only to think of her to feel again the craving urge and angry frustration which kept me chained to her during a period when all my energies and attention should have been focused upon my work.

It does not matter what I am doing now. No one has ever heard of me in this Pacific coast town where I came nearly two years ago after I had realized what a worthless and elusive will-o-the-wisp I had been chasing.

But it is not the present nor the future that is important. My story is to do with the past.

Although I am anxious to bring Eve upon my stage without delay, there are a few details about myself, as I have said before, that first must be told.

My name is Clive Thurston. You may have heard of me. I was supposed to be the author of that sensationally successful play *Rain Check*. Although I did not, in fact, write the play I did write three novels which were, in their way, equally successful.

Before *Rain Check* was produced I was, as I am now, a nobody. I lived in Long Beach in a large apartment house near a fish cannery where I worked as a shipping clerk.

Until John Coulson came to stay at the apartment house I lived a monotonous and unambitious existence; the kind of life that hundreds of thousands of young men lead who have no prospects and who will be doing the same work in another twenty years' time as they are doing now.

Although my life was monotonous and lonely I accepted it with apathetic resignation. I could see no escape from the routine on getting up in the morning, going to work, eating cheap meals, wondering whether I could afford this thing or that and having an occasional adventure with a woman if money allowed. There was no escape until I met John Coulson and even then it was not until he died that I saw my chance and took it.

John Coulson knew he was going to die. For three years he had been fighting tuberculosis and now he could fight no more. Like a dying animal who goes into hiding, he cut himself off from his friends and connections and came to live in the sordid apartment house in Long Beach.

There was something about him that attracted me and he seemed willing enough to share my company.

Perhaps it was because he was a writer. For a long time I had wanted to write, but the labour involved had always discouraged me. I felt that if I could once get started, my latent talents, which I was confident I possessed, would bring me fame and fortune. I suppose there are many of us who think like this, and like many of us, I lacked the initiative to begin.

John Coulson told me that he had written a play which, he assured me, was the finest thing he had ever done. I gladly listened to him, learning some surprisingly interesting things about the technique of play writing and the money that a good play will earn.

Two evenings before he died, he asked me to send his play to his agent. He was now bedridden and could do little to help himself.

"I don't think I'll live to see it produced," he said moodily, staring out of the window. "God knows who'll benefit, but that's something my agent will have to arrange. It's a damn funny thing, Thurston, but I have no one to leave anything to. I wish I had children now. It would have made all this work worthwhile."

I asked him casually whether his agent was expecting the play and he shook his head. "No one but you knows that I've even written it."

The following day was Saturday and the yearly Water Sports Carnival was being held at Alamitos Bay. I went down to the beach with the thousands of other weekenders to watch the yacht racing.

I disliked mixing with crowds, but it was obvious that Coulson was sinking and I felt I had to get away from the atmosphere of pending death that pervaded the house.

I arrived at the harbour as the tiny yachts were being prepared for the most important race of the afternoon. The prize was a gold cup, and competition ran high.

One particular yacht attracted my attention. She was a grand little boat with bright red sails and her lines were designed for speed. There were two men working on her. One, whom I gave only a cursory glance, was a typical longshoreman, but the other was obviously the owner. He was expensively dressed in white flannels and buckskin shoes and around his wrist I noticed a heavy gold bracelet. His big fleshy face had that arrogant expression which comes only from much wealth and power. He stood by the tiller, a cigar clamped between his teeth, watching the other man put the final touches to the boat. I wondered who he was and decided finally that he might either be a movie director or else an oil magnate.

After watching him for a few minutes, I moved away only to turn back at the sound of a heavy fall and a shout of alarm.

The longshoreman had slipped and was now lying in the harbour with a badly fractured leg.

The accident was immediately responsible for my extraordinary change of fortune. I had some experience of handling yachts and I volunteered to take the longshoreman's place and by doing so I shared the honours with the owner of winning the gold cup.

It was only after the race that the owner of the yacht introduced himself to me. When he told me his name I did not at first realize my good fortune. Robert Rowan was, at that time, one of the most powerful men behind the Theatre Guild. He owned eight or nine theatres and he had a long string of theatrical successes behind him.

He was childishly pleased to have won the cup and embarrassingly grateful for my help. He gave me his card and solemnly promised that if there was anything he could do for me he would do it.

You can now probably see the temptation that lay ahead of me. On my return to the apartment I found Coulson was unconscious; the next day he was dead. His play, ready to be mailed to his agent, lay on my bureau. I did not hesitate for long. Coulson had admitted that he knew of no one who would benefit by the play and I had felt at the time that he might at least have thought of me. It took me only a few minutes to reason with my protesting conscience and then I opened the parcel and read the play.

Although I knew little about play writing, I realized when I had finished it, that the play was outstanding. I sat for a long time considering the chances of detection, but I could see no danger at all. Then before I went to bed I substituted a new title page and cover to the manuscript. Instead of *Boomerang* by John Coulson, the title page now read, *Rain Check* by Clive Thurston. The following day I sent the play to Rowan.

It was almost a year before *Rain Check* was produced. By that time many alterations had been made to the original script as Rowan liked to have his personality impressed upon any theatrical venture that he financed. But in that time, I had become quite used to the feeling that the play was mine and when it was finally produced, scoring an immediate success, I was genuinely proud of my achievement.

It is a great feeling to walk into a crowded room and have someone introduce you and see by the people's faces that you mean something to them. Anyway, it meant a lot to me. It meant a lot too when I began to receive large sums of money, where previously I had to manage on forty dollars a week.

When I was assured that the play would enjoy a long run, I left New York for Hollywood. I felt that with my present reputation I should be in demand and perhaps establish myself as a top flight script writer. As I was now drawing almost two thousand dollars a week from royalties, I did not hesitate to take an apartment in a modern block off Sunset Boulevard,

Once I had settled down, I determined to exploit my opportunities and after considerable thought and planning I began work on a novel. It was a story of a man who had been hurt in the war and could not love his girl. I had known such a case and I knew what had happened to the girl. It was explosive material and it had made a big impression on me. Somehow I managed to get that impression over in the book. My name helped it, of course, but even at that, it wasn't such a bad piece of work. It sold ninety-seven thousand copies and was still selling by the time my second book was on the market. This one was not so good, but it sold. It was my first attempt at creative writing which I found exceedingly difficult. My third novel was based on the lives of a married couple I knew intimately. The wife had behaved outrageously and I had felt very bad about the final break up. All I had to do was to sit at my typewriter. The book wrote itself and when it was published it scored an immediate success.

I was sure after this that I had the golden touch. I told myself that I could have succeeded without John Coulson's play. I marvelled at my stupidity to have wasted so many years of my life on an office stool when I could have been writing and earning big money.

A few months later, I decided I would have to write a play. *Rain Check* had finished playing on Broadway and was now touring. It was still doing excellent business, but I knew that before long I would be receiving smaller royalties and I did not wish to lower my present standard of living. Besides that, my friends were asking me when I was going to write for the theatre again and my constant excuses were becoming threadbare.

When I began to plan a play I found I had no ideas that could be dramatized. I kept trying. I talked to people, but in Hollywood, no one gives away ideas. I thought and worried, but nothing came. Finally I said the hell with a play, and decided to write another novel. So I sat down at my typewriter and wrote another novel. I just cut into it and kept writing until I finished it. Then I sent it to my publisher.

Two weeks later, my publisher asked me to lunch. He was very direct and said bluntly that the book was no good. He did not have to convince me. I knew that the book was no good the moment I had finished it. So I told him to forget the book. I explained that I had rushed it, that I had been constantly interrupted and that I would let him have something up to standard in a month or so.

I began to hunt for a place where I could work without interruption. I told myself that if I could get away from the mob that demanded my time and attention, if I could find some quiet spot with a good view so that I could get my nerves right, I would write another best seller, and even a great play. I was so sure of myself now that I was certain that, given the right surroundings, I could do really good work. Eventually I found a place that I felt was ideal in every way.

Three Point was a one storey cabin which lay back a few hundred yards from the road to Big Bear Lake. It had a wide porch and a magnificent view across the hills. It had been furnished with every conceivable luxury and a number of modern labour saving devices had been installed, including a small, but powerful generating plant. I was delighted to hire it for the summer.

I hoped that Three Point would be my salvation, but it didn't work out that way. I would get up around nine o'clock and sit on the porch with a pot of strong coffee at my elbow and my typewriter before me. I would stare at the view and get nowhere. I would spend the morning smoking, looking at the view, writing a few lines and tearing them up. In the afternoon I would take the car over to Los Angeles, where I would wander around talking to the movie writers and watching the film stars. In the evening, I would try again, get irritated and finish off the evening by going to bed.

It was during this crisis of my career, when success or failure could be influenced by the slightest mental disturbance, that Eve came into my life. Her influence became so great that I was drawn to her as a pin is drawn to a giant magnet. She never knew the real extent of her power over me and if she had known, she would not have cared. Her arrogant indifference was the hardest part of her character I had to endure. Whenever I was with her, I had an overwhelming urge to obtain some moral surrender from her, to make her give up the secret strength that she had. The struggle between us was an infernal obsession with me.

But this is enough. My stage is set and my story can begin. I have long planned to write it. I have tried before and failed. This time I may succeed.

It may be that if this book is ever published, it will find its way into Eve's hands. I can imagine her lying in bed, a cigarette between her fingers, reading what I have written. Because her life is peopled by so many unidentified men, who must inevitably be shadowy figures in her mind, she will have forgotten most, if not all, of the things we did together. It may interest her to re-live the futile moments of our association and it may also give her confidence in her strength and ability to continue to stand alone. At least, she will learn when she has reached the end of my story that I have probed deeper into her life than she imagined, and, in stripping some of the camouflage from her, I have also stripped myself.

And when she has reached the last page, I can imagine her, with that contemptuous, wooden expression on her face I have seen so often, tossing the book indifferently aside.

CHAPTER TWO

At a gas station in San Bernardino, they told me there was a tornado warning out.

The attendant, in smart white overalls with a red triangular badge on his breast pocket, advised me to stay in San Bernardino for the night, but I wouldn't listen.

When I got into the hills, it began to blow. I kept going and a mile further on the stars were blotted out and then torrential rain came down like a black steel curtain shutting in the night with mist and water.

All I could see through the half crescent clearing made by the windshield wiper was the rebounding rain on the car's hood and a few feet of the shiny black road in the light of my headlights.

The noise of the wind and the rain against the car made me feel that I was imprisoned in a giant drum upon which some lunatic drummer was beating. All around me came the sound of trees falling and rocks shifting, and above all this, the noise of water against the wheels of the car. Rain flowed down the side windows and reflected my face, lit by the yellow light from the dashboard.

Then I nearly ran off the road. I had the hillside on my left and nothing but a clean drop into the valley on my right. My heart raced as I wrenched at the driving wheel and I fed more gas into the engine. The wind was so fierce that there was hardly any increase in the car's speed. The needle of the speedometer flickered between ten and fifteen miles an hour which seemed to be the best speed I could squeeze out of the engine.

Coming slowly around the next bend, I saw two men standing in the middle of the road. They had lanterns and they wore black slickers that shone in the rain and lantern light.

I slowed down to a crawl as one of them came over.

"Why, hello, Mr. Thurston," he said, rain from his hat dripping onto my sleeve, "Making for Three Point?"

I recognized him. "Hello, Tom," I said. "Can I get through?"

"I don't say you won't make it." His face was the colour of bruised meat from the wind and the rain. "It'll be bad though. Maybe you'd better go back."

I started the engine. "I'll take a chance. Do you think the road's open?"

"A big Packard went through two hours ago. It ain't come back. Maybe it's still all right, but you'd better watch out. The wind up there'll be hell."

"If a Packard can get through, I'm damned sure I can," I said and wound up the window and drove on.

I drove around the next sharp bend and edged up the hill, keeping close to the mountain-side. A few more minutes' driving brought me to the narrow mountain track that led through to Big Bear Lake.

The forest stopped abruptly at the foot of the track, and, except for a few jagged boulders on the mountainside, the rest of the track to Big Bear Lake was bare and exposed.

The wind crashed against the car as I drove out of the shelter of the trees. I felt the car rock. The outside wheels lifted a few inches before thudding back onto the road. I cursed. If that had happened when I was pulling around a bend, I would have been flung into the valley. I shifted into low gear and decreased my speed. Twice the car was brought to a standstill by a sudden gust of wind. Each time the engine stalled and I had to act quickly to stop from rolling backwards.

My nerves were badly frayed by the time I reached the crest of the hill. The rain drove against the windshield and I had to lean out of the window to see where I was going. The road was not more than twenty feet wide and I rounded the next bend more by luck than judgment with the wind tearing at the car, shaking and lifting it. Once around the bend, I found shelter. The rain continued to drum on the roof of the car, but I felt easier, knowing that the rest of the run was downhill, out of the wind.

Three Point was only a few miles further on and although I knew the worst part of the journey was over I continued to drive with caution. It was as well for, without warning, a stationary car suddenly appeared in my headlights and I only managed to slam on my brakes in time. The wheels locked and for one unpleasant moment, I thought I was going to skid off the road; then my bumpers hit the back of the other car and

I was thrown forward against the driving wheel.

Cursing the fool who had left this car in the middle of the road without a warning light I stood on the running board of my car while I groped for my flashlight. Rain poured down on me and before stepping to the ground, I turned the light down to see where I was going. Water was up to my hub caps and sending the beam of the flashlight over to the other car, I now realized why it had been left like that. Water was up to the front wheels and had probably got into the distributor.

I could not understand why there was a miniature lake in a road, which, I knew, went steeply downhill for the next few miles. Cautiously, I lowered myself into the water which rose to my calves. Gluey mud sucked at my shoes as I splashed over to the other car. By now, the rain had reduced my hat to irritating sogginess. Impatiently, I pulled it off and threw it away.

When I got over to the stationary car, I peered through the windows. It was empty. I climbed on its running board and worked my way towards the front of it so that I could see the road beyond. The beam from my flashlight showed me that the road had ceased to exist. Trees, boulders and mud completely blocked the track, forming a kind of dam.

The car was a Packard and I decided that this must be the car Tom had told me about.

There was nothing for me to do but walk. I went back to my car and lifted out the smaller of my two bags. I locked the car doors, climbed past the Packard and splashed through the water to the jungle of trees and rocks that blocked the road. Once out of the water, I continued to climb without difficulty. I soon reached the top of the rubble and could look down onto the road below which was, as far as I could see, clear of any further obstruction,

The climb down was more difficult and once I nearly fell. I had to drop my bag and clutch frantically at the roots of a tree to save myself and there was more delay before I found my bag again. But finally I reached the road.

Once past the obstruction, my progress was straightforward and in ten minutes or so, I reached the white gates of Three Point. I had not gone far up the drive before I saw a light in the sitting room. I immediately thought of the driver of the Packard and wondered a little angrily how he had got into the cabin.

I approached cautiously, anxious to catch a glimpse of my visitor before I made my own presence known. In the shelter of the porch, I put down my bag and peeled off my soaking wet bush jacket which I tossed onto the wooden bench against the log wall. I walked slowly to the window and looked into the lighted room. Whoever had broken into the cabin had lit a fire which blazed cheerfully. The room was empty, but as I stood hesitating, a man came in from the kitchen, carrying a bottle of my Scotch, two glasses and a syphon.

I looked at him with interest. He was short, but his chest and shoulders were powerful. He had mean blue eyes and the longest arms I had ever seen on anything more civilized than an orang-outan. I disliked him on sight.

He stood in front of the fire and measured out two stiff whiskies. One glass he put on the mantelpiece, the other he raised to his lips. He tasted the Scotch as if he were a connoisseur and was a little doubtful of this particular brand. I watched him roll the whisky round in his mouth, cock his head and eye the whisky thoughtfully. Then he nodded, apparently satisfied, and gulped down the rest of it. Having refilled his glass, he sat down in the armchair by the fire with the bottle on the table within reach.

I guessed he was on the wrong side of forty. He didn't look like the kind of man to own a Packard. His suit was a little shabby and his taste in ties and shirts, to judge from what he wore, was violent. I heartily disliked the prospects of spending the night in his company.

The second whisky on the mantelpiece also disturbed me. It could only mean that this intruder had a companion and I was in half a mind to remain where I was until this other person appeared. However, the wind and my wet clothes decided me. I wasn't going to stand out there any longer. I picked up my bag and walked around to the front door. The door was locked. I took out my keys, opened the door noiselessly and entered the lobby. I put my bag down and as I stood hesitating, wondering whether to go into the sitting room and make myself known or to go straight to the bathroom, the man appeared at the sitting room door.

He stared at me in ugly surprise. "What the hell do you want?" His voice was coarse and rasping.

I looked him over. "Good evening. I hope I'm not in the way, but I happen to own this place."

I expected him to collapse like a pricked balloon, but he became even more aggressive. His mean little eyes snapped at me and two veins at his temples began to swell.

"You mean this is your cabin?" he demanded.

I nodded. "Don't let it embarrass you. Have a drink—you'll find whisky in the kitchen. I'll run along and take a bath, but I'll be right back."

Leaving him staring blankly after me, I walked into my bedroom and shut the door. Then I became really infuriated.

Across the room, like stepping stones, lay various feminine garments; a black silk dress, lingerie, stockings, and finally at the bathroom door, a pair of black suede, mud-covered shoes.

A pigskin suitcase lay open on the bed from which spilled other feminine garments. A blue tailored dressing gown with short sleeves was draped over a chair before the electric heater.

I stood staring at this disorder, angry beyond words, but before I could do anything—I was on the point of walking into the bathroom and expressing an opinion of such bad manners—the bedroom door opened and the man came in.

I turned on him. "What's all this?" I asked, waving my hands at the scattered garments on the floor and the confusion on the bed. "Did you imagine this was a hotel?"

He fingered his tie uneasily. "Now, don't be sore. We found the place empty and—"

"All right, all right," I snapped, fighting down my annoyance. It was really no use making a fuss. They happened to be unlucky that I had returned. "You certainly know how to make yourself at home," I went on. "But never mind. I'm wet and irritable. It's a hell of a night, isn't it? Excuse me, I'll use the spare bathroom." I pushed past him and walked down the passage to the guest room.

"I'll fix you a drink," he called after me.

I liked that too. To have a stranger offer me my own Scotch is something I go for in a big way. I slammed the bedroom door and got out of my wet clothes.

After a hot bath, I felt better. After a shave, I felt sufficiently human to wonder what the woman would be like. But my mind recoiled when I thought of the man. If she were anything like him, I was in for an indescribable evening.

I put on a grey whipcord, fixed my hair and glanced at myself in the mirror. I did not look my forty years. Most people thought I was in my early thirties. All right, I was flattered by this. I'm as human as they come. I looked at my square jaw, my high cheekbones and the cleft in my chin. I was satisfied with what I saw. I was tall, rather on the thin side, but my suit fitted me excellently. I could still qualify as a distinguished playwright and novelist, although that was a tag a newspaper had yet to put on me.

I paused as I reached the sitting room door, The man's voice came faintly through the panels of the door, but I could not hear what he was saying, Squaring my shoulders and settling the casual, disinterested expression on my face that I reserved for press meetings, I turned the knob and went in.

CHAPTER THREE

I saw the woman, slight and dark haired, squatting on her heels before the fire. She had on the short-sleeved dressing gown that had been on the chair in my bedroom. Although she must have known that I had entered the room, she did not look round. As she held her hands towards the fire I saw her wedding ring. I also noticed that her shoulders were a shade wider than her hips and that is the way I like a woman to be built.

I did not mind her ignoring my entrance. I did not mind the wedding ring. But I did mind the dressing gown.

No woman looks her best in a dressing gown. Even if she did not know who I was, she might at least have dressed. It did not occur to me that she might not give a damn how she looked. I was judging her by the standards of the other women I knew. They would prefer me to see them naked than in a dressing gown.

With my reputation, looks and money, it was inevitable that women should spoil me. At first I enjoyed their attentions although I knew that the majority of them treated me as they treated any other eligible bachelor in Hollywood. They wanted me for my money, my name, my parties and for everything except myself.

Most women, if they had the right appeal, interested me. Good-looking, well-dressed women were an essential part of my background. They stimulated me, they were my recreation and they bolstered up my ego. I liked to have them around as some people like having good pictures on their walls. But, lately, they bored me. I found that my relations with them had developed into a series of strategical moves, in which both sides were expert, to obtain, on their part, the maximum entertainment, presents and attention, and on my part, a few hours of disillusioned rapture.

Carol was the one exception. We had met in New York when I was waiting for *Rain Check* to be produced. She was, at that time, Robert Rowan's personal secretary. She liked me and, oddly enough, I liked her. It was she who had encouraged me to go to Hollywood where she was now working as script writer for International Pictures.

I doubt if I am capable of loving any woman for long. In a way, I suppose, I should be pitied for this, as obviously there must be many advantages in which seems to me to be the stale routine of having one woman at your side for the rest of your days. If there are no advantages, then why do so many people marry? I feel then, that I have been cheated of something because I am not like the ordinary man in the street.

There was a time, before I came to Hollywood, when I did seriously consider marrying Carol. I enjoyed her company and considered her more intelligent than any other woman I knew.

But Carol was busy at the Studios and we seldom met during the day. I had a lot of women on my hands and my time was taken up not only during the day, but most nights as well. Carol kidded me about these women, but she didn't seem to mind. It was only when I was a little drunk one night and told her that I loved her that she gave herself away. She may have been a little drunk too, but I do not think so. For a couple of weeks, I felt like a heel when I went around with another woman, but after that, I stopped worrying. I suppose I became used to the idea that Carol loved me, in the same way as I became used to most things if they lasted long enough.

While I was looking at the woman, the man, who had been fixing drinks at the sideboard came over and gave me a Scotch and soda. He looked a little drunk and now that we were in a good light, I saw he needed a shave.

"I'm Barrow," he said, breathing whisky fumes in my face. "Harvey Barrow. I'm certainly embarrassed busting in like this, but there was nothing else I could do." He stood close to me, his thick set body between me and the woman by the fire.

I was not interested in him. I would not have noticed if he had dropped dead at my feet. I moved a few paces back so I could see the woman. She stayed by the fire as if she did not know I was in the room and oddly enough I found her attitude of deliberate indifference pleasantly exciting.

Barrow tapped my arm. I took my eyes off the woman and concentrated on him. He kept apologizing for breaking into my cabin so I told him curtly that it was all right and that I would have done the same thing myself if I had been in his place. Then casually I introduced myself, keeping my voice low so that the woman should not hear me. If she wanted to make an impression on me I would keep my identity from her to the last moment and then enjoy the look of dismay that would be certain to come when she realized whom she had been ignoring.

I had to repeat my name twice before he got it and, even then, it did not mean anything to him. I actually helped him by adding "the author", but I could see he had never heard of me. He was the kind of stupid ignoramus who has never heard of anyone. From that moment I was through with him.

"Glad to meet you," he said solemnly, shaking my hand. "It's pretty nice of you not to get sore. Some guys would have kicked me out."

Nothing would have pleased me more, but I said untruthfully, "That's all right," and locked past him at the woman. "Tell me, is your wife frigid, a deaf-mute or just coy?"

He followed my glance and his coarse, red face tightened. "This puts me in a bit of a jam, ol' boy," he said, his voice a mumble in my ear. "She ain't my wife and she's as mad as hell. She got wet and a dame like her doesn't like getting wet."

"I see." I felt suddenly disgusted. "Well, never mind. I want to meet her," and I walked over to the fire and stood close to the woman.

She turned her head, looked at my feet and then looked abruptly up at me.

I smiled. "Hello," I said.

"Hello," she returned and looked back into the fire.

I had only one brief glance at her heart-shaped face with its firm mouth, stubborn chin and strangely disconcerting eyes. But it was enough. I had a sudden stifled feeling, the kind of feeling you get when on top of a high mountain, and I knew what that meant.

It wasn't that she was pretty. She was, if anything, plain, but there was something magnetic about her that stirred me. Perhaps magnetic was not quite the right word. I instinctively knew that behind her mask she was primitively bad and there was something almost animal in her make-up. Just to look at her was like getting a jolt of electricity.

I decided that, after all, the evening was not going to be so bad. In fact, it looked as if it were going to exceedingly interesting.

"Won't you have a drink?" I asked, hoping that she would look up again, but she didn't. She lowered herself to the carpet and tucked her legs under her.

"I have one." She pointed to the glass that stood near her in the hearth.

Barrow came over. "This is Eve ... Eve ..." and he floundered, his face reddening.

"Marlow," the woman said, her fist clenched tightly in her lap.

"Yeah," Barrow said quickly. "I've a lousy memory for names." He looked at me and I could see he had already forgotten mine. I was not going to help him. If a man could not remember the name of his mistress then to hell with him.

"So you got wet," I said to the woman and laughed.

She looked up. I don't believe in first impressions, but I knew she was a rebel. I knew she had a hell of a temper, swift, violent and uncontrolled. Although she was slight, her whole make-up—her eyes, the way she held herself, her expression—gave the impression of strength. She had two deep furrows above the bridge of her nose. They were responsible to some degree for the character in her face, and could only have come from worry and much suffering. I became intensely curious to know more about her.

"I did get wet," she said and laughed too.

Her laugh startled me. It was unexpectedly pleasing as well as infectious. When she laughed, she glanced up and her expression altered, the hard lines went away and she looked younger. It was difficult to guess her age. Somewhere in the thirties; maybe thirty-eight, maybe thirty-three; when she laughed, she could have been twenty-five.

Barrow looked a little sick. He eyed us both suspiciously. He had reason. If he listened carefully he would have heard my glands working.

"I got wet too," I said, sitting down in the armchair close to her. "If I'd known it was going to be as bad as this, I would have spent the night in San Bernardino. I'm certainly glad now I didn't." They both gave me a quick look. "Have you come far?"

There was a pause. Eve looked into the fire. Barrow rolled his glass between his thick fingers. You could almost hear him think. "Los Angeles," he said, at last.

"I get around Los Angeles quite a bit," I said, speaking to Eve. "How come I've never seen you before?"

She gave me a hard, blank stare and then looked quickly away. "I don't know," she said.

Perhaps Barrow saw what I was going to do, for he suddenly finished his whisky and tapped Eve on her shoulder.

"You'd better go to bed," he said in a domineering voice.

I thought if she has got what I think she has then she'll tell him to go to hell; but she didn't. "All right," she said indifferently and rolled onto her knees.

"You mustn't go yet," I said. "Aren't you two hungry? I have some stuff in the ice box that wants eating. What do you say?"

Barrow was watching Eve with uneasy, possessive eyes. "We had dinner at Glendora on our way up. She'd better go ... she must be tired."

I looked at him and laughed, but he wouldn't play. He stared down at his empty glass, veins throbbing in his temples.

Eve stood up. She was even smaller and slighter than I had first supposed. Her head barely reached my shoulder.

"Where do I sleep?" she asked. Her eyes looked over my shoulder.

"Please keep the room you're in now. I'll use the guest room. But, if you don't really want to go to bed, just yet, I'd be glad to have you stay."

"I want to go." She was half-way to the door.

When she had gone, I said, "I'll see if she has everything," and followed her out before Barrow could move.

She was standing by the electric heater, her hands behind her head. She stretched, yawned and when she saw me in the doorway, her mouth pursed and a calculating expression came into her eyes.

"Have you everything you need?" I asked, smiling at her. "Sure you won't have something to eat?"

She laughed. I had a suspicion that she was mocking me and she knew why I was so concerned for her comfort. I hoped that she did know, because it would save time and dispense with the preliminary advances.

"I don't want anything ... thank you."

"Well, if you're sure, but I want you to feel at home. This is the first time I've had a woman in my cabin, so it's kind of an occasion." I knew I had made a mistake as soon as I had spoken.

The smile immediately went from her eyes and the cold quizzing look came back. "Oh?" she said, moving to the bed. She took a pink silk night dress out of her grip and tossed it carelessly onto the chair.

She knew I was lying and the way her expression changed told me she expected me to be a liar anyway. This annoyed me. "Is that hard to believe?" I asked, stepping further into the room.

She bundled various garments scattered on the bed into her bag and then moved it onto the floor. "Is what hard to believe?" she asked, going to the dressing table.

"That I don't have women here?"

"It's nothing to me who you have here, is it?"

Of course she was right, but I was irritated by her indifference. "Put like that," I said, feeling snubbed, "I suppose it isn't."

She patted her hair absently and looked hard at herself in the mirror. I felt that she had forgotten that I was in the room.

"You'd better let me have your wet clothes," I said. "I'll put them in the kitchen to dry."

"I can take care of them." She turned abruptly away from the mirror and pulled her dressing gown more closely to her. The two furrows above the bridge of her nose were knitted in a frown. But, in spite of her plainness, and she looked very plain with that wooden look on her face, she intrigued me.

She glanced at the door and then at me. She did this twice before it dawned on me that she was silently telling me to go. It was a new experience for me and I did not like it.

"I want to go to bed ... if you don't mind," she said and turned away from me.

No gratitude, no thanks, no question about taking my room, just a cool, deliberate brush-off.

Barrow was fixing himself a drink when I entered the sitting room. He lurched unsteadily as he made his way back to the arm-chair. He sat down and stared up at me, screwing up his eyes to see me more clearly. "Don't get ideas about her," he said, suddenly banging his fist down on the armchair. "You lay off. Do you understand?"

I stared at him. "Are you talking to me?" I said, outraged that he dared to take such an attitude.

His red face sagged a little. "You leave her alone," he mumbled. "She's mine for tonight. I know what you're up to, but let me tell you something." He edged forward and pointed a stumpy finger at me, his slack mouth working. "I've bought her. She cost me a hundred bucks. Do you hear? I've bought her! So keep off the grass."

I didn't believe him. "You couldn't buy a woman like that. Not a down-at-the-heel punk like you."

He slopped whisky over the carpet. "What was that?" He looked up at me with watery, mean eyes.

"I said you couldn't buy a woman like that because you're a down-at-the-heel punk."

"You'll be sorry for that," he said. The two veins in his temple beat faster. "As soon as I saw you, I knew you'd start trouble. You're going to try to take her from me, aren't you?"

I grinned at him. "Why not? There's nothing you can do about it, is there?"

"But I've bought her, damn you," he exclaimed, punching the arm of the chair. "Don't you know what that means? She's mine for tonight. Can't you act like a gentleman?"

I still didn't believe him. "Let's have her in," I said, laughing at him. "After all, a hundred dollars isn't a great deal of money. I might offer more."

He struggled out of his chair. He was drunk, but there was a lot of weight in his shoulders. If he caught me when I wasn't ready for him, he might do me some damage. I backed away.

"Now don't get excited," I said, giving ground as he crowded me. "We can settle this without fighting about it. Let's get her in …"

"She's had a hundred bucks from me," he said, speaking in a low furious voice. "I've waited eight weeks for this. When I asked her to come away with me she said all right. But when I went to her place her goddam maid said she was out. Four times she pulled that trick on me and each time I knew she was upstairs laughing at me and watching me from her window. But I wanted her. I was a sucker, see? I raised the price every time I called. And she came when I said a hundred bucks. It was all right until you turned up. Neither you nor any other monkey will stop me now."

He made me feel a little sick. I still only half believed him, but I was certain I could not have him in the cabin any longer. He had to go.

I took out my wallet and tossed a hundred dollar note at his feet. As an afterthought I added another ten. "Get out," I said. "There's your money with interest."

He stared down at the money, blood leaving his face. He made a soft choking noise as if he were trying to clear the phlegm in his throat. Then he raised his face and I saw I had a fight on my hands. I did not want to fight him, but if he wanted it that way, he could have it.

He shuffled toward me, his long arms held forward as if he were going to tackle me. When he was within reach, he made a grab at me. I did not avoid him, but stepped close and slammed my fist in his face and ripped down. The big signet ring I wore on my little finger ploughed a furrow in his cheek. He rocked back with a grunting gasp and I hit him again on the bridge of his nose. He went down heavily on his hands and knees. Then I walked over to him and deliberately taking aim, I kicked him under his chin. His head snapped back and he collapsed on the carpet. He was finished and he hadn't even touched me.

Eve stood in the doorway watching. Her eyes were wide with surprise.

I smiled at her. "It's all right," I said, blowing on my knuckles. "Go back to bed. He's leaving in a moment."

"You didn't have to kick him," she said coldly.

"No." I liked the flash of anger in her eyes. "I shouldn't have done that. I guess I got mad. I wish you'd go away."

She went then and I heard the bedroom door close.

Barrow sat up shakily and put his hand to his face. Blood ran down his fingers onto his cuff. He looked at it stupidly and then touched his throat.

I sat on the table and watched him. "You've got a two mile walk to Big Bear Lake. You can't miss the road. Just keep straight on downhill. There's a hotel before you reach the lake. They'll put you up. Now, beat it."

He did something I hadn't expected from him. He put his hands to his face and wept. That told me he was yellow right through.

"Get up and beat it," I said in disgust. "You make me sick."

He got up and moved to the door. His arm was across his eyes and he was snivelling like a kid who's hurt.

I picked up the hundred and ten dollar bills and shoved them into his top pocket.

He actually thanked me. He was as yellow as that.

I took him to the front door, gave him his bag that stood in the lobby and shoved him into the rain.

"I don't like your kind," I said, "so keep out of my way." I watched him move down the stoop, then the rain and the wind and the dark closed around him.

I shut and locked the door and stood in the lobby. I had a tight feeling in my chest and head and I badly wanted a drink. But there was one thing I had to know which wouldn't wait for a drink. I went to my bedroom and pushed open the door.

Eve stood by the dressing table, her arms locked tightly across her breasts. Her eyes were watchful.

"He's gone," I said, remaining in the doorway. "I gave him the hundred dollars you owed him and he actually thanked me."

There was no change in her expression, nor did she say anything. She had the stillness of a cornered, dangerous animal.

I eyed her. "Don't you feel sorry for him?"

Her mouth tightened in contempt. "Why should I feel sorry for any man?"

When she said that I knew what she was. I didn't have to kid myself any longer. I really hadn't thought that Barrow was lying. The stuff about the maid and how he had bargained was too smooth to be a lie. I was hoping it was a lie, but now, I knew it wasn't.

So she was anybody's woman. No one would have known it to look at her. She had ignored me. She—a woman who was looked upon by society as an outcast—had had the audacity to ignore me. I suddenly wanted to hurt her as I never had wanted to hurt anyone before.

"He told me he'd bought you," I said, moving into the room and closing the door. "You're very deceptive, aren't you? You know I really didn't think you would be for sale. A hundred dollars, wasn't it? Well, I've taken you over, only don't think I am paying any more. I'm not, because I can't imagine you could be worth more than a hundred dollars to me."

She didn't move nor did her wooden expression change. Her eyes were a shade darker and the sides of her nostrils had gone white. She leaned against the dressing table, one small white hand playing with a heavy brass ashtray that happened to be at her side.

I walked over to her. "It's no use looking at me like that. I'm not afraid of you. Come on, show me what you can do."

As I reached out for her, she suddenly whipped up the ashtray and smashed it down on my head.

CHAPTER FOUR

It is true to say that most men lead two lives—a normal life and a secret life. Society is, of course, only able to judge a man's character by his normal life. If he makes a mistake, however, and his secret life becomes public property, then he is judged by his own secret standards and is, more often than not, ostracized as a punishment. In spite of this, he is still the same man who, a moment before, received the plaudits of Society. At least, he is the same man with the one important difference: he has been found out.

By now, because of my complete frankness, you may have come to the conclusion that I am an exceedingly unpleasant person. You may even have decided that I am unethical, dishonest, vain and worthless. These conclusions are not due to your insight and perception, they are due entirely to my own frankness.

If you met me socially, if you became my friend, you would find me quite as agreeable as any one of your other friends because I should be most careful always to be at my best in your company.

I would not bother with such an elementary point as this if it were not for the fact that you may wonder why Carol loved me. Even now I remember her with deep attachment. She was a person of great sincerity and integrity. I would not like you to judge her by my standards because she loved me.

Carol knew only that part of my nature that I chose to reveal to her. Towards the end of our association, circumstances became so difficult to control that she did finally discover my faults. But up to that time, I hoodwinked her as successfully as some of you are hoodwinking those who love you.

It was because Carol was always understanding and sympathetic that, after staying two days at Three Point, following the night I first met Eve, I drove into Hollywood to see her.

The service station at San Bernardino had taken care of my car. They had told me that they had also taken care of the Packard. As I drove down the hill road from Big Bear Lake, I came upon a gang of men working on the obstruction in the road. They had nearly cleared it, but I had some difficulty in passing. The foreman of the gang knew me and he had planks laid across the soft ground and a bunch of men practically carried the car over.

I reached Carol's apartment off Sunset Strip about seven o'clock.

Frances, her maid, told me she had only just returned from the Studios and was changing.

"But come right in, Mr. Thurston," she said, beaming at me. "She won't be but a few minutes."

I followed her ample form into Carol's living room. It was a nice room, modern and quiet and the concealed lighting was restful. I wandered around while Frances fixed me a highball. She always made a fuss over me and Carol had once laughingly told me that Frances considered me her most distinguished visitor.

I sat down and admired the room. It was simply furnished. The chairs and large settee were of grey suede and the hangings were wine coloured.

"Every time I come into this room," I said, taking the highball Frances offered me, "I like it better. I must ask Miss Rae to get me out some designs for my place."

Carol came in while I was speaking. She was wearing a foamy negligée, caught in at her waist by a broad red sash, and her hair was dressed loosely to her shoulders.

I thought she looked pretty good. She wasn't a beauty—at least, she wasn't stamped from the Hollywood mould. She reminded me, as she came in, of Hepburn. She was the same build, nicely put together with the right things in the right places. Her complexion was pale which offset her scarlet lips and her skin seemed to have been pulled too tightly across her face, revealing the bone structure. Her eyes, her best feature, were big, intelligent and alive.

"Why, hello, Clive," she said gaily, coming swiftly across the room. She held a cigarette in an eighteen-inch holder. The long holder was her only mannerism. It was a clever one because it showed off her beautiful hands and wrists. "Where have you been these last three days?" Then she paused and looked questioningly at my bruised forehead. "What have you been doing?"

I took her hands. "Fighting a wild woman," I said, smiling down at her.

"I might have guessed that," she said, glancing at my knuckles, still skinned from the punch I'd given Barrow. "She must have been a very wild woman."

"Oh, she was," I said, leading her to the settee. "The wildest woman in California. I've come all the way from Three Point to tell you about her."

Carol settled herself in the corner of the settee and drew her legs up under her.

"I think I'll have a highball," she said to Frances. A little of her gaiety had gone from her eyes. "I have a feeling Mr. Thurston's going to shock me."

"Nonsense," I said. "I hope to interest you, but that's all. I'm the one who's shocked." I sat down by her side and took her hand. "Have you been working very hard today? There are smudges under your eyes. They suit you, of course, but do they mean tears and toil or are you, at last, becoming dissolute?"

Carol sighed. "I've been working. I have no time to be dissolute and I'm sure I'd be very bad at it. I am never any good at anything that doesn't interest me." She took the highball from Frances and smiled her thanks.

Frances went away.

"Now," she went on, "tell me about your wild woman. Are you in love with her?"

I looked at her sharply. "Why do you think I must fall in love with every woman I meet? I'm in love with you."

"So you are." She patted my hand. "I must remember that. Only, after three days without seeing you, I was wondering if you had dropped me. So you're not in love with her?"

"Don't be tiresome. Carol," I said, not liking her mood. "I'm most certainly not in love with her," and settling back against the cushions I told her about the storm, Barrow and Eve. But, I didn't give her all the details.

"Well, go on," she said as I paused to finger the bruise on my forehead. "After she had laid you out, what did she do? Pour water over you or skip with your wallet?"

"She skipped without my wallet. She didn't take a thing ... she wasn't the type. Don't get this woman wrong, Carol, she isn't the usual kind of hustler."

"They seldom are," Carol murmured smiling at me.

I ignored that. "While I was unconscious, she must have dressed, packed her grip and gone off into the storm. That was quite a thing to do ... it was blowing and raining like hell."

Carol studied my face. "After all, Clive, even a hustler has her pride. You were rather beastly to her. In a way, I admire her for knocking you on your conceited head. Who was the man, do you suppose?"

"Barrow? I have no idea. He looked like a travelling salesman. Just the kind of jerk who'd pay a woman to go out with him."

I hadn't told Carol about giving Barrow the hundred and ten dollars. I didn't think she'd understand that part of the story.

"I suppose you didn't want to get rid of him so you could have a heart to heart chat with the lady?"

I felt suddenly irritated that she should have touched truth so quickly. "Really, Carol," I said sharply, "a woman of that type doesn't appeal to me. Aren't you being a little ridiculous?"

"Sorry," she said, wandering over to the window. There was a pause, then she went on, "Peter Tennett said he'd be over. Will you have supper with us?"

I now regretted telling her about Eve. "Not tonight," I said, "I'm tied up. Is he calling for you?"

I wasn't tied up, but I had an idea at the back of my mind and I wanted the evening to myself.

"Yes, but you know Peter ... he's always late."

I knew Peter Tennett all right. He was the only one of Carol's friends who gave me an inferiority complex. But I liked him. He was a grand guy. We got along fine together, but he had too many genuine talents for me. He was producer, director, script writer, and technical adviser all rolled into one. Everything he undertook had, so far, been successful. He had the magic touch and he ranked as number one at the Studios. I hated to think what he made in a year.

"Can't you really come?" Carol asked, a little wistfully. "You ought to see more of Peter. He might do something for you."

Lately, Carol had been continually suggesting various people who might put something in my way. It irritated me that she should think I needed help.

"Do something for me?" I repeated, forcing a laugh. "What on earth could he do for me? Why, Carol, I'm getting along fine ... I don't need any help."

"Sorry again," Carol said, not turning from the window. "I seem to be saying all the wrong things tonight, don't I?"

"It isn't you at all," I said, going over to her. "I've still got a headache and I'm edgy."

She turned. "What are you doing, Clive?"

"Doing? Well, I'm going out to dinner. My—my publishers..."

"I don't mean that. What are you working at? You've been at Three Point for two months now. What's happening?"

This was the one subject I wanted to avoid with Carol. "Oh, a novel," I said carelessly. "I'm just laying out the blueprint. I start working seriously next week. Don't look so worried," and I tried to smile at her assuringly.

Carol was an extraordinarily difficult person to lie to. "I'm glad about the novel," she said, shadows in her eyes, "but I wish it were a play.

There's not much in a novel, is there, Clive?"

I raised my eyebrows, "I don't know ... film rights ... serial rights ... maybe *Collier's* will take it. They paid Imgram fifty thousand dollars for his serial rights."

"Imgram wrote an awfully good book."

"And I'm going to write an awfully good book too," I said. Even to me, it sounded a little lame. "I'll write another play in a little while, but I've got this idea for a book and I don't want it to grow cold on me."

I had an uneasy feeling that she was going to ask me what the book was about. If she'd done that, I would have been in a spot, but at that moment Peter came in and for once I was glad of the interruption.

Peter was one of the few successful Englishmen in Hollywood. He still had all his clothes made in London and the Sackville Street cut was right for his English type of figure, broad in the shoulders and slimming down at the hips.

His dark, thoughtful face lit up when he saw Carol. "Not dressed yet?" he said, taking her hand. "But looking very lovely. Sure you're not too tired to come out tonight?"

"Of course not," Carol said smiling,

He looked over at me. "How are you, my dear boy?" He shook hands. "Doesn't she look wonderful?"

I said she certainly did and noticed his eyes were question marks when he saw my bruise.

"Give us a drink, Clive, while I dress," Carol said. "I won't be long." She looked over at Peter. "He's being stuffy ... he won't dine with us."

"Oh, but you must ... this is an occasion, isn't it, Carol?"

Carol shook her head helplessly. "He's dining with his publishers ... I don't believe it, but I suppose I'd better be tactful and pretend I do. Look at that bruise ... he's been fighting a wild woman." She laughed, turning to me, "Tell him, Clive ... he may think it's a story."

Peter beat me to the door. He opened it. "Don't hurry," he said. "I'm feeling very leisurely tonight."

"But I'm hungry," Carol protested, "Don't let's be too late," and she ran from the room.

Peter came over to the little bar in the far corner of the room where I was fixing myself another drink. "So you've been fighting, have you?" he said. "That's quite a nasty bruise you have there."

"Never mind about that," I said. "What will you drink?"

"A little whisky, I suppose." He leaned against the bar and selected a cigarette from a heavy gold case. "Carol's told you the news?"

I gave him bourbon and water. "No ... what news?"

Peter raised his eyebrows. "Funny kid … now I wonder why …" He lit his cigarette.

I had a sudden sinking feeling. "What news?" I repeated, staring at him.

"She has been given the script of the year. It was arranged this morning. Imgram's novel."

I slopped whisky on the polished bar. Hearing him say that was wormwood to me. Of course, I knew I couldn't have handled Ingram's theme. It was too big for me, but it came as a blow to hear that a kid like Carol was to do it.

"Why, that's terrific," I said, trying to look pleased. "I've been reading it in *Collier's*. It's a great story. You producing?"

He nodded. "Yes, there are all sorts of angles. It's just the kind of story I've been looking for. Of course, I wanted Carol to do the script, but I didn't think Gold would agree. Then, while I was working out how best to persuade him, he actually called me in to say she's to do it."

I came around from behind the bar and carried my drink to the settee. I was glad to sit down. "What will it mean?"

Peter shrugged. "Well, a contract, of course … bigger money … screen credit … and another chance if she makes good." He tasted his whisky. "And she will, of course. She is very talented."

I was beginning to think that everyone in this game had talent except myself.

He came over and dropped into an armchair. He seemed to sense that the news had shaken me. "What are you working on now?"

I was getting tired of this interest in my work. "A novel," I said shortly. "Nothing of interest to you."

"That's a pity. I'd like to film something of yours." He stretched out his long legs. "I've been meaning to talk to you before. Ever thought of working for Gold? I could give you an introduction."

I wondered suspiciously if Carol had been getting at him.

"What's the use, Peter? You know me. I can't work for anyone. From what Carol tells me working at your Studio is refined hell."

"It's also big money," Peter said, taking the drink I handed to him. "Think it over and don't leave it too long. The public has a short memory and Hollywood an even shorter one." He didn't look at me, but I had a feeling that there was more to it than just casual conversation. It was almost a warning.

I lit a cigarette and brooded. There is one thing you don't tell other writers or producers in Hollywood. You don't tell them that you are out of ideas. They find that out quick enough for themselves.

I knew that if I went back to Three Point the same thing would happen as had happened these past two days. I'd think about Eve. I hadn't stopped thinking about her since I found myself lying on the floor in the deserted cabin with the sun coming through the curtains. I had tried to wash her out of my mind, but I couldn't do it. She was there in my bedroom, she was sitting with me on the porch, she was staring at me from the blank sheet of paper in my typewriter.

It finally got so bad that I had to talk to someone about her. That was why I had come into Hollywood to see Carol. But when I began to talk, I found I couldn't tell her the things that were really on my mind, I couldn't tell Peter either. I couldn't tell them how I was feeling about Eve. They would have thought I was crazy.

Maybe I was crazy. I had the pick of some twenty smart, attractive women. I had Carol who loved me and who meant a lot to me. But that didn't seem enough for me. I had to become infatuated with a prostitute.

Perhaps, infatuated wasn't the right word. I had sat on the porch, the previous night, with a bottle of Scotch at my elbow and I had tried to reason it out. Eve had hurt my pride. Her cold indifference had been a challenge to me. I felt she was living in a stone fortress and I had to storm that fortress and break down its walls.

I was pretty drunk by the time I'd come to these conclusions, but I'd made up my mind I was going to conquer her. All the women I'd played around with in the past had been too easy. I wanted a proposition that I could really get my teeth into. Eve would give me a run. She'd be difficult and the idea excited me. It would be a contest with no holds barred. She wasn't an innocent little thing who could be twisted around my finger without any effort. She had unconsciously thrown down the challenge and I was going to take it up. I had no doubts what the final results would be. Nor did I think of what would happen once I'd taken her by storm. That could take care of itself when the time came.

I snapped out of my thoughts as Carol came in. She had changed into an ice-blue evening dress over which she wore a short ermine coat.

"Why didn't you tell me?" I said, jumping to my feet. "I'm terribly glad and proud of you, Carol."

She looked at me searchingly. "It is exciting, isn't it, Clive? Won't you come now ... we ought to celebrate."

I wanted to, but I had something more important to do. If we'd been alone, I'd have gone with her, but with Peter, it wasn't quite the same thing.

"I'll join you later if I can," I said. "Where are you eating?"

"The Vine Street Brown Derby," Peter said. "How long will you be?"

"It depends," I said. "Anyway, if I don't turn up, I'll meet you both here after dinner .... all right?"

Carol put her hand in mine. "It'll have to be," she said, "You will try, won't you?"

Peter got up. "Well then, let's go. Are you coming our way?"

"I promised to meet my publisher at eight," I explained. It was only half-past seven. "Do you mind if I stay here for a few minutes? I'd like to finish my drink and I have some calls to make."

"No ... come on, Peter, we mustn't interfere with business." Carol waved to me. "Then we'll see you? Are you going back to Three Point tonight?"

"I think so, otherwise, if I'm very late, I'll go over to the penthouse, but, I want to start work tomorrow."

When they had gone, I poured myself out another whisky and picked up the telephone book. There were a number of Marlows in the book. Then with a sudden feeling of excitement I saw her name. The address was a house on Laurel Canyon Drive. I had no idea where that was.

For several seconds I hesitated, then I picked up the telephone and dialled her number. I listened to the steady burr-burr of the bell, then there was a click and my blood began to move around in me, like a prospective tenant looking over a house.

A woman, it wasn't Eve, said, "Hello?"

"Miss Marlow?"

"Who is calling?" The voice was cautious.

I grinned into the telephone. "She won't know my name."

There was a pause, then the woman said, "Miss Marlow wants to know what you want."

"Tell Miss Marlow to come off her high horse," I said. "I've been advised to call her."

There was another pause, then Eve came on the line. "Hello," she said.

"Can I come and see you?" I kept my voice low so she wouldn't recognize it.

"You mean now?"

"In half an hour."

"I suppose so." She sounded doubtful. "Do I know you?"

I thought this was a hell of a conversation. "You will before long," I said and laughed.

She laughed too. Her laugh sounded good on the telephone. "Then you'd better come along," she said and hung up.

It was as simple and as easy as that.

CHAPTER FIVE

Laurel Canyon Drive was a narrow street with a scattering of small-town style frame dwellings, partly hidden by hedges and shrubs.

I drove slowly down the street until I saw the number of Eve's house painted on a small white gate. I stopped and got out.

There was no one in sight and the house itself was discreet. Once I was through the gate, the high hedge hid me from the street. I walked down the path that went steeply to the front door which, in its turn, was screened by a built-in porch. The windows on each side of the door were curtained with cream muslin. I had to walk down several wooden steps before I was level with the front door.

The knocker on the door was an iron ring which passed through the body of a naked woman. It was a nice design and I studied it for a few seconds before I knocked. I waited, aware that my heart was thumping with suppressed excitement.

Almost immediately I heard an electric light switch click on and then the door opened. A tall, angular woman, almost as tall as myself, stood squarely in the doorway.

The light in the passage floodlit me while she remained in the shadows. I could feel her eyes crawling over me, then as if satisfied by what she saw, she stood aside.

"Good evening, sir. Have you an appointment?"

As I stepped round her into the lobby, I looked curiously at her. She was a red-faced woman of about forty-five or so. Her face was sharp with a pointed chin, pointed nose and small bright eyes. Her smile had just the right blend of friendly servility.

"Good evening," I said. "Miss Marlow in?"

I felt acute embarrassment and irritation. It was hateful to me that this woman should see me and should know why I had come to this sordid little house.

"Will you come this way, sir?" She moved down the passage and opened a door.

My mouth was dry and I felt a pulse beating in my temple as I entered the room.

It was not a large room. Facing me was a dressing table fitted with a bevelled mirror; on the floor in front of the dressing table, was a thick white rug. To the left of the rug was a small chest of drawers on which stood several tiny glass animals. On the far right was a cheap, white-painted wardrobe. A large divan bed, covered by a shell-pink bed-spread took up the remaining space.

Eve stood by the empty fireplace. Near her were a small armchair and a bedside table on which stood a reading lamp and several books.

She was wearing the same short-sleeved blue dressing gown and her face was wooden under careful make-up.

We looked at each other.

"Hello," I said, smiling at her.

"Hello." Her expression did not change nor did she move. It was a suspicious, indifferent greeting.

I stood looking at her, slightly embarrassed, puzzled that she showed no surprise at seeing me again and irritated about the dressing gown. But in spite of the hostile atmosphere, my blood moved fast through my veins.

"So we meet again," I said a little lamely. "Aren't you surprised to see me?"

She shook her head. "No … I recognized your voice."

"I bet you didn't," I said. "You're kidding."

Her mouth pursed. "I did … besides, I was expecting you."

I must have shown my startled surprise because she suddenly laughed. The tension eased immediately.

"You were expecting me?" I repeated. "Why?"

She looked away. "Never mind."

"But I do mind," I insisted, walking round her and sitting in the armchair. I took out my cigarette case and offered it.

Her eyebrows went up, but she took a cigarette. "Thank you," she said. She hesitated, and then sat down on the bed near me.

I also took a cigarette, thumped my lighter and as she leaned forward to light up, I said, "Tell me why you were expecting me."

She shook her head. "I'm not going to." She let smoke drift down her nostrils and she glanced uneasily round the room. She was on the defensive and I felt instinctively that she was nervous and unsure of herself.

I studied her for a few seconds. As soon as she felt my eyes on her face, she turned to look directly at me. "Well?" she said sharply.

"It's a pity you make-up like that. It doesn't suit you."

She stood up immediately and looked into the mirror over the fireplace. "Why," she asked, staring hard at herself. "Don't I look all right?"

"Of course, but you'd look better without all that muck on your face. You don't need it."

She continued to look at herself in the mirror. "I'd look an awful fright without it," she said, half to herself, then she turned and frowned at me.

"Did anyone tell you you're an interesting woman?" I asked, before she could speak. "You have character and that's more than most women have."

Her mouth tightened and she sat down. For a moment I had caught her off guard, but the wooden expression was now back again.

"You haven't come here to tell me I'm interesting, have you?"

I smiled at her. "Why not? If no one has told you before, then it's time someone did. I like to give women their due."

She flicked ash into the fireplace. It was a nervous, irritable movement and I could see she did not know what to make of me. As long as I could keep her in that frame of mind I held the initiative.

"Aren't you going to say sorry for this?" I asked, touching the bruise on my forehead.

She said what I expected her to say. "Why should I? You deserved it."

"I suppose I did," I said and laughed. "I'll have to be careful next time. I like a woman with spirit. I'm sorry about the way I behaved, but I did want to see what your reactions would be." I laughed again. "I didn't expect to feel your reactions."

She looked at me doubtfully, smiled and then said, "I do get wild sometimes ... but you deserved it."

"Do you always treat men like that?"

She hedged. "Like what?"

"Knocking them on the head if they annoy you."

This time she giggled. "Sometimes."

"No hard feelings?"

"No."

I watched her. She slouched as she sat, her head forward and her slim shoulders rounded. Again she looked sharply at me when she felt my eyes on her.

"Don't sit there looking at me," she said irritably. "Why did you come here?"

"I like looking at you," I returned, relaxing in the armchair and feeling completely at ease. "Can't I talk to you? Would that strike you as odd?"

She frowned. I could see she was in two minds. She did not know whether I was wasting her time or whether I was here professionally. It was obvious that she was controlling her impatience with difficulty.

"You have only come here to talk?" she said, looking at me and then immediately looking away. "Isn't that a waste of time?"

"I don't think so. You interest me and besides I like talking to attractive women."

She looked up at the ceiling with an exaggerated expression of exasperation. "Oh they all say that," she said impatiently.

That annoyed me. "If you don't mind I would rather not be classed with an anonymous 'they'," I said with acerbity.

She looked surprised. "You have a very good opinion of yourself, haven't you?"

"Why not?" It was my turn to be impatient. "After all, who'll believe in me if I don't?"

Her face darkened. "I don't like conceited men."

"Haven't you a good opinion of yourself?"

She shook her head emphatically. "Why should I?"

"I hope you're not just another woman with an inferiority complex?"

"Do you know so many?"

"Quite a few. Is that what you suffer from?"

She stared into the empty fireplace, her expression suddenly moody. "I suppose so." Then she looked up suspiciously. "Do you think that's funny?"

"Why should I? I think it's rather pathetic because there's no reason for you to."

She raised her eyebrows questioningly. "Why not?"

I knew then that she was unsure of herself and interested to know what I thought of her.

"You ought to be able to answer that if you are truthful about yourself. Now my first impressions of you ... no, never mind, I don't think I'll tell you."

"Come on," she said, "I want to know. What are your first impressions of me?"

I studied her as if I were making a careful assessment of her qualities. She stared back at me, frowning and ill at ease, but wanting to know. I had thought so much about her for the past two days that I was long past first impressions. "If you really want to know," I began with assumed reluctance, "only I don't suppose you'll believe me."

"Oh, come on," she said impatiently, "don't hedge."

"All right. I'd say you are a woman of considerable character, independent to a degree, hot tempered and strong willed, extraordinarily attractive to men and, oddly enough, sensitive in your feelings."

She studied me doubtfully. "I wonder how many women you have said that to?" she asked, but I could see she was secretly pleased.

"Not many ... none at all if you take it as a whole. I haven't met any one woman with all those qualities except yourself. But, of course, I really don't know you yet, do I? I may be entirely wrong ... they're just first impressions."

"Do you find me attractive?" She was in deadly earnest now.

"I would hardly be here if I didn't. Of course you're attractive."

"But why? I'm not pretty." She got up and looked in the mirror again. "I think I look awful."

"Oh no, you don't. You have character and personality. That's much better than insipid prettiness. There's something extraordinary about you. Magnetic is perhaps, the word."

She folded her arms across her small, flat breasts. "I think you're an awful liar," she said, anger in her eyes. "You don't really think I believe all this slop, do you? What exactly do you want? No one else comes here smarming over me like this."

I laughed at her. "Don't get angry. You know, I'm sorry for you. You certainly have a bad inferiority complex. Never mind, perhaps one day you'll believe me." I leaned forward to examine the books on the bedside table. There were copies of *Front Page Detective*, a shabby copy of Hemingway's *To Have and to Have Not*, and Thorne Smith's *Night Life of the Gods*. I thought they were an odd assortment.

"Do you read much?" I asked, deliberately changing the subject.

"When I can find a good bock," she returned, bewildered.

"Have you ever read *Angels in Sables?*" I asked, naming my first book.

She moved restlessly to the dressing table. "Yes ... I didn't like it much." She picked up a powder puff and dabbed at her chin.

"Didn't you?" I was disappointed. "I wish you'd tell me why."

She shrugged. "Oh, I just didn't."

She put down the powder puff, stared at herself in the mirror and then moved back to the fireplace. She was fidgety, impatient and a little bored.

"But you must have reasons. Did you find it dull?"

"I don't remember. I read so quickly I never remember anything I read."

"I see ... anyway you didn't like it." I was irritated that she couldn't remember my book. I would have liked to have talked to her about it and had her reactions, even if she did not like it. I began to realize that normal conversation with her was going to be difficult. Until we knew each other—and I was determined that we should know each other— topics of conversation were severely limited. Up to now, we had nothing in common.

She stood looking at me doubtfully and then sat down on the bed again. "Well?" she said, abruptly. "What now?"

"Tell me something about yourself."

She shrugged and made a little grimace. "There's nothing to tell."

"Of course there is," I said and leaning forward, I took her hand in mine. "Are you married or is this a phoney?" I was twisting the thin gold wedding ring on her finger.

"I'm married."

I was a little surprised. "Is he nice?"

She looked away. "Mmm-hmm."

"Very nice?"

She took her hand away. "Yes ... very nice."

"And where is he?"

Her head jerked round. "That's not your business."

I laughed at her. "All right, don't get high hat. I must say when you get mad, you look quite impressive. How did you get those two lines above your nose?"

She was up instantly, looking at herself in the mirror. "They're bad, aren't they?" she said, trying to smooth the furrows away with her finger tips.

I glanced at the clock on the mantelpiece. I had been in the room exactly a quarter of an hour.

"Then you shouldn't frown so much," I said, getting to my feet, "Why don't you relax?"

I moved towards her and as I did so the puzzled, rather worried look went out of her eyes, instead, there came a look of confidence and secret amusement. She undid the cord of her dressing gown and her slender fingers went to the silk loop that held the one button that kept the dressing gown closed.

"I must go now," I said looking pointedly at the clock.

Away went the look of confidence; her hands dropped to her sides. I was glad that I had decided not to meet her on her own ground. So long as I behaved differently from the other men who visited her, I was certain to hold her attention and keep her puzzled.

"I'd like to talk to you about yourself when you have the time," I said, smiling at her. "I might be good for your inferiority complex." As I passed the chest of drawers, I slid two ten dollar bills between the glass animals. One, a reproduction of Disney's Bambi, fell over on its side.

I saw her look quickly at the money and then she looked away. The sullen expression disappeared.

"Do you think I'll ever see you in anything but that dressing gown?" I asked at the door.

"You might," she said, blankly. "I do wear other things."

"One of these days you must give me a treat. And don't forget, the next time I call, leave off the make-up. It doesn't suit you. Good-bye now," and I opened the door.

She joined me. "Thank you for the—the present," she said, smiling. It was extraordinary how different she looked when she smiled.

"That's all right. By the way, my name's Clive. May I 'phone you soon?"

"Clive? But I know two Clives already."

During the past quarter of an hour I had completely forgotten that she was anyone's woman and that remark jarred me badly. "Well, I'm sorry. After all, it is my name. What do you suggest?"

She sensed my irritation and looked a little sullen. "I like to know who's coming," she said.

"Of course," I said sarcastically. "How about Clarence, or Lancelot or Archibald?"

She giggled and looked at me searchingly. "It's all right. I'll recognize your voice. Good-bye, Clive."

"Fine. I'll come and see you again soon."

"Marty ...." she called.

The big, angular woman came from an adjoining room. She stood waiting, her hands clasped, a faint smirk in her eyes.

"I'll call you before long," I said and followed the woman down the passage.

"Good evening, sir," she said politely at the door.

I nodded and walked up the path to the white wooden gate. When I reached my car, I paused and looked back at the house. There were no lights to be seen. In the dusk of the evening, it looked just like any other of the little houses that dotted the side streets of Hollywood.

I started the engine and drove to a bar off Vine Street, within sight of the Brown Derby. I felt suddenly deflated and I needed a drink.

The Negro bartender grinned cheerfully at me, his teeth glistening like the keys of a piano in the hard electric light.

"Evenin', sir," he said, spreading his big hands on the bar "What'll it be tonight?"

I ordered a straight Scotch and carried it to a table away from the bar. There were only a few men in the place, none of them I knew. I was glad of that because I wanted to think. I relaxed in the easy chair, drank a little of the whisky and lit a cigarette.

I decided, after brooding for a while, that it had been an interesting, if expensive, quarter of an hour. The first opening move in the game had been mine. Eve had been puzzled and I felt pretty sure, interested. I should have liked to have heard what she had said to Marty about me after I had left. She was smart enough to guess that I was playing some kind of a game, but I had given her no clue as to what it was.

I had made her curious. I had talked about her and not about myself; that must have been a change for her. The type of man she would mix with was certain to talk continuously about himself. Her inferiority complex was interesting. Possibly it was due to a fear of the future. She wanted to be reassured about herself. If she relied on her trade for money that would explain her anxiety about her looks. She wasn't young. She wasn't old, of course, but even if she were thirty-three, and I guessed she would be older than that, in her game that was the age when a woman did get anxious.

I finished my whisky and lit a cigarette. In doing so I broke the chain of my thoughts and began, almost against my will, to examine my own conscience.

Obviously something had happened to me. A few days ago, the idea of my associating with a prostitute would have been unthinkable. I have always despised men who go with such women. Everything they stood for was repugnant to me. And yet, I had spent a quarter of an hour with one of these women, treating her as I treated my other women friends. I had actually left my car outside her house, which must be notorious in the neighborhood, for anyone to identify and I had paid for the privilege of having a completely futile conversation.

It was my misfortune to associate with brilliant and talented people. I knew I was dross compared with them. But Eve had never known success. She had no talents and she was a social outcast. She was the only woman I knew whom I could genuinely patronize. In spite of her power over men, her strength of will and her cold indifference, she was for sale. As long as I had money I was her master. I realized now that it was essential for me to have such a companion, who was morally and socially my inferior, if I were not to lose all confidence in myself.

The more I thought about this, the clearer it became that I would have to leave Three Point. I was going to see a lot of Eve. Living so far from her would not simplify our meetings. Three Point would have to go.

I stubbed out my cigarette and walked over to the public telephone. I called my apartment.

Russell's voice floated over the line. "Mr. Thurston's residence."

"I'll be over some time tonight," I told him. "There's one thing I want you to do. You'll find one of my books, *Flowers for Madam*, somewhere around. I want it sent immediately to Miss Eve Marlow by special messenger. No card and nothing to show who sent it." I dictated the address. "Will you do that?"

He said he would and I thought I detected a faint note of disapproval in his voice. He was fond of Carol and always disapproved of any other woman I knew. I hung up before he could express an opinion which he was quite capable of doing. Then I left the bar and walked over to the Brown Derby.

CHAPTER SIX

I found Carol and Peter at a table away from the band. With them was a big, loosely built man in an immaculate tuxedo. He had a shock of iron-grey hair and his face was long and yellow with a thick loose under lip and a broad flattish nose. His grandfather could easily have been a lion.

Peter caught sight of me as I edged my way past the crowded tables. He rose to greet me. "Hello there," he said, looking surprised and pleased. "So you made it after all. Look who's here, Carol. Have you had dinner?"

I took Carol's hand and smiled at her. "No," I said. "May I join you?"

"Why, of course," she said. "I'm so glad you've come."

Peter touched my arm. "I don't think you've met Rex Gold," he said. He turned to the lion man who was still drinking his soup with fixed attention. "This is Clive Thurston, the author."

So this was Rex Gold. Like everyone else in Hollywood, I had heard a lot about him and knew him to be the most powerful man in pictures.

"Glad to meet you, Mr. Gold," I said.

Reluctantly, he gave over drinking his soup and half rose, offering a limp, boneless hand. "Sit down, Mr. Thurston," he said. His deep-set tawny eyes stared through me. "You'll find the lobster soup excellent. Waiter!" He snapped his fingers impatiently. "Lobster soup for Mr. Thurston."

I winked at Carol as the waiter slid a chair under me. "You see, I can't keep away from you," I murmured to her.

"Didn't your publishers want to see you after all?" she whispered. I shook my head. "I 'phoned them instead." Under the table I found and squeezed her hand. "It turned out to be nothing important so I'm seeing them tomorrow. I wanted to be in on the celebration."

While we were talking, Gold continued to spoon soup into his mouth, his eyes fixed in a glazed stare. It was obvious that he did not combine eating and talking.

"I wondered if you were going to see your wild woman," Carol whispered mischievously, "and that was the reason why you were passing me up."

"I wouldn't pass you up for anyone," I returned, trying to make my smile genuine. Carol had an uncanny knack of guessing the truth as far as I was concerned.

"What are you two whispering about?" Peter asked.

"Secrets," Carol replied swiftly. "Don't be inquisitive, Peter."

Gold finished his soup and dropped his spoon with a rattle. Then he scowled round for a waiter. "Where's Mr. Thurston's soup and what's coming next?" he called as a waiter came scurrying up. As soon as he was satisfied that neither he nor I were forgotten, he turned to Carol, "Are you coming to the club tonight?" he asked.

"For a little while," Carol said. "But I don't want to be too late. I've so much to do tomorrow."

The waiter brought me the soup.

"You should always let tomorrow take care of itself," Gold said, his eyes intent on my soup. I had a vague feeling that he would willingly take it from me and drink it if I gave him any encouragement. The feeling embarrassed me. "You must learn to play as well as work," he went on. "You can't divorce the two satisfactorily."

Carol shook her head. "I need my seven hours' sleep, especially now."

"That reminds me," Gold pursed his heavy lips. "Imgram will be at my office tomorrow morning. I'd like you to meet him." He was speaking now to Peter.

"Of course," Peter said. "Will he have much to do with the scenario?"

"No. If he is difficult to handle, just let me know." Gold looked suddenly at me. "Have you written for the screen, Mr. Thurston?"

"No ... not yet," I returned. "I've a number of ideas I'm going to work out when I have the time ..."

"Ideas? What ideas?" His face hung over the table as he hunched forward, "Anything I could use?"

I searched my mind frantically for a discarded plot that might be of use to him, but I could not think of anything. "There must be," I said, deciding to bluff. "I'll let you see some of them if you're interested."

I felt his eyes boring into me like drills. "See what? I don't understand."

"Treatments," I said, feeling suddenly hot and irritated. "A soon as I've time to dope out some treatments I'll let you see them."

He stared blankly over at Carol. She was crumbling bread casually and did not look up. "Treatments?" he repeated. "I'm not interested in treatments. I want a story. You're an author, aren't you? All I want you to do is to tell me a story ... tell me one now. You say you've ideas. All right, tell me one."

I wished I had not sat down at that table. I felt Peter eyeing me curiously. Carol still crumbled bread, but there was a faint flush or her face. Gold continued to stare at me while he stroked his loose jowls with his fleshly hand.

"I can't talk here," I said, "If you're really interested, perhaps could come and see you."

Just then several waiters closed in on us and began to serve the next course. Gold immediately lost interest in me and began to badger the waiters. Everything had to be just right even to the exact temperature of the plate on which his meal was served. For several minutes there was a feverish stir of activity round the table. Finally, he was satisfied and began to eat wolfishly as if he hadn't had a meal for several days.

Peter caught my blank look and grinned faintly. There seemed no point in attempting to make conversation while Gold was eating. Neither Carol nor Peter made any effort and I decided to follow their example. We all ate in silence. I wondered if, when he had finished his dinner, Gold would come back to his request for a story. Somehow I didn't think he would. In a way I was angry with myself for letting the opportunity slip, but as I had nothing to tell him. I decided to be thankful for the interruption.

The moment Gold finished eating, he pushed his plate impatiently away and took a toothpick from his vest pocket. He thoughtfully probed his teeth while he looked round the crowded room.

"Did you read Clive's book, *Angels in Sables?*" Carol asked suddenly.

Gold frowned, "I never read anything," he said shortly; "you know that."

"Then I think you ought to. The plot's not suitable for a picture, but the idea behind it is."

This was news to me and I looked sharply at her. She studiously ignored me.

"What idea?" His yellow face showed interest.

"Why men prefer wantons," Carol replied.

I was taken aback because I had no recollection of such a situation in *Angels in Sables*.

"Do they?" Peter asked softly.

"Of course they do," Gold said, snapping his toothpick between his fingers. "She's right. And I'll tell you why. They prefer them because a good woman is so tedious."

Carol shook her head. "I don't think so, do you, Clive?"

I didn't know what to say. I hadn't thought about it. Then Eve came to my mind. I thought of her and Carol. Eve was a wanton. While Carol was good in the sense that she was reliable, sincere, honest and lived by a code of sound ethics, I doubted if Eve even knew what ethics meant. This was as good a comparison as any. I had left Carol, lied to her even, to have a few minutes with Eve. Why had I done that? If I could answer that, I could answer Carol.

"A wanton has some qualities which a good woman lacks," I said slowly. "Those qualities—they're not necessarily good ones—appeal to the primitive instinct in man. Men lag behind women in controlling their instincts and as long as women have better control, so will men go after wantons. All the same, a man doesn't want a wanton for any length of time. She's here today and gone tomorrow."

Carol said sharply, "Absolute rubbish, Clive, and you know it."

I looked blankly at her. There was an expression in her eyes that I hadn't seen before. She was hurt, angry and ready for a fight.

"I don't disagree with Mr. Thurston myself," Gold said complacently. He took a large cigar from his case and examined it thoughtfully. "Men's instincts are important."

"They have nothing to do with it," Carol snapped. "I'll tell you why men prefer wantons." She glanced over at Peter as if to exclude him from the conversation. "I'm talking now about the majority of men who, if they are let off the lead, rush off and behave like promiscuous puppies. I've no quarrel with the minority of men who have set themselves a standard of moral behaviour and refuse to depart from it."

"My dear Carol," I protested, realizing that this could easily be a personal attack. "You ought to be in a pulpit."

"She'd look charming in a pulpit," Gold said, handing his cigar to a waiter to pierce. "Let her go on."

"A man prefers a wanton because he is vain," Carol said, speaking directly at me. "A wanton is usually decorative. She is sophisticated and glamorous. Men like to be seen with that kind of woman because their friends envy them ... the poor saps. A wanton is usually without brains. She doesn't need them, of course. All she needs is a pretty face, a nice pair of legs, smart clothes and willingness."

"You think men are more at their ease if women haven't brains?" Gold asked.

"You know they are, R.G.," Carol said shortly. "Don't think you can pull wool over my eyes. You're as bad as any of them."

Gold's yellow face softened into a smile. "Go on," he said, "You haven't finished, have you?"

"It makes me tired to see the worthless women men drag around with them. That's all most men think of ... looks, dress and bodies. A girl who hasn't looks is nowhere in Hollywood. It's disgusting."

"Never mind that. Keep to wantons," Peter said, his eyes alight with interest.

"All right... wantons. A man dislikes his woman to know more than he does. That's where a wanton scores. She's lazy by nature and she's no time to be anything else but wanton. She has no other subject to talk about but herself, her clothes, her troubles and, of course, her looks. Man likes that. He has no competition. If he wants to, he can be patronizing. He's a little tin god to himself, although, the wanton probably thinks he's a bore. All she's after is a good time and what she can get out of him."

"Very interesting," Gold said, "but where is the picture idea? I don't see it."

"A satire on men," Carol said. "*Angels in Sables* is a grand title. Never mind about Clive's plot. Use the title, and let him write a hundred per cent satire about men. Think how the women would eat it ... after all, women are our public."

Gold glanced across at me. "What do you say?"

I was staring at Carol. She had given me an idea. She had done more than that. She had fired my imagination which had been dead since I wrote my last book. I knew now what I was going to do. It had come in a flash. I was going to write the story of Eve. I was going to capture her warped, odd personality and put it on the screen.

"It's good," I said, excitedly. "Yes, I know I can do it!"

Carol looked at me and suddenly bit her lip. Our eyes met and I knew she had sensed what I was going to do. I looked quickly away and went on to Gold, "As Carol says it's a great title and a great subject ..."

Carol pushed back her chair. "Would you mind if I run away?" she said abruptly. "I've developed an awful head. It's been coming on all the evening....."

Peter was at her side before I could even stand up.

"You've been working too hard, Carol," he said. "R.G. will excuse you ... won't you?"

The tawny eyes had gone sleepy again. "Go to bed," he said a little curtly. "Mr. Thurston and I will stay here. See her home, Peter."

I stood up. "I'm seeing her home," I said, feeling angry and a little frightened. "Come on, Carol ..."

She shook her head. "Stay with Mr. Gold," she said, without looking at me. "Peter, I want to go home."

As she turned away I put my hand on her arm. "What's wrong?" I asked, trying to keep my voice. "Is it something I said?"

She looked steadily at me. The hurt, angry look was still in her eyes. "I just want to say good night to you now, Clive. Will you please understand?"

She knows, I thought, she knows everything. There's nothing I can keep from her. She sees through me as if I were made of glass.

There was an awkward pause. Gold stared down at his fleshly hands, a frown on his heavy face. Peter picked up Carol's ermine cape and stood, uneasily waiting.

"Of course," I said, surprised that my voice sounded so harsh, "if it's like that."

She tried to smile. "It is rather like that. Good night, Clive."

"Good night," I said.

"I'll see you at the club, R.G." Peter waved and they went away together.

I sat down at the table again.

Gold regarded the white ash of his cigar thoughtfully.

"Women are odd, aren't they?" he said. "Of course, you mean something to each other?"

I did not feel like discussing Carol with a comparative stranger. "We've known each other some time," I said flatly.

His thick lips pursed and his eyebrows came down. "That idea of hers is good. A satire about men. *Angels in Sables*. It's box office." He closed his eyes and brooded. "What's your angle?"

"A portrait of a wanton," I said, leaning back in my chair, my mind divided between Carol and Eve. "The men who pass through her hands, the power she exerts and her ultimate conversion."

"Who would convert her?" Gold asked casually.

"A man ... someone who is stronger than she."

Gold shook his head. "That's bad psychology. Carol would tell you that. If your character's a genuine wanton, then only another woman could convert her."

"I don't agree," I said stubbornly. "A man could do it. If a wanton could be made to love, then I believe the barriers would come down and you could do anything with her."

He touched off his cigar ash onto a plate. "I don't think you and I are thinking along the same lines," he said. "Describe to me your idea of a wanton."

"I'll describe the wanton I have in mind. She's the only one I could be interested in because I know her. She is real and I can study her."

"Go on." Smoke curled from his lips and partly obscured his face.

"The woman I'm thinking of lives on men. She is pitilessly selfish and very experienced. She is anti-social, amoral and interested only in herself. Men mean nothing to her except for the money they give her." I ground my cigarette butt into the ash tray. "That is my wanton."

"Interesting," Gold said, "but too difficult. You don't know what you're talking about. A woman like that could never love. She would have lost the feeling for love." He glanced up and looked at me fixedly. "You say you know such a woman?"

"I've met her. I can't say I really know her, but I'm going to."

"You are experimenting with her?"

I was unwilling to tell him too much. He might talk to Carol.

"Only from the point of view of writing about her," I said carelessly. "I have to mix with all kinds of people in my game."

"I see." His lips closed wetly over his cigar. "You weren't thinking of persuading this woman to fall in love with you?"

I eyed him. "I've something better to do with my time," I said, a little sharply.

"Don't misunderstand me," he said, fairly waving his hands. "You said this woman was the character you have chosen for your theme. You also said if she could be made to love then you could do anything with her? Isn't that so?"

I nodded.

"Then how can you be sure that you are psychologically right, unless you actually experiment? I don't think you are. I think such a woman as you have described is beyond the feeling of love. That is to me sound reasoning, while you are merely theorizing."

I sat back in my chair. I suddenly saw the trap he had laid for me. I had either to back out or else admit what I was planning to do.

"Now wait," Gold said, "don't say anything. Let me talk first. It is always better to know all the facts before you commit yourself."

He waved to a waiter. "We'll have a little brandy. I find brandy is very good for this kind of conversation."

When the brandy had been ordered, he sunk his head into his shoulders and hunched over the table. "I'm interested," he said. "I like *Angels in Sables*. I like the idea of a satire about men. I haven't made a psychological picture for a very long time. They are good box office. Women like them. Carol was right when she said women are our public." He fumbled inside his coat and took out his cigar case. "Have a cigar, Mr. Thurston?"

I took the long cigar although I really didn't want it. Something, however, told me that Gold didn't offer cigars to anyone but those he favoured.

"That cigar cost me five dollars," he said. "I have them specially made for me. You'll enjoy it."

The brandy came and he sniffed at the balloon-shaped glass and sighed. "Excellent," he murmured and held the glass cupped in both hands.

I was in no hurry. I cut the end of the cigar carefully and lit it. It was smooth, mild and satisfying.

"I am interested," Gold went on, "in a story based on facts. I like the idea of your modelling your character on someone you know. She sounds right. You will obviously bring her to life because she is already alive. All you have to do is to capture her likeness and put it on paper. I should like you to take a further step. I would like you to put yourself in your hero's place and, before you write, go through the experiences you have planned for your hero."

"Now look, Mr. Gold ..." I began, but he raised his hand.

"Let me go on. Hear what I have to say first. You may find that your ideas won't work out the way you think they will. But, that won't matter, the result will be psychologically right. You are a man of the world. I imagine that you have had considerable success with women in the past. This woman you have chosen as the subject for a story would be a worthy opponent, wouldn't she? Why don't you make her fall in love with you? It would be a very interesting experiment."

I didn't say anything. He was suggesting the very thing I had planned to do. All the same it made me uneasy because I had Carol at the back of my mind.

"I would buy such a story, Mr. Thurston," Gold went on quietly. "Whichever way it turned out it would be interesting. The experiment would be between you and me and, of course, the woman in question. No one else need know about it."

We looked at each other and I knew he realized that I was uneasy about Carol.

"I'll admit the idea had crossed my mind," I said. "But dealing so intimately with a woman of that reputation is a little tricky."

A flicker of a smile appeared in Gold's eyes. I had an uncomfortable feeling that he saw through me. "Then you'll do it?" he said, raising his eyebrows.

"Yes, as a business proposition, I'll do it," I said. "But I don't want to waste my time unless I receive some kind of compensation."

"Tell me the story in a few words."

I thought for a moment. "This will be the story of a successful wanton who preys on men. I will handle all the background stuff of her relations with men so that Hays won't kill it. The only thing we need really stress is that she takes money and presents from men who are infatuated with her. Then an entirely different type of man comes into her life, and this is where the drama really begins. At first, like the other men, he falls for her, but as he gets to know her, he realizes what a cheat she is and decides to play her at her own game. He does and he beats her in the end. Then tired of the game, he leaves her and goes off to hunt elsewhere. I see it as a Scarlet O'Hara and Rhett Butler set-up."

"And you really think it will work out that way?" Gold asked, pointedly disbelieving.

"Certainly. It's a question of the stronger will."

Gold shook his head. "Providing your woman is as bad as the one you have described, I am sure it will not work out that way."

"Well, let us experiment and see. As you say, whatever the result, it should make an interesting script."

Gold brooded. "Yes, I think it will. All right, do it. I will pay you two thousand dollars for the treatment. If it is what I want then I will pay a further fifty thousand for a complete shooting script. You can have all the help you want from the Studios, but, of course, you can please yourself about that."

I suppressed my excitement with difficulty. "May I have that offer in writing?"

"Certainly. I will tell my people to get in touch with you."

"Will you wait three months? If I don't succeed in three months, it won't be worth wasting any more time."

He nodded. "Three months then. It will be an interesting experiment in real life. You should have quite an exciting time before you." He signalled a waiter. "And now I must go to the club. Won't you join me, Mr. Thurston?"

I shook my head. "I'd rather not, thank you. You've given me quite a lot to think about and I have plans to make."

CHAPTER SEVEN

I did not see Carol for the next two weeks. I telephoned each morning and evening, but I was told that she was either at the Studio or at Mr. Gold's house. I did not know whether she was avoiding me or whether she was really busy with her script. If it had not been for the way she had walked out on me, I should not have given it another thought. She often disappeared for a week or so when she was working hard, but, now I was worried. I remember the look in her eyes when she had said, "It is rather like that." For the first time in two years, I knew I had hurt and angered her.

I could, of course, have gone to the Studio, but first, I wanted to talk to her on the telephone where she could not watch me while I talked. As I have already said, she was very difficult to lie to. If I were to convince her that there was nothing between Eve and myself, I would have to handle the situation with care. So I continued to the Studio.

I had settled in my apartment much to Russell's annoyance. He had hopefully believed that I would stay at Three Point for at least another month. I thought a lot about Eve. On the third night after our meeting I drove over to Laurel Canyon Drive and passed her house. There were no lights showing and I did not stop; but it gave me an odd feeling of satisfaction just to have seen the house again.

On the fourth day, immediately after lunch, I called her.

The maid Marty answered. When I asked for Eve, she wanted to know who was calling.

After a moment's hesitation, I said, "Mr. Clive."

"I'm so sorry," she said, "Miss Marlow's engaged right now. Can I take a message?"

"It's all right," I said. "I'll call later."

"She won't be long," she said. "I'll tell her you called."

I thanked her and hung up. I sat holding the telephone for several minutes, then I put it on the table with a little grimace. Why was I feeling bad? I asked myself. I knew what she was, didn't I? I did not ring her again that day and I did no work. I thought about Gold and I tried to work out a blue print for the script we had discussed. But I was not successful. Until I knew Eve better, I would not hope to make much progress.

I must have been a trial to Russell as he was used to my going out and leaving him the apartment to himself. I spent the rest of the day wandering between the large lounge, my bedroom and my small library. I had a date with Clare Jacoby, the singer, in the evening, and although I did not feel like listening to her incessant chatter, I could not very well put her off. I returned to the apartment just after midnight, a little drunk and irritable.

Russell was waiting up for me and after he had brought me a whiskey I sent him to bed. Then I telephoned Eve. I sat listening to the steady burr-burr of the bell, but there was no answer. I slammed down the receiver and went into my bedroom to undress. In pyjamas and dressing gown, I returned to the lounge and called her again. It was now twenty to one.

"Hello," she said.

"Hello yourself." I found my mouth had gone dry at the sound of her voice.

"You are very late, Clive."

She said she would recognize my voice, but I didn't think she would. That was one score for her.

"How are you?" I settled back in my armchair.

"All right," she said.

I waited, expecting her to say something else, but the line was silent. This was my first experience of the many unsatisfactory telephone calls I was to have with her, so I had no warning that her replies would be non-committal and monosyllabic.

"Hello?" I said, after waiting a moment. "Are you still there?"

"Yes." Her voice sounded remote and flat.

"I thought we were cut off." I settled back in my chair again. "Did you like the book I sent you?"

There was a long pause, then I heard her say something as if she were speaking to someone with her.

"What was that?" I asked.

"I can't talk now," she said. "I'm engaged."

A wild, unreasonable rage surged through me. "Good God!" I exclaimed, "Do you work all night as well as all day?" But I was talking to a dead telephone. She had hung up.

I sat thinking for almost an hour. It began to dawn on me that Eve was going to be an even harder proposition than I'd first thought. In fact, as I brooded about her and Gold's offer, I experienced a slight feeling of panic. It was four days since I had seen her and I had not even scratched the surface. The fact that she had hung up on me like that showed that she was not yet interested in me. She did not even say that she was sorry. "I can't talk now, I'm engaged," and down had gone the receiver. I clenched my fists.

In spite of my anger, her indifference made me all the more anxious to see her. During those two weeks that I saw nothing of Carol, I visited Eve three times. There is no point in recording those three meetings. They ran practically parallel with the previous meeting. We talked uneasily about the merest trifles and at the end of a quarter of an hour I left, being careful always to put two twenty dollar bills on the chest of drawers. Each time I called on her I brought her a book for which she seemed genuinely grateful. Although I tried to break down her reserve she remained wooden and suspicious. I realized that if I was to get anywhere with her I would have to try more forceful tactics. Finally I decided on my line of action.

The following morning I came down to the dining room to find Russell waiting to serve breakfast. It was now ten days since I had seen Carol and I knew that Russell was worried about this. I could tell that by his continuous disapproving looks.

"You might put a call through to Miss Carol," I said, as I flipped through my letters, "and see what she's doing. If she's at home I'll speak to her."

While he was making the call, I glanced at the headlines of the newspaper. There was nothing there to interest me and I dropped the paper on the floor.

Russell, after murmuring into the telephone, hung up and shook his head. "She's out, sir," he said, his round, fat face sagging with gloom. "Why don't you slip down to the Studio and see her?"

"I'm too busy to slip down to the Studio," I said shortly, "and what business is it of yours anyway?"

He stood opposite me, moving the toast within my reach. "Miss Carol's a nice young lady," he said, "and I don't like to see her treated badly, Mr. Clive."

"So you think I'm treating Miss Carol badly, do you?" I said, spreading butter on my toast and avoiding his disapproving glance.

"I do, sir. I think you should see her. She's a nice young lady and she deserves to receive better treatment than the other young ladies you know."

"You are poking your nose as usual into something that does not concern you. Miss Carol is extremely busy and has no time at the moment to be sociable. I'm not neglecting her and, if you will remember, I call her twice a day and have been doing so for the past two weeks."

"Then, all I can say, sir, is she's avoiding you," he returned obstinately. "You shouldn't allow it."

"I think you'd better do my bedroom now, Russell," I said coldly. "I have everything I want at the moment."

"This Miss Marlow, sir," he said, "she's a professional lady, isn't she?"

I stared at him in amazement. "And how did you know that?"

An almost pious look settled on his face. "Being a gentleman's man, sir," he said, a little pompously, "I feel it is part of my duties to know something of the worldly aspects of life. The name, sir, if I may presume, is a little obvious."

"You think so, do you?" I said, trying not to smile. "And what if she is?"

His bushy white eyebrows crawled to the top of his head. "I can only warn you, Mr. Clive. That sort of woman never did anyone any good.

And if I may say so, any attempt to establish a social relationship with her would be fraught with disaster."

"Do stop talking like a drip and get upstairs," I said, feeling this had gone far enough. "I am meeting Miss Marlow to get a background for a picture. Mr. Gold's commissioned me to write it."

"I'm surprised to hear that, sir. I always understood Mr. Gold was a person of intelligence. No one in his right senses would consider making a picture in connection with that subject. If you will excuse me, I will do your room."

I watched his dignified exit rather thoughtfully. On the face of it, he was right, yet Gold had definitely promised to do the story. I picked up my letters again and opened them, hopefully looking for a letter from the Studio. It was not here and I realized it was perhaps a little early to expect it. I went over to my desk and checked my bank balance. I was surprised to find it so low. After a moment's hesitation, I tossed the bills into the trash basket. They would have to wait for payment. Then I called Merle Bensinger, my agent.

"Look, Merle," I said, as soon as she came on the line, "what's happening to *Rain Check?* I haven't had this week's receipts."

"I was writing to you about that, Clive," she returned. Merle had a bright metallic voice which I always found a little overpowering on the telephone. "The cast has been given a week off. I think they deserve it, the poor dears. They've been at it now for twenty weeks."

"So while they disport themselves, I'm supposed to starve?" I said crossly. "Isn't there anything else coining in? How about my books?"

"You know there's nothing until September, Clive." She sounded startled. "Sellick's don't make up their accounts until September …"

"I know—I know," I said sharply. "Well, if you can't do anything for me, Merle, at least listen to my news. Gold's offered me a contract. I ought to have told you before. I outlined a story to him a couple of weeks ago and he's offering fifty thousand dollars for it."

"Why, that's wonderful." Her voice sounded even brighter and more metallic. "Do you want me to look after the arrangements?"

"I suppose so," I said, a little doubtfully. Ten per cent meant parting with five thousand dollars, but Merle did know her job and if Gold was going to try a double-cross, she would know how to handle him. "Yes, you'd better look after it. I'll send you the correspondence when I get it."

"How's the new book going?"

"Never mind about the new book. I've got Gold on my mind right now."

"But, Clive," her voice signalled alarm, "Sellick's are expecting it by the end of the month."

"Then they'll have to expect it," I returned. "I tell you I'm busy." There was a pause, then she said, "But haven't you begun it yet?"

"No, I haven't. To hell with Sellick's. I'm after Gold's fifty thousand."

"I shall have to tell Mr. Sellick. He'll be very disappointed. They've advertised it, you know, Clive."

"Tell whom you like. I couldn't care less. Tell the President if it'll make you feel any better, but for God's sake, Merle, don't bother me with Sellick's headaches," I snapped, feeling suddenly irritated with her. "Isn't Gold a better proposition?"

"The money's better, of course," she said slowly, "but, it's some time since you wrote a book and you must think of your name."

"I'll look after that," I assured her. "Don't worry about my name."

She remembered something. "Oh, Clive," she said, "I've an offer from the *Digest*. They want an article on the 'Women of Hollywood'. Three thousand dollars. Fifteen hundred words. Would you like to do it for them?"

It wasn't often Merle put anything in my way. I was pleased. "Sure," I said. "When do you want it?"

"Can you do it today? I've been holding it and it's urgent now."

That rather spoiled the offer. What she really meant was she had been trying to get someone to write it and had so far failed. "Well, all right. Leave it with me. I'll get Russell to bring it over first thing tomorrow morning." I said good-bye and hung up.

Russell came in just then to clear the breakfast things.

"I have an article to do for the *Digest*," I said. "Have I any dates today?"

Russell liked to be consulted about my appointments. "You promised to see Miss Selby at three, sir," he said. "And you're dining with Mr. and Mrs. Henry Wilbur tonight."

"Well, Miss Selby isn't important. She's a damn little nuisance anyway. Tell her I've had to go out of town. If I have the afternoon to myself I should be able to manage. I'll dine with the Wilburs."

I left him pottering about the living-room and went upstairs to dress. By the time I was through it was twenty to twelve. It was time to ring Eve.

The bell rang for quite a while before she answered. She sounded sleepy.

"Hello there," I said. "Did I get you out of bed?"

"You did, Clive," she said. "I was fast asleep."

"Well, I'm sorry, but look at the time. Aren't you ashamed of yourself?"

"I never get up before twelve. You ought to know that by now."

Well, anyway, she was at least stringing some sentences together for a change.

I drew a deep breath, "Eve," I said, "you wouldn't like to spend a week-end with me, would you?"

There was a long pause, then she said in a flat, indifferent voice. "If that's what you want."

"We might take in a theatre. How about this weekend?"

"All right."

If she would only sound just a little enthusiastic, I thought angrily. "Fine," I said, keeping the disappointment out of my voice. "Where would you like to dine?"

"I'll leave it to you." There was a pause and then she said, "But it mustn't be ..." and she ran through a bewildering number of restaurants and hotels which left me gasping.

"But there's nothing to choose from after that little lot's been eliminated," I protested. "For instance, why on earth can't we go to the Brown Derby?"

"I just can't," she said. I could imagine the two furrows above the bridge of her nose deepening. "Or any of the other places I've told you."

"Well, all right," I said, feeling that if I pressed her she would refuse to go altogether. "I'll send you a line. Then we definitely meet on Saturday?"

"All right," and down went the receiver before I could say how pleased I was.

CHAPTER EIGHT

As I drove round the corner of Fairfax and Beverley I saw a big crowd ahead. The boulevard was blocked with cars and people. It looked as if there had been an accident so I pulled into the curb and waited; but the crowd increased.

I said, "Hell !" and jumped out of my car and went to see what it was all about.

A small roadster was crossways in the street; one of its front fenders was crumpled up. Four men were pushing a big Packard over to the curb; it had a broken headlight and lot of scratches on its immaculate body and a flat tyre.

Peter Tennett stood in the middle of the group of arguing men.

He was speaking to an elderly man, and I could see he was worried and angry.

"Hello there, Peter," I said, shouldering my way through the crowd. "Anything I can do?"

His face brightened when he saw me. "Got your car with you, Clive?" he asked hopefully.

"Sure," I said. "It's parked over there. What happened?"

He waved his hand at the Packard. "I was pulling from the curb when our friend here cut across and hit me head on."

The elderly man muttered something about his brakes. He looked white and scared.

Just then there came the wail of a police siren and a radio car pulled up. A big red-faced policeman got out and pushed his way through the crowd.

He recognized Peter. "What's the matter, Mr. Tennett?" he demanded.

"I got clipped," Peter said, "but I don't want any trouble. I'm satisfied if this gentleman is."

The policeman looked coldly at the elderly man, "Well, if Mr. Tennett's satisfied, I am. Do you want to make anything of it?"

The elderly man backed away. "It's all right with me, officer."

Peter looked at his watch. "Will you take care of this, officer?" he said. "I'm late for the Studio as it is."

The policeman nodded. "That's okay, Mr. Tennett. I'll call the Studio garage for you."

Peter thanked him and then joined me. "Can you run me over to the Studio, or will it be out of your way?"

"Glad to," I said, pushing through the crowd. "You're sure you're all right?"

Peter laughed. "Yes, but the old fellow looks bad. I hope they take care of him."

I heard a girl who was standing nearby say to a little blonde with a bicycle, "That's Peter Tennett, the director."

I glanced at Peter with a grin, but he hadn't heard.

When we were driving towards the Studio, Peter said, "Where've you been, Clive? I haven't seen you for days."

"I've been around," I said. "How's the picture going?"

Peter lifted his hands expressively. "We're getting down to it," he said. "The first few weeks are always the worst. It's too early yet to say what's going to happen." He waved casually to Corrine Moreland, the movie star, as she passed us in a cream roadster. "I've been meaning to ring you, Clive. I'm damn pleased you're working for R.G."

I glanced at him quickly. "He told you?"

"He said he wanted you to get an angle on this idea of Carol's, but he didn't give me any details. What's behind it?"

I hedged. "I'm working on it now," I said. "It's going to be a satire on men. I can't tell you anything else because it's still up in the air."

"But is there anything really in it? R.G. usually talks to me about his plots, only this time he's gone mysterious on me."

"As soon as I've anything to show you." I said, "I'll let you in on it."

I slowed down before the Studio gates. The guard opened up and touched his cap to Peter as we drove through.

"You sure I'm not taking you out of your way?" Peter said as I crawled along the palm edged drive to the Studio offices.

"I'll drop you just here if you don't mind," I said, pulling up. "I've a whale of a lot of work ..." and I stopped because Carol was standing by my side. "Why, hello, stranger," I went on, taking off my hat and smiling at her.

She was wearing a dark brown shirt and brick red slacks. Round her hair she wore a flame coloured turban. She looked smart, neat and picturesque.

"Hello, Clive." Her dark eyes were wide and serious. "Have you come to see me?"

"It's time, isn't it?" I opened the car door and got out. "Do you know I've been ringing you twice a day?"

Peter broke in. "I'll leave you two. Thanks, Clive, for pulling me out of that mess." He waved and disappeared into the vast glass and wooden building that housed the Studio offices.

Carol suddenly put her hand in mine. "I'm sorry, Clive," she said with a rush. "I've been angry with you."

"I know," I said, thinking how lovely she looked. "I deserved it. Let's go somewhere and talk. I've missed you."

"I've missed you too." She slipped her arm through mine. "Let's go to my room, we can talk there."

As we moved towards the building, a call boy came running out. "Miss Rae," he said, a little breathlessly. "Mr. Highams wants you right away."

Carol snapped her fingers. "Oh, Clive, what a bore. But come with me. I want you to meet Mr. Imgram."

I hung back. "You don't want me around, Carol," I said. "You're busy now, aren't you?"

She pulled at my arm. "It's time you met the fellows," she said severely. "Jerry Highams is an important person. He's our production chief and you ought to meet him."

I allowed myself to be persuaded and followed her through the endless maze of wide passages until we reached a polished mahogany door on which was written in neat black letters *Jerry Highams.*

Carol went straight in.

Peter was sitting in an armchair with a mass of papers in a leather bound folder on his knees. By the window was a big fat man with hair like straw and tobacco ash all over his white and yellow sweater.

He turned as we entered. I noticed his slate grey eyes. They were humorous, sharp and penetrating.

"Jerry, this is Clive Thurston who wrote *Angels in Sables* and the play *Rain Check*," Carol said.

He looked swiftly at me and I could feel his eyes probing inside my skull. He took his hands out of his trouser pockets and came over. "I've been hearing about you," he said, shaking hands, "R.G. was saying you were working on a script for him."

Gold seemed to be generally advertising me. I didn't know whether to be pleased or not.

"Sit down. Have a cigarette," Highams went on, waving me to a chair. "What's the angle on this script? R.G.'s acting mysterious."

"She'll tell you," I said waving to Carol. "After all, it was her idea."

"Her idea?" Higham's face brightened. "Was it, Carol?"

"Well I did suggest that Clive should write a satire on men and use his title 'Angels in Sables'."

Highams shifted his attention to me again. "Are you doing that?"

I nodded. "That's the idea."

"Well, that isn't so bad." He looked hopefully over at Peter.

"The idea's right, and if Clive turns in a script like *Heaven Must Wait*, it'll be terrific," Peter said, putting the folder on the desk.

"Then why's R.G. being cagey?" Highams demanded.

"It's time he put one over you," Carol laughed. "Maybe he knows it's good and wants to surprise you."

Highams stroked his chin. "It could be that." He wagged his finger at me. "Now look, friend," he said, "I want you to get this straight. The people who'll make your picture'll be Peter and me ... not Gold. Before you turn your treatment over to Gold, let me see it. I'll help you in any way I can. I know what we can do and what we can't do, Gold doesn't. And if Gold doesn't like a treatment, he'll kill it. Let me see the treatment first and I'll vet it for you. You have a good idea to work on. Don't spoil it and don't listen to Gold. Okay?"

I nodded. "Okay."

I felt that I could trust him. He was sincere, and if he said he would help, I was sure he would without expecting anything in return.

A knock came on the door and when Highams called out, a thin little man, in a shabby suit edged cautiously round the door.

"Am I late?" he asked, looking at Highams anxiously.

"Why, come in," Highams said, going over to him. "No, you're all right. This is Clive Thurston. Thurston meet Frank Imgram."

I could scarcely believe that this insignificant little man was the author of *The Land is Barren*, the book every film company had fought for, and which, it was rumoured, Gold had finally bought for 250,000 dollars.

I got to my feet and offered my hand. "Glad to meet you, Mr. Imgram," I said, looking with interest at his pale, sensitive face.

He had large protruding blue eyes, a big forehead and thin, mouse coloured hair.

He looked at me searchingly, smiled nervously and turned back to Highams. "I'm sure Mr. Gold is wrong," he said, with a kind of feverish anxiety. "I've thought about it all this morning. Helen can't be in love with Lancing. It's too ridiculous. She could never have any feeling for such a complex character as Lancing. It's simply pandering to the happy ending."

Highams shook his head. "Don't worry," he said, soothingly. "I'll talk to R.G." He looked over at Carol.

"You had an angle, didn't you?"

Imgram went to her eagerly. "I'm sure you'll agree that I'm right," he said. "You've agreed with me up to now. Can't you see how impossible it would be?"

"Of course," Carol said gently. "The theme's so big I'm sure we could let the ending stand. Don't you think, Peter?"

"Yes, but you know what R.G. is about that kind of an ending."
Peter looked worried.

I felt out of this. "Look," I said, "I'll leave you to it ..."

Imgram immediately turned to me. "I'm so sorry," he said. "You see, I have so little experience and it all rather worries me. Don't let me drive you away. Perhaps, you can help us. You see....."

I stopped him. I had quite enough on my mind and I wasn't going to take on Imgram's headaches. "I'll only be wasting time," I said, smiling at him. "I know less about this than you do. And besides, I've a lot of things to do." I turned to Carol. "When do we meet?"

"Must you go?" she asked, disappointed.

"You want to get on and I've things to do," I said. "But, let's fix a date."

The three men were watching us. I could see Carol wanted me to stay, but I had enough of this concentrated interest in Imgram.

"Today's Thursday, isn't it?" She frowned over at the wall calendar.

"Tomorrow? Will you come tomorrow evening? I'm working tonight."

"Swell, I'll be there." I nodded to Highams, shook Imgram's hand and waved to Peter. 'Don't worry," I said to Imgram. "You're in very good hands." I tried not to sound patronizing, but it was there all right. Perhaps, it was his shabby suit that gave me a superior complex.

Carol came with me to the car. "He's so honest and sincere," she said as I slid under the wheel. "I'm so sorry for him, Clive."

I regarded her serious, upturned face with amusement. "Imgram? You should worry. He's bitten Gold for a quarter of a million, hasn't he?"

She waved this aside. "R.G. says he has no ideas, but he is full of them. Good ideas—great ideas, but R.G. doesn't understand them. If we left him alone, I do believe he'd make a far greater picture than anything Peter or Jerry could do. But Gold keeps interfering."

"Odd little guy, isn't he?"

"I like him. He's straight and this all means so much to him."

"Well, he needs to have something," I said coldly. "Did you notice the suit he was wearing?"

"It's not the suit that matters, Clive," she returned, colour coming to her face.

"Well, have it your own way." I reached forward and stabbed the starter button. "Don't work too hard. I'll see you around eight tomorrow."

"Clive." She stepped up onto the running board. "What did Gold arrange with you?"

"He wants me to do a story," I said carelessly. "I'll tell you about it tomorrow."

"About this woman?"

I twisted in my seat. "What woman?"

"When I suggested the idea, I knew I had made a mistake," she said a little breathlessly. "You want an excuse to see her, don't you? Oh Clive, I know you so well. You're just pretending that you want to write about her, but it isn't that. It's something far more complex than that. But, be careful, won't you? I can't stop you, but do be careful."

"I don't even know what you're talking about," I began, but she raised her hand.

"Don't Clive," she said and turning, she ran back into the building.

I drove slowly to my apartment. The hands of the clock on the dashboard pointed to three thirty when I drove into the garage. I had an uneasy feeling at the back of my mind. Although I told myself it wasn't anything to do with Carol, I knew I was playing a dangerous game. I wanted Carol. If she hadn't been such a worker, if she could have given me of her time, I guess I wouldn't have wanted any other woman. But with so much time on my hands I had to do something. Maybe, I thought, I'd better wash Eve out of my mind. Thinking like that was just kidding. I knew, even if I really wanted to—and I didn't—I should not be able to get free from her as easily as that.

I walked into my apartment, tossed my hat into the nearest chair and went to the library. I found a letter from International Pictures on my desk. I read it through carefully. There was no catch in it. Perhaps, the only suspicious thing about it was Gold's request to keep the arrangement confidential. But then, he might easily be asking it for my sake as well as his own. He had laid down in black and white that he would pay me fifty thousand dollars for a shooting script to be entitled *Angels in Sables*, provided the story was based on our discussions and that the script met with his approval.

I wrote a hurried note to Merle Bensinger and enclosed the letter. Then I turned my attention to the article for the *Digest*.

"Women of Hollywood" seemed, on the face of it, an easy subject. But, I was not used to writing articles and I approached my task with considerable uneasiness and doubt.

I lit a cigarette and considered the problem. Concentration was difficult. I kept thinking of Carol. It frightened me to know she could read my mind so completely. I did not want to lose her and I knew, if I was not careful, that was what would eventually happen.

Then Eve shouldered Carol out of my thoughts. I considered the coming weekend. Where should I take her? How would she behave? What would she wear? Why was she so cagey about appearing in public? If there was anyone to be cagey it should surely be me.

I picked up the newspaper and checked through the entertainments. I decided to take her to a theatre and after some hesitation I picked on *My Sister Eileen* as appropriate. The desk clock showed five fifteen and I hurriedly dropped the newspaper and threaded paper into my typewriter. I typed "Women of Hollywood by Clive Thurston" at the top of the page and then sat back to stare at the typewriter keys. I had no idea how to begin the article I wanted to say something sophisticated and witty, but my mind was completely barren.

I wondered uneasily if Eve would dress flashily and whether she would look what she was. It'd be an embarrassing situation if I ran into Carol when she was with me. I knew I was taking a risk. I had never seen Eve dressed and had no idea of her taste. I decided that I should have to select some small secluded restaurant where I was not known and where no one that I knew was likely to see me.

I lit another cigarette and tried once more to concentrate on the article. By six o'clock, the page in the typewriter was still blank, and I was in a slight panic.

Pulling the typewriter impatiently towards me, I began to hammer out words, hoping that they would make sense. I wrote like this until seven o'clock, then I gathered up the sheets of paper and pinned them together. I made no attempt to read them through.

Russell came in to tell me that my bath was ready. He eyed the sheets of paper in my hand approvingly.

"Gone all right, sir?" he asked in his most encouraging manner.

"Yes," I said, moving to the door. "I'll check it through when I come back and you can take it down to Miss Bensinger first thing tomorrow."

I did not arrive back from the Wilburs until one fifteen. It had been a good party and my head was a little heavy from the excellent champagne I had been drinking most of the evening. I forgot about the article lying on my desk to be checked and I went straight to bed.

Russell woke me at nine o'clock the following morning. "Sorry to disturb you, sir," he said apologetically, "but shall I take the article to Miss Bensinger now?"

I sat up with a grunt of dismay. My head felt heavy and my mouth like the bottom of a birdcage. "Hell!" I exclaimed. "I forgot to look it over. Get it, will you, Russell? I'll do it now."

I had finished my first cup of coffee by the time he returned.

He handed me the typewritten sheets. "I'll just clean your shoes, sir, then I'll be back."

I waved him away and began to read what I had written. In less than three minutes, I was out of bed and running downstairs to my study. I knew I could never send this stuff to Merle. It was hopeless. It was so awful that I could scarcely believe that I had written it.

I began hammering away at the typewriter, but my head ached and I could not string two sentences together. After a half an hour, I had worked myself into a furious rage. For the fourth time, I snatched the paper out of the typewriter and threw it angrily to the floor.

Russell put his head round the door. "It's after ten, sir," he reminded me apologetically.

I turned on him furiously. "Get out!" I shouted. "Get out and for God's sake stop worrying me!"

He backed out of the room, his eyes wide with surprise.

I turned savagely back to my typewriter. At eleven o'clock my head was nearly bursting and my temper was seething. Round me were crumpled balls of paper. I knew it was no good. I could not begin to write the article. Panic, rage and disappointment made me want to pick up the type-writer and smash it to the floor.

Then the telephone rang.

I snatched it up. "What is it?" I snapped.

"I'm waiting for the *Digest* article ..." Merle began plaintively.

"You'll go on waiting," I said, the whole of my concentrated rage and bitterness bursting from me. "Who do you think I am? Do you think I haven't anything better to do than to bother with a goddam mawkish article for the *Digest?* To hell with them! Tell 'em to write it themselves if they need it so much!" And I slammed down the receiver.

CHAPTER NINE

I did not see Carol that evening. I did not feel like it. I did not feel like doing anything after the way I had bawled out Merle. Once I had cooled down, I realized just how crazy I had been. Merle was the best agent in Hollywood. Writers and stars fought for her to handle their business. She was only interested in five-figured incomes and everyone knew it. So if she was your agent, your credit stood high everywhere. By bawling her out as I had done, it was likely that she would drop me. Right now, I could not afford to be without Merle. If there was any work to be had, it would come through her. In actual fact, she was my meal ticket. As soon as I had realized what a fool I had been and seen what a mess I had landed myself in, I telephoned her. Her secretary said she was out and she did not know when she would be back. She sounded as if she did not care. This did not look good to me so I wrote Merle a note, apologizing for what I had done and pleading a hangover. I said I hoped she would understand. I did everything in that letter except kiss her feet and I sent it to her office by special messenger.

After lunch, I still felt like hell. The idea of passing up three thousand dollars was wormwood to me. But what worried me more was that I could not sit down and write a simple article at a moment's notice. That was something to worry about. It told me, as nothing else could tell me, that I had not the equipment to make the grade as a first-class writer. The thought stuck in my throat like a fish hook.

Anyway, I did not feel like spending the evening with Carol. I knew she would start something about Eve and my temper was too jumpy to take anything from anyone. So I called her and told her I had to go into Los Angeles on urgent business. She wanted to see me on Saturday, but I lied myself out of that too. I could tell by her voice that she was depressed and disappointed, but I was determined to spend the weekend with Eve and no one was going to upset my plans. All the same I felt a heel when Carol tried to persuade me.

Then I wrote to Eve. I told her I would call for her at six thirty the following evening, that we would go to the theatre and have the rest of the weekend to get to know each other. I enclosed a hundred dollar bill saying it was for bed-and-breakfast charges. This was the first time I had ever paid a woman to go out with me. I did not like it. Somehow I began comparing myself with Harvey Barrow, but I told myself that she would come out with me before long just for the fun of it. That made things different.

The following morning while Russell prepared breakfast, I lounged in the big armchair by the window and idled with the newspaper.

"Russell," I said, when he brought the coffee and eggs, "I'll be away for the weekend. I want you to go out to Three Point and pack my things. I'm giving the place up. See the Estate agents and fix it with them."

He slid the chair under me as I sat down at the table. "It's a pity to give the place up, isn't it, Mr. Clive?" he said, spreading a snowy napkin across my knees. "I thought you liked it out there."

"So I do, but I have to cut down on something and Three Point is costing me plenty."

"I see, sir," His eyebrows crawled up his forehead. "I wasn't aware that we were financially embarrassed. I'm sorry to hear that."

"Maybe it isn't as bad as that," I said, not wishing him to be scared. "Let's face it, Russell, *Rain Check* is now only paying $200 a week. Last week, it didn't play at all. There'll be nothing from the books until the end of September and when I do get payment it won't be all that good. So I have to cut down for a while."

Russell looked vaguely alarmed. "Won't you be writing something else before long, sir?"

"I'm working on something now," I said, taking the cup of coffee he handed to me. "Once that's finished, we'll be on top of the world ... or we should be."

He didn't look impressed, "I'm glad to hear that, sir," he said. "Would it be another play?"

"It's this picture I was telling you about for Mr. Gold."

"Oh, I see, sir." His fat face became gloomy.

I still had Merle on my mind, so I called her office. Her secretary said she had gone away for the weekend. I asked for an appointment for Monday, but she said Merle was tied up all the week. I said I would call her later.

At six o'clock, just as I was leaving to pick up Eve, Carol rang. "Oh, Clive, I was scared I was going to miss you," she said, her voice was tense with excitement.

"Two more minutes and you would have missed me," I said, wondering what was coming.

"You really must come over, Clive."

With my eye on the clock, I said it was impossible.

"But I've been talking to Jerry Highams about *Rain Check*," she went on, her words stumbling over themselves. "He says Bernstien's looking for a story. They're both coming over to see me tonight and if you were there you might interest Bernstien in your plot. Jerry thinks it's right for him. I told him you'd be here."

I wondered if Carol had guessed what I was intending to do and had thought of this to prevent my seeing Eve. If Bernstien was really interested in *Rain Check*, it would be ridiculous to let such an opportunity slip. Bernstien was second only to Jerry Highams and he had a big reputation for slick, sophisticated pictures.

"Look, Carol," I said, trying to sound reasonable. "I'm really tied up tonight. Can't Bernstien see me on Monday?"

She said he had to make a decision over the weekend as Gold was getting impatient. He had two other stories he was considering, but if we all worked on him we might easily get him to do *Rain Check*.

"It's just his type of picture," Carol urged. "He'll listen to Jerry and if you're there and can give him an outline, I'm sure he'll go for it. Now do be sensible, Clive, this is so important."

But so was Eve. If I put her off at the last moment, I might never get the chance of taking her out again.

"I can't do it," I said, not bothering to keep the impatience out of my voice. "Don't I keep telling you? I have to go out of town."

There was a long pause and I heard Carol catch her breath in a little gasp. That told me she was losing her temper too. "What's so important, Clive?" she asked sharply, "Don't you want to get into pictures?"

"I am in them, sweetheart, remember?" I said. "Aren't I working for Gold?"

Was I working for Gold? Only God and Gold knew that. "Oh, do be sensible, Clive." There was an edge to her voice now. "What will they think if you don't show up?"

"That's not my headache," I snapped back. "I didn't make the arrangement. You knew I was tied up, didn't you?"

"I knew all right, but I thought your work came first. All right, Clive, have a good time," and she hung up on me.

That made two women who were sour with me. I slammed down the receiver and then shot three inches of bourbon into a glass and swallowed it at a gulp. Then I snatched up my hat and went down to my car.

By the time I turned into Laurel Canyon Drive, the bourbon was hitting me and I felt fine. I pulled up outside Eve's house and I flicked the horn. Then I lit a cigarette and waited. I waited exactly one minute and fifteen seconds which brought the hands of the dashboard clock to six thirty. Then Eve came out of the house.

When I saw her, I was out of the car and opening the white gate for her in a split second.

She was wearing a dark blue coat and skirt, a white silk shirt, no hat and under her arm, she carried a large handbag with her initials in platinum on the flap. That does not sound anything unusual, but if you could have seen the cut of that costume you would have stared as I was staring. Its severity and the way it was moulded to her trim figure made it the smartest outfit I had seen on a woman for a long time.

Then I noticed her legs. In Hollywood, legs are just commonplace. Ugly looking legs are as rare as natural platinum blondes. But Eve's legs meant something. They were not only pretty and neat and beautifully hosed, but they had a distinct personality of their own.

I realized with a shock of startled pleasure that I had a smart, sophisticated, well-groomed woman on my hands. Nor did she look plain. She was carefully made-up ... not too much... and her eyes were bright.

"Hello there," I said, taking her hand. "Are you always so punctual?"

She pulled her hand away as she asked, "Do I look all right?"

I opened the car door, but she made no move to get in. She stood frowning at me, her even teeth nervously chewing her under lip.

"You look terrific," I said, smiling at her. "Smart as paint. That costume's a knock out."

"Don't lie," she said sharply, although her frown went away. "You know you're just saying that."

"No kidding. What are you waiting for .... get in. If I'd've known you were going to look as good as this, I'd've been here yesterday."

She got into the car. Her skirt was so tight that it rode up as she settled down on the springy cushions. I took my time closing the door.

"Did anyone tell you that you've a swell pair of eyes?" I said, grinning down at her.

She hurriedly adjusted her skirt. "Now behave, Clive," she said, with a little giggle.

"That'll be hard work with you looking like you do," I said and slid under the steering wheel.

"You're sure I look all right?" She opened her bag and peered into a small enamel-backed mirror.

"Positive," I said, offering her a cigarette, "You could go anywhere with anyone."

She looked at me with malicious humour. "I bet you thought I was going to look like a tart, didn't you?" she asked. I could see she was pleased that she had surprised me.

I laughed. "I'll admit it," and I gave her a light.

"Do you know what?" She forced smoke down her nostrils. "I'm as nervous as a cat."

I was nervous too. Perhaps not nervous, but shy. This was a new experience for me and I was getting a big bang out of it.

"I don't believe it. Why should you be nervous with me?"

"Well, I am. Where are we going?"

"First the Manhattan Grill and then to see *My Sister Eileen*. All right?"

"Hmmm." She flicked ash from the cigarette. "I hope you've a table against the wall."

"Why?" I asked puzzled. "Why do you want a table against the wall?"

"I like to see people coming in," she said, not looking at me. "I have to be careful, Clive. My husband has friends all over,"

Now I was discovering things. "So that's why we can't go to the Brown Derby and the rest of the high spots," I said. "Would your husband object to me?"

She nodded. "It'll be all right once I've told him about you, but I don't want anyone to tell him first."

"You mean he wouldn't mind you going out with me if he knew about me?"

Again she nodded.

"Why wouldn't he? I'd mind like hell if I were your husband."

 Her lips tightened. "He trusts me."

That's more than I would do, I thought. If I were your husband I would not trust you further than I could throw you. "I see," I said. "Well, how are you going to put me right with your husband? You don't even know who I am."

She looked at me out of the corners of her eyes. "I was rather expecting that you'd tell me that."

I did some quick thinking. "Do all your other men friends tell you who they are?" I hedged.

"I don't go out with other men," she said. "You see, I do have to be careful."

"In your game with an unsuspecting husband, I suppose you do," I returned. "But where is he? What does he do, for God's sake?"

She hesitated for a moment. "He's an engineer. I only see him once in months. He's in Brazil now."

I didn't know whether I liked all this. "Suppose he takes it into his head to fly back tonight?" I asked jokingly, although at the back of my mind I thought it would be an awkward situation for me if he did.

She shook her head emphatically. "He won't. You don't have to worry. He always tells me when he's coming back."

I still was not too happy. "Maybe he might surprise you some day. Isn't it risky?"

"Why? You don't think that place is my home, do you? It's just my business address. I was thinking about taking you back to my real home tonight, but then I thought it would be better not to."

"So you've two homes? Where's the other one?"

"Los Angeles." By the way she said it I knew I wasn't getting any more out of her.

"So he doesn't know anything about Laurel Canyon Drive?"

"Of course, he doesn't."

"And you have to be careful?"

She hunched her shoulders. "He'd kill me if he found out," and she giggled suddenly.

I started the engine and engaged the gear. "You've an odd sense of humour."

She shrugged. "I suppose he'll find out. I always say my sins will find me out. They will too. Then I'll have to run to you for protection."

"Before I commit myself, I want to know just how big your husband is," I returned, knowing she was fooling.

"He's very big," she returned, sliding down in her seat so that her head rested against the cushioned back. "And tough and strong."

"Now you're getting me scared," I said grinning. "You'll be telling me he beats you next."

She smiled in a secret sort of a way. "He does sometimes."

I shot her a quick, startled glance. "You're the last woman I would have thought to stand for that."

"I'd stand anything for him except another woman."

I could tell by her voice that she meant it and I experienced an irritable pang of envy. I had not reckoned with a husband for a rival.

"How long have you been married?"

"Oh a long time." She turned her head so she could look at me. "And don't keep asking questions."

"I won't," I said and to change the subject, "do you know what would be swell?"

"What?"

"A large Scotch and soda. Don't you think that'd be swell or don't you drink?"

"I don't mind, but I don't drink much."

"How much?"

She giggled. "I can't take it. Three Scotches and I'm tight."

"I don't believe you."

"You don't have to. I'm just telling you." She flicked the cigarette butt out of the window.

"All right, then let's get tight," I said and turned the car into Vine Street and pulled up outside the little bar in sight of the Brown Derby.

She peered out of the window doubtfully. "Is this all right?" she asked. "I haven't been here before."

"It's all right," I said, getting out of the car and walking round to open the door for her. "I always come here when I want to do a Garbo." As she got out, I again admired her legs. "You should relax. After all, we haven't done anything wrong ... yet."

She followed me into the bar which was half empty.

The Negro bartender smiled at me.

"You sit over there and I'll get you a drink," I said. "Scotch?"

She nodded and moved across to a table in the far corner. I saw several men watching her with intent expressions. They watched her all the way to the table and one even turned in his chair to watch her sit down.

"Two double whiskies," I said to the bartender.

He shot them across the counter.

"And dry ginger."

As he went to the refrigerator, I leaned forward so that my back was to Eve and I emptied one of the whiskies into the other glass. If three whiskies made her tight, I thought, let's see what four can do.

The Negro gave me the dry ginger and I divided it between the two glasses.

"There you are," I said, joining Eve at the table. "To a lovely weekend." I drank some of the dry ginger. It tasted like hell without any whisky.

She looked at her glass. "What's this?"

"A whisky with a lot of dry ginger," I said. "What do you think it is?"

"There seems an awful lot of whisky."

"They leave the dry ginger out in the sun here. It gives it a suntan."

She drank half of the liquor, pulled a face and put the glass on the table. "There's more than one whisky in that."

"Can I help it if the barman gets the shakes? Come on, one more and we'll go."

"You're trying to get me tight," she said sharply.

I laughed at her. "Nuts," I said. "Why should I want to do that?"

She shrugged, finished the whisky and didn't protest as I went to the bar again. I went through the same process. For a time, anyway, I wanted to keep sober.

I kept my eye on her when we got into the street. As far as I could see, the whisky hadn't touched her. "Three whiskies and I'm tight," she had said. Perhaps I should have kept it to three. She was now carrying eight whiskies and she looked as sober as a coffin.

"How are you feeling?" I asked, when we had reached the Manhattan Grill.

"All right." She slid out of the car. "Why?"

"I just like to keep in touch with you," I returned, following her into the grill room.

There was a big crowd in the cocktail bar and Eve hung back. Her eyes scanned faces and the two lines above the bridge of her nose were now deep furrows.

I took her elbow in my hand and pushed her gently through the crowd. "It's all right," I said. "Don't get jumpy."

"I don't know if it is," she returned under her breath. "This is too crowded for me."

We worked our way into the restaurant and when she had settled down on the sofa seat against the wall, she looked happier.

"I'm always like this," she said, her eyes moving continuously round the room. "I'm sorry, but I do have to be careful."

"Not always," I reminded her. "You only go out with me. Your other clients don't take you out."

"Sometimes they do," she said without thinking. "You don't expect me to stay home every night, do you?"

That was lie number two. First she said three whiskies laid her out when eight whiskies left her cold. Then she had said she never went out with her clients and now she said she did. I was beginning to wonder just how much was truth that she told me.

We ordered dinner.

As she was eight drinks ahead of me, I thought I might as well begin to catch up. After a couple of stiff shots, I suddenly decided to tell her who I was. She would have to know sooner or later and there seemed no sense in delaying any longer.

"Let's get introduced," I said. "You know my name well."

There was immediate interest in her eyes, "Do I? Don't tell me you're famous."

"Do I look famous?"

"Tell me who you are." She wasn't the Eve I knew any more. She was human, very curious and a little excited.

"The name," I said watching her closely, "is Clive Thurston."

She wasn't like Harvey Barrow. I could see it meant something to her at once. For a second, a look of disbelief was in her eyes, then she turned to face me. "So that's why you wanted to know what I thought of *Angels in Sables*," she exclaimed. "Of course. And I said I didn't like it."

"That's all right," I said. "I wanted the truth and I got it."

"I saw your play *Rain Check* ... Jack took me. I was sitting behind a pillar and only saw half of it."

"Jack?" I was on to that quickly.

"My husband."

"Did he like it?"

"Yes ..." she looked at me half hesitating. "I'd better introduce myself... I am Mrs. Pauline Hurst."

"Not Eve?"

"Eve to you please."

"Yes ... although I like Pauline. It suits you, but so does Eve."

After dinner, we drove over to the theatre. The play amused her as I hoped it would. We had several quick drinks during the intermissions. As we were returning from the bar during the last intermission, I felt someone touch my arm. I looked round and found Frank Imgram behind me.

"Do you like it?" he asked, smiling.

I could have strangled him. He was certain to tell Carol that he had seen me.

"It's good," I said, nodding at him, "and beautifully acted."

His eyes were on Eve. "Yes—isn't it?"

Then the crowd separated us and I struggled back into my seat. Eve looked at me inquiringly. "Someone you know?"

"Imgram who wrote *The Land is Barren*."

"Does it matter that he saw me?"

I shook my head. "Why should it?"

She shot me another look and did not say anything. The rest of the act was spoiled for me. I kept thinking of what Carol would say.

We were lucky to be among the first out. I did not see Imgram again.

We got into the car and drove down Vine Street.

"Want a drink before we go home?" I asked.

"I think so."

We went into the same little bar and we stayed there for some time. We drank a lot, but Eve did not show it. I was feeling a little drunk and I thought it was time to stop. After all, I was driving. "One more and then we'll go. Have a brandy?"

"Why?"

"Just to see if you can take it."

Her eyes were bright, otherwise she seemed all right. "I can take it," she said.

I ordered a double brandy.

She looked at me. "Not for you?"

"I'm driving."

She drank the brandy neat.

We got into the car and I drove slowly to Laurel Canyon Drive.

"You can put the car in the garage," she said. "There's room for it."

She had opened the front door and was waiting for me in the hall. I took my small grip from the Chrysler's trunk and followed her upstairs.

We entered the bedroom and she clicked on the lights.

"Well, here we are," she said and I could see she was a little embarrassed. She stood with her chin almost on her shoulder, her eyes looking away from me, her right arm making a protective V over her chest, her left hand cupped under her right elbow.

I dropped my grip on the bed and put my hands on her biceps and pressed a little. Her arms were nice, but small. My fingers almost met round them.

We stood like that for a few seconds, then I drew her to me.

For a moment she tried to pull away, then she slowly lowered her arms from in front of her and put them round my shoulders.

CHAPTER TEN

I woke feeling hot and stifled. The grey light of the dawn came through the two windows facing me and shrouded the little room with a soft, mysterious light. For a moment, I could not remember where I was, then I saw the glass animals on the chest of drawers and I looked immediately at Eve who was sleeping at my side.

She slept curled up, one arm above her head. Her eyes being closed, youth had descended on her face. I propped myself up on my elbow and watched her, marvelling that she could look so young and child-like. Sleep had smoothed the lines in her face and softened the hard, defiant chin. She looked, in sleep, more elfish than ever, but I knew when her eyes opened this would all go. It was her eyes that gave the clue to her character. They were the windows through which you could see her rebellious spirit and the secret shadows of her life. Even in sleep, she did not rest. Her body jerked and twitched and her mouth moved as if she were talking to herself. She moaned softly and her fingers clenched and unclenched. She slept like a woman who lived entirely on tortured, tightly strung nerves.

I lowered her arm from above her head. She sighed heavily and reaching out, she put her arms round me and gripped me tightly. "Darling," she murmured, "don't leave me."

Of course, she was asleep. Of course, she was not speaking to me. Perhaps she was dreaming of her husband or a lover; but I wanted it to be me she was speaking to and I held her close, her head on my shoulder.

Her body suddenly gave a great bound as if her nerves had bunched themselves together like a coiled spring and snapped apart. Then she woke and pushed away from me.

She blinked at me, yawned and flopped back on her pillow. "Hello," she said. "What time is it?"

I looked at my wrist watch. It was five thirty-five.

"Oh God!" she exclaimed. "Can't you sleep?"

I again realized how hot and stifling it was in the bed. "How many blankets have we got on?" I asked, counting them. There were five and a quilt. I must have been pretty drunk not to have noticed that last night.

"Do you want all these?" I asked her.

She yawned again. "Of course I do. I feel cold in bed."

"I'll say you do." I slid out and began to strip the blankets back. She sat up in alarm, "Don't do that, Clive ... you're not to!"

"Don't get excited," I said. "You'll get 'em back."

I folded the blankets so that I had only two over me. The rest I laid on her side. "How's that?"

She curled down in the bed again. "Mmmm," she sighed. "I've got an awful head. Was I tight last night?"

"You ought to've been."

"I think I was." She stretched luxuriously. "Oh, I'm so tired. Do go to sleep, Clive."

My mouth felt stale. I wished I could ring for Russell and have coffee. Obviously there was no service here.

She looked up. "Do you want coffee?"

I brightened. "Not a bad idea."

"Well, put the kettle on. Marty's left it all ready," and she drew the blankets to her chin.

It was a long time since I had made coffee for myself, but I wanted it, so I went into the other room. It was sparsely furnished with only one easy chair. The small kitchen was just beyond. I put on the kettle and lit a cigarette.

"Where's the bathroom?" I called.

"Upstairs on your right."

I climbed the steep stairs. There were three doors leading off the landing at the top of the stairs. Cautiously I looked into all three rooms. Except for the bathroom, the other two rooms were unfurnished. Dust lay on the floor and obviously no one ever went into them.

I went into the bathroom, sponged my face and brushed my hair; then I wandered downstairs again and found the kettle was boiling. I made coffee. A tray was on the table in the sitting room containing cups, sugar and cream. Then I returned to the bedroom.

Eve was sitting up in bed, a cigarette between her lips. She looked at me sleepily and scratched her head.

"I bet I look awful," she said.

"A little tousled, but oddly enough, it suits you."

"Don't lie, Clive."

"One of these days you'll get over your inferiority complex," I said, pouring out the coffee. "If this is bad, don't blame me."

I gave her a cup and sat on the bed.

"I'm going to sleep after this," she warned me. "So don't start talking."

"Okay," I returned. The coffee was not bad and the cigarette began to taste less like brown paper.

She stared out of the window at the fading stars. "You're not falling in love with me, are you?" she asked abruptly.

I nearly dropped my cup. "What on earth makes you ask that?" I said.

She looked at me, pursed her mouth and looked away again. "Well, if you are, you're wasting your time."

Her voice was brutal in its cold, flat finality.

"Why don't you admit it?" I said. "You've a hell of a hangover and you're looking for someone to pick on. Finish your coffee and go to sleep."

Her eyes darkened. "Don't say I didn't warn you. There's only one man in my life, Clive, and that's Jack."

"Just as it should be," I said lightly and finished my coffee. "So he means a lot to you, does he?"

She put her coffee cup down impatiently on the bedside table. "Every-thing," she said, "so don't think you can mean anything to me."

I found it difficult to control my rising irritation, but in her present sullen mood, so different from last night, I knew we would quarrel un-less I humoured her.

"All right," I said, taking off my dressing gown and sliding under the blankets, "I'll remember that Jack means everything to you."

"You'd better," she snapped and turning her back on me, she curled further down in the bed.

I stared up at the ceiling, savagely angry. I was angry with her because she had seen through me. She had sensed that she now meant something to me. She did. I did not want to admit it, but, there it was. I found her exciting, mysterious and I wanted her for myself. I knew it was lunacy. Perhaps if she had encouraged me it might have been different; but her calculated indifference made me want her all the more. It went beyond sex. I wanted to break down the wall she had erected between us. I wanted to make her care for me.

I woke again when the sun streamed through the cream blinds. Eve was in my arms, her head on my shoulder and her mouth against my throat. She was sleeping peacefully and her body was limp and still.

I held her, feeling good. She was easy to hold, light and small and warm. I liked her breath against my throat and the smell of perfume in her hair. She slept like that for almost an hour and then she moved, opened her eyes, raised her head and looked at me.

"Hello," she said and smiled.

I touched her face with my fingers. "Your hair smells nice," I said. "Did you sleep well?"

"Mmmmm." She yawned and rested her head back on my shoulder. "Did you?"

"Yes ... how's the head?"

"All right. Are you hungry? Shall I get you something to eat?"

"I'll get it."

"You stay here." She broke away from me and slid out of bed. In her blue nightdress, she looked slight and childish. She put on her dressing gown, looked in the mirror, grimaced and left me.

I went up to the bathroom, and after a leisurely shave, I returned to find her in bed. On the table by the bed was the tray containing fresh coffee and a plate of thinly cut bread and butter.

"You don't want me to cook you anything, do you?" she asked as I stripped off my dressing gown and slid into bed beside her.

"No, thank you. Don't tell me you can cook," I said, reaching for her hand and turning it over in mine.

"Of course I can," she returned. "Do you think I'm quite helpless?"

The palm of her hand was fleshless and hard and I could easily encircle her wrist in my thumb and forefinger. I examined the three sharply etched lines in her palm.

"You're independent," I said. "That's the key to your character."

She nodded. "I am independent."

I released her wrist and she examined her palm herself. "What else?" she asked.

"You're moody."

She nodded again. "I have an awful temper. I go crazy when I'm really angry."

"What makes you really angry?"

"Lots of things." She dumped the plate of bread and butter on my chest.

"Does Jack make you angry?"

"More than anyone." She sipped her coffee and stared blankly out of the window.

"Why?"

She pursed her lips and shrugged. "Oh, he's jealous of me and I'm jealous of him." She suddenly giggled. "We fight. Last time I went out to dinner with him, there was a woman he kept looking at. She was only a silly little blonde—she had a good figure though. I said he could go with her if he wanted to. He told me not to be a fool, but he didn't stop looking. I got mad then." Her eyes sparkled. "Do you know what I did?"

"Tell me."

"I grabbed the table cloth and I jerked everything onto the floor." She put down her coffee cup and laughed. "Oh, Clive, I wish you'd been there to see it. The mess—the noise—and Jack's face! Then I walked out and left him. I was still mad when I got home so I went into the sitting room and smashed everything that would smash. It was marvellous! You have no idea how marvellous it was. I went up to the mantelpiece and swept everything off it. The clock, Jack's glass animals," she pointed across to the chest of drawers, "those are the only ones that survived. I keep them here because he thinks they're all smashed. And there were photographs and—well you know—everything." She lit a cigarette and inhaled deeply. "Of course he was furious when he came back. I'd locked myself in the bedroom but he kicked the door down. I thought he was going to kill me but he just packed his bag and walked out without even looking at me."

"And you haven't seen him since?"

"Oh, he knows me." She tapped ash into her empty coffee cup. "He knows what I'm like. I'm always getting into tempers. I've no time for anyone who hasn't a temper ... have you?"

"I like a peaceful life."

She shook her head. "When Jack gets wild ..." she threw up her hands and laughed.

I found she was quite willing to talk about her husband. In fact, she seemed anxious and pleased to have someone who would listen. By asking her a few leading questions and by letting her talk, I pieced together much of her background.

I knew by now, that she was a skilful liar, but some of the things she told me I felt must be true.

She had been married for ten years. Before her marriage I gathered she had been pretty wild. She met Jack at a party and they took one look at each other and that was enough. It must have been one of those rare violent physical clashes that left no doubt that they were meant for each other. They were married almost immediately.

At that time, she had money of her own. She did not say how much she had, but she must have been fairly well off. Jack was a mining engineer whose work took him to many distant countries—places where a woman could not go. The first four years of their married life must have been dull and lonely for a woman like Eve. She was, of course, neurotic and highly strung. She had extravagant tastes and Jack was not making big money. That did not matter at the time because she kept her independence and refused to accept any of his money. He knew she was comfortably off and the arrangement suited him. But Eve was a gambler. She admitted that both Jack and she were born gamblers. She played the races while he concentrated on poker for big stakes. Because he was an expert player he made a little more than he lost.

While he was in West Africa—this would be some six years ago—she got in with a fast set and she began to drink heavily and to plunge recklessly on horses. She had continued bad luck, but it did not stop her. Always at the back of her mind, she believed that she could recoup her losses. Then one morning, she discovered that she had worked through every nickel of her capital and was high and dry. She knew Jack would be furious with her, so she did not tell him.

She was popular with men and it only needed this financial pressure to make her what she was now.

She had been living on men for the past six years. The unsuspecting Jack still thought that she had her comfortable income and she kept up the illusion.

"I suppose some day he'll find out ... then I don't know what'll happen," she concluded with a fatalistic shrug of her shoulders. "Why don't you give it up?" I asked, lighting my tenth cigarette.

"I must have money... and besides what shall I do with myself all day? It's lonely enough as it is."

"Lonely? Are you lonely?"

"I have no one ... except Marty. She goes about seven o'clock and I'm here by myself until she comes the following morning."

"But you have friends .... surely?"

"I've no one," she repeated flatly; "and I don't want anyone."

"Not even now that you know me?"

She twisted round in bed so she could look at me. "I wonder just what your game is," she said. "You're up to something. If you're not in love with me ... then what is it?"

"I've told you, I like you. You interest me and I want to be your friend."

"No man's my friend," she said.

I stubbed out my cigarette and slid my arm round her, pulling her close to me. "Don't be so suspicious," I said. "Everyone needs a friend some time or other. I might be able to help you."

She relaxed against me. "How? I don't need any help. The only trouble I might have is from the police. I have a judge who would take care of that."

She was right of course, apart from money there was nothing I could really do for her.

"You might be ill ..." I began, but she just laughed at me. "I've never been ill and if I was no one would care. That's a time when men always leave a woman. She's no use to them when she's ill."

"You're a hell of a cynic, aren't you?"

"So would you be if you'd lived my life."

I rested my face against her hair. "Do you like me, Eve?"

"You're all right," she returned indifferently; "and don't fish, Clive."

I laughed. "Where shall we lunch?"

"Anywhere ... I don't mind."

"Shall we take a movie in tonight?"

"All right."

"That's fixed then." I looked at the clock on the mantelshelf. It was after twelve. "You know I could do with a drink."

"And I must have a bath." She slid away from me and got out of bed. "Make the bed, Clive. That's one thing I can never do."

"All right," I said, watching her fuss before the mirror.

I got up and made the bed. Then I went into the other room and telephoned the Barbecue Restaurant and reserved a sofa table against the wall.

Eve had come down by then.

"The water's running," she called. "What shall I wear?"

"Oh, a dress, I think," I said. "Although I liked that costume last night."

"Costumes suit me better than a dress." She came to the door as I was going upstairs. She put her hands on her flat chest. "They suit my figure," she added and giggled.

"All right," I returned, "you please yourself."

The rest of the day passed too quickly for me. I seemed to have gained her complete confidence and she talked about her experiences with men and her husband was never far from her conversation. We enjoyed ourselves. But I had a feeling that I could only get so far. There was still this invisible wall which every now and then I came up against. She would not tell me how much she earned. When I asked her if she saved money, she said, "Every Monday I go to the bank and deposit one half of what I've made. I never touch that."

This came out so glibly that I did not believe her. I knew how careless and extravagant this kind of woman always is. I was willing to bet that she had not saved a nickel, although of course, I could not give her the lie.

I tried to persuade her to take out an endowment policy. "It'll be something when you are old and when you'll be glad of the money," I explained.

But she wasn't interested. I doubt if she even listened. "I can't be bothered," she said. "I'm saving money... besides what business is it of yours?"

One thing she said, pleased me. It was after we had seen Bogart's latest picture and we were driving back to Laurel Canyon Drive. We had both been drinking heavily and she had slipped low down in the cushioned seat of the car with her head back and her eyes closed. "Marty said I'd be bored with you," she said. "She thought I was crazy to spend a whole weekend with you. She'll be surprised when she hears I didn't throw you out."

I put my hand over hers. "Would you have thrown me out?"

"I would have if you bored me."

"So you've enjoyed the weekend?"

"Mmmm ... very much."

Well, that was something.

We lay in the dark and talked far into the night. I do not think she had talked with such complete freedom to anyone for a long time. It was as if she had opened the gates of a dam and words came from her at first haltingly and then in an uninterrupted flow. I cannot remember everything she said. Although most of it was about Jack. Their life seemed to be made up of endless quarrels and wildly exciting reunions. From what she told me, his relations with her were based on a kind of brutal affection which appealed to her odd, complex nature. The fact that he occasionally beat her made no difference so long as he was faithful to her. Of this, she was sure. She told me how one evening they had come home from a party and she had slipped and fallen in the street. She had turned her ankle which immediately swelled up. Jack had laughed at her and had left her sitting on the curb. He was tired and he wanted his bed. When she did finally limp home, she found him asleep and the following morning, he drove her out of bed, when she could hardly walk, to bring him coffee. She seemed to admire him the more for this kind of treatment.

This defeated me. It was so outside my normal relations with women that I could not understand it.

"Are you telling me that you don't like considerate treatment?" I asked her.

I felt her shoulders lift. "I hate weakness, Clive. Jack's strong. He knows what he wants and nothing will stop him."

"Well, if you like to be treated like that ..." I gave up.

When she talked about the men who came to see her, she did not mention names. I admired her for her discretion. At least, it meant that she would not talk about me.

CHAPTER ELEVEN

I reached my apartment around noon. As I entered the elevator the boy gave me one of those it's-six-months-to-Christmas smiles. "Good morning, Mr. Thurston."

"Morning," I said and experienced the inevitable lift in my stomach as the elevator raced between floors.

"Did you see about the two guys who killed themselves last night outside Manola's?" The elevator boy asked as I left the cage.

"No."

"Sure thing. They got fighting over a dame and they fell off the sidewalk, bang under the wheels of a truck. One of the guys had his face stove in."

"That should give him a new outlook," I said and opened my apartment door.

Russell was in the lobby. "Good morning, Mr. Clive," he said in a voice that told me he thought it was anything but a good morning.

"Hello." I was about to go to my bedroom when I caught his eye. I stopped. "What's wrong?"

"Miss Carol's waiting in the lounge," he said reproachfully. His whole body, his face, his eyebrows oozed reproach.

"Miss Carol?" I stared at him. "What's she want? Why isn't she at the Studio?"

"I don't know, sir. She's been waiting more'n a half an hour."

I gave him my bag. "Put that in my bedroom," I said, and walked across the lobby to the lounge.

Carol was by the window as I entered. She did not turn although she must have heard me. I admired her slim back and the cool white and red check frock she was wearing. "Hello," I said, closing the door.

She stubbed her cigarette in the ashtray and swung round on her heels. She looked steadily at me and my eyes gave ground. "Aren't you working this morning?" I went on, crossing the room and standing by her side.

"I wanted to see you."

"Swell." I waved to the settee. "Sit down."

As she walked to the settee, I said, "Nothing wrong, is there?"

She sat down. "I don't know yet." She reached for another cigarette, fitted it in her holder and lit up.

I suddenly felt a little tired and not in the mood to be lectured. I stood over her. "Look here, Carol ..." I began, but she held up her hand.

"It's not going to be a 'Look here...' kind of conversation," she said sharply.

"I'm sorry, Carol, but I'm on edge this morning." I didn't want to quarrel with her. "There's something wrong. You'd better give it to me straight."

"I met Merle Bensinger this morning. She's worried about you."

"If Merle Bensinger's been discussing my affairs with you," I said coldly, "she's forgetting she's my paid agent."

"Merle likes you, Clive. She thought we were engaged."

I sat down slowly in an armchair away from Carol. "Even if we were married, it's still not Merle's business to talk about my affairs," I said, cold fury tripping my words.

"She didn't talk about your affairs," Carol said quietly. "She asked me to try to persuade you to work."

I lit a cigarette and tossed the match into the empty fireplace. "But I am working," I said. "If she's worried about her goddam commission, why doesn't she say so?"

"All right, Clive, if that's the way you feel about it."

"That's just the way I do feel about it. For God's sake, Carol, no writer can be bullied into writing. You know that. It's either there or it isn't. Merle wanted me to do a cockeyed article for the *Digest*. I just didn't feel like it. That's why she's sore."

"She didn't say anything about the *Digest*, but never mind about Merle then." She crossed her slim ankles. "About Bernstien, Clive."

"What about him?"

"You know he came round to my place on Saturday?"

"Yeah, you told me."

"I did what I could. I read him parts of your play. I even persuaded him to take it away with him."

I stared at her. "You gave him a copy of the play?" I repeated. "Where did you get the script from?"

"Oh, I got it," she said, a little impatiently. "That doesn't matter. I did so hope ..." She broke off with a gesture of despair. Then she said, "If you had been there, it would have made all the difference. I'm afraid you've missed a great chance, Clive."

I dragged down a lungful of smoke. "I don't believe it," I said. "If Bernstien was all that anxious to do *Rain Check*, he'd have done it. A guy who has to be talked into buying a story doesn't stay hot. He cools off after making a lot of promises. Don't tell me Imgram had to talk Gold into buying his story."

"There's a big difference between *Rain Check* and *The Land is Barren*," Carol said sharply. Then as I shifted impatiently, she went on, "I'm sorry, Clive. I didn't mean it in that way. You can't compare ... I mean ..."

"All right, all right," I said angrily. "You don't have to handle me with kid gloves. You mean my stuff isn't good enough to stand up by itself. It needs you and Jerry Highams and me to slop over Bernstien before he'll even look at it."

She bit her lip nervously, but she didn't say anything.

"Well, that's not the way I want to sell my stuff. When I do sell it, I'll sell it because it's worth selling. I won't need to peddle it like a street salesman. So to hell with Bernstien."

"All right, Clive, to hell with Bernstien. But, you're not getting anywhere, are you?"

"I'm all right. Can't you lay off worrying about me? Now, look here, Carol, let's get this straight. When I want anyone's help, I'll let you know.

There're too many people taking an interest in me. It embarrasses me."
So as not to hurt her feelings, I added, "Of course, I am grateful, but,
after all, it is my business. I'm getting along fine."

She again looked steadily at me. "Are you?" she said. "You've written nothing for two years. You're living on the past, Clive. That's just one
thing you can't do in Hollywood. A writer's only as good as his next
book or picture."

"But my next picture is going to be good," I said, trying to smile.
"Don't fuss, Carol. After all, Gold has made me an offer. That ought to
tell you I'm not on the slide."

"Oh, do stop posing, Clive," she said, colour coming into her face. "It's
not a question of whether you can write. It's a question of when you're
going to work."

"Okay, suppose you leave that to me?" I said. "What are you doing
away from the Studio? I thought you were tied up with Imgram."

"So I am. But I had to see you, Clive. People are talking." She got to
her feet and wandered across the room. "We're supposed to be engaged,
aren't we?"

That was something I didn't want to go into just them. "What do you
mean ... people are talking?"

"About this weekend." She turned to face me. "How could you,
Clive? How could you do such a thing? Have you gone crazy?"

Here it comes, I thought. "If I knew what you were talking about ..."

"Why lie to me? I know what happened. I should have thought by now
you'd got all that out of your system. You still don't think you're a col-
lege boy, do you?"

I stared at her. "What do you mean? Got what out of my system?"

She sat down again. "Oh, Clive, at times, you are stupid and hateful,"
she said, wearily. Anger had gone out of her voice. She was now desperately unhappy. "You want to be irresistible, don't you? You want to
be the big charmer and sweep all the women off their feet. Why do you
pick on a woman like that? Where do you think it'll get you?"

I reached impatiently for a cigarette. "You're saying some pretty hard
things, Carol." I was controlling my temper with difficulty. "I'm not in
the mood to stand much more of this. Maybe you'd better go back to
the Studio before we say something we'll be sorry about later."

She sat still for a few seconds, her hands clenched on her knees and her
body tense. Then she drew a deep breath and relaxed. "I'm sorry,
Clive," she said. "I'm going the wrong way about it. Can't you stop all
this? Can't you just drop the whole thing? It's not too late, Clive."

I flicked ash angrily onto the carpet. "You're making a fuss about nothing," I said. "For God's sake, Carol, you must be sensible."

"Did you get anywhere with her over the weekend?" she asked abruptly. "Has she fallen for your charms yet?"

I jerked to my feet. "Now look, Carol, I've had enough of this. I'd much rather you go. We'll hurt each other in a moment."

"Rex Gold has asked me to marry him."

Years ago I was kicked by a horse. It was my own fault. I had been warned of its viciousness, but I thought I could handle it. But it suddenly had lashed out and I remembered lying on the wet, muddy ground, pain twisting at my guts and staring at the horse, not believing that it could have done this to me. I felt the same twisting pain in my guts now.

"Gold?" I said and sat down again.

Carol beat her fists together. "I shouldn't have told you now," she said. "It's blackmail, isn't it, Clive? No, I shouldn't have told you now."

"I didn't think that Gold ..." and I stopped.

Why not? She was lovely. She was good at her job. She would make Gold a fine wife.

"What are you going to do?" I asked, after a long silence.

"I don't know," she said. "Not after this weekend."

"What has the weekend to do with it?" I asked. "I'd've thought it was whether you loved him or not."

"Not in Hollywood," Carol said. "You know that as well as I do. If I thought that you and I ..." She stopped, hesitated, and then went on, "You're making it very hard for me, aren't you?"

I didn't say anything.

"You see, I love you, Clive."

I reached out to take her hand, but she drew away. "No, don't touch me. Let me talk. I've stood an awful lot from you. We've known each other for two years now. I suppose it's silly of me to live in the past, but I can't help remembering you when you first came to see Robert Rowan. Neither of us were anybody then. I liked you the moment I saw you. I thought your play was fine. I thought anyone who had these kind of sentiments must be good and kind and decent. I liked the scared, embarrassed look you always had when Rowan talked to you. You were simple and nice and not like the other men who came to that office. I thought you were going to do great things; that's why I told you to come out here and leave New York and everything it stood for. There was a time, before you found all your other friends, when you were glad to have me for company. We went everywhere and did everything. Once you asked me to marry you and I said yes. But, you'd forgotten about it the next morning. You didn't even bother to call me. I don't know, even now, how you feel about me, but I know how I feel about you. But that doesn't mean that I'm holding you to anything. That's not the way I want you."

I wished she had not started this. I knew a decision had to be made and I wanted time to think. Until Saturday night, I loved Carol, now I was not sure. I knew I could not let her go on talking like this, stripping herself in front of me, unless I met her half way. Otherwise, it would finish when she left me and I did not want it to finish. She was important to me. She represented the past two years which were the best years of my life. She represented understanding and kindness. She gave me confidence. It scared me to think what it would be like without her.

"I believed you when you said you loved me," she went on. "I suppose it was because you meant so much to me. There was something fine about you, Clive, when you were poor. I suppose success is bad for some people. It's been bad for you. You see, I'm worried about you. I can't really see how you're going to get anywhere now. You haven't learned anything new since you first began to write. You think you have the magic touch, but you haven't. No one has ... there isn't such a thing. It all comes from working and never being satisfied and moving on to a bigger theme each time you write. Then, of course, you must feel you want to say something and that something must be worthwhile saying."

"That's a terrific speech," I said impatiently, "but we'll take it as read if you don't mind. What about you? Are you going to marry Gold?"

She closed her eyes. "I don't know," she said. "I don't want to, but it has many advantages."

"Are you sure?"

"Gold has imagination .... power ... money. He would give me a free hand. There are some great pictures to be made. Perhaps that is something you won't understand, Clive. But I'm ambitious. Not for myself. I want to see better pictures made. I could influence Gold. He would listen to me."

"Never mind about educating the world, let's concentrate on ourselves. You don't have to marry Gold to educate the world, do you?"

"Would you mind?"

I had to talk now or I'd lose her. "Of course I'd mind, but I want you to try to see it from my angle. I love you. I've loved you for a long time, but there isn't much I can do about it right now. Something's gone wrong. I can't write any more. If something doesn't happen soon, I'll be in a fix. I've been in a fix before, of course, but I've always been alone. I couldn't stand being in a fix with you."

She examined her slim brown hands. "It's only because you are out of touch with the things that matter. You've been having too good a time."

She paused, adjusted her cuffs so that they hid her wrists, and then jerked out, "Why did you have to take that woman where you would be seen together?"

Rage swept through me. "So that goddam success-writer squawked, did he?" I said. "I thought he would. That's just about his weight—making mischief and gossiping."

"Jerry Highams saw you too," Carol said wearily.

"Well, what of it? Highams knows why I'm seeing her. There's nothing else to it Carol. I wouldn't lie.to you. I've a whale of a story I want to write about her. But that's all."

Carol stood up. "I must get back to the Studio," she said. "I'm sorry about all this, Clive. There's nothing we can do, is there?"

"Don't you believe me?" I asked, going to her. "Gold commissioned this story. How else can I write it if I don't meet the woman?"

She shook her head. "I don't know, Clive, and I don't particularly care. I'm rather tired of your women friends. I've had to share you with so many of them. I don't feel like competing with professionals. Until you've dropped her, I think we'd better not meet."

"You can't mean that, Carol," I said in alarm. "Don't you want me to have a break? Gold's offering fifty thousand dollars. I can't write the story if I don't see her." As she turned away, I took her arm. "Look, I tell you there's nothing in it except the story. Can't you believe that?"

She pulled her arm free. "No ... but don't forget to be careful, Clive. You'll get hurt. She knows how to handle a man like you."

My temper boiled up at this. "All right," I said, furious with her now. "You're a dear, sweet girl. Thank you for the warning. I'll be careful. Every time I see her, I'll think of you and your warning and I'll be very, very careful."

She flushed. "You can keep your cheap sarcasm. You are asking for trouble and I'm very much afraid you'll get it."

"You don't have to be afraid of anything. As long as I have your pity, I'll get along fine," I said. "We don't have to quarrel about it, do we? It's nicer for us to be agreeable and sort of phony about all this, isn't it?"

"You're the authority on phony, of course," she retorted, stung to anger. "But, if that's really how you feel, then we don't have to quarrel about it."

"Swell." I was determined to make her as angry as I was. "And ask me to the wedding. I won't come, but ask me because that'll be the one time I'll be able to turn Gold down. But I'm not turning down his fifty thousand dollars."

There was contempt in her eyes and I suddenly wanted to hurt her.

"I can imagine the kind of wedding that Gold'll give you," I went on, smiling at her. "It'll be a technicolour wedding. You know the sort of stuff. The bride looked lovely. She gave herself to Rex Gold so she could educate the world by making better pictures. That'll get a hell of a laugh." I took out my cigarette case and selected a cigarette. "You did say you weren't competing with the professionals? Is that quite true, my sweet?"

"I hope she hurts you," Carol said, her face white. "You need hurting. You need a woman like that who can prick your mean, horrid little ego. I think she'll do it. I hope so. I hope so very much."

"You know, I'm glad you're a girl. I'm glad you're in my apartment and under my protection, because it stops me doing what I feel like doing."

"I suppose you'd like to punch me in the face?"

"That's it. That's just what I'd like to do, my pet."

"Good-bye, Clive."

"That's terrific. That's what they call restrained drama. It'd make a great curtain. Nothing vulgar ... final, of course, but definitely not vulgar. You're a swell script writer and you've a swell sense of the theatre. But you'll have to watch your lines on your wedding night, my sweet."

She was at the door. She didn't look back. Then she was gone. When the door closed behind her, the room seemed very empty. I went over to the sideboard and poured myself a whisky. I drank it without putting the bottle down and I immediately poured another. I did that four times. Then I put the bottle back and walked into the lobby. I was feeling a little tight and I wanted to cry.

As I put my hat on, Russell came down the stairs. He looked at me mournfully, but he didn't say anything.

"Miss Carol's marrying Mr. Rex Gold," I said, carefully pronouncing my words. "I know you like these snappy little gossip items, Russell. You've heard of Mr. Rex Gold, haven't you? Well, she's marrying him. She's marrying him so she can make good pictures and educate the lower classes." I leaned on the banister rail. "Do you think the lower classes want to be educated? Do you think the sacrifice is worthwhile? I don't. I don't think they give a goddam whether she marries Gold or whether they have better pictures. But you can't argue with women."

Russell looked as if I had hit him in the face. He tried to say something, but words would not come. I left him and took the elevator to the street.

I got in the car.

"You poor guy," I said to myself. "I feel so sorry for you."

Then I pressed the starter and drove to the Writers' Club. The usual crowd was not in the club this day. I said hello to the steward and went into the bar.

"A double Scotch," I said, pulling up a stool and sitting down.

"Yes, Mr. Thurston," the bartender said. "Would you like a little ice?"

"Listen," I leaned forward, "if I wanted ice, I'd ask for ice. I don't want a lot of talk from you or anyone else."

"Certainly, Mr. Thurston," he said, going red.

I drank the whisky neat and shoved the glass back at him. "I'll have it again without ice and without a lot of talk. You don't even have to mention the weather."

"Certainly, Mr. Thurston."

If I did not sell Gold my story I would be like this guy before long. I would be so hard up for money that I would have to take anything anyone liked to hand out to me.

I finished my whisky. "Fill it up again."

Just then Peter and Frank Imgram came in.

It was too bad that they had to come in at that moment because I was very angry and rather drunk. I got off my stool.

Peter smiled at me. "Hello there, Clive," he said. "Have one with me? You know Frank Imgram, don't you?"

I know him all right.

"Sure," I said and took a step backwards and got into position. "The Hollywood gossip writer, isn't he?" And I let Imgram have it, full in the mouth. He fell back and gurgled and reached fingers in his mouth to keep from choking on his bridgework. He may have written *The Land is Barren,* but his teeth weren't his own. That was something I had over him.

I didn't wait to see what happened. I just walked out of the bar. I went through the lobby and into the street. I got into my car and started the engine. I had to control myself because I wanted to go back and hit the little louse again. I wanted to hit him again so badly that I ached behind my eyes and nose and at the back of my neck.

I thought: Merle Bensinger, Carol, dear, sweet Carol and now Frank Imgram ... possibly Peter Tennett. They would all hate my guts now. I was certainly making a mess of things. If I went on like this I would be getting quite a name for myself.

I drove fast down Sunset Boulevard. In a few days, perhaps, no one would want to talk to me. Perhaps I would have to resign from the Club. Never mind, I said to myself, you still have Eve. I slowed down, because I suddenly wanted to talk to Eve. That was something no one was going to do anything about. They might stop me from beating up Imgram, but they certainly would not stop me telephoning Eve.

I pulled up outside a drugstore, left my car and went in.

I had trouble with the dial. I was tighter than I thought. I misdialled three times before I got it right. By that time I was sweating and angry.

Marty came on the line.

"Miss Marlow," I said.

"Who is that?"

What the hell was it to do with her? Why didn't Eve answer the telephone herself? Did she think I wanted to talk to her servant every time I called? Did she think I wanted to give my name to a servant who would tell the milkman, the iceman and all the guys she got drunk with?

"The man in the moon," I said, "that's who it is."

There was a pause, then she said, "I'm sorry, but Miss Marlow's out."

"No, she isn't," I said, angrily. "Not at this time, she isn't. Tell her I want to talk to her."

"What name shall I give?"

"Oh, for God's sake. Mr. Clive ... now are you happy?"

"I'm so sorry, but Miss Marlow's engaged."

"Engaged?" I repeated stupidly. "But it's not yet two o'clock. How can she be engaged?"

"I'm sorry," she said again. "I will tell her you called."

"Now wait a minute," I said, feeling sick and empty, "you mean she has some guy with her?"

"I will tell her you called," Marty said and hung up.

I dropped the receiver and left it swinging on its cord. I felt like hell.

CHAPTER TWELVE

I came out of a heavy sleep to find Russell drawing the curtains. I sat up with a groan, aware that my head was aching and my tongue was like a strip of leather.

"Mr. Tennett's asking to see you, sir," Russell said, plodding over to stand at the foot of the bed. His fat face was full of foreboding. Then I remembered Imgram.

"Oh hell," I said, flopping back on my pillow. "What's the time?"

"It's just after ten thirty." He continued to look accusingly at me.

"Do come off your high horse, Russell," I exclaimed. "I suppose you've heard what happened at the Writers' Club?"

"I did, sir," he said, compressing his lips. "I am very sorry to hear about it."

"I bet you are," I said, wishing my head did not ache so violently. I must have got pretty drunk when I had returned to the apartment. I could not even remember going to bed. "The little louse asked for it."

Russell cleared his throat. "Mr. Tennett's waiting, sir," he reminded me.

I groaned. "Very well. Tell him to wait. But I've no idea what he can do. I don't think there's anything anyone can do."

When he had gone away, I got up and crawled into the bathroom. A cold shower eased my aching head. After I had shaved, I mixed myself a brandy and soda and by the time I had dressed I felt more myself.

I found Peter in the sitting room.

"Hello," I said, going to the sideboard and mixing myself another brandy and soda. "I was sleeping. Sorry to have kept you waiting."

"That's all right," he said.

"Drink?"

He shook his head.

I came over and sat down on the settee near him. There was an awkward pause. We looked at each other and then looked away. "It's about Imgram of course?" I said.

"Well, yes, it's about Imgram. I suppose you were tight?"

"Do I have to defend myself?" I demanded, trying to keep calm about the whole thing, but feeling my temper rising.

"Don't think I'm here to criticize," he said quickly. "Although I must admit I'm surprised you could have done such a thing. I came to tell you that Gold intends to sue you."

I stared at him. "Gold intends to sue me?" I repeated. That was something I had not expected to hear.

Peter nodded. "I'm afraid so. You see Imgram's hurt. He won't be able to work for some days. The delay's going to cost the Studio money and Gold's furious."

I felt a sudden stab of satisfaction. At least, I had hurt the little louse. "I see," I said.

"I thought I'd better come round and talk to you," Peter went on. He was uneasy and embarrassed and I could see by his expression that he found the whole business very distasteful. "R.G. says it'll cost him a hundred thousand."

"Quite an expensive punch," I returned, feeling suddenly cold and scared. "He wasn't thinking of suing me for that amount, was he?"

"Technically speaking, he couldn't sue you at all. Imgram would have to do that," Peter explained. He stared down at his perfectly polished shoes, then added, "R.G.'s seen Imgram."

"So he's seen Imgram." I drank half the brandy and soda. It did not taste so good. "And Imgram's going to sue me for a hundred thousand dollars? I don't think he'll get the money."

Peter carefully touched off his cigarette ash with his little finger. "Imgram won't sue you," he said. "He told Gold he wouldn't."

I put my glass down. "What's the idea?"

"I don't know," Peter said frankly. "I think I would have sued you. It was a pretty filthy thing to do, wasn't it, Clive?"

I waved that aside. "Do you mean he's turning the other cheek?"

Peter nodded. "Something like that."

I got to my feet. "Why the greasy little beast!" I exclaimed furiously. "He can't treat me like that. Let him sue! Do you think l care? Do you think I care what he does?"

"Look here, Clive, you'd better sit down. You've done enough harm as it is without adding to it. What's the matter with you? Do you realize that Carol's gone to pieces?"

I stood over him. "Now look, Peter, I don't have to take anything from you. That's one thing I am sure of. So keep out of this. Keep right out of it."

"I wish I could," Peter said, lifting his hands in a despairing gesture. "Do you think I like any of it? You don't seem to realize how serious this is. You're up against Gold. Anything that affects Gold affects the Studio. That punch has caused a lot of trouble, don't know why you did it. Probably you had every reason for punching Imgram. I don't know and I don't want to know. It's done now and it's upset our working schedule. To add to our troubles, Carol's gone haywire. She can't concentrate and I believe you're at the bottom of it all."

I sat down again. "It looks as if everything's going to be blamed on to me," I said bitterly. "What the hell am I going to do?"

"I think you'd better get out of town for a few days," Peter said. "Can't you go to Three Point? I don't want you to run into R.G. ... not in his present mood. You see Imgram won't take any action and we're trying to persuade R.G. to leave you alone. At the moment, Clive, he's after your blood."

If that's the way he's feeling, I thought, then it looks like curtains for my film script.

"I can't leave town just now," I said, after a moment's thought. "I've too much on hand, but I'll be careful to keep out of his way."

Peter looked worried. "It'll probably work out," he said, getting to his feet. "I'd better be getting over to the Studio. We're in a frightful mess at the moment and R.G.'s like a bear with a sore head. Be a good chap and lie low for a few days."

"I will," I promised. "By the way, Peter, you know I'm working on a story for Gold. Do you think this'll upset it?"

Peter shrugged. "It may. It depends how long we are held up. If it blows over quickly and the story's good, then it should be all right. R.G.'s a business man. He's not likely to pass up a good story. But it has, of course, to be outstanding."

"Yes." I walked with him to the door, feeling depressed and worried. I began to realize what a fool I had been to have punched Imgram. It might easily influence my future career.

"Can you do anything about Carol?" Peter asked abruptly.

"I guess not."

He looked steadily at me and I felt suddenly ashamed,

"She loves you, Clive," he said quietly. "She's a great kid and she doesn't deserve to be treated like this. There was a time when I thought you two were serious about each other. I know it's not my business, but I hate seeing her go to pieces."

I didn't say anything.

He stood hesitating, then said with a little shrug, "Well, I'm sorry. Perhaps she'll get over it. Good-bye, Clive. Lie low for a while. I'm sure it'll blow over if you're careful."

"Sure, I said. "And thanks for coming."

When he had gone I returned to the sitting room and had another drink. I wanted to go to Carol, but, somehow I just could not bring myself to face her. I had hurt her and was sure that if I went to her now, my task would be much harder than if I gave her time to recover. Besides, I had too much on my mind. I was not worried about Imgram, but I was worried about Gold. He could be dangerous if he wanted to be. I sat down and thought about it. Perhaps I should see him and try to explain, but I finally decided that Peter knew best. I would have to make up my mind to keep out of sight until things quieted down.

I looked angrily round the big sitting room, knowing that I could not bear the idea of spending day after day caged in these four walls. I would go mad. It was not as if I could settle down with a book as I did in the old days. Hollywood had made me restless and the thought of being alone, even for a few hours, was intolerable.

I glanced at my watch. It was eleven forty-five. Then I thought of Eve. She would be in bed—probably asleep. I knew what I was going to do. I would call on her and persuade her to have lunch with me. As soon as I had decided to do this, I felt a great surge of relief. Eve would be the solution to my loneliness. As long as I had her I did not care what happened.

I reached Laurel Canyon Drive a few minutes after noon. I pulled up outside Eve's house, left the car and walked quickly down the path. I knocked and stood waiting.

The door was opened almost immediately and Eve stood there, blinking in the strong sunlight. She stared at me. "Clive!" she said and giggled. "I thought you were the milkman." She had obviously just got out of bed. Her hair was ruffled and she was without makeup. "What on earth are you doing here at this time?"

I smiled down at her. "Hello, Eve," I said. "I thought I'd give you a surprise. Can I come in?"

She pulled her dressing gown about her and yawned. "I was just going to take a bath. Oh Clive, you are the limit. You might, at least, have 'phoned."

I followed her into her bedroom. The room smelt faintly of perfume and stale perspiration. She went over and jerked open the windows.

"Phew! It stinks in here, doesn't it?" she said, sitting on the bed and scratching her head. "Oh I'm tired."

I sat on the bed close to her. "You look as if you've had a hectic night," I said. "What have you been up to?"

"Do I look awful?" she asked, rolling back on the pillow and stretching. "I don't care. I don't care about anything this morning."

"I feel like that too. That's why I came to see you," I said, looking down at her white, pinched face. There were smudges under her eyes and the two lines above the bridge of her nose were very pronounced. "Let's be bored together. Come and have lunch with me."

She screwed up her face. "No," she said, "I can't be bothered."

"Now, don't be obstinate," I said. "We'll have an early lunch and then you can come back here if you want to. Come on, don't be a crab."

She looked up at me and there was hesitation in her eyes. "Oh I don't know," she said, a sulky expression darkening her face. "It's such a bore to get dressed. No, Clive, I don't think I will."

I reached down and took her hands, pulling her up so that our bodies were close. "You're coming," I said firmly. "I want to see you in your clothes for a change. Now, what will you wear?"

She pulled away from me and slouched over to the wardrobe. "I don't know," she said and yawned again. "Ooh I'm tired and I don't want to go out."

I opened the wardrobe. Hanging from the centre rail were a half a dozen tailored suits of various patterns.

"Why not wear a dress?" I asked. "Why must you always dress so severely? I'd like to see you in something flimsy and feminine for a change."

"At least, Clive, let me decide what suits me," she said, pulling a pinhead grey suit off the hanger. "I'll wear this. All right?"

"Sure, now go ahead and take your bath," I said, sitting on the bed. "I'll smoke a cigarette and wait for you."

"I won't be long," she said, closing the cupboard.

While she was upstairs in the bathroom, I wandered around the little room. I opened drawers, glanced inside, then closed them. I moved the glass animals and in doing so I thought about her husband. There was a dark secret atmosphere about the room and I could not help thinking of the many men who came here. Secretive, furtive men who would be ashamed if their friends knew where they had been.

I was worried by these thoughts and I began to feel angry and frustrated. I hated to think that so many men shared Eve with me. The whole atmosphere of the room finally became so unbearable that I went into the passage and called to her to hurry.

"I'm coming," she said. "Don't be so impatient!"

At this moment I heard the front door open and Marty came in.

She gave me a quick, surprised look and then she smiled. "Good morning, sir," she said. "It's a lovely morning, isn't it?"

"Yes," I returned, not looking at her.

I hated seeing her. I hated her servile, knowing expression. I wondered if Eve told her about me. I wondered if these two women discussed the men who came to this little house and whether they sniggered about them. I could not stay in the same room with this woman, suspecting that sometimes she sniggered about me.

"Tell Miss Marlow I'll be in the car," I said curtly and let myself out of the house.

Eve joined me in less than a half an hour. She was smart and trim, but in the hard sunlight I thought she looked older and a little tired.

I opened the car door and she slid in. We looked at each other. "Do I look all right?"

I smiled at her. "Wonderful."

"Don't lie. Do I really look all right?"

"You could go anywhere, Eve, and with anyone."

"Do you really mean that?"

"Of course. The trouble with you is you're ashamed of what you do," I said, stubbing the self-starter. "That's one of the reasons for your inferiority complex. You want it both ways, don't you? Well, so far, it's all right. You have nothing to worry about."

She looked searchingly at me, decided that I was telling the truth and sank back against the cushions. "Thank you," she said, with a little nod. "Where are we going?"

"Nikabob's," I said, turning into Sunset and going in the direction of Franklin. "All right?"

"Mmmm, I suppose so."

"I tried to call you yesterday at two o'clock, but Marty said you were engaged."

She grimaced, but did not say anything.

"You must work all day and all night," I said, secretly torturing myself.

"Don't let's talk about it," she said shortly. "I wonder why you men must always talk about it."

"Sorry ... I was forgetting it was shop to you." I drove in silence for a couple of blocks and then said, "You puzzle me, Eve. You're not really hard, are you?"

She pursed her mouth. "Why do you say that?"

"I think you could easily be hurt."

"But, I'd never let you know," she countered quickly.

"You're an oddity. You're always on guard against an unkind word. You think everyone is your enemy. I wish you'd relax and accept me as a friend."

"I don't want friends," she returned impatiently. "Anyway, I never trust men. I know too much about them."

"That's because you know only the rottenness in men. Won't you let me be your friend?"

She looked at me indifferently. "No, I won't and do stop talking such nonsense. You can never mean anything to me. I keep telling you, so why don't you stop?"

It seemed pretty hopeless to me. Again I felt the dark stirring of frustrated anger against her. If there were only something I could do to move her, to get behind that cold, completely indifferent attitude she hid behind.

"Well, you're blunt enough," I said. "At least, I know where I am."

"I wish I knew what you were up to," she said, giving me a searching look. "There's something going on behind all this smoothness. What do you want, Clive?"

"You," I said simply. "I like you. You intrigue me. I want to feel that I've a place in your life. That's all."

"Oh, you're crazy," she said impatiently. "You must know hundreds of women. Why bother with me?"

Yes ... why bother with her? Why bother with her when I had Carol? Why waste my time beating against a stone wall when every time I met her it became clearer that she would never accept me? I did not know.

But I had to go on, although I knew that unless something unexpected happened we would always be on the same hopeless footing.

"Never mind the other women," I said, pulling up outside Nikabob's. "They don't count. It's you that matters."

She made an impatient gesture with her hands. "You must be crazy," she said. "I've told you you mean nothing to me. I can't keep telling you, can I? You mean absolutely nothing to me and you never will mean anything to me."

I got out of the car and walked stiffly round to open the door for her. "All right," I said. "What have you got to worry about? And besides, if you're so sure about that, why do you come out with me?"

She gave me a quick, hard look. For a moment I thought I had gone too far and that she was going to leave me flat. Then she suddenly giggled.

"Well, I've got to live, haven't I?"

I felt the blood leave my face, but I did not pause nor look at her. We entered Nikabob's and sat down at a table away from the entrance.

Everything that I suspected and did not wish to admit was in that one damnable sentence. "Well, I've got to live, haven't I?"

After I had given the order I told the waiter to bring me a bottle of Scotch. I wanted a drink badly. We did not speak until the whisky came.

"You're a cold blooded little thing, aren't you?" I said, pouring out two large drinks.

"Do you think so?" She looked bored.

It was all going wrong. I would have to make an effort if the lunch was going to be at all successful. It was no use leaving it to her.

"Heard from Jack?" I asked, abruptly changing the subject.

"I hear every week."

"Is he all right?"

"Mmmm he's fine."

"Coming home?"

"Mmmm."

"How long will he stay?"

"Oh ... a week ... ten days, I don't know."

"So I shan't see you?"

She shook her head. There was a blank faraway look in her eyes and I felt she was scarcely listening to what I was saying.

"I would like to meet your husband," I said deliberately.

She looked at me sharply. "Would you?"

"Why not?"

"You would like him." Her eyes became animated. "Everyone likes him ... but, I'm the only one who really knows him. They think he's such a nice person." She pretended to sneer, but it did not come off. "It infuriates me sometimes to see the way people flock around him ... if they only knew how he treated me." I could see she did not mind how he treated her. Whatever he did would be all right with her. I could see that in every line in her face and in the expression in her eyes.

"Well, do we meet?"

"All right. I'll speak to him."

The waiter brought lobster soup. It was very good, but Eve scarcely touched it.

"You're not eating."

She lifted her shoulders. "I'm not hungry. After all I've only just got up."

I pushed my plate impatiently away. "Are you sorry you came?"

"No ... I wouldn't have come if I hadn't wanted to."

"You've never learned to say anything complimentary, have you?"

"I don't need to. You can take me as I am, or leave me."

"Do you always treat your men like this?"

"Why not?"

"Not very wise, is it?"

"Well, they always come back. Why should I worry?"

She had no need to worry. I knew she was speaking the truth. If her other men were like me, then they always would come back.

I looked at her. The arrogant expression in her eyes made me want to hurt her. "You know best, of course," I said evenly, "but, after all it's not as if you're getting any younger. A time'll come when they won't come back."

Her mouth twisted and she shrugged. "It's too late to learn new tricks now," she said. "I've never run after any one yet and I don't intend to start now."

"You know, Eve," I went on. "I don't think you're happy. This is a pretty ghastly kind of life you lead, isn't it? Why don't you give it up?"

"You're all the same," she said. "They all say that, but they don't do anything about it. Besides, what do you think I'd do? Become a drudge around the house? Not me!"

"Is Jack going to keep travelling? Isn't there a chance that he'd make a home for you?"

She looked past me across the room. Her eyes softened as she brooded. "We had planned to open a roadhouse." She lifted her shoulders rather hopelessly. "Oh, I don't know."

The waiter brought the second course and then when he had gone away, she said suddenly, "You wouldn't believe it, but I cried last night." She looked quickly at me to see if I were going to laugh at her. "You wouldn't think I'd do that, would you?"

"Why did you?"

"I was lonely ... I'd had a rotten day." Her face tightened. "You don't know how rotten some men can be. You don't know how lonely this life is. You can't trust anyone. They're all after what they can get."

"Of course, it's a rotten life," I said. "No good can possibly come from it. Can't you earn money in some other way?"

Her face became cold and wooden. "No," she snapped. "How can I? I'm a fool to grumble, only I just feel low today." She drew a deep breath and said, "How I hate men!"

"Something's upset you. What is it?"

"Oh, nothing. Never mind, Clive, I'm not going to talk about it."

"Someone treated you badly last night."

"Yes. He tried to gyp me..." She snapped her fingers irritably, "I'm not going to talk about it."

"I hope he didn't get away with it," I said curious to know what happened.

Her eyes showed deep anger and spite. "He didn't and he'll never be allowed in my house again." She suddenly pushed her plate away. "We'd better go back." She had only picked at her food.

I beckoned to the waiter. "Look, Eve," I said, "let's have lunch or dinner together from time to time. It'll be good for you. I want you to treat me as a friend. Maybe you don't think you want a friend, but it does give you a chance to unbottle. I'm trying to treat you like a human being. None of your other men treat you like that, do they?"

For a moment she looked a little startled, then she said, "No, I suppose they don't."

"Well, will you? Can't you see that a little time off from all this muck will be good for you?"

She pursed her mouth. "All right," she said, then she brightened a little. "Thank you, Clive. Yes, I'd like to."

I felt as if I had won a major battle. "That's fine," I said. "I'll call you next week and we'll get together."

I paid the bill and we went back to the car.

As we turned into Laurel Canyon Drive, she said, "I've enjoyed this. You're odd, aren't you, Clive?"

I laughed. "Am I? Only in comparison with the other men you know. You still think I want something from you. I don't. You intrigue me. I like having you around."

We stopped outside her house. I got out and we stood by the car. "You're coming in?" she said, smiling at me.

I shook my head. "No ... I won't today. It's been nice, Eve. I want you to come again."

She stood looking at me. The smile was still on her lips, but it had gone from her eyes. "Don't you want to come in?"

"I want to be your friend," I said. "I'll take you out next week, but I don't want to treat you as other men treat you."

Her eyes were very cold now, but the smile still persisted. "I see," she said. "All right. Thank you, Clive, for the lunch."

This was, for me, a crucial moment. I could see she was disappointed and annoyed that I was not going to pay her for her company. I could clearly read that in her eyes. If I were to continue on the lines I had planned, I would have to reach this point sooner or later. In spite of what she had said as we had entered the restaurant, I was determined to go through with it. I was not going to be like Harvey Barrow and pay for her company. I would give her a good time; I would listen to her talk about Jack and about her troubles, but I was not going to give her any more money.

"You'll call me then?" she said.

"I will. Good-bye, Eve, and don't cry any more."

She turned from me and walked quickly to the house.

I returned to the car, lit a cigarette and started the engine. Then I drove slowly down the street and, as I turned the corner, I saw a man walking towards me. For a moment I did not recognize him, then I noticed the long arms that seemed to reach almost to his knees. I looked quickly at him as I drove past. It was Harvey Barrow.

I pulled to the curb and stopped. What was Harvey Barrow doing in this district? I knew, of course, but I refused to admit that he was going to see Eve.

I slid out of the car and ran back. Turning the corner I could see him walk purposely down Laurel Canyon Drive. He slowed down outside Eve's house and stood hesitating at the gate.

I wanted to shout at him. I wanted to break into a run, reach him and slam my fist into his ugly, brutal face. But, instead, I just stood there, watching. He pushed open the gate and walked quickly down the short path to the house.

CHAPTER THIRTEEN

I had forgotten Harvey Barrow. He had seemed to me to be such a cheap, insignificant creature that I had dismissed him from my mind after I had driven him from Three Point. It did not occur to me that he would again associate with Eve. She had treated him so ruthlessly and I had so humiliated him before her that it was inconceivable that he could ever again face her. Yet there he was, going to her, sharing her with me, and bringing me down to his own sordid level.

I was still feeling shocked and depressed as I opened my front door. Russell came down the passage to meet me. One look at his worried face told me that more trouble was on the way.

"Miss Bensinger's waiting to see you, sir," he announced.

I stared at him. "Waiting to see me?" I repeated. "How long has she been here?"

"She has only this moment arrived. She said it was urgent and she would wait ten minutes."

I wondered why Merle Bensinger had come all the way from her office to see me. It must obviously be urgent and important as she scarcely ever left her desk.

"All right, Russell," I said, handing him my hat. "I'll see her at once."

I walked into the sitting room. "Hel-lo, Merle," I said, going to her. "This is a surprise."

Merle Bensinger was big, red haired and tough. She carried her forty years well and there was no smarter business woman in Hollywood. She had planted herself before the empty fireplace and she looked at me with stormy eyes.

"If this is a surprise you'd better get yourself some brandy," she said, ignoring my hand and sitting down on the arm of the settee, "because you'll certainly need it."

"Now look, Merle," I began, "I'm sorry about the *Digest* article ..."

"Never mind the *Digest* article," she snapped. "You've enough grief without bringing that up." She fumbled in her handbag and produced a battered packet of Camels. "I haven't much time, so we'll get right down to business. Just tell me one thing ... did you punch Frank Imgram?"

I ran my fingers through my hair. "Suppose I did? What's it to you?"

"He asks what's it to me?" Merle raised her eyes beseechingly to the ceiling. "That's a laugh. He socks the biggest money making proposition in Hollywood, breaks his bridgework, and asks what's it to me?" She regarded me, her green eyes almost savage. "Listen, Thurston, you've been dumb. You've been so goddamn dumb that I can't imagine what kind of parents produced you. The *Digest* was pretty bad, but this ... well, it's murder!"

"Come on," I said impatiently, "just how bad is it?"

She threw her cigarette away and walked over to the window. "Couldn't be worse, Thurston. You're up against the biggest, toughest guy in pictures ... Gold. He's out to break you and he'll do it. Between you and me and my dog's fleas you might just as well pack your bag and skip. As far as Hollywood's concerned ... you're out!"

I went to the sideboard and mixed myself a strong highball. I felt I needed it.

"Make that out in duplicate," Merle snapped. "Do you think you're the only one with nerves?"

I gave her a whisky and sat down. "How about that contract between me and Gold?" I said. "You're not going to let him get away with that?"

Merle shook her head hopelessly. "The way this guy talks," she said, addressing a vase filled with carnations. "Contract! He thinks he's got a contract." She swept round on me. "I couldn't hold a blind, half-witted baby of two months to a contract like that. It means absolutely nothing. If Gold doesn't like the story, it's out."

"Maybe he will like it," I said uneasily. "Don't tell me Gold'd be dopey enough to turn down a good story just to get even with me."

She looked at me pityingly. "Don't you understand your drunken frolic has cost Gold something like a hundred grand? A story's got to be mighty good to make a guy like Gold forget a hundred grand. If you ask me I don't believe there's a writer in Hollywood who could make him forget all that money,"

I finished my drink and lit a cigarette. "Well," I said, trying not to feel scared, "what do I do? You're my agent. Can't you suggest anything?"

"There's nothing to suggest. Gold's blacklisted you and that's all there is to it. You'll have to write novels. The stage and movies are out."

"Oh, no," I said, suddenly angry. "He can't do that to me. Why, it's crazy....."

"Maybe it is, but I know what he can do. Gold's the one guy in Hollywood I can't handle," She suddenly snapped her fingers. "But there is someone who could do it."

I stared at her. "Do what? What are you talking about?"

"Put you right with Gold again."

"Who?"

"Your girl friend ... Carol Rae."

I stood up. "And what the hell do you mean by that?"

She waved me to my chair. "Now don't get upset," she said soothingly. "Carol Rae could fix it for you. She and Gold are like that." She crossed her fingers.

"Since when?" I asked, hardly trusting my voice.

Merle stared at me. "You know Gold wants to marry her, don't you?"

"I know that, but it doesn't mean anything."

"It doesn't? What's the matter with you? Let me tell you something. Gold's never been married. He's nearly sixty. Suddenly he falls for a girl and you say it means nothing. It means everything to Gold. A guy his age when he falls, comes down like a ton of pig-iron dropped from the Empire State building. Right now, that girl could do what she liked with Gold. I tell you ... she could even fix you."

I drew a deep breath and controlled my temper with an effort that made me sweat. "Well, okay, Merle, thanks for the tip. I'll think it over." How I kept my hands off her I don't know, but I knew I couldn't afford to make any more enemies. "I'll watch it."

She got up. "You'd better do more than that, Thurston," she said. "I've told you how to handle it. It's up to you now. If I were you, I'd drop this film script and get a novel out. Already some of your creditors have been on to me to know whether you're on a spot with Gold. I've stalled them, but that won't last long."

I was too dumbfounded to do anything but stare at her.

"And another thing," she said, turning back from the door, "what's all this about you going around with a tart?"

I felt myself flinch. "I've taken enough from you, Merle, for one morning. You keep your snout out of my business," I snapped, turning away.

She eyed me and then raised her hands in a gesture of hopeless exasperation. "Then it's true?" she said. "Are you crazy? Aren't there enough women in this cesspool of glamour without picking on a floozy? They're talking about you, Thurston. No writer can afford that kind of scandal. Pull yourself together, for God's sake, or you and me'll have to part."

Blood drained from my face. "Hollywood's not going to dictate to me!" I said furiously. "And that goes for you too, Merle! I'll damn well please myself who I associate with and if you don't like it, you know what you can do."

"What a sucker you are," she said, her own temper rising. "I thought you and me could make money, but I was wrong. Okay, if that's how you feel. It means nothing to me because you're on the slide. You know me, Thurston, I'm frank. If you continue to kick around with this woman your name's going to stink like a month-old corpse. Get wise. If you can't do without her, for the love of Mike, don't flaunt her before the public. Keep her out of sight."

I was so angry I could have hit her. "So long, Merle," I said, opening the door. "There's plenty other vultures who'll be glad to handle my affairs. As far as I'm concerned, you're through."

"So long," she returned. "Watch your nickels, Thurston, you'll need 'em."

She was gone before I could think of a suitable reply.

I began to pace up and down. What did she mean about my creditors? I did not owe any big amounts. What did she mean? I rang for Russell.

"Have we any outstanding bills, Russell?" I asked when he came.

"There are a few, sir," he said, his eyebrows crawling to the top of his forehead. "I thought you kept check on them."

I gave him a hard look and then went over to the desk. I opened one of the drawers and took out an assorted bundle of papers.

"You should have watched this, Russell," I said angrily. "You can't expect me to do everything in this damned apartment."

"But I've never seen this lot before, sir," Russell protested. "If I'd known they were here ..."

"All right, all right," I said irritably, knowing that he was right. I had been in the habit of putting all my bills in this drawer, promising myself to have a grand settling up at the end of the month. Somehow, I never got around to going through them.

I sat down at the desk.

"Here, get a pencil and paper and write the amounts down as I call them," I said.

"Is—is anything wrong, sir?" Russell asked, suddenly anxious.

"Just do as I say and for God's sake stop talking."

At the end of a quarter of an hour, I found I owed thirteen thousand dollars to various stores and tailors.

I looked at Russell. "Not so good," I said with a grimace. "No, it's certainly not so good."

"Well, at least, they'll wait, sir," he said, stroking his chin uneasily. "It's just as well Mr. Gold has given you an offer, isn't it? I mean you can't go on much longer like this. I thought ..."

"Never mind what you thought," I broke in. "You're not paid to think, Russell. Okay, beat it. I've got things to do."

When he had gone I took out my bank book. I had fifteen thousand dollars in hand. If what Merle had said was true and my creditors were getting anxious, I would be down to nothing in no time. As I put the bank book away I noticed my hand was shaking.

For the first time since I had come to Hollywood I suddenly experienced a feeling of doubt. Up to now, with *Rain Check* bringing in a steady income, and my books selling well I had been confident of the future. But the play and the books could not go on forever. I simply had to make a success of this story for Gold. There were no two ways about it.

I spent the next three days trying to work out the blue print of my script. I worked hard, but at the end of the third day I found I had produced nothing of value. The main reason why my work was abortive was that, for the first time in my life, I knew that I had to succeed. This feeling created a spark of panic which finally prevented me thinking clearly and as I became more and more worried I found myself filling pages with meaningless words.

I finally pushed the typewriter aside, mixed myself a stiff whisky and soda and began to pace the room.

I looked at the clock. It was ten minutes past seven. Almost without thinking, I reached for the telephone and called Eve. She answered immediately. "Hello."

A great weight rolled from my mind when I heard her voice. I knew then that I had been wanting to call her for the past two days. I needed her to share my loneliness and through her, I wanted to regain my lost confidence in myself.

"Hello," I said. "How are you?"

"I'm all right, Clive. And you?"

"Fine. Look Eve, will you have dinner with me? Can I come round right now?"

"No … you can't."

My mind grew dark and heavy again.

"Now don't say that. I want to see you."

"I can't."

"But I want to see you tonight," I persisted, feeling blood mounting to my head.

"I can't tonight, Clive."

Couldn't she at least say she was sorry? I thought, furious with her. "You mean you've a dinner date?"

"Yes … if you must know."

"All right … all right … I still want to see you. Can't you cancel it?"

"No."

I nearly slammed down the receiver, but thinking of the long hours I had on my hands, I tried again. "Wouldn't it be possible to meet you after your dinner date?" I thought if she said no to that God knows what I'm going to do.

"Well I might," she said reluctantly. "Do you really want to see me?"

What did she think I was crawling on my hands and knees for? "Yes," I said. "What time shall we say?"

"About nine thirty?"

"Suppose you call me when you're back? Then I'll come on over."

"All right"

I gave her my number.

"Then about nine thirty. I'll wait here for you."

"All right," and she hung up.

I put the receiver down. There had been no encouragement in that conversation. It had been flat, depressing and impersonal, but I did not care. I had to see her. It was like grinding down on an aching tooth, but I knew I could not face another night alone.

Russell came in as I was brooding about her. He glanced at me, then at the litter on my desk and his mouth pursed.

"All right, Russell," I said irritably. "Don't look like a bishop. Things aren't so good. In fact, everything's going to hell."

His eyebrows began to crawl up his forehead. "I'm sorry to hear that, sir," he said. "Is there anything particularly wrong?"

"I'm not getting the breaks," I went on, after a pause. "Carol's left me, Miss Bensinger's quit, I can't get going with my story and I'm in debt. That's my hell for today. How do you like it?"

He rubbed his bald head with the palm of his hand. "I don't know what's come over you, Mr. Clive," he said. "At one time you used to be working all hours of the day. Now, you haven't worked for I don't know how long. It's been worrying me. If you don't mind my saying so ever since you sent the book to that Miss Marlow, there's been nothing but trouble."

"Everyone's trying to blame it on her," I said, getting to my feet and pacing up and down. "But you're all wrong. I don't know what I'd do without her."

He permitted himself a respectful smile. "I hope I have not offended you, Mr. Clive," he said, taking out his handkerchief and mopping his forehead. I could see he was very earnest and embarrassed. "I do hope, sir, you will give this woman up. She can do you no good in the long run. There's Miss Carol. She's a fine young lady, if I may say so. Why don't you see her? Why don't you tell her what has happened and ask her to help you? She won't desert you if she's sure you really want her."

I thought of my date with Eve. It was no good. I had to see Eve tonight. It was no good listening to Russell. Perhaps he was right, but even if he was, I could not draw back now that I was making some progress with Eve.

"I'll think about it, Russell," I said, getting to my feet. "Maybe it'll come out all right. I don't know. Maybe I will see Carol. Right now I feel it's hopeless, but I may change my mind by tomorrow." I began to wander round the room. "Be a good fellow and get me some supper, will you? I shan't be going out until late."

He got to his feet, giving me a quick, shrewd look. I saw his lips compress and his face clouded with gloom, but he went off without saying anything further.

I felt a sudden affection for him. I was sure that he meant well and was genuinely worried about me. In my present mood, it was comforting to think at least someone cared about me.

I was restless for the next hour and as the minute hand crept round the face of the clock, I became increasingly nervy.

I glanced at the clock again. It was nine thirty-seven. Of course, I told myself, I could not expect her to be punctual, but any moment now the bell would ring.

I could no longer concentrate on my book and I sat waiting, a cigarette between my fingers and a sick hollow emptiness in my stomach.

Russell looked in to see if I wanted anything. I waved him impatiently away.

"Shall they put your car away, sir?"

"No. I'm going out any minute now. Tell them to leave it."

"Will that be all, sir?"

I restrained the temptation to shout at him. "Yes, thank you, Russell," I said with studied calm. "Good night and don't fuss if I'm late."

When he had gone, I was about to glance at the clock, but stopped myself in time. You wait until she calls, I said to myself. It's no use looking at the clock. That won't get you anywhere. She'll ring. She said she would and she will.

I closed my eyes and waited. I waited a long time, feeling doubt, disappointment and frustration gathering in my mind like a clot of blood. I even began to count and when I reached eight hundred I opened my eyes and looked at the clock. It was five minutes past ten.

I walked to the telephone, dialled her number and waited. I let the bell ring for a long time, but there was no answer. I hung up. Damn her, I said, damn her to hell.

Then I poured myself a whisky and lit a cigarette. While I was doing this my mind crawled with cold, disappointed fury. I cursed her. All along she had been like this. Unreliable, selfish, indifferent. She had promised to call me. She had no thought that my evening would be spoilt. She just didn't care what happened to me.

At ten thirty I rang again, but there was still no reply.

I began to pace up and down, trembling with anger. She didn't care a damn. Independent, was she? I'd show the slut! I'd teach her to make a sucker out of me! Then I threw my cigarette away in frustrated disgust. How was I going to teach her? I couldn't even hurt her. There was not a damn thing I could do to her that'd make any difference. Not one single thing.

If I ever get you where I want you, Eve, I said to myself, I'll make you suffer for this.

Even as I said it, I knew that I would not get her where I wanted her. If we were to continue to know each other, I would be the one to suffer. I would be the one always to give way, because she did not give a damn and never would give a damn for me.

I called her number every ten minutes after that. I was determined to speak to her even if I continued to call her all night. At eleven thirty, she answered.

"Hello?"

"Eve ..." I stopped because I could not put my thoughts into words. Rage, relief and hysterical exhaustion left me speechless.

"Oh hello, Clive."

The flat, indifferent note in her voice galvanized me to say, "I've been waiting. You said nine thirty. Look at the time. I've been waiting and waiting ..."

"Have you?" There was a pause, then she said under her breath, "God! I'm tight."

"You're tight, are you?" I almost shouted at her. "Haven't you any thought for me?"

"Oh Clive, stop it. I'm tired ... I can't talk now."

"But we were going to meet. Why did you do this?"

"Why not?" she snapped back. "You take too much for granted. I tell you I'm tired ..."

She'll hang up in a moment, I thought, in sudden panic. "Wait, Eve, don't cut me off." I was half crazy with rage, frustration and fear that I could not see her. "If you're tired—well, I'm sorry, but couldn't you have just telephoned me? I've been waiting. I mean, after the weekend, couldn't you have treated me a little differently?"

"Oh do stop it!" she exclaimed. "Come now if you want to. But don't keep on and on. It's not too late, is it? Come now and stop talking."

Before I could say anything, she hung up.

I did not hesitate. Picking up my hat, I ran to the elevator. A few minutes later I was in my car speeding towards Laurel Canyon Drive.

It was a bright moonlight night and the traffic on the streets was heavy, but I reached her house in thirteen minutes.

She opened the door when I knocked.

"You're awful, Clive," she said, leading the way into the bedroom. "What's the matter with you? I only saw you a few days ago."

I faced her, struggling to control my temper. She was wearing her blue dressing gown and a strong smell of whisky came from her. She peered at me, her eyes dazed, then she pulled a little face.

"Oh, God !" she said, yawning. "I'm tired."

She flopped across the bed, her head on the pillow and stared up at me. I could see she had difficulty in focusing.

I stood over her, feeling a sudden revulsion for her. "You're drunk," I said accusingly.

She put her hand to her head. "I must be," she said, yawning again. "Anyway, I've had quite enough," and she closed her eyes.

"How could you do this to me?" I burst out, wanting to shake her and go on shaking her, "I've been waiting and waiting. Haven't you any feeling at all?"

She struggled up on her elbow, her face wooden and her eyes like wet stones. "Feeling?" she repeated. "For you? Why should I? Who do you think you are? I warned you, Clive. There's only one man I've any feeling for—that's Jack."

"Oh, shut up about your goddamn Jack!" I said violently.

She suddenly giggled. "If you could only see how silly you look," she said and fell back onto the pillow again. "Do sit down and stop standing over me like the wrath of God."

I suddenly hated her. "Where have you been all this time?"

"I couldn't get away. I was working. What's it to you anyway?"

"You mean you forgot all about me?"

"No, I didn't," she giggled again. "I remembered, but I thought it'd do your conceit good to wait. So I let you wait and now perhaps you won't take me so much for granted."

I could have struck her. "All right," I said, "If that's the way you feel. I really don't know why I've come, I think I'd better go."

She struggled up from the bed and put her arms round my neck. "Don't be silly, Clive. Stay ... I want you to stay."

You mean you want my money, you rotten little slut, I thought and I pulled her arms away and shoved her back on the bed.

"You are in a state," I said, stepping away from the bed. "I didn't think, after the weekend, you could have treated me like this."

She locked her hands behind her head and giggled up at me. "Do stop pitying yourself. I warned you how it would be if you fell in love with me, didn't I? Now be nice and come to bed."

I sat on the bed by her side. "Do you think I'm in love with you? You don't give a damn anyway, do you?"

She pursed her lips and looked away from me. "I'm sick of men falling in love with me, I don't want them. Why can't they leave me alone?"

"You might easily be left alone. If you treat all your men as you treat me, you deserve to be left."

She shrugged. "They come back. It doesn't matter how I treat them, they always come back. If they didn't, I wouldn't care. I'm independent, Clive. There are plenty of other fish."

"You're only independent because you've got Jack," I said, wanting to smack her face. "Suppose something happened to him? What would you do then?"

Her face seemed to sag. "I'd kill myself," she returned. "Why?"

"That's easy talk. But you wouldn't have the guts when the time came."

"That's what you think," she retorted, stung. "I did try to kill myself once. I drank a bottle of Lysol. Do you know what that means? It didn't kill me, but I was bringing up chunks of my inside for months."

"Why did you do that?" I asked, momentarily shocked out of my anger.

"I'm not going to tell you. Come on, Clive, don't keep talking. Come to bed. I'm tired."

Her spirit-laden breath fanned my cheek and I turned away, suddenly revolted. "All right," I said, anxious now only to find an excuse to get out of this disgusting little room. "I'll stay. I shan't be a moment. I want to use the bathroom."

As I moved to the door, she took off her dressing gown and slid between the sheets. "Hurry up," she said, closing her eyes and blowing through her lips.

I stood looking at the other pillow. There were faint grease marks on it and it was slightly soiled. So she was inviting me to sleep in sheets that had been used by some other man. That finally decided me. Without looking at her, I went upstairs to the bathroom and sitting on the side of the bath, I lit a cigarette. I knew this was the end between us and my first reaction was of overwhelming relief. I had seen her as she really was.

I knew nothing that I did, nothing I said would make any difference to her feelings for me. I was, to her, merely a means of earning money. I might have put up with her heartlessness and her drunkenness, but the soiled bed killed my infatuation for her once and for all.

I remained in the little bathroom for some time and then I went downstairs and softly entered the bedroom.

Eve lay sprawled across the bed, her mouth open and her face flushed. As I looked down at her, she began to snore.

There was nothing in me now except a weak, drained feeling of disgust. I took two twenty dollar bills from my wallet and put them among the glass animals. Then I tiptoed out of the house and drove back to my apartment.

CHAPTER FOURTEEN

Lying in my bed, with the pale dawn sunlight coming through a gap in the curtains, I marvelled that my association with Eve had lasted so long. She had done everything in her power to destroy my feelings for her. She had behaved with incredible selfishness and brutal indifference and it was only because I had been so utterly infatuated with her that the association had lasted as long as it had.

I had had a narrow escape. It frightened me to think what might have happened if I had continued to associate with her. And while I thought of this, I took time to consider my past life as a whole and I realized what an unscrupulous, dishonest fool I had been. I thought of John Coulson. I thought of Carol. I thought of Imgram. I thought of the many mean and cruel things I had done in the past and, in something like panic, I searched my memory for some deed that could go on the credit side of my page of self-judgment. I could think of nothing. At the age of forty I had not one single thing to be proud of—except perhaps one. I had walked out of Eve's life. Since I had been strong minded enough to do that surely there was still time for me to recover my self-respect and my position as a writer.

But I knew that the task was too overwhelming for me to undertake alone. There was one person who could help me. I must see Carol. I experienced a sudden feeling of tenderness and affection for her. I had treated her shamefully and I was determined I would never again hurt or grieve her. It was unthinkable that she should marry Gold. I would see her today.

I rang for Russell.

He came a few minutes later with my morning coffee which he put on the table by my bed.

"Russell," I said, propping myself up on my elbow, "I've been an incredible fool. I've been thinking about it half the night and I'm going to pull myself together. I'm seeing Miss Rae this morning."

He gave me a long searching look, raised his eyebrows and walked over to the windows to pull the curtains.

"I take it Miss Marlow was not accommodating last night, Mr. Clive?"

I had to laugh. "How did you guess?" I asked, lighting a cigarette. "You know everything, don't you? Well, I did see her last night. I saw her as she really is and not as I've been trying to imagine she is. It's a hell of a difference. She was tight and ... but never mind the details. My God, Russell, I've had a narrow escape. I'm through with her and I'm going to start work today. But first, I'm seeing Carol." I looked at him. There was a sudden brightness in his eyes and I knew that he was pleased and relieved. "Do you think she'll have anything to do with me?"

"I hope so, sir," he said gravely. "It will depend on how you approach her."

"I know." I experienced a sudden feeling of doubt. "After the way I've treated her I can't expect it to be easy, but if she'll only listen to me, perhaps I'll make her understand."

It was just after nine thirty when I walked into Carol's sitting room.

Carol came in after a few minutes. She was pale and there were dark smudges under her eyes.

"I'm glad you came, Clive," she said and sat down with her hands in her lap.

"I had to come," I said, not moving from the window, but turning to look at her, suddenly scared that I was going to lose her. "I've been an awful fool, Carol. May I talk to you about it all?"

"I suppose so," she said listlessly. "Sit down, Clive, there's no need for you to be nervous with me."

There was something in the flatness of her voice that worried me. I had a feeling that she might not care very much what I was going to say.

I sat down near her.

"I can't tell you how sorry I am for the rotten things I said to you. I was crazy. I didn't know what I was saying."

She held up her hand. "There's no need to go over that. You're in trouble, aren't you, Clive?"

"Trouble? Do you mean Gold? No, that's all right. I couldn't care less about Gold. I've thought it all out, that's why I've come to see you."

She looked at me sharply. "I thought ..." she began but stopped and looked down at her hands.

"You thought I was coming to ask you to plead my case with Gold, didn't you? Merle wanted me to, but I said no. It isn't that at all. I don't care what Gold does. I don't care if he buys my script or not. In fact, I don't think now I'll even write it. I'm through with all that. I've come to say I'm sorry for the beastly things I said and to tell you that I'm beginning work in a day or so."

She sighed and fluffed up her hair with her slender fingers. "I wish I could believe you, Clive. You've said that so many times in the past."

"I deserve that. I've been pretty rotten about all this. I've been utterly rotten to you. I don't know what came over me, but I've chucked it for good. I'm sorry about this woman, Carol. It was just a physical madness. There was nothing else to it. Her way of life is something I could never understand nor could I share it with her. It's all over, Carol. Last night ..."

She stopped me, "No, please Clive, I don't want to hear. I can imagine what happened." She got up and walked over to the window. "If you say it's over, then I'll believe you."

I went to her and turning her, I pulled her to me in spite of her gesture of protest. "Forgive me, Carol," I pleaded. "I've been worthless and rotten to you. I want you so much. You're the only one who means anything to me. Can't you forget this ever happened?"

She pushed me away gently. "You're in a jam, my dear, and so am I. You see R.G. knows I am fond of you. He wants me to marry him. He thinks if you're out of the way, he stands a chance. He'll do everything in his power to get you out of the way. I'm scared of him. He's so utterly ruthless and his power is so immense."

I stared at her. "You're scared because Gold's gunning for me? Then you do care for me? Be generous, Carol, say it if it's true."

She suddenly smiled. "I've been fond of you for a long time, Clive," she said. "If you're through with this woman, then ..." she stopped, looked at me and went on. "Well, I'm glad. I couldn't believe that a woman like that could hold you for long."

I took her in my arms. "I can't do without you, Carol." I said. "I'm so lonely and so unsure of myself. If you'll forgive me I don't care what happens."

She slid her fingers through my hair. "You silly old thing," she said softly. "I've always loved you."

The feel of her slim young body in my arms was a new and exciting experience.

I pulled myself together and holding her away, I anxiously searched her face. "I've been leading a rotten life, Carol, and it has made an awful mess of me, but if you really love me, I'll make good."

"I love you."

It was all going to be all right. I saw it in her face and I took her in my arms and kissed her.

"That settles it," I said.

She looked up at me, her eyes bright. "Settles what?"

"Our marriage."

"But Clive ..."

I kissed her again. "You're going to walk out on the Studio and we're going to have a marvellous week all to ourselves. Then you'll go back and face the music, but you'll go back as Mrs. Clive Thurston and if Gold sacks you, he'll be sacking one of the best Hollywood script writers and some other producer will grab you."

She shook her head. "I couldn't do that," she said, her eyes dancing. "I've never let anyone down yet and I'm not going to start now. I'll tell him. I'll ask him for a week off and I'll tell him why."

I did not realize until she had finished speaking that she had said yes.

"Carol!" I exclaimed, taking her in my arms.

I kissed her.

After a moment I said, "But you're not seeing Gold until we're married. I'm not taking any chances of him pulling a fast one. We'll get married now. This very moment and then you can go to the Studio and tell him. I'll get everything ready. We'll take Russell. You and me, and Russell to look after us. Let's go to Three Point. It's still empty and I can work there. It won't be too far for you to reach the Studio and you'll love the drive and we'll be away from everybody."

She shook me a little, smiling at my enthusiasm and excitement, "Do be sensible, darling. We can't be married today. We haven't got a licence."

"We're going to drive down to Tijuana where you don't need a licence. All you need is five dollars and a girl as lovely as you. We'll get married and then next week, just to keep the record straight, we'll get married at the City Hall, then I'll feel doubly sure of you."

She suddenly laughed. "You're crazy, Clive, but I'm wild about you." She clung to me for a few seconds. "Ever since I first saw you, looking so nervous and sweet in Rowan's office, I've been wild about you. That was two years ago. You villain, Clive, to have kept me waiting such a long time!"

"I've been a blind fool," I said, kissing her throat. "But I'm going to make up for it now. Go and put on your hat. We're off to Tijuana this very minute."

My urgency and excitement was infectious and she almost ran from the room. As soon as she had gone, I picked up the telephone and called Russell.

"You've got a busy day before you, Russell," I told him, not bothering to keep the excitement out of my voice. "Pack enough stuff for both of us for one week. I want you to open Three Point again. You can fix that with the agent by telephone. The place can't be let yet. And then there's the apartment. Johnny Neumann would take it off our hands. He has always wanted it. From now on, Russell, we're going to make Three Point our home and we're keeping away from the temptations of night life. I'm going to work. When you've done all that, take a taxi out to Three Point and put things in order for us when we arrive some time this afternoon. Can you do that?"

"Certainly, sir," he replied, his voice a triumph of restrained delight. "Your bags are already packed, sir. I foresaw what might happen and I knew you would be in a hurry. Everything will be in order for you and Mrs. Thurston when you arrive this afternoon." He coughed a little pompously and added, "I should like to be the first to congratulate you, Mr. Clive. I hope with all my heart that you will both be very happy," and he hung up.

I stared at the telephone blankly, "Well, I'll be damned," I said aloud. "I believe he planned it all along."

I ran from the room, shouting to Carol to hurry.

I sat in the Chrysler outside the main office buildings off International Pictures. Extras, show girls, carpenters and technicians walked past me in a steady stream. Some glanced curiously at me, some were too busy talking to notice me, while others eyed the lines of the Chrysler with envious admiration. I drummed on the driving wheel and waited impatiently.

Everything was ready. Our bags were in the trunk of the Chrysler and we were on our way to Tijuana, but Carol had insisted on seeing Gold before we were married.

"It's all right," she said seriously. "I'll make him understand. He's been good to me, Clive, and I don't want to do anything underhanded. For goodness' sake don't look so worried. R.G. can't stop us getting married. There's nothing he can do about it and all he will want me to do is to get back to the Studio as quickly as I can."

I would not believe it. "He'll run you out. When a guy has his power and his money and reaches his age, he just hates being thwarted. I'm sure he'll do something mean."

But she laughed at me and had gone in to see him. She had been with him twenty minutes now and I was becoming anxious.

I suddenly had a sinking feeling of doubt. If Carol lost her job and I couldn't stage a comeback, what was to happen to us? The idea of returning to the almost forgotten routine of going to work every morning, the cheap meals and wondering whether I could afford this thing or that appalled me.

I stubbed out my cigarette with an irritable shrug of my shoulders and told myself that such a thing could not happen. I was sure that I would write something worthwhile with Carol at my side. She would help me and I would help her. As a team we would be unbeatable.

"Still worrying?" Carol said, putting her hand on my arm.

I started because I had not heard her come down the few stone steps that led from the office buildings.

I looked at her anxiously. She was serious but calm, and she met my eyes with unruffled serenity.

"It's all right," she said, smiling. "Of course, it was a shock to him, but he was rather fine about it. I wish he wasn't so fond of me." She drew a sharp little breath and shook her head. "I hate hurting people, Clive."

"What did he say?" I asked, opening the car door for her. "Is he letting you off for a week?"

She nodded. "Yes. The picture's held up anyway. Jerry Highams's ill. It's nothing much, but it'll mean a delay and—and, of course, Frank is still away." She glanced back at the office building embarrassed when she mentioned Imgram's name. "Clive—" she paused uneasily.

"'What is it?"

"R.G. wants to see you."

My heart gave an uneasy lurch. "Wants to see me?" I repeated, staring at her. "What on earth for?"

She got in the car and adjusted her dress over her knees. "He wanted to know if you were out here and when I said you were, he asked if you would see him. He didn't say why."

"He's going to back out of his contract," I said, suddenly angry. "That's how he's going to get even."

"Oh no, Clive," Carol said, quickly. "R.G.'s not like that. I'm sure he—"

"Then why is he asking to see me? My God! You don't think he wants to lecture me on how I should treat you? I'm damned if I'd stand that from him."

Carol looked worried. "I think you should see him, Clive. He's important and—" She stopped, hesitated and then went on, "but it's up to you. If you don't want to—well, you must please yourself."

I got out of the car and slammed the door. "All right, I'll see him. I won't be a minute," I said and ran up the steps into the office building.

I did not like this. It wasn't that I was scared of Gold, but when a man is as powerful and arrogant as he was, he would automatically dominate the situation.

I walked down the long corridor with my heart bumping uneasily against my ribs. I knocked on his office door and went in.

A tall, lovely looking girl with a Veronica Lake hair style, dressed in a well-cut black silk frock glanced up as I entered. She was sitting at a glass topped desk on which was scattered a mass of papers.

She gave me a quick, shrewd look and then smiled. "Good morning, Mr. Thurston. Will you go right ahead? Mr. Gold is expecting you."

I thanked her and crossed the office to another door and entered. Gold's office was furnished like a sitting room. There was no desk. A large table at which some twenty people could comfortably sit occupied the far end of the room. Around the big, antique fireplace were armchairs and a large settee. Above the fireplace was an original Van Gogh which supplied the only bright colouring in the room.

Gold sat in an armchair facing the door. At his elbow was a small table on which were a few papers, a telephone and a large ebony cigar box.

He looked up as I came in and his massive head sank further into his shoulders.

"Sit down, Mr. Thurston," he said, waving his hand to the armchair opposite me.

I was aware that my heart was beating rapidly and that my mouth was dry. This annoyed me and I tried to control my nerves without success. I sat down, crossed my legs and eyed him as calmly as I could.

He did not look at me for a moment, but drew on his cigar, blowing a thin stream of smoke to the ceiling. Then his sleepy, tawny coloured eyes met mine.

"I understand, Mr. Thurston," he began, his low pitched voice was bland, "that Carol and you are getting married this afternoon."

I took out my cigarette case, selected a cigarette, tapped it once or twice on my thumb nail and lit it before replying. "We are," I said shortly and put my cigarette case back into my pocket.

"Is that wise?" he asked, raising his eyebrows.

A muscle in my calf began to quiver. "That is something for us to decide, Mr. Gold," I returned.

"I suppose it is," he said, "but I have known Carol for some time and I don't want to see her unhappy."

"I appreciate how you feel," I said, my anger struggling with my awe of the man. "I assure you that Carol will be very happy." I drew a deep breath and went on a little too hurriedly to be really effective. "Much happier, Mr. Gold, than if she had married a man twice her age."

He looked at me. "I wonder," he said, tapping ash into the tray near the cigar box. He brooded for a moment, then went on, "I haven't a great deal of time, Mr. Thurston, so you will forgive me if I come to the point."

"I haven't got any time to waste either, Mr. Gold," I snapped back. "Carol is waiting for me."

He placed his finger tips together and eyed me with sleepy indifference. "I am surprised that Carol could have fallen in love with anyone quite so worthless as you," he said with disconcerting directness.

"Do we have to be personal?" I felt a sudden rush of blood to my face.

"Oh, I think so. You might ask me why I find you worthless. I'll tell you. You have no background. You have succeeded by an extraordinary chance—call it a fluke if you like—in getting a certain amount of notoriety, and in earning more than you ever thought possible. It is, to say the least, a lucky flash in the pan, more extraordinary, perhaps, because your first play was excellent, although your novels are pure sensation. I have often wondered how you came to write that play. You see, Mr. Thurston, when I heard that Carol was fond of you I made it my business to find out something about you."

"I don't think I'm going to listen to any more of this," I said, between my teeth. "My private life is my affair, Mr. Gold."

"It would be if you were not attempting to share it with Carol," he returned quietly. "As you have been foolish enough to do that, you have no private life as far as I'm concerned." He regarded his cigar for a moment and then looked over at me. "You are not only a bad writer with no future, Mr. Thurston, but you are also an exceedingly unpleasant character. I can't, of course, prevent you marrying Carol, but I can watch her interests and I will do so."

I got to my feet. "This has gone beyond a joke," I exclaimed, my nervousness overcome by anger, "You want Carol for yourself and you're being disagreeable because I've beaten you to it. All right, I can get along very well without you, Mr. Gold. I don't want your fifty thousand dollars. You and your Studio can go to hell as far as I'm concerned."

He still regarded me with an absent minded, indifferent expression. "Keep away from that Marlow woman, Mr. Thurston, or you and I will have another little talk."

I stared at him, shocked. "What the devil are you talking about?"

"Come, don't let us waste time. I know you have been making a fool of yourself with this woman. At first, I thought it was one of those unfortunate failings that men have who either have become bored with the usual run of women or else are suffering from some odd kink that the ordinary woman cannot satisfy. But I find you do not come under these categories. You have actually been stupid and weak enough to let this woman infatuate you. Surely there can be no better example of spineless degeneracy than that? When I heard of this, Mr. Thurston, I was not disappointed, I felt you were running to type."

"Okay," I said, furiously embarrassed to know that he had found out so much about me, "you've had your say. I hope you've enjoyed it. Now I'm going and I'm marrying Carol. Think of me tonight, Mr. Rex Gold, and say 'that might've been me.' "

"No doubt I shall," Gold returned, his loose lips closing wetly over his cigar. "I shall certainly think of you both. In fact, I'm not going to forget either of you. If Carol is unhappy because of you, you will be sorry. I promise you that, Mr. Thurston."

CHAPTER FIFTEEN

Looking back now as I hammer out this story in a sordid little bedroom with pieces of wallpaper peeling from its damp walls and dust upon the table on which only a typewriter stands, I realize that the first four days of my marriage with Carol were the high lights in my life. In her I found a companion who gave me confidence and spiritual peace; who amused me and who seemed to satisfy me physically as well as mentally.

We would get up about ten o'clock and have breakfast on the verandah with the valley spread out below us like a magnificent natural carpet. Away to the right, we could see the still waters of Big Bear Lake reflecting the fir trees and the lazy white clouds that drifted like balls of whipped cream in the brilliant sky. After breakfast we would put on shirts and slacks and take the car to the lake where Carol would swim in a simple white swimsuit while I lounged in the boat, a rod in my hand, watching her. When the sun got hot I would go in after her and we would wrestle in the water, swim races and behave like a couple of kids on their first vacation. Then we'd go back for lunch which Russell would bring to us on the verandah and we'd talk and look at the view and talk some more. Then we'd go for a long walk in the woods, the pine needles making a carpet for us to walk on and the sunlight coming through the heavy foliage overhead making patterns on the ground. In the evening we would listen to the gramophone. It was grand to have Carol alone, lying on the big settee which we had dragged out onto the verandah, the moon shining down on us and the stars like diamond dust and the sound of music coming from the sitting room.

I told Carol much of my past life. I did not mention John Coulson nor did I speak of Eve, but I told her about the apartment house in Long Beach and how I had always wanted to write and my early struggles as a shipping clerk. I had to tell her a few lies to make the story stand up, but as I had now completely accepted Coulson's play as my own I had no difficulty not only convincing Carol how I had written *Rain Check* but also myself.

In our big, airy bedroom with the windows wide open and the curtains pulled back and the moonlight making a bright patch of light on the white carpet, I would lie in bed with Carol in my arms. She slept with her head on my shoulder and one arm thrown across my chest. She always slept peacefully, scarcely moving until the sunlight woke her. Holding her in my arms, listening to her light breathing and thinking of the things we had done together during the day gave me many hours of satisfied contentment.

And yet, in spite of this contentment and happiness, I was aware that I was not entirely fulfilled. In some deep recess of my subconscious mind every now and then something stirred. I experienced from time to time a feeling of physical dissatisfaction. At first it was vague and undefined; then later this feeling became stronger and I knew that the physical impact that Eve had had upon my senses had left an indelible mark.

As long as Carol kept close by me, this hankering for Eve did not cause me any misgivings. Carol's personality and kindness and affection was strong enough to override Eve's remote influence, but if Carol went into the garden and left me alone, I found myself struggling against the temptation to call Eve on the telephone and to hear once again the sound of her voice.

You may find it difficult to understand why I could not completely dismiss Eve from my mind. I have already said that most men lead two lives—a normal life and a secret life. It follows then that most men have two mentalities. If the truth must be told, I began to realize that although Carol meant so much to me she was only able to satisfy part of my mental life. Eve's corrupting influence was necessary before I was completely fulfilled.

You must not think that I weakly accepted this situation without a struggle. During those four days and nights I did succeed in putting Eve out of my mind, but I knew that I was waging a losing battle. My sublime happiness with Carol was not to last. I suppose it was too much to expect considering that I was never able to withstand temptation for long. The change came abruptly and without warning on the night of our fourth day together.

The night was perfect. A big, glittering moon hung above the hills, casting black sharp etched shadows and lighting the lake, making it look like a burnished mirror. It had been hot all day and even on the verandah, it was still too hot to think of going to bed.

Carol had suggested a midnight swim and we took the car to the lake. We stayed in the warm water for over an hour and by the time we returned to Three Point it was after one o'clock. We were undressing in the bedroom when the telephone began to ring. We both paused and looked at each other in surprise. The bell sounded shrill and impatient in the silence of the night and I had a sudden feeling of suffocating excitement.

"Who can it be at this time?" Carol asked. I can see her now. She had just taken off her white and red sports frock and was sitting on the edge of the bed in her brassiere and shorts, looking lovely, her skin tanned a golden brown and her eyes bright.

"It's bound to be a wrong number," I said, slipping into my dressing gown. "No one knows we are here."

She smiled at me and went on undressing while I hurried into the lounge and picked up the receiver.

"Hello?" I said. "Who is it?"

"Hello, you stinker," Eve said.

I gripped the telephone, aware of a sudden stifled feeling and a thickness in my throat. "Why hello, Eve," I said, keeping my voice low and looking over my shoulder across the lounge to the bedroom.

Carol had gone into the bathroom and I could hear water running. There was no fear of her hearing me.

"You stinker," Eve was saying in a flat expressionless voice. "Why did you walk out on me like that?"

I scarcely understood what she was saying. Excitement and desire for her surged up in me and my blood pounded in my ears.

"What?" I said, struggling to control my feelings. "What are you saying?"

"When I woke and found you weren't there, it gave me an awful shock. I couldn't make out where you had got to."

"So it gave you a shock, did it?" I said and laughed. "Well, you've given me a shock or two in the past, so we're quits."

There was a pause, then she said angrily, "Oh, so we're quits? Well, let me tell you something, Clive. I've returned your rotten rnoney. I don't want it. I think it was a stinking trick to say you were going to stay and then to sneak off like that."

"You've returned the money?" I repeated blankly, not believing her. "But, why?"

"I don't want it from you. I don't want your rotten money."

"What did you want to do that for?" I asked, not knowing what I was saying.

"I've told you. I just don't want your rotten money. I can get on all right without it, thank you. I'm not going to be treated like that, so I've sent it back to you."

"I don't believe you, Eve, I haven't had it. You're lying and you know it."

"I tell you I sent it back."

"Where did you send it to?"

"I put it in an envelope and sent it to the Writers' Club. That's your club, isn't it?"

I relaxed against the back of the chair, feeling a little sick. "But why did you do it? I wanted you to have the money."

"I tell you I don't want your money," she snapped back. "And Clive, I don't want to see you any more. So don't either telephone or call again. I'm telling Marty she's not to let you in and if you telephone she's to cut you off."

The barriers that I had so half-heartedly tried to erect against her influence crumbled completely, and the beauty of the past four days was washed away in the flood of bitter repression that engulfed me when I heard those words.

"Don't be impulsive, Eve," I said, gripping the telephone until my hand ached. "I want to see you again."

"You're not going to, Clive. You're making a fool of yourself. I've warned you before, but it doesn't seem to make any difference. So we're not going to see each other again."

"Don't let's be final about this, Eve," I said, trying to keep the feverish desperation out of my voice. "May I see you tomorrow? I'd like to talk this over with you."

"No, Clive, I don't want to talk to you any more. I don't want you to call me. And if you do, I will hang up. You've got to stop all this nonsense. You take me too much for granted. You take up too much of my time and I don't want it that way."

"But look, Eve, I'm sorry I walked out on you. I can explain everything if only you'll let me. I didn't mean anything by it. It was just that I couldn't sleep and I was restless and I didn't want to disturb you, Eve, we've got to meet again. We can't break this up ... it's too important. Please, Eve, don't treat me like this ..."

"I'm tired and I'm not going to keep on talking. I don't ever want to see you again. It's good-bye." There was a pause, then she repeated, "Good-bye, Clive," and she hung up.

"Eve..." I began and then I sat very still staring at the telephone. I felt sick with frustration. It could not end like this. Good God, I thought, what kind of a rat must I be for a prostitute to return me my money and refuse to see me? I had never felt so completely and utterly humiliated. I replaced the receiver with a trembling hand. I had to see her again. She couldn't do this to me. My confidence in myself had gone and I was in black despair.

"Who was it, Clive?" Carol called from the bedroom.

"Just a fellow I know," I called back, my voice husky and unsteady.

"What did you say?" She came to the door and ran across the lounge in her flimsy nightdress. "Who was it?"

I walked over to the sideboard and mixed myself a drink. I did not dare let her see my face. "Just a fellow I know. He was a little tight, I guess."

"Oh." There was a long pause. I did not look round but drank the whisky quickly.

"Drink?" I asked, looking for a cigarette.

"No, thank you."

I lit the cigarette and turned. We looked at each other. Carol's eyes were full of questions.

"Come on," I said, forcing a smile. "Let's go to bed. I'm tired."

"What did he want?" she asked suddenly.

I glanced over at her, frowning. "What did who want?"

"Your friend ... the one who phoned."

"He was tight, God knows what he wanted. I told him to get to hell off the line."

"Sorry."

I looked at her sharply and then stubbed out the cigarette and went over to her. "I'm sorry if I sounded like a crab. It annoyed me that a drunk should interrupt us like that."

Again she looked searchingly at me, but I looked away and took off my dressing gown. I got into bed beside her and snapped off the light.

She came close, her head on my shoulder. I put my arm round her and we lay for a long time in the dark, not saying anything. In my mind, I kept saying to myself, you fool, you fool. You are throwing your happiness away. You are crazy. You have not been married five days and you're cheating already. This woman in your arms loves you. She will do anything for you. What do you think Eve will do for you? Nothing. You know she never will do anything for you.

"Is something wrong, Clive?" Carol asked.

"Of course not."

"Sure?"

"Sure."

"You're not worrying about anything? Tell me, Clive, if there's anything wrong. I want to share things with you."

"Nothing, darling, really. I'm tired and that guy annoyed me ... go to sleep. I'll be fine tomorrow."

"All right." She sounded doubtful and troubled. "But you will tell me if anything ever goes wrong, won't you?"

"I will."

"Promise?"

"Promise."

She sighed and clung to me for a moment. "I do love you, Clive. You won't let anything spoil this, will you?"

"Of course not," I said, thinking what a swine I was. I was lying deliberately because I wanted to have them both. It wouldn't work out that way ... it couldn't work out that way. "Now stop talking rot and go to sleep. I love you; everything's perfect and there's nothing to worry about."

She kissed me and then there was silence. Eventually I could tell by her breathing that she was asleep.

The next two days passed slowly. We continued to go to the lake. We swam, we talked, we listened to the gramophone and we read books. We both knew now that something was missing, something was not quite right, but neither of us said anything. I knew, of course, what it was. I don't think Carol guessed. I'm sure she did not, but she was troubled and I caught her looking at me from time to time with puzzled, hurt eyes.

Now that I had let the barriers down, Eve came into the house. As I sat reading, her face would suddenly appear on the page of my book. If I were listening to the gramophone, instead of the music, I would hear her voice saying, "I don't want your rotten money," over and over again. I would wake up at night thinking that I had her in my arms and then realizing, with a violently beating heart, that it was Carol and not Eve whom I was holding so tightly.

I began to long for her as a drug addict longs for a "shot" in the arm. I began to count the hours when Carol would get in her car and drive away to the Studio and yet, I still loved Carol. It was as if two people were living in my body, one clamouring for the cold indifference of Eve and the other content with the love that Carol gave me. Over these two people I had no control.

It was Saturday afternoon and we were sitting in the boat. Carol had on a red swimsuit and it looked nice with her golden skin and dark hair.

"It would be wonderful if we could always be happy like this, Clive, wouldn't it?" she said.

I rowed a few strokes before I said, "We'll always be happy, darling."

"I don't know. Sometimes I'm afraid something will happen and spoil all this."

"Nonsense," I held the oars against my chest and stared across the big expanse of blue water. "What could happen?"

She was silent for a moment, then she said, "Don't let's get like other couples we know and cheat and lie to each other."

"Don't worry," I told her, wondering if she had guessed what was going on in my mind. "We won't get like that."

She was quiet for a minute or two, her fingers playing in the water. "If you get tired of me, Clive, and you want someone else, will you tell me? I could stand it better if you told me than if I found you were cheating."

"What's got into you?" I demanded, leaning towards her and staring at her. "Why are you talking about such things?"

She looked up and smiled. "I just want you to know. I think if you ever cheated on me, Clive, I'd walk out and never see you again."

I tried to make a joke of it. "Swell," I said. "Now I know how to get rid of you."

She nodded. "Yes, now you know how to get rid of me."

When we returned to Three Point, there was a big, black Packard parked in the drive. I pulled up and stared at the car.

"Who can this be?" I asked.

Carol peered across me. "Let's go up and see. What a bore having people call on our last day but one."

I drove on up to the cabin. A short, dark fat man was sitting on the verandah with a highball on the table near him. He waved to Carol and got up.

"Who the hell's this?" I asked Carol in an undertone.

She clutched at my arm. "Bernstien," she whispered back. "Sam Bernstien of International Pictures. I wonder what he can possibly want."

We went up together and Bernstien patted Carol's arm affectionately before turning to me.

"So you're Thurston?" he said, offering a limp, fat hand. "Well, I am glad and happy to know you, Mr. Thurston. Glad and happy, and I don't often say that to writers, do I, my pet?"

Carol looked at him with a twinkle in her eyes. "You don't, Sam," she said. "At least, you don't say it to me."

"And you're honeymooning. Isn't that romantic? You're happy—both of you? That's swell. I can see it. My, my, it's done her good. You know, Thurston, I've watched this little girl ever since she came to Hollywood. She can write. Sure, she can write, but there was something frozen inside. 'Carol, my pet,' I said to her over and over again, 'what you want is a man. A big, strong man and then you will really write.' But she takes no notice." He pulled at my sleeve and whispered, "The trouble is she did not think me big enough," and he laughed, patting Carol's shoulder and putting his arm around her. "Now she will do great things."

I thought this was all pretty nice, but I was wondering what he wanted. He hadn't come all the way from Hollywood just to tell me that he was glad and happy to see me and that Carol wanted a big, strong man.

"Let's sit down," he said, going over to the table. "Let's all have drinks. I have come to talk to your clever husband, Carol. I have a lot of important things to talk to him about, otherwise I would not interrupt your honeymoon. You know me, don't you, my pet? Romantic ... a lover ... I do not spoil a honeymoon unless it is important."

"Come on, Sam," Carol said, her eyes sparkling with excitement. "What do you want to talk about?"

Bernstien rubbed his hand over his fat face, pushing his small, beaky nose almost at. "I have read your play, Mr. Thurston," he said. "I think it is very good."

A cold trickle ran down my spine. "You mean *Rain Check?*" I said, staring at him. "Why, why of course, it's very good."

He beamed. "And by golly, it'll make a grand picture. That's what I want to talk to you about. Let us, you and me make this play of yours into a picture."

I looked quickly at Carol. She put her hand on mine and squeezed it. "I told you, Clive. I told you Sam would like it," she said breathlessly.

I looked over at Bernstien. "Do you mean it?"

He waved his hands. "Mean it? Why should I come all this way if I didn't mean it? Of course, I mean it. But wait, there is one little thing. It's nothing, but it is something."

"So there's a catch in it?" I said, my excitement dying on me. "What is it?"

"You can tell me." He leaned forward. "What has Gold against you? Tell me that. Let me put that right and we make the picture. We give you a contract. Everything will be all right. But first I must put you right with Gold."

"That's a hell of a chance," I said bitterly. "He hates my guts. He loves Carol. Now do you understand what he's got against me?"

Bernstien looked at me and then at Carol and began to laugh. "That is very funny," he said, when he had recovered sufficiently to speak. "I had no idea. I would hate you too if I were in his place." He drank half his highball and then raised a short, fat finger. "There is a way. Not so good, but in the end—," he shrugged his shoulders, "it'll be all right. You write the treatment and I will take it to Gold and tell him that I do the picture. He does what I say, but first I must have the treatment."

"But first I want a contract."

He frowned. "No. Gold gives the contracts. I can't give you that. But I get you a contract when you have finished the treatment. I promise." He offered his hand.

I looked at Carol.

"It's all right, Clive. Sam always gets his own way. If he promises to give you a contract, he'll give it to you."

I shook hands with Bernstien. "Okay," I said. "I'll do you a treatment and you'll sell it to Gold. Right?"

"Right," he said. "Now I go. I have already stolen too many minutes of your honeymoon. We will work together. Your play is very fine. I like your mind. I like the way you express yourself. I like your drama. It is good. You will make a fine treatment. Come and see me at the Studio on Monday at ten o'clock. Carol will show you where to come. Then we get to work."

When he had gone, Carol threw herself into my arms. "Oh, I'm so pleased," she said. "Bernstien will make a marvellous picture for you. You two working together will make a marvellous team. Isn't it wonderful? Aren't you thrilled?"

I was scared and dismayed. I heard Bernstien's voice ringing in my ears. "I like your mind. I like the way you express yourself. I like your drama. It is good. You will make a fine treatment." He wasn't talking about me. He was talking about John Coulson. I knew I couldn't possibly write the treatment.

Carol pushed away from me and looked at me, her eyes troubled. "What is it, darling?" she asked, shaking me a little. "Why are you looking like that? Aren't you pleased?"

I turned away. "Of course I am," I said, sitting on the settee and lighting a cigarette. "But, Carol, let's face it. I don't know much about film treatments. I'd much sooner sell the thing and let Bernstien get someone to do it. I—I don't think somehow—"

"Oh, nonsense," she said, sitting by me and reaching for my hand. "Of course you can do it. I'll help you. Let's do it now. Let's make a start this very minute."

She was away to the library before I could stop her and I heard her calling to Russell to prepare a sandwich supper.

"Mr. Clive's going to turn his play into a picture, Russell," I heard her say. "Isn't it marvellous? We're going to start right in now."

She was back again with a copy of the script and we sat down and began to go through it. In an hour or so Carol had mapped out the first rough treatment. I did nothing except agree because her mind was so quick and her experience so sure that I knew that any suggestion from me would be valueless.

While we paused to eat chicken sandwiches and drink iced hock, she said, "You must do the script, Clive. It would mean so much if you did the actual shooting script. With your gift for dialogue ... You must do it."

"Oh no," I protested, getting up and pacing the floor. "I couldn't. I don't know how ... no, that's absurd."

"Listen ..." she held up her hand, "Of course you can. Listen to this dialogue ..." and she began to read from the play.

I stopped walking up and down, held by the power and strength of the words. They were words that I could never write. Words that had beauty, rhythm and drama. And as I listened, the words seemed to burn themselves into my brain until I thought I must snatch the play from her or go mad.

What a fool I had been to imagine that I could step into Coulson's shoes. I thought of what Gold had said. "It is, to say the least, a lucky flash in the pan, more extraordinary, perhaps, because your first play was excellent. I have often wondered how you came to write that play."

This was too dangerous. If I made a slip now I might be found out. Already Gold was suspicious. Why else had he said such a thing? If I began to write the script they would know at once that I had never written the play. God knows what would happen to me if they found out.

"Aren't you listening, darling?" Carol asked, looking at me.

"Let's not do any more tonight," I said, pouring hock into my glass. "I think we've done quite enough. I'll talk it over with Bernstien on Monday. Maybe he has someone in mind to do the script."

She looked at me, puzzled. "But darling ..."

I took the play from her hands. "No more tonight," I said firmly and walked out onto the verandah, unable any longer to meet her eyes.

The moon rode high. I could see the lake, the valley and the hills. But at that moment they meant nothing to me. My attention was concentrated on a man who was sitting on the wooden seat at the far end of the garden. I could not see his features, He was too far away for that, but there was something strangely familiar about the way he sat and the way he held himself, his shoulders rounded and his clasped hands gripped between his knees.

Carol came out and joined me.

"Isn't it lovely?" she said, slipping her arm through mine.

"Do you see ... ?" I asked, pointing to the man sitting on the garden seat, "Who is that man? What is he doing there?"

She looked, "What do you mean, Clive? What man?"

A cold wave of blood surged down my spine. "Isn't there a man sitting on the garden seat down there in the moonlight?"

She turned to me quickly. "There is no one there, darling."

I looked again. She was right. There was no one there.

"That's odd," I said, suddenly shivering. "It must have been a shadow ... it looked like a man."

"You're imagining things," she said, her voice troubled. "There honestly was no one there."

I drew her closer to me. "Let's go inside," I said, turning back to the sitting room. "It seems cold out here."

It was a long time before I fell asleep that night.

CHAPTER SIXTEEN

Sam Bernstien whipped off his horn-rimmed glasses and gave a wide, expansive smile. "Yes," he said, slapping the treatment Carol and I had written with his small fat hand, "this is what I want. It is not right. It is not nearly right, but it is something to work on. It is a good beginning."

I looked expectantly at him from where I was sitting in a low comfortable armchair in his big office. "I thought that'd be something on which to base a discussion. After all, you have ideas of your own so I kept it to the briefest outline."

Bernstien pulled a box of cigars towards him, selected one, offered it to me but I shook my head. He lit up and rubbed his bands. "I didn't expect you'd be so quick," he said. "Now let us go through this point by point. When we have agreed, I suggest you take it away, expand it and let me have it when you are ready. Then I will see R.G."

"You're going to have some difficulty there," I said, pessimistically.

He laughed. "That is something I can take care of," he said. "For the past five years R.G. and I have had our little fights. They mean nothing because, in the end, I get my own way. You leave him to me."

"All right," I returned, not convinced. "I'll leave it to you, but I warn you, Gold hates my guts."

He laughed again. "I don't blame him," he said. "Carol's a very lovely girl and you are a very lucky man. But if he hates your guts, he also loves a good story." He slapped the treatment again. "This is a good story!"

I caught a little of his enthusiasm. "Just as you say." I pulled my chair closer to his desk. "Suppose we go through the treatment."

"It's swell," he said, grinning delightedly at me. "Take all this stuff away and give me a second treatment. I think then it will be time to go to R.G."

I got to my feet. "Well, thanks a lot, Mr. Bernstien," I said. "I've enjoyed this immensely and I won't be long in letting you have the second treatment."

"Just as soon as you can," He walked with me to the door.

"I suppose Carol will be tied up all day?" I said, as we shook hands.

He lifted his shoulders. "I do not know. Go along and see for yourself. She's with Jerry Highams. You know his office?"

"Sure," I said, "I know where it is. Well, so long, Mr. Bernstien. I'll be seeing you,"

I walked quickly down the corridor and although I had to pass Highams' office I did not pause. I had no intentions of meeting Frank Imgram again and the chances that he would be with Carol were too great a risk.

I passed a public call box at the end of the corridor and I slowed my steps, stopping outside it. I looked at my wrist-watch. It was eleven fifty-five. With any luck, Marty would not have arrived. I wanted to be sure that Eve would answer the telephone. I entered the call box and shut myself in. While I dialled her number I was aware that my heart was pumping against my side with suppressed excitement.

The bell rang several times before she answered.

"Hello."

I recognized her voice.

"Eve," I said. "How are you?"

"Good morning, Clive," she said. "How are you? You're early, aren't you?"

"Did I wake you up?" I asked, startled that she sounded so friendly.

"No, it's all right. I was having some coffee. I've been awake some time."

"When am I going to see you?"

"When do you want to come?"

"Now wait a minute, Eve," I said, too puzzled to be cautious. "The other day you said you didn't want to see me again."

"All right, then I don't want to see you again," she returned and giggled.

"I'm coming right away," I said. "You are a devil. You gave me a bad two days. I really thought you meant it."

She giggled again. "Well, you are the limit, Clive. Anyway I did mean it at the time. I was angry. You were a stinker to go off like that."

"All right, I was a stinker," I said, laughing. "But I've had my lesson and I won't do it again."

"You better not," she warned. "I shan't forgive you so easily next time."

"Come and have lunch with me."

"No." Her voice hardened. "I'm not going to do that, Clive. You can come and see me professionally if you want to, but I'm not coming to lunch."

"That's what you think. You are coming to lunch and you're not going to argue," I said.

"Clive!" There was a startled, annoyed note in her voice. "I tell you I'm not coming to lunch."

"We'll talk about that when we meet. I'll be along in half an hour."

"It's too soon, Clive. I shan't be ready by then. Come about one o'clock."

"All right and wear something nice."

"I'm not coming to lunch."

"You're going to do what you're told for a change," I said, laughing at her. "You put on something smart—" but the line suddenly went dead as she hung up.

I looked at the telephone and grinned. Okay, sweetheart, I thought, we'll see who's going to be boss.

I went to the parking lot and drove the Chrysler slowly through the Studio gateway. I felt good. I felt confident that I could master Eve. She could hang up on me if that pleased her vanity, but she was going to have lunch with me, if I had to drag her to the restaurant in her nightdress.

I drove to the Writers' Club and asked the Steward for my mail. He gave me a few letters and I walked over to the bar and ordered a Scotch and soda. A quick look at the letters convinced me that there was nothing from Eve. Leaving my drink on the bar table I went back to the Steward and asked him if he was sure that there was nothing else for me.

"No, sir," he said, after looking again in my pigeonhole.

And yet Eve had been so emphatic that she had returned the forty dollars I had given her on the night I had walked out on her.

I went to the telephone and dialled her number.

"Hello," she said, almost immediately.

"I hope I didn't get you out of your bath, Eve," I said. "But you remember you told me you had returned my money?"

"Well, I did." Her voice was sharp.

"To the Writers' Club?"

"Yes."

"Well, it isn't here."

"I can't help that," she returned indifferently. "I sent it and when I say a thing I mean it."

"But Eve, I want you to have the money. I came here to get it. Are you quite sure you sent it?"

"Of course I am and, anyway, I don't want it. You annoyed me, so I returned you the money. I shan't accept it if you do give it to me."

I stared thoughtfully at the pencil scribblings on the wall. There's something wrong here, I decided.

"Did you put a note inside?"

"Why should I?" She was on the offensive now. "I put the money in an envelope and addressed it to the Club."

She was lying. I knew now that she never had any intentions of sending the money back. She had wanted to show her power. She knew that she would hurt me by sending the money back to me, but, in spite of wanting to get even with me, her greed had been too strong. She had tried to compromise and hoped that by telling me she had returned the money I would believe her and she would get her revenge cheaply. Well, she had made me suffer for two days, but now I realized that she'd not been big enough to go through with it, my contempt for her was in itself a victory.

"Maybe it's been lost in the mail," I said, half jeering at her. "Well, never mind, I'll make it up to you."

"I don't want it, Clive," she snapped. "I must go now. My bath's running."

"We'll talk about it when we have lunch," I said and tried to get the receiver down before she did, but she beat me to it.

I reached Laurel Canyon Drive at five minutes to one. I pulled up outside the little house and sounded my horn. Then I got out and walked down the path. I rapped on the door, took out a cigarette and lit it.

I waited a moment or two and then realized that there was no sound coming from the house. Usually as soon as I knocked 1 would hear Marty coming down the passage.

I frowned, then I knocked again. Nothing happened. I waited, a cold sinking feeling coming over me as I stood there.

I knocked four times and then I went back to the Chrysler. I got in and drove slowly down the street. When I got out of sight of the house, I pulled up and lit another cigarette. My hands were trembling as I held the match.

I suddenly thought of Harvey Barrow. I remembered what he had said. "I said I'd take her away and she said all right. But I went to her place four times and each time her damn maid said she was out. But, I knew she was upstairs laughing at me."

My hands tightened on the steering wheel. She hadn't even had the decency to send Marty with some lie. I could see her in the little bedroom, her head on one side, listening to me knocking on the door. Marty would be with her and they would exchange glances. They would smile. Let him knock, Eve would whisper, he'll soon get sick of it.

I drove slowly along Sunset Boulevard, not thinking of anything, but feeling numb and sick. I pulled up outside a drugstore, went in and dialled her number. The bell rang for a long time, but there was no answer.

I could imagine her about to pick up the receiver and then stop. She would know who it was. I leaned against the wall of the stale smelling call box, listening to the bell ringing. Quite suddenly I wanted to kill her. It was a cold, almost impersonal thought that dropped unexpectedly into my mind and I found myself considering it with interest and pleasure. Then, horrified at even contemplating such a thing, I hung up and walked out into the sunlight.

Was I going crazy? I asked myself, as I drove towards Three Point. It was one thing to be furiously angry with her, but to kill her ... what a mad, stupid, dangerous thing even to think of for a moment.

All the same, 1 knew I would get pleasure out of killing Eve. There was no other way that I could touch her. Her armour was too strong. Again I hurriedly dismissed the thought but it kept coming back, and, in my mind, I went throughout the details of killing her and it gave me a lot of pleasure.

I saw myself, some night, getting into that little house when she was out and waiting for her. I would hide upstairs in one of the empty rooms until I heard her key in the lock. Then I would come out of my hiding place onto the landing to make sure that she was alone. I knew I could see her quite easily by leaning over the banisters and that she couldn't see me.

Before going to bed, she would want to use the bathroom. I would slip back into one of the other empty rooms and wait until she went downstairs again. It would give me a lot of pleasure to think she was moving about the lonely little house, believing that she was alone, while, all the time, I was hiding upstairs, waiting to kill her.

Perhaps she would return drunk as she had on the night I had walked out on her. If she were drunk, then it would be easy for me to kill her. I would have no pity nor feeling for her if I found her snoring and smelling of whisky.

I would creep out onto the landing and listen. I would hear her prepare for bed. I knew enough of her routine now to picture exactly what she would do. First she would take off her skirt. She did that the moment she got indoors because it was cut so tight that she could not sit down comfortably in it. Then she would go to her wardrobe and take out a clothes hanger. She would put the coat and skirt away methodically. Perhaps she would light a cigarette while she slid out of the rest of her flimsy underclothes. She would put on her nightdress and flop into bed.

By listening carefully, I would be able to follow all these details. Each of them had their own individual sound to the final creaking of the bed as it received her slight body. Perhaps she would read or perhaps she would turn out the light and smoke in the darkness. Whatever she did, I would give her plenty of time to fall asleep. What did I care if I had to wait hours up there in the darkness? I would come down eventually. I would come down like a ghost, holding onto the banister rail and trying each stair before I put my full weight upon it. I would not wake her until it was too late for her to save herself.

I would edge round the door and peer into the darkness. I would not be able to see her, but I would know just where her head lay and I would sit gently on the bed by her side. Even then she would not awaken. I would find her throat with one hand and with the other I would switch on the little bedside lamp.

Then would come the moment that would heal all the wounds she had inflicted on me. That brief moment when her senses would awake from sleep and her eyes would recognize me. We would look at each other and she would know why I was there and what I was going to do. I would see the helpless, terrified look that would come into her eyes and I would see her for the first time without her wooden mask or without her professional mannerisms.

It would be only for two or three seconds. But it would be enough. I would kill her quickly with my knee on her chest and my hands about her throat. Pinning her to the bed with all my weight, she would not have a chance. She would have no time to steel her body against me or even scratch at my hands.

No one would know who had done it. It would have been any of her men friends.

I was shaken out of this horrible daydream by the violent sound of a
motor horn and I only managed to avoid a head-on collision with a
Cadillac. I had been so absorbed that I had allowed the Chrysler to wander over to the left side of the road. I heard the driver of the other car
curse me as he swept past and I hastily pulled over to my right side and
continued on my way with caution.

When I reached Three Point I was still disturbed by the uncontrolled
feeling of pleasure I had experienced while imagining how I might settle all my differences with Eve. As it was now almost three o'clock, I
asked Russell to bring me sandwiches and a whisky on the terrace.

While I waited, I paced up and down, savagely angry by the way Eve
had treated me and yet alarmed to realize to what an extent my mentality had been affected by her callous indifference towards me. The fact
that I had actually contemplated murder down to the last details and had
derived pleasure in doing so shocked and frightened me. Such a thought
would never have entered my mind some three weeks ago, but in that
unguarded moment in the call box it had seemed to be the one solution
of our struggle.

I must pull myself together, I thought, as I paced up and down. She's
no good to me. She never will be and I might just as well admit defeat
and forget her. I can never hope to get on with any work if I allow her
to influence my mind, to occupy my thoughts and to irritate my nerves
in this way. This nonsense must stop.

Russell came with a tray which he put on the table.

"Get my typewriter, Russell," I said turning. "I've some work to do."

He beamed at me. "I do hope, sir, you had a good morning at the Studio."

"It was all right," I said, without enthusiasm. "Be a pal and let me get
to work."

He gave me a quick, disappointed glance and hurried into the library
for my typewriter.

I sat down and began to read through Bernstien's notes but I found concentration difficult. I could not erase from my mind the humiliation of
standing outside Eve's door like some street salesman. The more I
thought about it, the more angry I became. When Russell put the typewriter at my elbow and had gone away, I could not bring myself to work.
Instead I finished the sandwiches and began to drink steadily.

I'll make her pay for this, I thought, pouring more whisky into my glass
with an unsteady hand. Somehow I'll find a way to get even with her. I
drank the whisky at a gulp and immediately refilled my glass. I did this
several times until I felt a slight numbness in my legs. I knew I was get-

ting drunk. I pushed the decanter away and pulled the typewriter towards me. To hell with her, I said aloud. She can't stop me. Nobody can.

I made an attempt to write the first scene along the lines suggested by Bernstien and after struggling with it for over an hour I tore the sheet from my typewriter and ripped it angrily to pieces.

I was in no mood for creative thought and, leaving the terrace, I wandered through the empty rooms of the cabin. Russell had taken himself off somewhere. He had probably hidden himself away for an afternoon nap in the woods. The cabin was unbearably lonely and I began to wonder if I had not been a fool to have settled in such an out of the way place.

It was perfect so long as I had Carol to keep me company, but now that she was going to spend most of her days at the Studio I was going to find it pretty dull.

My mind kept returning to Eve. I made a feeble effort to think of something else, but I did not succeed. I picked up a novel and tried to read, but after turning a half a dozen pages I realized that I had no idea what I had been reading and I threw the book across the room.

By now, the whisky I had drunk was hitting me and I felt heavy in the head and reckless. I suddenly got to my feet and went over to the telephone. I'll tell her exactly what I think of her, I decided. If she thinks she can do that to me and get away with it she's got a surprise coming to her.

I dialled her number.

"Who is that please?" Marty asked.

I hesitated, then quietly replaced the receiver. I wasn't going to be snubbed by Eve through Marty. I lit a cigarette and wandered unsteadily onto the terrace again.

I could not go on like this, I thought. I must try to do some work. I again sat down at the table and began reading through Bernstien's notes, but my mind kept wandering and I finally gave it up in despair.

Carol returned in time for dinner. She got out of her cream and blue roadster and came running across the lawn towards me.

I felt a great weight roll from my mind at the sight of her and I held her tightly against me for several seconds before letting her go.

"Well, my dear," I said, smiling at her, "How did you get on?"

She heaved a sigh. "I'm tired, Clive. We've been at it without a stop. Do come in and get me a drink. I want to hear all your news."

We walked to the cabin while I listened to her account of the story conference.

"R.G. is delighted so far," she said. "It's going to be a marvellous picture. Jerry has never been better and even R.G. has made one good suggestion."

I fixed her a gin and lime and gave myself another whisky.

"I say, Clive," she exclaimed suddenly, "You haven't drunk all that whisky yourself, have you? The decanter was full this morning."

I gave her a drink and laughed. "Of course not," I said. "What do you think I am … a soak? I upset the damn thing and wasted half of it."

She gave me a quick, searching look but I met her eyes and her face cleared. "So you're not a soak," she said, smiling at me. She looked tired and pale. "Well, tell me, did Sam like the treatment?"

I nodded. "Sure he liked it. Why not? You wrote it, didn't you?"

"We wrote it, darling," she said, again looking troubled. "You're not sore about it, are you? I mean—I won't interfere if you don't—"

"Forget it," I said shortly. "I know I'm not so hot when it comes to a picture treatment, but I don't mind learning." I sat down by her side and took her hand. "But I'm not going so well with the second rewrite. You know, Carol, I wish Bernstien would get someone else to do it. I don't seem to be getting anywhere."

"Give me a cigarette and tell me what Bernstien said."

After I had lit her cigarette I explained Bernstien's suggestions. She listened attentively, nodding her small dark head every now and then with approval.

"He's terrific," she said, when I had finished. "It is enormously improved. Oh, Clive, you simply must work at it. I know you can do it and it'll mean so much to you."

"It's all very well for you to talk, Carol," I returned bitterly, "but now I haven't any feeling for the story. I've been messing with it all the afternoon and I've got nowhere."

She looked at me for a moment, her eyes searching and puzzled. "Perhaps tomorrow you'll feel more like it," she said hopefully. "Sam will expect something soon. He's late for production as it is."

I got up irritably. "Oh, I don't know. You can't force these things."

She came and put her arms round me. "Don't worry, Clive. It'll come, you see."

"Oh, the hell with it." I turned to the door. "I'll put on a dressing gown and settle down for the evening. Have you a book?"

"I've some work to do," she said quickly. "I want to draft out a few scenes."

"You can't go on working all day and night," I returned, irritated that she could give her mind to creative thought. "Have a rest. It'll do you good."

She pushed me to the door. "Don't tempt me. You sit on the terrace. It's lovely out there and I'll come as soon as I'm through."

I sat on the darkening terrace for a long time brooding about Coulson. I knew I was doing a mean thing by turning his play into a picture, but I had gone too far to stop. I should never have stolen his play in the first place. But if I had not done that I should not be where I was, sitting on the terrace of an expensive cabin in one of the loveliest spots in California. I should never have met Carol. I drew a sharp breath—and I should never have met Eve.

"What are you doing out there in the dark?" Carol said as she stepped onto the terrace. "You've been sitting there hours, my dear. It's after twelve o'clock."

I pulled myself together with a start. "I've been thinking," I said, getting up. I felt stiff and a little cold. "I had no idea the time had gone so quickly. Have you finished?"

She slipped her arm round my neck and kissed me. "Don't be cross, darling," she whispered, her lips touching my ear. "I've roughed out the second treatment for you. You can do it now and it's really good. You're not angry, are you?"

I stared down at her, sick with envy that she could do so easily what I had failed to do. "But, Carol, you can't do my work as well as your own. This is absurd. I'll be living on you next."

"Don't be angry," she pleaded. "All I've done is to put your ideas and Sam's ideas down on paper. Why a stenographer could do that. You must polish it tomorrow and take it to Sam. Then R.G. will okay it and you can really start work. Give me a kiss and take that frown off your face."

I kissed her.

She gave me a quick hug. "Come on to bed," she said. "I must be up early tomorrow."

"I'm coming," I said, feeling flat and depressed.

CHAPTER SEVENTEEN

During the next four days I became increasingly aware that I had made a bad mistake in coming to live at Three Point. By doing this I had cut myself off from all social contact and now, without any form of amusement, I was rapidly becoming bored with this self-imposed isolation. Although I had hoped to write a novel in the quiet of these surroundings when the time came to begin I found that inspiration was lacking.

I had managed, with a considerable effort, to rewrite Carol's second treatment of the play. As she had done most of the necessary work, my own particular job amounted merely to copying what she had written.

Although I had no actual creative work to do, it still required an effort of will to sit at my typewriter. Several times while I worked, I was tempted to telephone for a stenographer to come out and finish it. But, in the end, I managed to complete the treatment and it was now in Sam Bernstien's hands. I was waiting with mixed feelings to hear what Gold was going to say. It was my intention, if he accepted it, to insist that someone—anyone but me—should do the shooting script. I knew that I was incapable of doing it and besides, I dare not take the risk of writing the additional dialogue and script required. I had no hope of imitating John Coulson's brilliant phrases and, if I did make the attempt, it would at once become obvious to a man of Gold's shrewdness that I was not the author of the original play.

My financial position was beginning to worry me. My capital was dwindling, my royalties were becoming depressingly smaller each week and my debts were increasing. I gave Carol no hint of the true position since I knew that she would insist on paying her share. She was, of course, earning big money at the Studio and, although she used a certain amount of this for pocket money and for her wardrobe, the bulk was being carefully invested in real estate. Whatever else were my faults, I was determined never to take a dollar from her.

While she was at the Studio, the day seemed interminable. I spent many hours shut up in my library and when I could no longer bear this seclusion I went into the woods and roamed about in a mood of black depression. Eve and John Coulson were never far from my thoughts.

I did attempt to write a shooting script of *Rain Check* but no sooner had I begun than I experienced an eerie feeling that John Coulson was in the room by my side, watching me struggle with his creation and silently laughing at my clumsy efforts. It was an absurd fancy but it persisted and made concentration impossible.

For three days I fought against a strong desire to telephone Eve, but on the fourth day, soon after Carol had gone to the Studio, I gave way to temptation.

As it happened I had allowed Russell a few days off as a relative of his was dangerously ill. I had finished my coffee which I had prepared for Carol and myself and I could still hear the distant sound of Carol's car as she drove down the mountain road. Suddenly, acting on impulse, I threw down the newspaper I was reading and reached for the telephone.

Eve answered almost at once.

"Hello?"

It was extraordinary that, even after the way she had treated me, the sound of her voice quickened my blood and caused my heart to beat rapidly.

"Eve," I said. "How are you?"

"Hello, stranger," she returned gaily. "Where have you been all this time?"

I could hardly believe that this was Eve speaking. Her voice was bright and I sensed that something had happened to make her happy. In some odd perverse way, this annoyed me.

"You're not confusing me with someone else, are you?" I asked sarcastically. "This is Clive. The guy you don't see when he knocks on your door."

She giggled. "I know."

So she thought it was amusing, did she? I clenched the receiver until my knuckles turned white. "I think it was a pretty rotten trick to play on me. I arranged lunch. At least you might have seen me and made an excuse."

"It was a pretty rotten trick to sneak off in the middle of the night too," she returned. "And I didn't want to have lunch with you. I won't be told what to do by any man. I hope it's taught you a lesson."

I gritted my teeth. "You're always trying to teach me a lesson."

She giggled again. "And you don't seem to learn, do you, Clive?"

"At least, I'm a trier."

"You are. I've never known anyone so difficult to get rid of."

"So you want to get rid of me?"

"Have you only just found that out?"

Her flippancy infuriated me. "You'll succeed one of these days and then you'll be sorry," I said angrily.

"That's what you think," she returned, laughing.

This was Eve in an entirely new mood and my curiosity got the better of my temper. "You sound pretty good this morning. Have you come into a fortune?"

I waited but she offered no further explanation.

"I think I'll come and see you, Eve," I said.

"I can't see you today."

"Now don't be like that, Eve. I want to see you."

"I shan't be in, so don't come. You won't find me if you do."

"Where are you going?"

"That's my business."

I felt blood mounting to my face. "Well, when shall I see you?"

"I don't know. If you want to come you'd better ring me in a few days."

I had an idea. "Is Jack coming home?"

"He is. Now are you satisfied?"

The old feeling of jealousy came to me again. "I'm glad," I lied. "I suppose you're going back to your other house, is that it?"

"I am." Her voice sounded a little curt.

"For how long?"

"I don't know. I do wish you wouldn't ask so many questions. I don't know how long he'll be staying."

"You expect him today?"

"Hm-hm. I had a telegram last night."

"Don't forget I want to meet him."

There was a moment's pause. "I won't."

"Do we meet this time?"

"No—not this time."

"When then?"

"Some time. I'll see."

"So you're going to forget all your boyfriends? What will they do without you?"

"I don't know and I don't care. They'll come back when I'm ready."

Her indifference tortured me. "Well, have a good time. I'll call in a few days."

"All right. Good-bye," and she hung up.

I slammed down the receiver and walked onto the terrace. Every time we met, every time I telephoned her, it became more obvious that I meant nothing to her. Yet I could not give her up. I knew I would never mean anything to her, but still I had to pursue her.

I couldn't stay in the cabin all day with the thought that she was meeting her husband on my mind. It would drive me crazy.

I decided I would drive over to the Studio and see if Bernstien had any news for me.

After my bath, I dressed and got the Chrysler from the garage, then I drove leisurely down the mountain road through San Bernardino to Hollywood. I was in a black mood of depression, hating the thought of the long afternoon and evening that lay before me.

I reached the Studio by noon and as I drew up outside the main office buildings, Carol came hurrying down the steps.

"Why, hello, darling," she said, jumping on the running board and kissing me. "I've been trying to get you."

I looked at her sharply. "Anything wrong?"

"It's such a bore, but we're flying to Death Valley and I won't be back until tomorrow morning. Jerry insists that we get the right desert atmosphere and he, Frank and I are leaving immediately."

"You mean you won't be coming home tonight?" I asked blankly.

"I can't, my sweet. Oh, and Russell won't be there to look after you. What are we going to do?"

I tried to conceal my dismay, but I did not succeed too well. "I can look after myself. Don't worry about me, besides I have a lot of work to do."

"I hate your being all alone," she said, worried. "Why don't you stay in town or better still, come with us?"

I thought of Imgram and I shook my head. "I'll go back to Three Point," I said. "Don't worry, I'll get along fine."

"Oh, do come with us," she pleaded. "It'll be fun."

"Now don't fuss," I said a little irritably. "I tell you I'll be all right. Have a good trip. I'll see you tomorrow night then?"

"I wish I hadn't to go. It does worry me to think of you being all alone. You're sure you won't stay in town?"

"I'm not a child, Carol," I said, a little curtly. "I can look after myself. I must run. I want to talk to Bernstien." I had seen Highams and Imgram coming down the long avenue to the office buildings and I was anxious not to meet them. "Have a good time." I kissed her. "Good-bye and bless you." I hurried into the building, leaving her looking after me with a worried expression in her eyes.

I walked down the long corridor to Sam Bernstien's office, feeling depressed. If only Eve had been free. I would have persuaded her to take the day off and we would have had fun together. I could have spent the night with her. But now, I was faced with a hopelessly blank twenty-four hours unless Bernstien had something for me.

"Go right ahead," his secretary told me as soon as I gave her my name. "Mr. Bernstien has been trying to get you."

I brightened. This sounded promising.

"Hello there," I said as I entered the office.

Bernstien jumped to his feet. "I've been calling you. It's all right. R.G. agrees. What do you know? A contract for one hundred thousand dollars. I congratulate you."

I stared at him speechless.

"I thought that would surprise you," he said grinning. "Didn't I tell you I would get round Gold? I know him. I know all his little ways." He opened a drawer and took out a contract form. "Everything has been agreed to. I have had my way in everything. See for yourself."

With unsteady hands I picked up the contract and began to read. Then quite suddenly my heart gave a lurch and I went cold.

"But it says here I'm to do the shooting script," I stammered.

"Of course," Bernstien beamed. "Carol suggested the idea herself and when I mentioned it to R.G. he made that the condition of the contract.

He said that the picture would be no use unless it had your brilliant dialogue. Those were his very words.”

I sat down limply. Gold knew then. No wonder he was offering a hundred thousand dollars. He knew that I would not dare attempt to produce any dialogue.

“But aren’t you pleased?” Bernstien demanded, staring at me with puzzled eyes. “Is anything wrong? Don’t you feel well?”

“I’m all right,” I said dully. “This—this has been a bit of a shock to me.”

Bernstien brightened at once. “Of course. You did not expect so much. But it’s a grand play and it will make a fine picture. Have a drink?”

I was glad to gulp down the stiff whisky he gave me. All the time he was fussing around mixing the drink, I was trying to think of a way out. There was no way out. Gold had got me where he wanted me.

The next couple of hours meant nothing to me. I drove around aimlessly, my mind stunned by the trick Gold had devised, wondering how I was going to explain to Carol that I could not go through with it.

I had to make money some way. I just could not go on without money. Then I remembered *Lucky Strike*.

When I first came to Hollywood I had been a keen gambler and I used to go out to the gambling ships which were anchored off the California beaches. There were more than a dozen of these ships which avoided the regulations by staying outside the three mile limit and I had been out to the *Lucky Strike* a number of times. It was about the best equipped gambling ship of the lot and I had at one time or another won considerable sums of money. I would try my luck again.

Whether it was because I had faith in my luck or because I had something to do I brightened up and I drove to the Writers’ Club and cashed a cheque for a thousand dollars.

I had a few drinks and some sandwiches and spent the rest of the afternoon looking through the illustrated papers and brooding about Gold.

I had a light supper at the club and it was just after nine o’clock when I drove down to Santa Monica Bay. I turned into the parking lot on the pier and for several minutes I sat in the Chrysler looking across the bay.

I could see the *Lucky Strike* anchored outside the three mile limit. It was a mass of lights and already taxi boats were going out to the ship.

It was a good ten minutes’ ride out to the *Lucky Strike*. The taxi boat rolled and pitched a little, but it did not bother me. There were only five other passengers with me. Four of them were well dressed, rich looking, middle-aged businessmen and the other was a girl. She was tall and a redhead. Her skin was creamy and soft looking. Her body in her tight yellow dress was soft looking too. She was voluptuous and sensual and she had a high-pitched, slightly hysterical laugh.

I sat opposite her. She had good legs although they thickened abruptly above her knees. She was with a grey haired man with a hooked nose. He seemed kind of embarrassed when she laughed. I looked at her and she looked at me. I could see she knew what I was thinking because she suddenly stopped laughing and began pulling her skirt over her knees. It was too short and tight, so she kept her hands on her knees and did not look at me any more.

The *Lucky Strike* was about two hundred and fifty feet long. It looked big from the little taxi boat and there was trouble with the redhead before she got aboard. I guess she was kind of self conscious climbing up the wind swept ladder. Anyway she made a lot of fuss and the man with the hooked nose got mad at her.

There was a big crowd on board and I lost sight of her. I was sorry. She was like a candle burning in a dark room.

I mixed with the crowd, but I did not see anyone I knew. I wanted a drink badly so I headed for the bar. It was packed with people, but I managed to catch the bartender's eye. I got part of a double whisky which was handed to me over the heads of the crowd. It was no good trying to get another, so I went into the main cabin where the dice tables were.

I edged through the crowd until I reached the centre table. I had to use my elbows, but the crowd seemed good tempered and let me through. Green dice rolled across the green cloth, struck the rim together and bounced back. One stopped short showing five white spots. The other tumbled out to the centre of the table and came to rest with six spots on top.

A sigh went up as the winner cleared the table of money.

I watched the play for about five minutes and then the dice came to me.

I put down two twenties and threw snake eyes. I put down another twenty and threw a five. After four throws I made it and let it ride. Then I threw an eleven and began to coast.

I made five straight passes, then I lost the dice. I began to bet on the board.

I found the redhead was standing at my side. She was wedging her hip against mine. I leaned against her, but I did not look at her. The dice came around to me again. I put down two fifties and made it. I made two more passes. Then I crapped out.

"You're losing a lot of weight," the redhead said.

I wiped my forehead with a handkerchief and looked around for the man with the hooked nose. He was wedged against the table opposite us. He could not hear what she was saying.

"Do you like that guy?" I asked. I was betting ten dollars at a time and I had just won again.

She crowded me. "Would it make any difference?"

I got the dice again and upped the ante. "It might," I said and made three straight passes.

"I'm bringing you luck," she said. "It's my red head."

My next throw was seven. I waited until they paid me and then passed the dice.

"Let's go somewhere," I said, my pockets tight with money.

"Have you been here before?"

The man with the hooked nose had the dice now. He threw two sixes. They took his money.

"I know all the places," she said and squeezed herself out of the crowd. I noticed a lot of men enjoyed that. I did not blame them.

I took a quick look at the man with the hooked nose, but he was busy. So I forced myself through the crowd and joined her.

She led me along the deck, through the crowds, up an iron ladder. I could not see her, but I could smell her perfume. I followed her with my nose.

The crowds suddenly disappeared and we were alone. I felt the rail against my back and she was pressing against me.

"The moment I saw you ..." she said.

"That's the way it is," I said and took hold of her. She was big and soft. My fingers sank into her back.

"Just kiss me," she said and she put her hands under my coat.

We stayed like that for a minute.

Then she jerked away. "Whew! Come up for air," she said.

I hated her suddenly more than anyone ever hated anyone.

I took hold of her again, but she shoved me off. She was terribly strong. I did not think she could be so strong.

"Don't rush me," she said, giggling. "Just take it easy."

I wanted to slam my fist in her face, but I stood away and said nothing.

I could see her fiddling with her hair. She turned round and looked at the moon that was coming up fast.

"I'd better get back," she said.

"That's all right with me."

She made no move. "He'll be wondering where I am."

"I guess he will."

It was a pushover.

She put her hands on her lips. "I believe you bruised me."

I did not care a great deal. "Not you," I said.

She laughed. "The moon looks all right now," she said, turning back to me.

"Were you waiting for the moon?"

"Hm-hm." Her hands reached out and I pulled her against me. "I don't neck with every guy I meet," she said as if excusing herself.

"I should worry what you do so long as you do it now," I said, still hating her, but overwhelmed by her.

She bit my mouth.

Someone laughed on the deck below. I knew that laugh. No one but Eve could laugh like that. I shoved the redhead away.

"What's the matter?" Her voice was a mumble.

I stood listening.

Eve laughed again. I looked over the rail but the crowd was too dense. I could not see her.

"Hey!" The redhead sounded angry.

"To hell with you," I said.

She swung at me, but I caught her wrist. It felt soft and flabby in my grip. She gave a kind of squeal.

I called her a name and left her.

Down on the deck I looked around for Eve. I saw her at last standing by the lighted doorway that led to the roulette room. By her side was a tall hard-faced man in a well fitting tuxedo.

I knew who he was.

As I moved towards them, they went into the roulette room. He had his hand on her elbow and she was looking happy.

CHAPTER EIGHTEEN

I did not want Eve to see me. Anyway, not just yet. I was not able to stand in the doorway because people kept crowding in. The room, although large, was pretty tightly packed. From the door, I could not see the tables, although I could see the shaded arc lights that illuminated them.

I moved cautiously forward until I reached the first table. I was wedged then, and looking around, I saw Eve was not there. I guessed she would be at the far table and I tried to make my way there. The crowd was too thick and I had to wait.

The croupier was singing out, "*Faites vos jeux, Messieurs.*" There was a concerted movement towards the table and I was carried along with it.

A moment later the croupier said, "*Les jeux sont faits.*" The pressure eased and I was able to back away from the table and drift down the room. Even then it was not easy. I picked up some black looks as I squeezed through the crowd, using my elbows and trying to be pleasant about it.

It was a full ten minutes before I reached the other table. Eve was standing behind Jack Hurst who had managed to get a seat. The croupier was saying, "*Onze, noir, impair.*"

After he had raked in the losing stakes, he pushed a small pile of chips across to Hurst.

"*Messieurs, faites vos jeux.*"

Eve leaned forward and whispered in Hurst's ear. Her eyes were bright and she looked almost beautiful. He shook his head impatiently, but did not look around. He staked on black and *Impair*.

While other players were staking, I eyed him with interest. He was big, broad shouldered and powerful looking. His eyes were deep set and his nose straight. He had no top lip. His mouth looked like a hard line drawn with a ruler and pencil. His tuxedo fitted him well and his linen was flawless. I guessed he would be about forty.

So this was the guy Eve had fallen for. I did not blame her. Whatever else he was, he was a man. I found it hard to admit, but Jack Hurst looked all right.

I glanced at Eve. She had her hand possessively on his shoulder and she never took her eyes off him for one second. Every move he made she watched excitedly. I hardly recognized her. She was animated and I had never seen her look so happy.

All the same, I was sick with jealousy. If Hurst had been a little rat of a man, it would not have been so bad. But he wasn't. I could not help comparing him with myself. The comparison wasn't so good. He was better looking, more interesting and more powerful. He looked like a man who would get his own way in everything he did.

The wheel spun and Eve leaned forward. Hurst just sat with his eyes on the wheel, cold and disinterested.

The croupier said, "*Rien ne va plus.*"

The ball gradually slipped down the ledge and finally lodged in one of the compartments of the bowl.

The croupier paid out. He shoved more chips at Hurst and smiled at him. Hurst didn't catch his eye.

I began a slow move around the table. It was difficult and Hurst won more chips before I got behind Eve. I had to elbow a fat old woman out of the way before I got right behind her. I could smell the perfume in her hair. I wanted to touch her, but I didn't.

She said in a whisper to Hurst, "Double your stakes."

"Shut up," he said.

He put down six chips on the line between 16 and 13. I reached over and put three one hundred dollar chips down on the red. Eve turned. We looked at each other.

"Hello," I said.

Her face became wooden and she turned away.

All right, you slut, I thought. If that's the way you want to play it.

The croupier said, "*Les jeux sont faits*," and tossed the ivory ball into the wheel.

It came up red.

The croupier took Hurst's chips before he shoved mine over to me.

"I'll leave it there," I said, "O.K.?"

The croupier nodded.

Hurst had lost about fifty dollars. He put more chips on the table. It came up red again.

"Leave it there," I said.

Hurst lost his chips.

He glanced over his shoulder at me and a slight smile came into his eyes. I grinned right back at him. I could afford to.

He did elaborate things with his chips this time laying them out on the first and third dozen.

The red came up and they took Hurst's chips again. I guessed he had lost about two hundred dollars. I had about eight hundred dollars on the red now. The croupier looked at me inquiringly. I nodded.

As Hurst was about to stake again, Eve said, "It's no good tonight. Let's go." She looked worried.

"Shut up," Hurst said.

That seemed to be the only thing he could say to her.

Again the red came up and again Hurst lost his chips.

I put two hundred dollar chips on *Passe* and left the pile of chips on red.

People crowded close behind me. I had quite a piece of money on the table now.

Hurst didn't stake.

The wheel spun. The ivory ball hovered over red 36, then dropped lazily into black 13.

The croupier raked in all my chips and shook his head at me. I tried to grin, but it didn't quite come off.

I'd seen fifteen hundred dollars slide through my fingers and that hurt. I let it ride.

Hurst began to stake again. This time he won. It looked like he couldn't win when I was playing. I waited a couple of rounds then I staked two hundred on the black.

The red came up.

All right, I thought, then I'll play red. I was crazy not to play the red. I was four hundred dollars down.

As I reached forward to place my stake, I touched Eve's hip. It was like touching a live wire. She moved quickly away and that told me she knew who was touching her. I didn't care. It was enough just to stand by her and watch the man she loved losing his money.

I put down five hundred dollars on the red.

Hurst staked too.

The red came up and Hurst lost.

It went on like that for fifteen minutes. I did not stake every time. Twice I was going to take the pile of chips off the table, but something stopped me.

The red came up eleven times. I could hear all the people letting their breath out.

"Leave it on the red," I said. There were fifty two hundred dollar chips there.

The croupier said, "No bet." He didn't start the wheel.

Then, right off, an argument started. A little man with a scar across his face started shouting that they had to take the bet and spin the wheel.

The croupier just sat there and shook his head.

Hurst said suddenly, "Spin that goddam wheel." There was a crack like a whip in his voice.

The croupier whispered something to a tall, thin bird who had pushed his way up to the table.

Hurst said, "Tell him to spin the wheel, Tony."

The tall thin bird looked at my pile of chips and his lips pursed. He looked at Hurst and then at me. Then he said to the croupier, "Well, what the hell are you waiting for?"

The croupier lifted his shoulders. *"Messieurs, fates vos jeux."*

Everyone crowded forward. It was an exciting moment. I put my hand down and found Eve's. She did not look at me, but she let me hold it. I got more of a bang out of that than I did watching the wheel spin.

The ball seemed to be taking a long time to make up its mind. It dropped into the red and seemed about to settle, then at the last moment, almost as if an unseen hand had given it a flip, it rolled into the black.

There was a long drawn-out sigh from the crowd.

"Why didn't you stop, you weak fool?" Eve said, snatching her hand away.

Hurst looked over his shoulder, stared at her and then at me. Everyone was looking at me. I just stood there, feeling weak at the knees. By just one throw too many I had gypped myself out of ten thousand dollars.

"Okay?" The thin bird asked, sneering at me.

I pulled myself together. "Yeah," I said and without looking at Eve, I forced my way across the crowded room to the bar.

There was scarcely anyone in the long low room. The crowd had begun to gamble and they would not start drinking again until later on in the evening. It was still early. The clock above the bar said ten five.

I ordered a double Scotch and when I had drunk it I told the bartender to leave the bottle. It was going to be a hell of an evening after all.

I stayed there for half an hour and I drank steadily. Then I saw Eve come in. She was alone. I was pretty high by now and as I was about to leave the bar and go over to her she went into the Ladies' Room. A few minutes later she came out with the redhead. They passed close to me without seeing me.

The redhead was saying, "He's terrific, isn't he? He looks like a sailor and I adore his thin lips."

Eve giggled. "He doesn't go for redheads," she said, her face animated.

"I'd dye for him," the redhead said and her high-pitched laugh grated on my nerves.

I watched them cross the room and go back into the roulette room. I pulled out a handful of change and shoved it at the bartender and went after them. I could not see Eve nor Hurst. The redhead wasn't there either. I went into the dice room and the card room. There was no sign of them. I went up on deck. The wind was still cold, but there were a number of couples up there.

I walked around, but I could not see them, so I went up on the top deck.

The redhead was there.

"Hello," she said.

I joined her at the rail. "Haven't you found your friend?"

"He's gone. I came up here to see the moon again."

I looked at her. Perhaps she was not so bad after all. I remembered how my fingers had sunk into her back.

I moved closer. "How are you getting back?"

"By boat ... do you think I'd swim?" She laughed and I laughed too. I was plastered so anything could be funny right now; even losing ten thousand dollars.

I manoeuvred her against the rails. She did not seem to mind.

"I'm sorry I tried to hit you," she said.

"I liked it," I said and pulled her towards me.

She came willingly enough. This time I hurt her mouth. "Is that all you can do?" she asked, pushing me away.

"I can drive a car and play the gramophone. My education has been intensive."

"You mean extensive don't you?"

"What the hell does it matter? Who was the dark girl you were talking to?"

"Eve Marlow? Oh, she's a tart."

"So what? ... so are you."

She giggled. "Only to my friends."

"How did you come to know her?"

"How did I come to know who?"

"Eve Marlow."

"How do you know I know her?"

"You just said so."

"Did I?"

"Look, let's not go on like this. Let's go somewhere for a drink."

"All right. Where?"

"I've got a car. Let's get off this lousy boat."

"I'm not free."

"But you said your gentleman friend had left you."

She giggled. "I mean you'd have to pay me."

I grinned at her. "Course I'll pay you." I pulled out my roll of money and counted it. I had fifteen hundred dollars. Well, I had won five hundred dollars so it wasn't so bad. I gave her two twenties.

"Oh, I want more than that."

"You shut up. That's just a retainer. I'll pay you more later on."

She put her arms around me, but I shoved her off.

"Come on," I said impatiently. "Let's go."

When we got back to the pier, we walked to the parking lot.

"Some car," she said with open admiration when she saw the Chrysler.

I slid under the steering wheel and let her find her own way in. We sat side by side and looked at the moon. It was a nice moon and I was drunk, so right at that moment I felt pretty good.

"Is your wife having you watched?" the redhead asked suddenly.

I turned my head to stare at her. "What the hell are you talking about? Who said I had a wife anyway?"

She giggled. "A dick's been tailing you all evening," she said. "Haven't you spotted him? I thought maybe your wife was wanting a divorce."

"What guy?" I asked sharply.

"He's over there waiting for us to go."

"How do you know he's been watching me?"

"He's never let you out of his sight since you were on the boat and now he's waiting for you to go so he can follow you in that heap," she said. "I can smell a dick a mile off."

I remembered what Gold had said at our last meeting. "I shall certainly think of you both. In fact, I'm not going to forget either of you. If Carol is unhappy because of you, you will be sorry. I promise you that, Mr. Thurston." So the heel was having me tailed.

"I'll fix him," I said, cold with fury. "Just you stick around and watch me."

"Atta boy!" the redhead said, clapping her hands. "Give the little louse a sock from me."

I crossed the parking lot and went over to him. As soon as he saw me, he straightened and took his hands out of his pockets. I stood before him and peered down at him. It was dark, but not all that dark. He was a fat faced mild little man with rimless spectacles on his small fat nose.

"Good evening," I said.

"Good evening, sir," he returned, edging away.

"Has Mr. Gold hired you to watch me?"

He started to bluster, but I cut him short.

"Save it," I said. "Mr. Gold told me about you."

He looked sulky. "Well, if Mr. Gold told you, why ask me?"

I smiled at him. "I don't like being watched," I said. "You better take your glasses off."

He began to get alarmed and looked wildly round the parking lot. But it was still early and there was no one but ourselves in sight. I reached forward and flicked off his spectacles, then I trod on them. They crunched on the concrete.

"I can't see without my glasses," he almost wailed.

"That's too bad," I said, taking him by his collar. I slammed my fist in his face. I was getting good at hitting people in the mouth. Like Imgram, this little stool pigeon had trouble with his bridgework. It got caught up in the roof of his mouth and he tried to hook out the broken pieces of bridgework, but I would not let him. I took his small hands in one of mine and I rammed him against the wall. His hat fell off and I shifted my hands to his ears and banged his head hard against the wall, using his ears as handles.

His knees sagged, but I held him up.

"Maybe you won't be so anxious next time to watch me," I said, shaking him. "If I see you again, I'll smear you on a wall."

I gave him a quick shove and he lost his balance and sprawled on the oily concrete. He picked himself up and began to run blindly down the street.

I lurched back for the Chrysler.

The redhead was hanging out of the window.

"That was terrific," she said, as I slid under the steering wheel. "You're a great, big, beautiful savage."

"You talk too much," I returned and drove out of the parking lot and headed towards Hollywood.

Although I was pretty high, I wasn't reckless enough to take any chance of being seen with this tramp. You didn't have to look at her twice to know what she was, but she knew Eve and I was hoping she would tell me what I had always been wanting to know about her.

We stopped at several bars on our way to Hollywood and I tried to get her to talk, but she hedged. I was careful not to press her because I didn't want her to know how anxious I was to talk about Eve. The redhead preferred to talk about herself and that was a subject in which I had not the slightest interest. I let her chatter away, scarcely listening to what she had to say, but I kept buying her drinks hoping that if she drank enough liquor she might be persuaded to talk about Eve.

Every bar we went into was crowded and I kept losing her and then finding her and that did not help in getting her to tell me what I wanted to know.

"I'm sick of this," I said, leaning against the bar and holding her arm just above her elbow. "We've got to go some place quiet. All this noise and talking confuses me."

"Well, if we go some place quiet it's going to cost you money," she returned, resting her small turned-up nose on the rim of her glass. "It's going to cost you a stack of dough."

"Don't let's keep talking about money," I said. "To hear you talk you'd think that's all there is in the world to talk about."

She leaned heavily against me. "S'matter of fact," she said, "that's all I am interested in, only I wouldn't let everyone know. It's not ladylike, is it?"

I regarded her. She was getting tight all right. If she had a few more drinks she wouldn't know what she was talking about. I bought two more double whiskies and while we were drinking them I had a bright idea. I'd take her out to Three Point. It was a bright idea because it killed two birds with one stone. I would get her to talk about Eve and she would keep me company. I was not going to stay at Three Point all night by myself. Why should I? Why should Carol and Russell suddenly leave me flat without caring whether I'd be lonely or not? I decided it was the brightest idea I had thought up for a long time and I got quite excited about it. I would take this big, soft-bodied redhead on the terrace and we'd watch the moon lighting the hills and Bear Lake and we'd talk all night about Eve. That seemed to me to be a pretty good way of passing the time until Carol returned.

I explained my idea to the redhead.

She leaned more heavily against me. "Suits me," she said, "but it'll cost you a stack of dough and I'd like some of it now."

I gave her two twenty dollar bills to keep her quiet and steered her through the crowd into the moonlit street.

"You'll have to do better than this," she said as she almost fell into the Chrysler. "You can't make a girl tight and drag her off some place to look at the moon without it costing you a stack of dough."

I told her not to worry and she said that she never worried, but it would be a good idea if I began to worry because although she was alone in the world and tried to act like a lady she had a lot of expenses and she just had to have a lot of money. After she had said all that she went to sleep and she did not wake up until I stopped the Chrysler on the sloping ramp of the garage at Three Point.

She yawned and followed me along the short path that led to the cabin.

She clung on to my arm and stumbled as she walked but after a moment or so, the mountain air steadied her up and she began to look around.

"Gee" she exclaimed. "Isn't this elegant."

"Well, here we are," I said. "Come out on the terrace and look at the moon."

But she was wandering around the lounge staring at everything, a little incredulous and a little bewildered.

"This must have cost a stack of dough," she muttered to herself. "I've never seen anything to beat this. It's terrific."

She was overwhelmed and so envious that I decided to give her a little time to get used to the room before we settled down to talk. So I let her wander around while I fixed drinks in a large cocktail shaker.

Even after I had fixed the drinks, she was still pawing my books, my pictures, my furniture and my ornaments.

"What are you staring at?" she demanded, turning suddenly.

"You," I said.

She came over and flopped down on the settee by my side. She put her soft arms round my neck and tried to bite my ear. I pushed her off.

She blinked at me. "What's the matter?"

"Come out on the terrace," I said, suddenly disgusted with her. I wanted her to tell me about Eve and then to go.

"I'm all right here," she said, laying back, her red hair making a startling splash of color against the white suede cushion.

"Have a drink." I gave her half the contents of the cocktail shaker in a tumbler.

She spilt some of it on the carpet before she gulped it down. Then she hit herself on her chest with her clenched fist and let out a long gasping breath. "Whew!" she exclaimed, "that went right down to my feet."

"That's where it was meant to go," I said and got up to refill the shaker.

"You know you're the first guy who's ever taken me to his home," she said, stretching out full length on the settee. "I can't understand it."

"Don't try to," I said, "There are some things that pass all understanding."

She giggled, "I bet your wife would be wild."

"Shut up, you little slut," I said.

"If I were your wife and I found out you brought women back to my room I'd be wild," she said. "I think it's a filthy trick to pull on a girl."

"All right," I said, coming back to her and shoving her legs away so I could sit down, "it's a filthy trick, but I'm lonely. My wife left me alone. That's a filthy trick too, isn't it?"

She brooded for a moment. "You're right. A wife should never leave her man alone. I'd never leave my man alone if I kept one long enough to call him my man," and she giggled.

"I bet Eve Marlow never leaves her husband alone," I said casually,

The redhead giggled. "She gave him the bird years ago."

"Oh no, she didn't. She was with him tonight."

"Who? Don't talk wet. That's not her husband."

"Oh yes he is."

"That's all you know about it."

"Now don't let's argue, I know Eve better than you do. I tell you that was her husband."

"That shows you don't know her better than I do," the redhead said. "I've known her for years. Her husband's Charlie Gibbs. She left him flat seven years ago. The poor little bastard. The only thing he ever did wrong was never to have any money. She still sees him from time to time when she wants to practise cursing. Can't she curse, too." The redhead threw back her head and laughed until she had to mop her eyes which she did on her sleeve. "I've heard her curse poor little Charlie. It's made my ears burn. Instead of smacking her one on her kisser, he just cringes."

Now I was getting somewhere. "Tell me about her."

"There's nothing to tell. She's a tart. You wouldn't want to know about a tart, would you?"

"Yes I would. I want to know all about her."

"Well, I'm not going to tell you."

"Oh yes you are, because I will give you a hundred dollars if you do and you'd like that, wouldn't you?"

Her face lit up. "It'll cost you more than that," she said without much conviction.

"No, it won't." I took a hundred dollar bill from my pocket and flicked her nose with it. "Tell me."

She grabbed at the note, but I was too quick for her.

"When you've told me and not before. I'll keep it so you can see it and I promise you you'll have it."

She lay back and looked at the bill with such intensive greed that she sickened me.

"What do you want to know?"

"Everything."

She told me and all the time she was speaking her eyes never left the hundred dollar bill I was holding.

CHAPTER NINETEEN

There is no point in telling you Eve's story as I learned it from the red-headed girl as she lay on the settee, maudlin with drink and anxious to earn the money I dangled before her. At first, in order to please, she mixed fact with fiction and I had to ask her many questions and go over the same ground many times before I finally learned enough of the details which, added to what I knew already, enabled me to form what I believe to be an accurate account of Eve's life.

It was only after the redhead had fallen asleep—the hundred dollar bill tucked safely in the top of her stocking—and I had gone onto the terrace and had turned over in my mind what she had told me that the story finally took shape. It was like solving a difficult jigsaw puzzle and some of the pieces only appeared after I had thought back and remembered certain things that Eve had said, certain things she had hinted at and certain things that she had denied.

I had known, of course, that the key to Eve's extraordinary behaviour to me was her strong inferiority complex. I had guessed all along that this was the psychological pivot upon which her behaviour turned, but up to now, I did not realize why she should suffer from such a strong inferiority complex. When I learned that she had been illegitimate and, as a child, had had that fact continually brought home to her, I began to understand things that had previously puzzled me.

The stigma of illegitimacy can be most harmful to a child's psychological make-up if the parents show in any way that the child is unwanted. No more crushing blow can be given to a child's sensibilities if it is allowed to think that its birth is different from that of other children. Its companions—little savages that children are—are quick to seize upon any hint of illegitimacy and the child can suffer much misery by their brutal persecution.

Her parents—she was her father's daughter by another woman—had no patience with her. Her foster mother hated her since she was a living sign of her father's infidelity, and when she was young, she whipped her, and locked her in her room in the dark for long hours when she became too big to flog.

When Eve was twelve years of age, she was sent to a convent school where the Mother Superior believed that the rod exorcized evil spirits and Eve was mercilessly thrashed practically every day in the endeavour to break her rebellious spirit. But the Mother Superior was not only a sadist, she was also a bad psychologist. This treatment only brutalized Eve's mentality where a kind word might easily have saved her.

When she was sixteen, she ran away from the convent and obtained employment as a waitress in an eating house in one of the Eastside streets in New York.

There is a blank in her story for the next four years but we pick up the threads again in a shady hotel in Brooklyn where she now worked as a receptionist. The past four years had been hard on Eve. She was utterly sick of being a drudge and when Charlie Gibbs came along, she married him.

Charlie Gibbs, an inoffensive, unambitious truck driver, had no idea what he was marrying. Eve's temper and hard little soul crushed him as effectively as if he had been fed through a wringer. She soon tired of keeping house for him and after a series of nightmare scenes which haunted Charlie for years after, she packed her bag and returned to the Brooklyn hotel.

It was not long before she became the mistress of a well-to-do business man who gave her a small apartment and visited her whenever he happened to be in the locality. He soon began to regret his choice. Eve was too much of a rebel to be at the beck and call of an elderly man who believed, quite wrongly, that he was still physically attractive. Her temper became ungovernable and the least little thing he did that annoyed her caused her to smash everything within reach. Finally the business man grew tired of her unreliable moods and giving her a generous sum of money, he got rid of her.

Having no background, no anchor, no idea of ethics, she naturally drifted to the bad. Prostitution was an antidote for her inferiority complex. So long as men came to her, she must have felt that she could not be as dull and stupid as she imagined she was. She still made a pretence to find work, but as time went on, she became more and more dependent on men for a living, until, finally, she took the little house in Laurel Canyon Drive and set up in business as a full time professional.

So much for the history of Eve which has no special point of interest with the exception of her inferiority complex. It is a story that any woman of the streets might tell you, only Eve makes it interesting because of her psychological reaction to life.

It is obvious that, in spite of the brutalizing effects of the beatings, convent life had instilled in Eve a streak of respectability which had never been entirely eradicated. She lived—and for all I know still lives—in two worlds: the sordid existence of her profession, and the make-believe existence that her secret urge to be respectable makes her wish were true.

Jack Hurst, whom she claimed to be her husband, was not a mining engineer. He was a professional gambler who lived by his wits and his skill at cards. Eve and he had met at a party and had been immediately attracted to each other. This had happened a year or so after she had set up in Laurel Canyon Drive. Hurst was married to a woman who had grown tired of his reckless gambling and his sadistic, domineering ways. She had left him a few months before he met Eve. He was not the type of man to bother with the complicated intricacies of divorce and even if he had taken the trouble to get rid of his wife legally, I do not believe that he would have married Eve. A man has to be very sure of himself to marry a prostitute and although he found her intriguing and associated with her for such a long time, he did not appear anxious to make her his wife.

Even now I do not quite understand why Hurst remained Eve's lover for so long. He was, of course, a sadist. I knew he was that when Eve had told me of his behaviour when she had twisted her ankle. To have left her sitting on the curb and to have driven her from her bed the next morning when she could scarcely walk to get him coffee was obviously an act of a sadist. There were other times, so the redhead told me, when he treated Eve abominably, but the worse he treated her the more she seemed to admire him. There was nothing he could do that would turn her against him. She was his slave. It seems scarcely credible that Eve, in spite of her own ruthlessness and strength of character, should be a masochist beneath her wooden exterior. It is doubtful, however, whether any other man but Hurst could have roused in her this twisted heritage of a brutalized childhood. That he had done so explains why he continued the association.

Apart from Hurst, no other man stood a chance with Eve. She was simply an empty shell, devoid of any feeling, except for those twisted emotions inspired by Hurst. For ten years she had lived on men. She knew all their tricks, all their subterfuges and all their weaknesses. This existence killed her feminine instincts as surely as arsenic will kill weeds. It killed her instinct for love. I do not believe she even loved Hurst. She was drawn to him because he was the only man she had ever met who mastered her and I believe there were times when she actually hated him. The astonishing thing was that she did not show in her face the brutalizing life that she led, but there can be no doubt that it scarred her mind. She had nothing to look forward to, nothing to look back upon. Little wonder then that she tried to build around herself a world of illusion. She liked to believe that she was married to a professional man. She liked to believe that she did not live in two rooms but had a house in Los Angeles. She liked to believe that every Monday she went to the bank and put half her earnings away for the time when Hurst and she would buy their roadhouse. Although these fancies never materialized they made her existence possible and soothed the running sore of her inferiority complex.

I had no way of finding out whether she paraded these fancies before her other clients. No doubt she did. I now realized that the weekend we had spent together had been a weekend of lies. She had lied cleverly and I had not suspected for a moment that she was telling me anything but the truth. Perhaps the most artistic of her lies had been when she listed the number of luxury restaurants which she could not be seen in with me in case her "husband's" friends might tell him that she was going around with strange men.

As I sat on the terrace, a bottle of Scotch at my elbow, and the moon like a dead man's face, shedding its silver light on the hills, I tried to reconstruct Eve's character now that I knew so much more about her.

So well had she created her make-believe background that even now I wondered whether the redheaded girl had been telling me the truth. Eve had been so emphatic that Jack Hurst did not know of the existence of the house in Laurel Canyon Drive and that he did not know how she had earned her living. I remembered her saying, "He'd kill me if he knew. But I suppose he will find out one day. I always say my sins will find me out and they will too. Then have to run to you for protection."

Was she lying when she had said that? It would be easy to trap her now. I had only to telephone the house in Laurel Canyon Drive to find out if she were still there.

I poured myself out another whisky, drank it and then looked at my wrist watch. It was twelve fifteen.

I stood up. My legs were a little unsteady, but my brain was clear. I went along the terrace to my study and opening the french windows I entered and turned on the light. I had forgotten the redhead in the sitting room so absorbed had I become in stripping aside the curtain of secrecy that Eve had erected. I sat at the desk and dialled her number, The bell rang for a long time and as I was about to hang up, thinking that after all I had guessed wrong and that the house was empty, there was a sudden click and Eve said, "Hello?"

So it was true. I need not have spoken but I could not resist letting her know that I had found her out.

"Did I wake you?" I asked.

"Oh, Clive, can't you leave me alone for five minutes?" Her voice was thick and blurred.

"You're tight," I said.

She giggled. "Beautifully tight, I've drunk everything in the world tonight."

"I like the look of your husband."

"Everyone likes him. But go away, Clive. I can't talk now."

"Is he with you?"

"Hm-hm ... he's here all right."

"I thought he didn't know you had that place," I said.

There was a pause and I could not help smiling to myself. I would have liked to have seen her face. She must have realized that she had talked too much."

"I was tight ... I brought him here without thinking," she said, at last, almost as if she were trying to convince herself. "He's furious ... I guess it's all over with us now."

I nearly laughed. "You can't mean that, Eve," I said, trying to assume an anxious note in my voice. "Whatever will you do?"

"I don't know." She tried to sound worried, but she did not succeed. "Please hang up, Clive. I've got an awful head and things are all going wrong."

"Is he staying long?"

"No … no … not after this. He'll go tomorrow."

"So he knows everything now?" I asked, determined to give her no respite.

"I can't talk now." Her voice had sharpened and I could imagine those two furrows above her nose knitted in a frown. "I must go … he is calling," and she hung up.

"I've been looking all over for you," the redhead said from the door.

I got to my feet. "I'll drive you back," I said, determined to get rid of her at once. "Come on, let's go."

She stared. "Are you crazy?" she asked. "I'm going to bed. To hell with going all that way back. I'm tired. You told me you wanted me to stay the night and I'm damn well going to stay."

Now that she had told me what I wanted to know about Eve I could not wait to see the last of her. To have brought such a woman into my home had been the craziest thing I had yet done.

"Oh no, you're not," I said sharply. "I shouldn't have brought you here in the first place. I'll get you home in an hour. Let's go."

She sat down heavily in an armchair and kicked off her shoes. "I'm not going," she said obstinately.

I stood over her, cold with anger and alarm. "Don't be a slut," I said, "I shouldn't have brought you here."

She smiled. "You should have thought of that before," she said and yawned. She had a lot of gold work in her mouth. "And don't look like that. I can take care of myself and I'm not scared of you."

I suddenly wanted to get my hands round her soft fat throat, but I turned away.

"What's the matter with you?" she went on, watching me suspiciously. "Don't you want a good time? Why have you got sore all of a sudden?"

I faced her. "I've changed my mind," I said, speaking slowly and deliberately. "I'll give you one more chance. Are you going quietly or do you want me to use force?"

We eyed each other for a long moment and then she shrugged. "All right," she said and called me a bad name. "Give me a drink and I'll go."

I went onto the terrace for a bottle of Scotch.

John Coulson was sitting on the wooden seat at the bottom of the garden. As I watched him, he turned and the moonlight lit his face. He was laughing at me.

I filled a glass with whisky and drank it standing.

"You haven't anything to laugh at," I said. "You may think you have, but you haven't. The laugh's on you, but you're such a poor dumb cluck you don't even know it."

I went back to the study, but the redhead wasn't there.

I stood staring round the empty room for several minutes. Whisky fumes clouded my brain and I began to wonder whether I had imagined that the redhead had been in this room. I began to wonder, after I had taken another drink, whether she had ever been in this cabin and after a few moments I had an obstinate idea at the back of my mind that I had never met her at all.

As I crossed the room to the settee I lurched against a table and sent it over with a crash. A cut glass ash tray and a big vase of carnations smashed on the carpet.

'Where are you?" I shouted. "I know you are hiding somewhere."

I stumbled into the lobby and called again. "Come out, wherever you are. Come-on-out!"

I waited, but the cabin was silent. Then I knew where she was. It was only because I was drunk that I hadn't thought of it before. She was in Carol's and my bedroom. I felt a great surge of hot blood rise to my head and I walked down the passage to my bedroom and turned the door knob. The door was locked.

"Come out," I shouted, hammering on the panels. "Do you hear? Come out!"

"Go away," she called. "I want to go to sleep."

"I'll kill you if you don't come out," I said, a vicious, desperate note in my voice.

"I'm going to sleep," the redhead shouted back. "I'm not coming out for you or any other tight fisted punk."

I went on hammering on the door for several minutes until my hands throbbed and burned.

Then I had an idea, "I'll give you five hundred dollars if you'll go home," I said, with my head against the panel of the door.

"Honest?" I heard her scramble out of bed.

"Honest."

"Push it under the door and I'll believe you."

"Here you are," I said and I began to force the notes under the narrow space between the carpet and the door.

She could not wait to get it that way and she jerked open the door.

I stepped back, staring at her in horror. She had wedged her big soft body into a pair of Carol's pyjamas and over her heavy shoulders was Carol's short ermine coat.

I let the rest of the money slip out of my fingers and I stood there unable to move or unable to say anything. She bent down and began to gather up the money. As she did so her knees burst through the thin silk of the pyjamas.

She giggled, "Your wife must be a skinny bitch," she said, not pausing as she grabbed at the money.

Then something made me look round.

Carol was standing in the lobby, watching us. Her eyes looked like two big holes cut in a sheet. She drew in a sharp, shuddering breath and the redhead looked up. She stared at Carol and then at me.

"What the hell do you want?" she snapped, standing up and trying to cover her heavy breasts with the ermine coat. "Me and my boyfriend are engaged."

I shall never forget the look on Carol's face. I took a step towards her, but turning swiftly, she ran down the short passage and the front door slammed.

I went after her.

As I jerked open the door, I heard her car start up and I was in time to see the red tail light flashing down the long winding drive.

I blundered out into the moonlight and began running after the car.

"Come back, Carol," I shouted after her. "Come back ... don't leave me, Carol," I shouted after her "... come back!"

The red tail light disappeared round the corner where the drive entered the road.

I raced on to the gate and stood panting in the middle of the road that led to San Bernardino. The road ran straight for a mile and then turned sharply with the curve of the mountain.

I could see the red tail light moving like a ruby fired from a gun. Carol was driving very fast ... too fast. I knew the road better than she did and I suddenly began to run again, shouting after her.

"You're going too fast," I yelled. "Look out, Carol, my darling. You're going too fast. You won't make the turn... slow down! Carol! You won't make the—"

Even from that distance I heard the tires squeal on the road as the mountain curve suddenly sprang at her from out of the darkness. I saw her headlights swing out to the left and I could hear stones rattling inside the mudguards as the tires skidded.

I stopped running and fell on my knees. The noise of the tires rose to a high pitched scream and then the car suddenly leaped off the road and went straight through the white palings. I heard a crunching, ripping noise and I watched the car hang for a second in mid-air, then it went down through the darkness into the valley.

CHAPTER TWENTY

It was Eve. From the very beginning it had been Eve. If it had not been for her none of this would ever have happened.

I walked down Laurel Canyon Drive and passed her house. There were no lights showing. I paused, then retraced my steps. A distant clock struck midnight. Perhaps she was asleep; perhaps she was still out; perhaps she was at the back of the house. I would have to find out.

I looked up and down the street, but there was no one in sight except John Coulson. He stood in the shadows across the road, his hands in his pockets and his head a little on one side, watching me.

I stood outside Eve's house and again looked up and down the street. It was quiet, even the distant traffic sounded muffled. I pushed open the gate and groped my way down the path. I fumbled my way around to the back of the house and kicked against a number of bottles that were stacked against the wall. One of them rolled and smashed against something in the dark. I stood still and listened. The back of the house was in darkness. No one called out so I edged forward cautiously until I reached a window. It was half open. I pushed it right up and listened. No sound came from inside the house.

I leaned inside the window and struck a match. I was looking in at the small kitchen and it was as well that I had a light because the sink, full of dirty crockery, was immediately under the window.

I threw the match away and stepped onto the window sill. Then I struck another match, I climbed over the sink and lowered myself to the floor.

There was a faint smell of stale cooking and a fainter smell of Eve's perfume in the room. The smell of that perfume gave me a cold feeling of hate deep in my guts. I went to the door, opened it and stood in the passage. I listened, but I could hear nothing.

I was sure now that the house was empty, but I was still cautious. I edged my way to her bedroom. The door was open and I stood outside, holding my breath and listening. I stood like that for a long time until I was sure there was no one in the room. Then I went in and turned on the light.

By her bed was a large photograph. It was turned face down on the little table. I picked it up. Jack Hurst looked at me. It was a good portrait and I studied it for some minutes, then in a sudden spasm of rage, I nearly smashed it against the wall. I stopped myself in time. That would be the first thing she would miss when she entered the room. I put the photograph back as I had found it and as I did so I wondered whether Hurst would care when he heard that Eve was dead. I wondered too with a sense of malice whether the police would suspect that it might have been Hurst who had killed her.

The clock on the mantelpiece ticked softly. It was twenty minutes past twelve. Any moment now, I could expect her to return. In this quiet little room, I had no feeling of time and I sat down on the bed and picked up her dressing gown. I buried my face in it, smelling her scent and the faint odour of her body.

I remembered the first time I had seen her in it. She had been squatting before the fire at Three Point. That picture conjured up a flood of bitter memories. So much had happened since then.

It did not seem that five nights ago I had watched Carol die. It had taken me more than two hours to scramble down the mountainside to reach her. I knew when I looked at the smashed car that she would not be alive. It had been very quick; her lovely little body had been jammed between a great boulder and the side of the car. I could not move her and I sat by her side with her head in my arms, feeling her grow cold until they came and took me away.

Nothing seemed to matter after that. Even Gold did not matter. He took his revenge, but I was past caring. It did not matter that he stripped me of everything. He knew, as I suspected, that *Rain Check* wasn't my play. Somehow he found out about Coulson and reported what I had done to the Writers' Guild. They sent a stiff necked little man to see me. He said they would not prosecute if I repaid all my royalties. I scarcely listened to him and when he gave me a paper authorizing my bank to pay 75,000 dollars to Coulson's agent to dispose of as he thought fit, I signed it.

I had not the money of course, so they took everything I had. My Chrysler, books, furniture, clothes—everything I had, and even then they wanted more, but there was nothing more to give them.

I did not even care when they took Carol's clothes. I did not need to have anything of hers to remember her by. She was in my mind as I had last seen her, jammed between the boulder and the car with a scarlet thread of blood from her lips to her chin. That memory of her will always be with me.

I think I could have borne her loss if I had been able to tell her before she died that the redhead had meant nothing to me. But I reached her too late and she died thinking that big soft bodied slut of a woman had taken her place while she was away. That knowledge unhinged my mind. If I could have told her that she was the only person who had ever given me any real happiness and if she had believed me, I might not now be in this sordid little house waiting to commit murder.

Everything had happened because of Eve. I had nothing to live for, why then should she? During the past five days I had thought a great deal about her and I had decided that it would be very satisfying and final to kill her.

I went to the door, turned off the light and fumbled my way upstairs. As I reached the head of the stairs, the telephone began to ring.

I was a little unnerved now and I walked unsteadily across the landing. I went into the front room, next to the bathroom. My feet scraped on the bare boards and the moon breaking through the clouds suddenly sent a shaft of light through the uncurtained window. The room was unfurnished. From the window I could see the street, the garden and the little path that led to the house.

I leaned against the window and stared down into the street. John Coulson was still there. He had moved closer to the house and was looking up at me.

I watched him for a few minutes, then I turned away from the window. I wanted a drink. I wanted to smoke too, but I was afraid Eve would smell the burning tobacco as she came in. She must have no warning that I was in the house, waiting to kill her.

The minutes dragged slowly by and I grew impatient. I wondered where she was. Would she bring a man back with her? I had not thought of that. It was more than likely that she would do so and it would, of course, ruin all my plans.

Suddenly, without warning, something soft and yielding moved against my leg. My nerves bunched together like a coiled spring and my mouth went dry. I blundered away from the window with a faint cry.

Beside me was a large black and white cat. It looked up at me and its eyes sparkled in the moonlight.

The shock had driven the blood from my face and my heart thumped against my ribs. When, at last, I had controlled my fluttering nerves, I bent down to touch the cat, but it slid away from me and disappeared through the half open door.

Still quivering from the shock, I closed the door and as I came back to the window I heard a car coming down the road. I flattened myself against the wall and peered through the window. John Coulson had gone and the road seemed desolate without him.

A taxicab pulled up and the driver leaned out and opened the door. The moonlight lit the darkness inside the cab and I caught a glimpse of Eve's immaculate legs. There was a long pause before she got out. She was alone and she stood for several seconds searching in her bag before she paid the driver. He did not touch his cap, but slammed the door and then drove off without looking at her.

I watched her as she moved down the path. She walked wearily, her shoulders sagging and her bag clutched firmly under her arm.

In a few seconds, she and I would be alone together.

I was no longer afraid and my hands were dry and steady. I crept across the room and opened the door. I heard her snap back the lock and enter the lobby.

I crossed the landing and looked cautiously over the banisters and caught a glimpse of her as she disappeared into her bedroom. A light sprang up and flooded the lobby.

I heard her strike a match and I guessed she was lighting a cigarette. Then I heard her yawn. The sound ended in a groan of exhaustion, but I had no pity for her, only a cold, sullen anger and that overpowering desire to get my hands around her throat.

She moved about the room while she undressed. The house was so silent that I could hear her take off her coat, skirt and blouse. She unlocked her cupboard and I guessed she was putting her clothes away. Then she came out of the bedroom and walked into the kitchen. I saw her distinctly as she passed from room to room. She looked very slight and forlorn down there by herself. Her hair looked neat and her blue dressing gown was wrapped tightly around her.

I heard a rattle of crockery from the kitchen and, later, she returned carrying a tray for her morning coffee. She took it into her bedroom and I guessed that before long she would be coming upstairs. I stepped into the front room and closed the door.

I had not been in the room more than a few seconds before I heard her come up the stairs. She moved slowly and at the head of the stairs, she stumbled. She said "Oh, hell!" loudly and I knew then that she was drunk.

I heard her stumbling around in the bathroom and then I heard water running. She was in there for some time, but eventually I heard her come out and go downstairs.

I edged once more onto the landing. Below me, she was bending over the cat. As I watched her, she sat on her heels and stroked the cat with quick, light movements. "Poor old Sammy," she said softly. "Did I leave you all alone?"

The cat twined itself around her and I could hear its deep throated purr. I watched Eve's slim hands as she fondled the animal and I listened as she talked to it. She talked as only a lonely woman will talk to an animal, speaking to it as if it were a child.

The cat suddenly stopped purring and looked up at me. Its tail became bushy and it spat. For a moment I stared down into its yellow eyes, then I drew back out of sight.

"What's the matter, you silly old thing?" Eve asked. "Are there mice up there?"

My hands became clammy.

"Come on, my beauty, I'm not going to play any more with you. No, you're not going up there. I'm tired, Sammy, oh I'm so very, very tired."

I glanced over the banisters again. Eve had picked up the cat and was disappearing into the bedroom.

I took out my handkerchief and wiped my face and hands, then went to the head of the stairs and listened.

Eve was talking to the cat. I could not hear what she said. It seemed strange to hear her voice in the silent house and not to hear anyone answer her. Then the bed creaked and I knew that she was settling down for the night.

I sat on the top stair and lit a cigarette.

As I sat there, I remembered our first weekend together. It had been exciting and intriguing because I did not then know how false and what a liar she was. I had thought that I had won her confidence and I had enjoyed her company. It was a memory that would remain with me for a long time.

I clenched my fists. If she had given just a little instead of taking all the time, this would never have happened. I wanted to be her friend but she had frustrated me at every point.

Then the light snapped off and I started to my feet; but I controlled my eagerness with an effort and sat down again. I would have to wait just a little longer. One false move now, after waiting so long, would spoil everything.

I sat there and waited for her to fall asleep.

Then out of the darkness came a new sound. Eve was crying. It was not a pleasant sound. It was so unexpected that it set my teeth on edge and gave me a cold feeling under my heart. It was the sound a woman makes who has lost everything and who is desperately lonely and miserable. Eve lay in the darkness and sobbed without any effort to control herself. She sounded tragically unhappy. At last I was face to face with the real Eve without the make-believe, without the wooden expression or the professional mannerisms. This was the Eve I had wanted to know, the real Eve who lurked behind the stone fortress, its door now open for me to see inside. This was a prostitute taking a vacation.

I sat for a long time in the darkness and listened to her. I heard her toss about in the bed and once she said, "Oh damn and damn and damn!" and I heard her beat her fists together as her unhappiness tormented her.

At last she quieted down and there was silence. Very faintly, she began to snore. It was a strangled, gasping sound that was almost as bad as her sobbing.

My cold, vicious calm returned. I stood up and flexed my fingers. Now, I thought, I will put you out of your misery. This is the moment for which I have been waiting.

I paused outside the bedroom. I could hear Eve jerking about in bed, moaning and muttering to herself. I edged into the room and moved quietly around the bed until I was sure I was near her. I put my hand out cautiously and felt the top of the quilt and then, very slowly, I sat down on the bed. It creaked under my weight, but the movement did not wake her.

I felt her body twitch and jerk under the bedclothes. I could smell the whisky on her breath. My heart began to pound, I reached out and found the lamp switch. Holding it in my shaking fingers, I groped for her throat.

My hand hovered in the dark, then I touched her hair. She was under my hand. I drew a deep breath, clenched my teeth and snapped on the light.

She was there, close to me, my hand a few inches from her throat, but I could only sit and stare at her. I could not move. She looked so utterly helpless. She lay on her back, her lips parted and her face twitching as she slept. She looked very young and unhappy and there were dark shadows under her eyes. My hand dropped limply and I felt all the viciousness drain out of me. I knew then, as I looked down at her, that I had been out of my mind and at the sight of her I was suddenly sane again.

I could not kill her. My mouth went dry when I realized how close I had come to doing so. I wanted to take her in my arms and feel her respond to me. I wanted to tell her that I would look after her and she need never be unhappy again.

I looked down at her, seeing her elfish, heart-shaped face with its determined chin and the two deep furrows above her nose. I thought if only she always looked like this—helpless and needing protection, the hard lines smoothed from her face and her eyelids hiding the windows of her dreadful, callous, selfish little soul. If I could only trust her not to lie or cheat or drink or to be cruel to me. But I knew that was impossible. She would never change.

The cat came and rubbed itself against my arm. I stroked it and for the first time since Carol had died, I felt relaxed and content. As I sat close to Eve, with the cat pushing its head into my hand, I realized a fulfillment of a desire that I wanted to go on and on.

Then suddenly Eve opened her eyes. She stared at me with bewildered, terrified hatred. She did not move and she seemed to have stopped breathing. We looked at each other for a full minute.

"It's all right, Eve …" I began, reaching for her hand.

I did not think it was possible for anyone to move so quickly. She whipped out of bed, snatched up her dressing gown and was by the door before I could touch her. There was a scraped, bony look on her face and her eyes glinted strangely in the shaded light of the lamp.

"I didn't mean to frighten you," I said, cold with panic. "Eve, I'm sorry I did this …"

She mouthed at me, but no sound came. I could see she was heavy with sleep and the whisky was still stupefying her. It was only an instinct for self-preservation that had made her leave the bed so quickly. And yet, as I watched her, she frightened me more than I was frightening her.

"It's all right, Eve," I went on, soothingly. "It's Clive. I'm not going to hurt you."

She said in a croaking whisper, "What do you want?"

"I was passing and I had to see you," I said. "Come and sit down. It's all right, there's nothing to be afraid of."

Her eyes were becoming alive. She licked her dry lips and when she spoke again, her voice was clearer. "How did you get in?"

"You left a window open," I said, trying to make a joke of it. "I couldn't resist surprising you, but I didn't mean to frighten you."

She still stood by the door. Her eyes began to glitter and her nostrils became pinched and white. "You mean you broke in here?"

"I know I shouldn't have done it, but … well, I did want to see you."

She drew in a deep breath and her face went livid. "Get out!" she screamed, throwing open the door. "Get out, you snivelling cur!"

I flinched away from her. "Please, Eve," I implored. "Don't be angry with me. I can't go on like this any more. I want you to come away with me. I'll do anything for you. Only don't be angry."

She took a step forward, her face twisted with insane rage. "You crazy, sloppy fool," she said in a low, vicious voice and then filth spewed out of her mouth.

I put my hands over my ears sickened and terrified by her obscenities.

She crouched before me, her eyes blazing in a chalk white face. She looked hideous in her crazed fury. Her tongue lashed, soiled and burned me. "Do you think I'd waste my time with a little, two-bit jerk like you?" she finally screamed at me. "Get out! You're never to come here again. Get out! You've hung around me until I'm sick of the sight of you. You're so thick-skinned you don't know when you're not wanted. Do you think I want your lousy twenty dollar presents? Get out and stay out and never show your ugly face here again!"

My fear of her suddenly left me. Suffocating rage and a vicious desire to hit back brought me to my feet. "You slut! I'll teach you to talk to me like that," I shouted at her.

She screamed me down. "I know what your game is. You're worse than any of them. You're trying to get me for nothing. So you want me to go away with you? Why, you cheap heel, I've men with more dollars than you've got nickels who want to marry me. But I don't want them and I don't want you! I'm sick of men! I know all their filthy little tricks and their rotten little minds. I wouldn't be found dead in a ditch with a man. I know what you want, but you're not going to get it from me!"

We stood and glared at each other. The only sound in the room was the cat's deep-throated purr. I wanted to smash her now. A cold, murderous rage seized me and I wanted to hit, rend and mangle her with my hands.

"I'm going to kill you," I said softly. "I'm going to hammer your rotten little head against the wall until your skull cracks. You'll never torment any more men after I've finished with you."

She drew her white lips off her teeth and spat at me.

I came slowly round the bed and moved towards her. She stood her ground, her eyes blazing and her small hands like fleshless claws. Then as I reached for her, her hooked fingers slashed at my face, like a cat striking.

Her nails missed my eyes only because I jerked my head back in time, but they clawed down my nose and cheek. I was blinded with pain and fury. I struck at her, but she was too quick for me. My fist missed her head and slammed against the wall. I reeled back, crying out with pain.

She slipped out of the room and ran into the kitchen. The telephone was in there, but I gave her no time to call for help. There was no exit in that little room except through the door by which she had entered and already I was standing in the doorway.

I looked at her, feeling warm blood running from the furrows she had clawed in my face. She had pressed herself against the far wall, her hands behind her and her eyes glittering. She showed no sign of fear as I rushed at her.

As I crossed the room, she raised her arm. In her hand was a knotted dog whip. She lashed me across the face. The suddenness of the attack and the blinding pain sent me staggering back. I threw up my arms as she slashed at me again. The whip came down across my shoulders like the touch of a red-hot iron. I cried out and swearing at her, I tried to seize the thong as it whistled once more down on my head. But she moved like a lizard and she had crossed the room, turned and cut at me again as I was trying to recover my balance.

She drove me before her, her lips drawn back and her eyes like glowing embers, systematically slashing at me, hitting me round the head, back and neck.

I was stunned by the pain and I tried to get out of the room into the passage, but she headed me off.

There was no escape from that whistling thong that cut at me with white-hot streaks of pain. I stumbled over a chair as the whip curled across my eyes. The pain was excruciating and I screamed out and fell on my knees.

As she continued to slash at my unprotected head, I dimly heard someone pound on the front door. Then she stopped her insane, vicious attack and I lay on the floor, blood pounding in my ears and my body hot and in agony. Way back in my head somewhere, way back in the dark, I heard voices and I felt a hand seize my arm. I was dragged to my feet.

I lurched forward, half crying with pain. Harvey Barrow stood before me. His whisky-laden breath fanned my face.

"Suffering snakes!" he exclaimed. "You've half killed him," and he burst out laughing.

"Throw him out," Eve said viciously.

"I'll throw him out," Barrow grinned, folding his fist in my shirt front. He jerked me towards him. "Remember me?" he demanded, his coarse face close to mine. "I haven't forgotten you. Come on, you're going for a little walk."

He shoved me into the passage. At the front door, I tried to break away, but he was too strong. We struggled for a moment, then as he forced me out of the house, I glanced back at Eve. She stood in the lighted doorway and stared fixedly at me. I can see her now. She had pulled her blue dressing gown tightly round her and her arms were folded across her flat breasts. Her face was wooden. Her eyes were wide and glittering and her mouth was set in a hard thin line. As our eyes met she tossed up her head in an arrogant gesture of triumph. Then Barrow shoved me into the street and that was the last I ever saw of her.

"Now, you masher," Barrow said, showing his short yellow teeth. "Maybe you'll leave her alone." He drew back his fist and hit me in the face.

I sprawled in the gutter and lay there.

He bent over me. "I owe you that," he said, "and I owe you something else." He dropped a hundred dollar bill and a ten dollar bill in the gutter beside me.

I watched him walk down the path and into the house. Then the front door slammed behind him.

As I reached for the notes, John Coulson burst out laughing.

CHAPTER TWENTY-ONE

A story never ends.

You throw a stone into a pond and in a few seconds it has disappeared. But that is not the end of it. Your action affects the surface of the pond and circular ripples begin to form at the point where the stone has hit the water. These ripples gradually widen until the whole surface of the pond is in gentle motion. It takes a long time for the pond to become still again.

I sit at my typewriter in my shabby room and look out of my window at the waterfront of this small Pacific coast town. Russell is waiting patiently for me to begin the day's work, but, today, I am in no hurry to join him.

We have a boat and for the past year we have taken hundreds of tourists to the chain of small islands that skirt this Pacific coastline. I run the boat and Russell sits in the bow and tells the tourists stories of gun runners and Chink smugglers who used these islands many years ago. The tourists seem to like Russell and he, in his turn, seems to like them. Personally I hate their stupid sheep-like faces and the sound of their strident voices, but as I remain on the bridge during the trips I do not have any contact with them.

We do not make a great deal of money, but we get along all right. Russell is very thrifty and has already put enough by to see us through the slack season.

No one has ever heard of me in this town. My name means nothing to the tourists, but perhaps if this book is ever published, I will see my name in print again. Oddly enough I do not mind being a nobody. I did at first, but as time passed I realized that I would not have to worry about writing a new novel or a play. I would have no bills to pay and I would not have to entertain and do the hundred and one things that a celebrity has to do. I was now free of all that and, although I missed some of the trappings of fame, I decided that I was happier as a nobody.

I don't know what I should have done without Russell. I owe everything to him. It was he who found me, half-crazed, lying in the gutter outside Eve's house. I was lost and if he had not come along at that crucial moment I believe that I would have taken my life.

It was Russell who had bought the boat. It was a fine thirty-foot job fitted with a hundred horse Kermath. He bought it with his savings. I did not like his buying it, but it either meant that or starving. So I let him buy it.

At first, I thought it was a crazy idea, but Russell had it all worked out. He said that an outdoor life would put me on my feet again, and besides, he liked an outdoor life himself.

At that time I did not care what happened to me, but I felt I had to point out that he was sinking his money in a forlorn hope, but he just let his eyebrows crawl up his forehead which was as good as saying, "Wait and see."

I was much more enthusiastic, however, when we went down to the harbour and inspected the boat. Although Russell had paid for it out of his own pocket, he managed to make me feel that I had as big a share in it as he had. Although we were now no longer master and servant, it seemed only right that I should be the captain and he should be the mate.

We had only one awkward moment before we settled down to our new roles. It happened when we decided to rename the boat. I said right away that we should call it "Eve." I pointed out that the tourists would remember a name like that and since it did have rather a wicked flavor they would even gain some harmless amusement from it. Anyway that's how I put it to him.

But Russell would not hear of it. I had never known him to be obstinate before and after trying to persuade him for some time, I finally lost my temper and told him he could call the boat anything he damn well pleased.

When I went down to the harbour the next morning, I found a sign writer had put Carol's name on the stern of the boat in red, two-inch high letters. I stood looking at her name for several seconds and then I went to the end of the deserted jetty and sat with my back to the waterfront and looked out at the Pacific.

It was nearly an hour later when Russell joined me. I told him that he was right about naming the boat after Carol. He didn't say anything, but from that moment we got along fine together.

Well, that's how it is with me. I don't know how long it'll last. I don't know if this book is going to be a success or not. If it is, I might go back to Hollywood. Without Carol I know Hollywood would be an unfriendly place. I don't know whether I could face it again. Carol's death has strangely affected me. It is only now that I realize how much she really meant to me. It is so often the case that the thing you value most in life is not appreciated until you lose it. By losing Carol I found myself and I feel that I can face up to my future with confidence, knowing that Carol's influence will always be with me.

Although it is now two years since I last saw Eve, I still think of her. Not long ago I had a sudden desire to find out what had happened to her. I had no intentions of renewing our acquaintanceship, but I did want to satisfy my curiosity and to discover, if I could, how she had fared during the past two years.

I found the little house on Laurel Canyon Drive empty. The windows were uncurtained and the garden was a wilderness; that furniture that I had come so used to seeing had vanished.

The people next door could not tell me where Eve had gone. The woman who came to the door smiled in a superior, secretive way. "A midnight flit," she explained, "and about time too. No, I don't know where she's gone. I don't care. Good riddance, I say. I shouldn't be surprised if the police weren't looking for her. Anyway she's gone. We don't want her sort in this road, thank you."

I have no means now of finding Eve. It is a pity. I would like to keep in touch with her, without her knowing, of course, since I couldn't imagine what her end will be. Will she give up her profession? Will she go back to Charlie Gibbs? Or will she hang on until she becomes just another worn out, drink sodden hag hopelessly plying for hire on the streets? I don't know.

Perhaps one day we will meet again; although I feel that it is not likely. If she is in trouble with the police she will change her name and vanish from her usual haunts.

It was only recently I picked up a copy of Voltaire's *Candide* and found in it some lines that seemed appropriate not only to Eve's future but to the future of that regiment of women who follow a profession which occupies a definite place in our present society.

I was obliged to continue that abominable trade which you men think so pleasing, but which to us unhappy creatures, is the most dreadful of all sufferings. Ah, sir, did you but know what it is to be obliged to lie with every fellow; with old tradesmen, with counsellors, with monks, watermen, and abbes; to be exposed to all their insolence and abuse; to be robbed by one gallant of what we get from another; to be subject to the extortions of civil magistrates; and to have for ever before one's eyes the prospect of old age, an hospital, or a dunghill, you would conclude that I am one of the most unhappy wretches breathing.

As I say, I don't know. I feel that Eve's destiny is largely in her own hands. She is not a weak woman and I feel hopeful that a time will come when she will face up to her future as I am facing up to mine. I should not like to be far away when that happens.

I have often wondered why I did not succeed in gaining her confidence. I now realize that it was too much to expect that I would ever gain her affection, but I should at least have gained her confidence. I have always believed in the theory that a woman's emotions can hold out only for so long against the impact of a man's mind. But, obviously, Eve was no ordinary woman. Perhaps I had been over anxious. Perhaps I gave up too soon. I don't know. It was a difficult task not only because Eve knew every move in the game, but because the line that divides loathing and loving in a woman's heart is very fine, I may have had too clumsy a touch.

Now that I can look back in our association over a bridge of two years, I can say that although she caused me much pain and bitterness, it was an experience that I would not have missed. Our weekend together was in itself an intense physical impact that few men have experienced. And I do believe that she enjoyed it as much as I did. But I made the mistake of continuing our association when I should have seen her no more after that weekend.

But why go on? I have gained experience from the past and I must prepare for the future. I must stop now. Russell is looking anxiously up at my window. I can see the sun catching the glass of his watch which he holds in his hand. Already *Carol* has her full complement of tourists. They are waiting for me.

THE END

MORE DEADLY THAN THE MALE

. . .

JAMES HADLEY CHASE

For Sylvia

CHAPTER ONE

They were all there—Capone, Dillinger, Nelson, Karpis and Charlie Lucky. The table at which they sat was littered with poker chips, playing cards, whisky bottles and glasses. A green-shaded lamp hung low over the table; its harsh light fell on their faces, while the rest of the room remained dark and shadowy.

Several men, almost invisible in the gloom and haze of tobacco smoke, lounged behind the group at the table. They were small men, with eyes like wet stones, swarthy complexions and granite faces.

The group at the table and the men in the shadows suddenly stiffened when George Fraser walked into the room. He stood a few feet from the table, his hands in his coat pockets, his jaw thrust forward and his eyes threatening and cold.

No one spoke; no one moved.

"If any of you guys wants to start something," George Fraser said, after a long pause, "I'll take care of his widow."

Very slowly, very cautiously, Capone laid his cards down on the table. "Hello, George," he said in a husky whisper.

George Fraser eyed him coldly. There were few men who would have had the nerve to walk alone into that back room and face five of the biggest and most dangerous bosses in the booze racket, but George Fraser was without nerves.

"It's time we had a little talk," he said, biting off each word. "You guys have been running this show too long. You're through—the lot of you. From now on, I'm taking over this territory, and I'm running it my way."

There followed another long pause, then Dillinger, his eyes glowing and his face white with rage, snarled, "Who said?"

George Fraser smiled. "I said," he returned, in his clipped, cold voice.

Dillinger made a growling noise deep in his throat and his hand flashed to his hip pocket.

Capone, sitting next to him, grabbed frantically at his wrist. His fat face was blue-white with fear. "Do you want to commit suicide?" he yelled. "You don't stand a chance with Fraser!"

Dillinger, swearing under his breath, tried to break Capone's grip, and the table rocked as the two men wrestled. A bottle of whisky toppled and smashed to pieces on the floor.

"Let him alone, Al," George Fraser called. "If he wants to play it that way, you'd better give him some air."

Capone shot a terrified look at George Fraser. The pale set face and the eyes that were now like chips of ice completely unnerved him. He nearly fell over himself to get away from Dillinger.

"Look out!" he cried. "He's going to shoot!"

The other three at the table kicked their chairs away and jumped clear, while some of the men who had been standing in the shadows threw themselves on the floor.

Dillinger, alone at the table, sat motionless, glaring at George Fraser.

"Okay, Johnny," George Fraser said mockingly, "go for your gun. What are you waiting for?"

Dillinger rose slowly to his feet. He swept his chair out of the way and crouched.

"Bet you a hundred bucks I can put five slugs in your pumper before your rod shows," George Fraser said, letting his hands hang loosely at his sides.

Dillinger cursed him, and then his arm moved with the speed of a striking snake. A heavy, snub-nosed automatic jumped as if by magic into George Fraser's hand. The room rocked with the sound of gunfire.

Dillinger, his eyes wide and sightless, crashed to the floor and rolled over on his back.

"Take a look at him, Charlie," George Fraser said, his eyes on the group of men huddled against the wall.

Charlie Lucky, after a moment's hesitation, reached forward, pulled Dillinger's coat back and ripped open his shirt.

"Five slugs," he said, his voice cracking; "all in the same spot."

"Good morning, Mr. George," Ella said, putting a cup of watery tea on the bamboo table by the bed. "Did I wake you?"

"Hmm?" George Fraser asked. He looked up with blank astonishment at Ella in her frowsy blue uniform and her ridiculous cap perched on the top of her mouse-coloured hair. "Good Lord! You gave me quite a turn. I didn't hear you come in. I must've been dozing ..."

"It's ever such a lovely morning," Ella went on, crossing the drab little room, and pulling up the blind. "The sun's shining and there ain't a cloud in the sky."

George Fraser closed his eyes against the bright sunlight that streamed through the grimy windowpane. The image he had been creating of himself as "Machine-Gun Fraser," millionaire gangster, still gripped his imagination, and Ella's unexpected intrusion fuddled him.

"Shall I tidy up a bit?" Ella asked, her plain, shiny little face resigned as she surveyed the disordered room. "Coo, Mr. George! Your socks are in the coal scuttle.”

George Fraser sighed. It was no good. He would have to leave the back-room, the smell of cordite, the terrified faces of Capone, Nelson, Karpis and Charlie Lucky until later. He could always pick up his fantasy when Ella had gone.

“Oh, all right,” he said, pushing the blankets from his shoulders and sitting up. “Only don’t make too much noise. I’ve got a bit of a head this morning.”

Ella looked at him hopefully. “Did you have any adventures last night?” she asked as she busied herself about the room.

George resisted the temptation to give her a fictitious account of his evening. He did not feel quite up to it this morning, and after the story he had told her the day before, which had been his best effort to date, he did not think it wise to risk an anticlimax.

“I can’t tell you yet,” he said. “A little later perhaps; but it’s too secret right now.”

Ella’s face fell. She was thin, sharp-featured, wistful—a typical prod-uct of the East End slums. For three years she had been the general help at this boarding house off the Edgware Road. Most mornings, provid-ing he hadn’t a hangover, George would keep her entranced with lurid tales of G-men, gangsters and their molls. He assured her that, when he lived in the States, he had known them all. At one time he had worked with Frank Kelly, the bank robber; at another time he had been the body-guard of Toni Scarletti, the booze racketeer. His name was known and feared by all the big shots of the underworld, and he had experienced enough adventures to fill a dozen books.

These stories which George recounted so glibly were the figments of his extraordinary imagination. He had never been to America, let alone seen a gangster; but, being an avid reader of the lurid American pulp magazines, and having seen every gangster film ever made, he had ac-quired a remarkable knowledge of American crime. The gunmen as de-picted by such magazines as *Front Page Detective* and *True Confessions* completely obsessed him.

Like so many other men and women who live in a secret world of their own, George suffered from an acute inferiority complex. He had always lacked confidence in himself, and believed that whatever he planned to do was bound to end in failure.

This inferiority complex was the direct result of the treatment he had received in his early childhood from his parents. His birth had been an “accident,” and his parents, music hall artists by profession, had no place for a child in their rather selfish, extremely mobile lives. They regarded him as a calamity, and had made no attempt to conceal the fact from him. He was always the last to be considered, his babyhood was loveless, and at the earliest possible moment he was handed over to an elderly couple who had reluctantly taken on the role of foster parents in return for the much-needed addition to their meagre income. They were too old to be bothered with a small child, and it was not long before George realised that they considered him to be an unnecessary burden to them.

It says much for George's character that this unhappy, unwanted existence did not entirely affect his nature, but it certainly made him extremely shy and unnaturally sensitive. Because of his shyness he had a wretched time at school. As he grew older he became more reserved and repressed. He made no friends, and consequently had no outlet for his thoughts and desires. It was not surprising, then, that he became an introvert: as an antidote against loneliness and as a bolster to his drooping ego, he filled his mind with stories of adventure and violence, imagining himself as the hero of whatever story he happened to be reading. When he was at school he imagined himself as Bulldog Drummond; later, he saw himself as Jack Dempsey, and now, at the age of twenty-seven, he pictured himself as the all-powerful gang leader, amassing millions of dollars, terrorizing other mobs, racing the streets in a black armoured car, and being the idol of dazzling, beautifully dressed blondes.

For some time George Fraser had been content to live, in his mind, this role of a gangster; but these mental pictures became so vivid and exciting that he could no longer keep them to himself. Cautiously he tried them out on Ella, and was gratified to find that he had an immediately enthralled audience.

Ella had previously regarded George as just another boarder who seldom got up before eleven o'clock, and who expected a cup of tea just when she was occupied in making beds. But when George casually mentioned that he had lived in Chicago and had rubbed shoulders with most of the notorious Public Enemies, Ella was instantly intrigued. She went regularly to her local cinema, and was well acquainted with the savagery of American gangsters. Now here was someone, it seemed, who had actually met these men in the flesh, who had fought with and against them, and whose experiences were much more exciting and fantastic than the most exciting and fantastic film.

Ella was profoundly impressed. Not that George Fraser was impressive to look at. He had a tall, beefy, ungainly figure. His complexion was sallow and his eyes were big, blue and rather sad. In spite of his size, he could not entirely hide his timidity and shyness. If someone spoke to him suddenly he would change colour and become flustered, looking anywhere but at the person addressing him. His landlady, Mrs. Rhodes, terrified him, and whenever he ran into her he would talk complete nonsense while endeavouring to escape, leaving her staring after him, completely bewildered.

In spite of his manner, the stories he had to tell fascinated Ella. Not for a moment did it cross her mind that George was deceiving her. When he told her that he had been forced to leave the States in a hurry and that even now, if a certain mob knew where he was, they would come after him, she spent restless nights in fear for him. She must not, he had warned her, tell anyone of his past. He was, he explained, doing important and secret work, and his life would be in danger if anyone so much as suspected what his activities were.

All this was so much nonsense. In actual fact, up to four months ago George Fraser had been a bank clerk. He had been with the bank for ten years, and he would have been quite satisfied to remain a bank clerk for the rest of his days, but it did not turn out that way. One evening he had wandered into a pub—he was always wandering into pubs—a few minutes before closing time. There he met a flashily dressed individual who had, rather obviously, been in the pub since it had opened. This individual proposed to do George a good turn. Lowering his voice, he conveyed to George the name of a horse that was certain to win the next day's two o'clock handicap.

Now, George was no gambler, nor was he interested in horse racing, but he was flattered that his companion had mistaken him for a sportsman. He decided to have a flutter. The horse finished a length ahead of the field, and George received twenty pounds from a disgruntled bookmaker. He immediately jumped to the conclusion that he could make his fortune by backing horses. Before long he was in debt, and in desperation he turned to a moneylender to get him out of the mess. Then he couldn't pay the moneylender's charges, and the bank heard about it. George got the sack.

He was out of work for two miserable weeks, and he soon discovered that a discharged bank clerk was not a proposition an employer cared to consider. Things looked pretty black for George. He tramped the streets looking for work, and just as he was giving up hope, he obtained a job with the World-Wide Publishing Company. It wasn't much of a job, but, by now, George was glad to take anything.

He was, however, a little dismayed to find that the company expected him to sell a set of children's books from door to door on a "commission only" basis.

George had no confidence in his ability to sell anything. But the sales manager assured him that he need not worry about that. They would train him, and by the time they were through with him he would be able to sell coals to Newcastle. George was introduced to Edgar Robinson, head of the group of salesmen on whose territory George was to work. Robinson, an odd, aggressive creature with a shock of black hair and a blotchy complexion, took George aside and earnestly congratulated him on his good fortune to be working with him. What he did not know about selling the *Child's Self-Educator*, Robinson told him, could be written on his thumbnail. Every salesman who worked on his territory received personal tuition, and there was not a man trained by Edgar Robinson who was not earning at least ten pounds a week.

George became much more enthusiastic after he had heard this, and greatly encouraged when he realized that he was going to be shown how to obtain orders. He was, in fact, given an intensive two-day course in salesmanship along with the other applicants, and then he went out with Robinson and saw for himself how orders could be obtained.

A week later George was canvassing on his own, and by sheer hard work managed to earn three pounds ten shillings a week. He soon discovered that Robinson's stories about salesmen earning more than this amount was so much sales talk, but, as George knew that he was not likely to get anything else, he stuck to the job, and continued to make enough to keep himself going.

The job of calling from door to door was a great blow to George's pride. At first his shyness and timidity were a handicap. He would stand outside a house, screwing up his courage for such a time that people would become suspicious of him, and once one old lady telephoned for the police. Many people slammed the door in his face, while others were extremely rude to him. This treatment greatly increased his inferiority complex: there were moments when he suffered from moods of black depression, and he was driven more and more to rely on his fantasies of violence and adventure to sustain his bruised ego.

While Ella was tidying the room, George wrestled with his hangover. He had spent the previous evening at the "King's Arms," and had drunk one too many beers. Feeling the tea might help him recover, he reached for the cup.

"Seen Leo this morning?" he asked, for something to say. Ella gave the dressing table a final flick and moved to the door.

"He's somewhere around," she said indifferently. She was plainly disappointed that George wasn't in a talkative mood. "The silly thing! Wot you see in that cat I can't imagine. Not that I don't like cats meself, but not an old stupid like Leo. Leo indeed! I wonder who gave 'im that name.

As much like a lion as I am. 'E's frightened of 'is own shadow. I reckon it's crool to keep 'im alive. 'E never comes near anyone but you, Mr. George. But I must say 'e does seem to 'ave taken a proper fancy to you, doesn't 'e?"

George's face lit up. "Animals like me," he said simply. "Poor old Leo! He must have had a pretty rotten time as a kitten, I should think. He's all right once he knows you."

Ella sniffed. "He's 'ad enough opportunity to know me," she returned, "but 'e bolts as soon as 'e sees me. 'E's daft, that's wot 'e is," and she reluctantly took herself off to make the ten beds and clean the ten bedrooms of the other boarders who had, three hours since, gone off to their various offices.

As soon as she had gone, George slipped out of bed and opened the door. He left it ajar, went over to the dressing table, found his cigarette case and then returned to bed. He left his door ajar every morning, for as soon as Ella was out of the way, Leo would come to see him.

When George first came to the boarding house, Leo had been as terrified of him as of everyone else. The room George took over had been vacant for some little time, and the cat had used it as a kind of sanctuary. Several times George, coming home late, had found Leo curled up on his bed. The moment he opened the door the cat had sprung from the bed and had shot past him out of the room, a terrified streak of black fur.

George had been sorry for Leo. He saw, with a startling flash of intuition, that Leo was very much like himself. The cat was big and imposing, but its soul was as timid as George's. He understood the cat's fear of strangers, and he made up his mind that he would win its confidence.

For two months George wooed Leo's affection. He bought fish, which he left under his bed. He was always careful to enter his room slowly and without noise, and he would sit motionless if the cat ever visited him. It took a long time before Leo would stay with him. Even then the cat would spring away if he came near. But gradually, with inexhaustible patience, George won its affection. Now Leo came regularly every morning and kept him company.

This was a major triumph for George. He was not only flattered, but his interest, filling many hours of otherwise lonely boredom, developed into an intense love for the animal. He depended on Leo for company, and their association afforded an outlet for his own repressed affection.

While he was thinking about the cat, he felt a weight on the bed and, opening his eyes, he found Leo looking at him. The cat was a big black Persian with enormous yellow eyes and long whiskers. It stood on

George's chest, padding with its paws while it sniffed delicately at George's face.

"Can't stay long, old boy," George said, stroking its head with tender fingers. "I've got work to do this morning. Come on, settle for a moment," and he pulled the cat down beside him.

He continued to talk to it, stroking and fondling it, feeling at peace with life, grateful to the cat for its company, lavishing on it the urgent, rather overpowering love which unconsciously he yearned for himself.

CHAPTER TWO

George Fraser wandered into the saloon bar of the "King's Arms" at ten minutes to one o'clock. He walked to his favourite corner at the far end of the long bar-counter and propped himself up against the wall.

The bar was not particularly full, and after a moment or so, Gladys, the barmaid, a big, good-natured-looking girl, detached herself from a group of men with whom she had been gossiping and came towards him, wiping the counter with a swab as she did so.

"How's yourself ?" she asked, giving George a fleeting smile as she drew a pint of mild and bitter, which she set before him.

George tipped his hat and returned her smile. He liked Gladys. She had served him regularly for the past four months, and he had a vague feeling that she was interested in him. Anyway, George always felt at home with barmaids, considering them to be friendly, comfortable women, not likely to jeer at him nor to pass unkind remarks about him behind his back.

It gave him considerable pleasure to enter the saloon bar of the "King's Arms" and receive a pint of beer without actually asking for it, and for Gladys to inquire how he was. These trifling attentions made him feel that he was one of her special clients, and he regarded the "King's Arms" as a kind of second home.

"I'm fine," he said. "No need to ask how you are. You always look wonderful." He paid for his beer. "Don't know how you do it."

Gladys laughed. "Hard work agrees with me," she confessed, glancing in the mirror behind the bar. She patted her mass of dark, wavy hair and admired herself for a brief moment. "Your Mr. Robinson was in last night. Oo's his new friend—young, white-faced feller with a scar? I haven't seen him around 'ere before."

George shook his head. "Don't ask me. Robo's always picking up waifs and strays. He can't bear his own company for more than five minutes."

He winked and went on, "Case of a bad conscience, if you ask me."

"Well, I dunno about that," Gladys said, polishing that part of the counter within reach of her arm. "But this feller looked like a bad conscience if ever anyone did. 'E fair gave me the creeps."

"Go on." George's rather vacant blue eyes widened. "How's that?"

Gladys sniffed. "Something fishy about 'im. I wouldn't like to run into 'im in the dark."

George was mildly intrigued. "Oh, come off it," he said, smiling. "You're imagining things."

An impatient tapping on the counter reminded Gladys that she was neglecting her duties.

"Shan't be a jiffy," she said. "There's old Mr. Henry. I mustn't keep 'im waiting."

George nodded understandingly. He was used to carrying on interrupted conversations with Gladys. It was understood between them that customers should not be kept waiting no matter how pressing the topic of discussion happened to be.

He glanced at Mr. Henry, who was waiting impatiently for a small whisky. Mr. Henry, like George, was a regular customer of the "King's Arms." He was a thin, red-faced little man, and he kept to himself. George often speculated what he did for a living. This morning, George decided that there was something rather mysterious about Mr. Henry. He drank a little of his beer and relaxed against the wall.

...Gladys served Mr. Henry with a whisky and soda, exchanged a few words with him, and then came towards George Fraser. Her eyes were alight with excitement, her face had paled.

"Something's up," George Fraser thought as he pushed his empty tankard towards her.

Gladys picked up the tankard, and while she filled it, she said in a voice scarcely above a whisper, "That's Davie Bentillo. I recognized him in spite of his disguise."

George Fraser stiffened. He glanced quickly at the little, red-faced man. Davie Bentillo! What a bit of luck! Every cop in the country was looking for Davie. It could be, although the disguise was superb. He was the same height as Scarletti's ferocious gunman. Yes, it was the same nose and eyes . . . Gladys was right!

"Nice work, kid," George Fraser said, and his hand crept to his hip pocket to close over the cold butt of his gun.

"Be careful, Mr. Fraser," Gladys breathed, her face waxen with fear. "He's dangerous."

Edgar Robinson jogged George's elbow. "Wake up, cock," he said, settling himself comfortably on a stool. "You look like sleeping beauty this morning. Bin on the tiles?"

George Fraser blinked at him, sighed and said, "Morning."

Robinson took off his thick glasses and polished them with a grimy handkerchief. Without his glasses his eyes looked like small, green gooseberries. "Be a pal and ask me what I'll have," he said, showing his yellow teeth as he beamed at George. "I've bin and left me money at home."

George eyed him without enthusiasm. "Well, what'll it be?" Robinson put his glasses on again and looked round the bar.

"Well, I'd like a double whisky," he said, after a moment's thought, "but seeing as 'ow you're paying, I'll make it a beer." George signalled to Gladys.

"What's up?" Robinson asked, eyeing George keenly. "Very strong and silent this morning, aren't you? Gotta touch of pox or something?"

"I'm all right," George said shortly. He disliked Edgar Robinson, while admiring his ability as a salesman.

"That's the spirit," Robinson returned, beaming again. "Must have my boys on the top line. The right mental attitude gets the business, you know. If you're worrying about anything, 'ow can you hope to get orders?" He smiled his horsey smile as Gladys joined them. "Hello, my pretty," he went on; "'pon my soul, she gets more desirable every day. Wouldn't you like a little session with our Gladys in the park, George?"

George looked uncomfortable. Sex embarrassed him, and Robinson was always making him feel awkward by his loose talk in mixed society.

"Oh, shut up," he growled, and without looking at Gladys he muttered, "Give him a mild and bitter, please."

Robinson grinned. "Glad, my girl, I believe we've the privilege of drinking in the company of a virgin. Not being one meself, and knowing from the saucy look in your eye, my pretty, that you'd make no false claims, we knows who we're talking abawt, don't we?"

Gladys giggled, drew another pint of beer and set it before Robinson. She glanced at George's red face, winked at him and said, "Don't you take any notice of him. It's those who talk the most that do the least."

Robinson dug George in the ribs. "She's calling you a dirty old man, George," he cackled. "Maybe you are. What's your particular vice, old boy? 'Ere Glad, don't go away; you might learn something."

"I can't waste my time talking nonsense with you," Gladys returned. "I've got my work to do."

When she had gone to the other end of the bar, Robinson stared at her broad back for a second or so and then winked at George.

"Rather fancy her meself," he said, his small green eyes lighting up. "Think she's a proposition?"

George scowled at him. "Oh, dry up," he snapped. "Can't you get your mind off women for five minutes?"

Robinson gave him a sneering, amused smile. "Funny bloke, aren't you, George?" he said, taking out a crumpled packet of Woodbines. "'Ere, have a smoke. The trouble with you, me boy, is you're repressed. You're scared of sex, and if you ain't careful, it'll fester inside you, and then anything may happen. Me—I'm as free as the air. It's just a cuppa tea to me. When I want it, I have it, and that way it don't do me any 'arm."

George lit his cigarette, cleared his throat and produced a big envelope from the "poacher's" pocket he had had made inside his coat.

"Now then," he said. "Let's see what I've got to do." He took from the envelope a packet of printed forms and a sheet of paper containing the addresses of the local schools. "I'm planting more forms this afternoon. I've to collect others from Radlet Road School. Ought to get something from them, and this evening I'll make some calls."

Robinson glanced down the list of addresses and grunted, "All right," he said. "Still working Wembley? Where are you going next?"

"Alperton, Harlesden and Sudbury," George returned. "I've got it all doped out. There's a good bunch of Council houses in all those districts, and they haven't been worked for some time now."

"I almost forgot," Robinson said, blowing a thin stream of smoke to the ceiling. "I've taken on a new salesman. Thought I'd put him under your wing, George. You can show him the ropes, and he'll be company for you."

"You mean you want me to train him?" George asked eagerly, his big face lighting up.

Robinson nodded. "That's the idea," he said. "He's new to the game, and you know all the tricks by now; so I thought you might as well give me a hand."

"Why, certainly," George said. He was delighted that Robinson should pay him such a compliment. "Yes, I think I can teach him a few tricks. Who is he?"

"Chap named Sydney Brant. Rum kind of a bloke, but he might get some business." Robinson glanced at the clock above the bar. "He ought to be here any minute now. Take him out this afternoon and show him how to plant the forms, will you? And then take him with you when you make your calls tonight. Anyway, I don't have to tell you what to do, do I?"

"You leave it to me," George said, straightening up and feeling important. "Have another beer, Robo," and he signalled to Gladys.

Robinson gave him a sly, amused look. He could see that George was delighted to be given some responsibility. That suited Robinson, as he was getting tired of showing new men how to get orders. If George wanted to do it, so much the better. Robinson had long since given up serious canvassing. He relied on his salesmen to get orders, and took from each an overriding commission. Now that George was showing promise as a reliable salesman, Robinson planned to shift the training onto his shoulders, and in time he hoped he would not have to do any of the work at all.

Gladys gave them two more pints, and George, who was hungry, ordered a beef sandwich.

"Want one?" he asked Robinson.

"Not just now," Robinson returned. "It's a bit early for me. I've only just got up."

While George ate his sandwich, the bar began to fill up, and soon the place was crowded.

Suddenly, edging through the crowd at the bar, George noticed a thick-set young fellow with an untidy shock of straw-coloured hair coming towards them.

There was something about this young man that immediately arrested George's attention. He had a livid scar—a burn—on his right cheek. The skin was raw and unsightly. George guessed the burn had only just been freed of its dressing. Then there was a look of starved intensity in his face, and his grey-blue eyes, heartless and bitter, were the most unfriendly George had ever seen.

This young man—he could not have been more than twenty-one or -two—came up to Robinson and stood at his side without saying anything.

He was wearing worn grey flannel trousers and a shabby tweed coat. His dark blue shirt was crumpled and his red tie looked like a piece of coloured string.

Robinson said, "Ah! There you are. I was wondering where you'd got to. This is George Fraser, one of my best salesmen. George, this is Sydney Brant, I was telling you about."

George flushed with pleasure to be called one of Robinson's best salesmen, but when he met Brant's eyes he experienced a strange uneasiness. There was something disconcerting about Brant's blank face, the indifferent way he stood, as if he didn't give a damn for anyone. The raw, puckered wound upset George, who had a slightly squeamish stomach in spite of his fascination for violence and bloodshed.

"How do you do?" he said, looking away. "Robo was just saying he wanted me to show you the ropes. I'll certainly do my best."

Brant stared at him indifferently and said nothing.

"You'll find old George knows all the tricks," Robinson said breezily.

Why couldn't the fellow say something? George thought. He glanced down at his tankard, swished the beer round in it and looked up abruptly at Brant.

"Robo says he wants you and me to work together," he said. "We—we might do some work this afternoon."

Brant nodded. His eyes shifted to Robinson and then back to George. He still appeared to find the situation called for no comment.

Robinson was not at his ease. He picked his nose and smiled absently at himself in the big mirror behind the bar.

"You couldn't do better than work with George," he said, addressing himself in the mirror. "You'll be surprised when you see old George in action." He patted George's arm. "We'll make a big success out of young Syd, won't we?"

"Don't call me Syd," the young man said in a low, clipped voice. "My name's Brant."

Robinson flashed his toothy smile, but his eyes looked startled. "Must be matey," he said, looking into the mirror again. He adjusted his frayed tie. "Can't do business if we aren't matey, can we, George? You call me Robo, I'll call you Syd—right?"

"My name's Brant," the young man repeated and stared through Robinson with bored, cold indifference. ,

There was an awkward pause, then George said, "Well, have a drink. What'll it be?"

Brant shrugged his thin shoulders. "I don't drink," he returned. "Still, I don't mind a lemonade," and his eyes went to Gladys, who came along the bar at George's signal.

George, seeing her give a quick, alarmed look at Brant, realised that this was the fellow she had been telling him about. Well, she was right. He could understand now what she meant when she had said that he'd given her the creeps. George scratched his head uneasily. He was reluctant to admit it, but the fellow gave him the creeps too.

"A lemonade for Mr. Brant," he said, winking at Gladys.

Gladys poured out the lemonade, set it before Brant and, without a word, walked away to the far end of the bar.

Again there was an awkward pause, then Robinson finished his beer, wiped his thick lips on his coat sleeve and slid off the stool.

"Well, I'm off," he announced. "I've got several little jobs to do. I'll leave you in George's capable hands. Don't forget, boys, every door is a door of opportunity. The right mental attitude gets the business. If you haven't the right M.A., you can't hope to conquer the other man's mind. You want your prospect to buy the *Child's Self-Educator*. He doesn't want to have anything to do with it because he doesn't know anything about it. It's your job to convince him that the *C.S.E.* is the best investment he can buy. Get your prospect agreeing with you from the very start of your sales talk. Get inside the house. Never attempt to sell a prospect on his doorstep. Know when to stop talking and when to produce the order form." He beamed at George and went on, "George knows all about it. Follow those rules and you can't go wrong. Good luck and good hunting." His toothy smile faltered a trifle as he felt Brant's sneering eyes searching his face. With a wave of his hand, Robinson pushed his way through the crowd and out into the street.

George stared after him, an admiring look in his eyes. "He knows the business all right," he said enthusiastically. "Believe me, he's one of the best salesmen I've ever met."

Brant sipped his lemonade and grimaced. "You can't have met many," he said, staring past George at the group of men at the end of the bar.

George started. "What do you mean? Why, Robo knows every trick in this game better than any salesman working for the Wide World."

Brant's expressionless eyes shifted from the group of men to George's flushed face.

"He's living on a bunch of suckers who're fools enough to let him get away with it," he said in flat, cold tones, like a judge pronouncing sentence.

George's sense of fair play was outraged. "But it's business. He trains us, so naturally we pay him a small commission. We couldn't sell anything unless he tells us where to go and how to get our contacts. Be fair, old man."

The white, thin face jeered at him. "What do you call a small commission?"

"He told you, didn't he?"

"I know what he told me, but what did he tell you?" Brant jerked a long lock of hair out of his eyes.

George put his tankard down on the bar. He felt it was time this young fellow was taken down a peg or two. "We give Robo ten per cent of what we make. That's fair, isn't it? We get a quid for every order and we pay Robo two bob. Can't call that profiteering, can you?" He studied Brant anxiously. "I mean Robo trains us and arranges our territory. Two bob isn't much, is it?"

Brant again jerked the lock of hair out of his eyes, impatiently, irritably. "What makes you think the Company doesn't pay more than a pound for an order?"

George stared at him. He felt he was on the brink of an unpleasant discovery; something that he didn't want to hear. "What are you hinting at?" he asked uneasily.

"The Company pays thirty bob on every order sent in. That's why your pal Robinson makes you send your orders through him. He not only takes two bob off you, but ten bob as well. I took the trouble to 'phone the Company and ask them what they'd pay me if I sent in my orders direct. They said thirty bob."

George suddenly hated this young man with his straw-coloured hair and his disgusting scar. Why couldn't he have left him in peace? He had trusted Robinson. They had got along fine together. Robinson had been his only companion. Robinson had said that George was his best salesman, and he had given him responsibility. He had always been at hand to smear a paste of flattery on George's bruised ego. George thought of all the past orders he had given him, and he felt a little sick.

"Oh," he said, after a long pause, "so that's how it is, is it?"

Brant finished his lemonade. "Should have thought you'd found that out for yourself," he said in his soft, clipped voice.

George clenched his fists. "The dirty rat!" he exclaimed, trying to get a vicious look in his eyes. "Why, he'd 've been taken for a ride for that if he'd been in the States."

Brant smiled secretly. "Is that where you come from?"

"Sure," George said, realizing that this was a chance to reestablish himself. "But it's some time ago. I must be slipping. Fancy letting a cheap crook like Robinson pull a fast one on me. If ever Kelly got to hear about it, he'd rib me to death."

The thin, cold face remained expressionless. "Kelly?"

George picked up his tankard and drank. The beer tasted warm and flat. Without looking at Brant, he said, "Yeah—Frank Kelly. I used to work for him in the good old days."

"Kelly?" Brant was still and tense. "You mean, the gangster?"

George nodded. "Sure," he said, feeling an infuriating rush of blood mounting to his face. "Poor old Frank. He certainly had a bad break." He set his tankard down, and in an endeavour to conceal his confusion, he lit a cigarette. "But, of course, that was some time ago."

Brant's thin mouth twisted. "Still, now you know, you're not going to let Robinson get away with this, are you?"

George suddenly saw the trap he had dug for himself. If Brant was to think anything of him, he'd have to go through with it.

"You bet I'm not," he growled, scowling fiercely into his empty tankard.

"Good," Brant said, a veiled, jeering look in his eyes. "That'll save me some trouble. You'd know how to talk to him, wouldn't you?"

"I'll fix him," George threatened, feeling a growing dismay. "No one's ever pulled a fast one on me without regretting it."

"I'll come with you," Brant said softly. "I'd like to see how you handle him."

George shook his head. "You'd better leave this to me," he said feebly. "I might lose my temper with him. I don't want witnesses."

"I'll come with you all the same." Brant's thin lips tightened. "You don't have to worry about me."

They looked at each other. George felt himself wilt under the baleful look that had jumped into Brant's eyes.

"Okay," he muttered uneasily. "You can come along if you want to."

There was a long pause and then he said, "Well, we'd better do some work. You ready?"

Brant nodded. "Yes." He pushed himself away from the counter. "Tonight'll be interesting," he added, and followed George out of the bar.

CHAPTER THREE

George Fraser had little to say while he and Brant travelled by underground to Wembley. Talking was difficult in the swaying, roaring train, and he wanted time to think over what Brant had told him.

If what Brant had said were true, then Robinson had cheated him out of at least twenty pounds. George considered what he could have done with all that money. Twenty pounds! Why, he could have bought a second-hand car, he thought dismally. He had always wanted a car. He had no idea what he was going to say to Robinson when he saw him that night. If it hadn't been for Brant, he probably wouldn't have had the nerve to raise the matter at all; but now he had to make a show before this unpleasant, disturbing intruder. He would have to make a shot at persuading Robinson to fork up the twenty pounds. He hadn't much hope, as Robinson never seemed to have any money, but it might be worth trying. Of course, Robinson might turn nasty. He might even demand the return of all George's specimen copies of the *Child's Self-Ed-*

ucator and then tell George to go to blazes. Then what would he do? It'd mean he'd be out of work again, and that thought appalled George.

Well, it was no good worrying, he decided gloomily. After all, Robinson was cheating him, and he couldn't expect to get away with it. He'd tackle him politely and firmly, and hope for the best. It wouldn't do for Brant to think he couldn't handle the situation. Brant seemed now to be regarding him with a little more respect since George had mentioned Frank Kelly. George pulled a face. He hoped Brant wouldn't say anything about that to anyone. He shot a furtive look at the blank, hard face. All he could see was the disagreeable, raw-looking scar and one vacant, glittering eye. Nasty young customer, he thought uneasily. Proper dead-end kid. He wondered if Brant believed him. You couldn't tell where you were with a fellow with such an expressionless face. Anyway Brant hadn't asked any questions, and he seemed to have accepted Kelly after a momentary glimmer of surprise.

The train pulled into Wembley station, and with a sigh of relief George got to his feet. He was glad to have something to do. He didn't want to think about Brant nor what he was going to say to Robinson that night. He forced this disagreeable prospect to the back of his mind and shambled along beside his companion.

"Now, our first job is to call at Radlet Road School," he said, as they walked briskly up the High Road. "I called in there yesterday and planted our circulars. You see, unless we know where the kids live, we can't get any orders. It isn't like selling vacuum cleaners, for instance. With vacuum cleaners it's a straight door-to-door canvass. But in our line we have to know which homes have children and which haven't." He paused while he fished a cigarette from a crumpled carton and offered it to Brant.

"I don't smoke," Brant said shortly. They were the first words he had uttered since leaving the train.

"Oh, all right," George looked at him blankly, and lit up. They moved on, and George said, "Well, we've got to get the names and addresses of all the kids at the various Council schools. It isn't easy, because the teachers don't want to help us. You'd think they'd be glad for the kids to have the books, wouldn't you? But not they." George breathed heavily through his thick nose. "Of course, some of 'em do help, otherwise we'd get nowhere. But the majority are a lazy, suspicious lot. We have to persuade the teacher to pass our forms round the class and get the kids to put their names and addresses on them; then we collect the forms next day and make our calls. It sounds simple, doesn't it, but you wait ... you'll see what I mean before long."

All the time he was talking, Brant strode along at his side, his face expressionless and his eyes blank. For all George knew, he hadn't heard a word George had said.

This indifferent attitude annoyed George. All right, he thought, lapsing into a sulky silence, you think it's child's play, but just you wait. You'll find it's not all beer and skittles. You wait until you try to get an order. Be as superior as you like, but with a dial like yours you don't stand a hope. Do you think anyone will want to look at you when you try to talk to them? They'll slam the door in your ugly mug, you see if they don't, and it'll serve you right. Take you down a peg or two, my lad. That's what you want. Be superior if that's how you feel, but you're riding for a fall. You can't say I haven't tried to be friendly, but I'm damned if I'm going to put myself out if you don't meet me halfway.

He was glad when they reached the school. Now he could show Brant how successfully he had cultivated the headmaster the day before. They crossed the deserted playground and approached the red-brick school building. In spite of his outward show of confidence, George could never enter a school premises without a feeling of guilt. The L.C.C. had forbidden canvassers to call on Secondary and Council schools, and George always had it at the back of his mind that he would run into a visiting school inspector one of these days and be ordered ignominiously from the school.

He paused at the main entrance, and with an uneasy smile pointed out the notice pinned to the door.

"See that?" he said, anxious that Brant should share his own secret uneasiness. "'Canvassers and salesmen are not permitted on the school premises. I told you it wasn't easy, didn't I? It's only when the headmaster's friendly that we can get anywhere."

Brant didn't say anything. He glanced at George with sneering contempt in his eyes.

George pushed open the door and entered the long passage, which smelt of disinfectant, floor polish and stale perspiration. They walked down the passage, past a number of classrooms. They could see through the glass partitions into the small rooms, each containing a number of children at desks. The children spotted them, and heads turned in their direction with the precision of a field of corn moving in a wind.

George shrank from their inquisitive, staring eyes. He hunched his great shoulders and hurried on towards the headmaster's office.

The headmaster looked up from his desk and frowned at them. He was a little man, thin and old. Two or three strands of greying hair had been carefully plastered across the baldness of his head. His large, mild eyes were tired, and his shoulders, under his shabby coat, drooped as if the burden of his responsibilities were too much for him.

"Good afternoon, Mr. Pickthorn," George said, with the overpowering heartiness he always assumed when working. "What a magnificent day! Too good to be in, but we've all got our living to make, haven't we?" He stood over the headmaster, large, friendly, anxious to please. "We can't all go gadding about when there's work to be done, can we? Noses to the grindstones, eh?" He lowered his voice and winked. "Not that you and me wouldn't like to be at Lord's today."

It had taken George some time to conquer his shyness when meeting strangers, but now that he was sure of what he was going to say, he was becoming quite a fluent, if automatic talker. He hoped that Brant was being impressed. That'd show him how to talk to prospects. Brant would have to shake up his ideas if he thought he was going to make a successful salesman. People liked to have someone call on them who was cheerful and bright.

Mr. Pickthorn smiled vaguely and blinked up at George. "Ah," he said, shaking his head sadly. "Yes, Lord's." Then he glanced at Brant, and the friendly look drained out of his eyes. He glanced hurriedly away, his thin mouth tightening.

There! George thought triumphantly. See what happens when they look at your ugly mug. Go on, be superior. I don't care. At least, they don't look away when I talk to them.

Feeling the changing atmosphere, he went on hurriedly, "I was passing, Mr. Pickthorn, so I thought I'd pick up those forms I left yesterday. Are they ready?"

Mr. Pickthorn fiddled with his pen tray, placing the pens and coloured pencils in their racks with exaggerated care. "No," he said, without looking at either of them. "No, I'm afraid they aren't."

George felt his heartiness, bolstered up by the feeling that Mr. Pickthorn liked him, oozing away like air from a leaking balloon.

"Well, never mind," he said, with a fixed smile. "You don't have to tell me how busy you are. I know what you headmasters have to do. Work, work, work, all day long. Suppose I call back tomorrow? Perhaps you'll find time to get them done tomorrow."

Mr. Pickthorn continued to fiddle with his pens and pencils. He did not look up. "I've changed my mind," he said abruptly. "As a matter of fact, Mr. Herring, my assistant, drew my attention to it. He's quite right, of course. I wasn't thinking. Of course, the books are good. No doubt about that. I've known the *Child's Self-Educator* for many years, but as Mr. Herring pointed out, it's encouraging canvassers, and the Council doesn't approve." He opened a drawer and took out the packet of printed forms that George had left with him the day before. "I'm sorry," he went on, pushing the forms across the desk to George. "Now, if you'll excuse me ..." He gave George a fleeting embarrassed smile, again glanced at Brant, and then pulled a pile of papers towards him.

"You see?" George said, when they were in the street again. "Now we've got no calls for tonight. The rotten little rat! Couldn't do enough for me yesterday. I spent a whole hour listening to him talk about his blasted garden. As if I cared! He promised me faithfully to distribute those forms. Oh, well, it only goes to prove." He fished out his carton of cigarettes and lit one. "We'll have to do a cold canvass tonight. It means wandering up and down a street looking out for kids, asking them where they live, or spotting toys in the windows or gardens. That's a job I hate! Everyone watches you, and sometimes if you do ask the kids who they are, they get scared and start howling."

Brant shoved his hands in his pockets and stared down at his shoes. His indifferent expression infuriated George.

"Well, what do we do?" Brant asked, as if to say, this is your mess, and it's up to you to find a way out.

Choking back his irritation, George took out his list of schools and studied it. "We'd better go over to Sherman Road School," he said. "It's about half a mile from here. That's the best school in the district. If we don't get our forms in there, we're properly in the soup."

Brant shrugged. "All right," he said, falling in step beside George. "So long as we get something done today."

George shot him an angry glance. "It's all very well to criticize," he snapped, "but if you think you can do better, you'd better try."

"I'll take over if you make another mess of it," Brant returned in his clipped, indifferent voice.

George could scarcely believe his ears. He walked on in silence, fuming with rage. If he made a mess of it! Of all the cheek! And he was teaching this smug brat—that's all he was—a smug brat! He'd take over, would he? All right, they'd see about that. Perhaps it'd be a good idea to let him make a fool of himself. As if anyone would listen to him, with his scar and his straw hair and his shabby clothes. Then George's caution asserted itself. The kids at Sherman Road were of a better class than in any of the other schools. He couldn't afford to take chances with this school. Every form that was filled up might mean an order.

In the school lobby they found the same depressing notice warning canvassers and salesmen that they were trespassing Underneath this official notice was another notice written and signed by the headmaster.

Can you read? Then keep out! No canvassers or salesmen will be seen during school hours. Any attempt to enter school premises without an official permit will be immediately reported to the local authorities.
Chas. Eccles.

Headmaster.

George read this notice and experienced a sinking feeling in his stomach. "I've never seen anything like this before," he whispered, furtively looking down the passage that led to the classrooms. "Doesn't look very hopeful, does it?"

Brant shrugged. "You can always tell him you can't read," he said with a sneer. "He might even believe you."

George flushed, and without a word walked down the passage to the headmaster's office. He wished that Robinson was with him. Robo would know what to do. He didn't care a damn whom he tackled or how rude people were to him.

George tapped on the door and waited.

"Come in," roared a voice.

They entered a small, bare room. A big, fleshy man, with a large blonde moustache on a round, flat face, frowned at them.

"Who are you? What do you want?" he shouted in a voice made harsh by constant bullying.

George gave him a nervous smile. "Good morning, Mr. Eccles," he said, his heartiness wavering. "Forgive me for intruding like this, but I was passing, and I felt that you'd be interested to hear that the new edition of the *Child's Self-Educator* is now ready."

Mr. Eccles leaned across his desk, his hard little eyes boring into George. "What?" he shouted. "Selling something? Where's your permit?"

George took an involuntary step back. "Now, please don't misunderstand me, Mr. Eccles," he said, trying to control his rising colour. "We're not selling anything. It's just that we thought you'd be interested to hear that the new edition of the *Child's Self-Educator* is—er—ready. It's a magnificent job. Two hundred additional coloured plates, and all the maps have been revised. There's more than two hundred thousand additional words, bringing this wonderful work of reference right up to date."

"Hmm," Mr. Eccles grunted. "You people are not supposed to be on the school premises, you know. I haven't the time nor the inclination to talk to salesmen. All right, thank you for calling. Good afternoon," and he picked up his pen and began to write.

Had George been alone, he would have slunk out of the room, but the cold, still, hateful figure of Brant made retreat impossible.

"If you'll excuse me, Mr. Eccles," George said, his face now the colour of a beetroot, "there's just one other point I would like to raise with you. You know the *C.S.E.*, of course. You'll agree with me, I'm sure, that it is a most useful set of hooks and its reputation in the world of letters is second to none. Any child possessing this magnificent work of reference has an obvious advantage over the unfortunate child who is without it. The task of the teacher is considerably lightened if a child can turn to the *C.S.E.* and find for itself the answer to those awkward questions that a child is always asking his teacher."

Mr. Eccles laid down his pen and pushed back his chair. His movements were deliberate and ominous.

"If I thought you were trying to sell something on these premises," he said with deadly calm, "I would give you in charge."

George shuffled his feet. "I assure you, Mr. Eccles," he stammered, "I—I have no intention of selling anything, no intention at all. It's just that I hoped for your co-operation. Unless teachers are prepared to assist us, we are unable to let parents know how valuable the *C.S.E.*—and who would deny it?—would be in the home."

Mr. Eccles rose to his feet. To George, he seemed to grow in stature, and broaden like a rubber doll that is being inflated. "You're canvassing," Mr. Eccles said in an awful voice. "I thought as much. What is the name of your firm?"

George had visions of a complaint being lodged by the L.C.C. Although the World-Wide Publishing Company was fully aware of the methods used by their salesmen, officially these methods were not recognised. They were all right, so long as there were no complaints. If there were complaints, then the salesmen were sacked.

George stood staring stupidly at Mr. Eccles, his face red, his mouth dry and his eyes protruding. He visualized the arrival of the police and being marched through the streets to the police station.

"Well?" Mr. Eccles shouted at him, seeing his confusion and enjoying it. "Who's your firm? I'll get to the bottom of this! I'm going to stop you touts bothering me and my staff. Everyday someone calls. If it isn't vacuum cleaners, it's silk stockings. If it isn't silk stockings, it's expensive books that no one can afford to buy. I'm going to put a stop to it!"

From somewhere in the rear, where he had been standing, Brant suddenly appeared in front of George. He walked straight up to Mr. Eccles and fixed him with his cold, expressionless eyes.

"There is no need to shout," he said, in his soft, clipped voice. "We've been received at all the other schools in this district with courtesy, Mr. Eccles. Surely, we are entitled to your courtesy too."

Mr. Eccles glared at Brant, then quite suddenly moved back a step.

"We are men trying to do a job of work," Brant went on, his eyes never moving from Eccles' face. "Just as you are trying to do a job of work. As representatives of the World-Wide Publishing Company we are entitled to a hearing. The World-Wide Publishing Company has been dealing with the teaching profession for two hundred years. Its reputation for integrity and good work is known and commented upon by the London County Council. The *Child's Self-Educator* is known all over the world."

Mr. Eccles sat down slowly. It was as if he had suddenly lost the strength in his legs. "World-Wide Publishing Company," he muttered and wrote on his blotting-paper. "All right, I'll remember that."

"I want you to remember it," Brant said. "I'm surprised that a man of your experience does not know who published the *Child's Self-Educator.* Have you a set yourself?"

Mr. Eccles looked up. "Who—me? No, I haven't. Now, look here, young man—"

"Then you will be glad to hear that you are going to be presented with a set. That's why we've come to see you."

"Presented with a set?" Mr. Eccles repeated, his little eyes opening. "You mean—*given* a set?"

"Certainly," Brant said, his hands on the desk. "We're anxious that every teacher should have a set of the *C.S.E.*, but, for obvious reasons, it is not possible to give so many sets away. It has been decided, however, that the headmaster of the best school of each London borough is to be presented with our deluxe, half-calf edition, free, gratis and for nothing."

If Mr. Eccles was surprised by this news, George was utterly flabbergasted.

"Well, 'pon my soul," Mr. Eccles exclaimed, a sly smile lighting up his face. "Why didn't you say so before? Sit down, young man. I'm sorry I was so abrupt just now, but if you only knew how I'm pestered all day long, you'd appreciate I've got to do something to protect myself."

Brant drew up a chair and sat down. George, standing by the door, was forgotten.

"I understand, Mr. Eccles," Brant went on, after a moment's pause, "that your children's handwriting is of an exceptionally high standard. Mr. Pickthorn of Trinity School also boasts of a high standard. We are organizing a harmless competition between schools, and I suggest you might like to co-operate. All we need is a specimen of each of your pupils' handwriting, which will be sent to our head office, and the pupil with the best handwriting will be given a beautifully inscribed certificate and ten shillings. Mr. Pickthorn has been happy to help us in this scheme, and we would like your pupils to compete against his. Whatever you decide, of course, will not influence my Company's decision to send you the C.S.E., which should reach you early next month."

"Pickthorn?" Mr. Eccles snorted. "That old muddler! None of his brats can write. He's got no method. Why, in a competition, it'd be a walkover." He frowned down at his blotting pad. "I'd like to do it. 'Pon my word, I would. I'd like to wipe old Pickthorn's eye, but it'll disorganise my day. A thing like that'd need a bit of arranging."

Brant shifted in his chair. "It took less than ten minutes at Radlet's," he said quietly. "All you have to do is to get the children to write their names and addresses on a piece of paper, and we will judge their handwriting from that. It is a simple system, and we shall not need to bother you further, as we shall have the name and address of the prize winner. Surely, that's not going to upset your school?"

Eccles looked a little blank. "Well, if that's all it is," he said doubtfully. "I suppose I could arrange that. All right, I'll do it. Will you call back sometime tomorrow?"

Brant stared at him with bored eyes. "We have a lot of ground to cover, Mr. Eccles. Could we wait? It shouldn't take a few minutes." He paused, and before Mr. Eccles could speak, he went on, "By the way, I suppose you would like a bookcase for your set of the *C.S.E.?* I think I could persuade the Company to part with one. It's a nice piece of furniture, light oak with glass panels."

Mr. Eccles got to his feet. "Yes," he said, beaming, "that sounds magnificent. Hmm, yes, by all means." He rubbed his hands together. "Well now, you wait here and I'll get these kids to work. I'll be as quick as I can."

As soon as he left the room, George said, "Have you gone mad? What are you playing at? The Company doesn't give sets away, let alone bookcases. They don't even sell bookcases."

Brant stared at him in a bored, detached way. "He doesn't know that," he said, and his thin mouth sneered.

"Well, he soon will when the books don't turn up," George said, now thoroughly agitated. "He'll report us. Why, he might even tell the police. There'll be a hell of a stink about this. And what's all this about handwriting competitions? I really think you must be out of your mind."

Brant looked out of the window. "Can't you see?" he said with that patient voice that people reserve for tiresome, questioning children. "We're going to get the names and addresses of all the brats in this school. That's what you want, isn't it? You made a mess of it, so I've fixed it. I said I would, didn't I?"

"You'll jolly well pay the ten bob out of your own pocket. I'm not going to throw money away like that," George snapped, flushing angrily.

The cold eyes flickered. "Don't be wet," Brant said. "No one's going to pay ten bob. Let the brat whistle for it."

"What?" George exclaimed, starting forward. "You're not even going to give a prize—after telling all those lies?"

"You dumb, or something?" Brant's face showed a faint curiosity. "Your pal Kelly wouldn't pay 'em a nickel, would he? What's the matter with you—slipping?" He stared at George until George had to look away. "Anyway, why should you worry? We won't be here next month. They don't know our names, and if they complain to the Company, we can deny it. It's their word against ours."

The enormity of such a swindle paralysed George. He sat down and stared stupidly at Brant.

"It's cheating," he said at last. "I—I don't know what to say."

"Aw, dry up!" Brant said, a vicious snarl in his voice. "The whole business is a racket. The Company doesn't care how you get business so long as you don't tell 'em. They don't pay you a salary and they don't care if you starve. All they're interested in is to get a mug to sell their books. Robinson cheats us out of ten bob on every order we get. Do you think he cares? He doesn't give a damn so long as he gets his rake off. These teachers are only out for what they can get. It's a racket from start to finish." He leaned forward, two faint red spots on his thin cheeks. "It's us or them. If you don't like it, then get the hell out of it and leave me to handle it. I'm out for what I can get, and I'm going to get it. So, shut up!"

George flinched away from the savage anger that faced him, and for a long time the room was silent except for the distant sound of children's voices coming from the classrooms.

CHAPTER FOUR

"If it rains," George had said to Brant, looking at the mass of black cloud slowly creeping across the sky, "we shan't be able to work tonight. It's no good calling on people if you're dripping wet. They don't ask you in, and just try selling anything standing on a doorstep with rain running down the back of your neck."

Well, it was raining all right. From his bedroom window George looked down at the deserted street, the pavements black and shiny with rain, and water running in the gutters.

It was a few minutes past six. The little, dingy room was dark and chilly. George had moved the armchair to the window so that he had at least something to look at. It was extraordinary how lonely this room could be. No one seemed to be moving in the house. George supposed that Ella and Mrs. Rhodes were in the basement preparing supper. The other boarders seldom came in before seven o'clock: that was the time when George went out. He had the house, as far as he knew, to himself.

He decided that the results of the afternoon's work had been satisfactory. On the mantelpiece was a packet of names and addresses neatly mounted on card and sorted into "walking order." All good calls.

George was rather pleased that it was raining. It would be nice to have an evening off. He had done well the previous evening, and he was three pounds in hand. If he did no further work that week, he would still be all right. At half-past six, he decided, he would go over to the "King's Arms" and spend the evening in his favourite corner. He liked the atmosphere of the pub. He was quite content to remain there until closing time, watching the lively activity, listening to the snatches of conversation and seeing Gladys cope, astonishingly efficient, with the constant demand for drinks. Perhaps he would be lucky tonight and find someone who would talk to him. He would have his supper there, and when closing time came he would have an early night.

After staring out of the window for several minutes, he became bored with the rain-swept, deserted street, and, leaving his armchair, he crossed the room to his dressing table. Pulling open the bottom drawer, he fumbled beneath his spare shirts and underwear until his hand closed over a cardboard box. He took the box back to the window and sat down, placing the box carefully on his knee.

As he was about to lift the lid of the box, he heard a distinct noise, as if someone were pushing at his door.

An extraordinary expression of guilt and fright crossed his heavy features. Springing quickly to his feet, he thrust the box out of sight under the chair cushion. He stood listening, his head on one side and his eyes half closed. Again the door creaked. Cautiously, noiselessly, he walked to the door and jerked it open. Leo came languidly into the room, glanced up at him with enormous yellow eyes and then leapt up onto the bed.

"Hello, old son," George said, closing the door. "You gave me quite a fright."

He stroked the cat for several minutes. His thick, gentle fingers probed the cat's body, moving caressingly over its head, into the hollow of its shoulder blades, under its chin. The cat remained still, its eyes closed and its sleek body vibrating as it purred.

The room seemed to George to be suddenly cosy now that he was no longer alone. The rain against the window no longer looked depressing. He was grateful to Leo for coming all the way from the basement to see him, and, bending down, he rubbed his face against the cat's long fur.

Leo rolled on his side, stretched, touched his face lightly with his paw, his claws carefully sheathed. When at last he had settled itself on the bed in a big, furry ball, George returned to his chair. He recovered the cardboard box from under the cushion and sat down again. A glance round the room, a glance out into the darkening street and a moment to listen, assured him that he would not be disturbed. Then he opened the box and took from it a heavy Luger pistol. As his hand closed over the long wooden and metal butt, his face lit up. He laid the box on the floor at his side and examined the pistol as if he had never seen it before.

The cat watched him with sleepy, bored eyes.

George's foster father had brought this Luger pistol back from France as a souvenir of the Battle of the Somme. It was in perfect working order, and with it was a box of twenty-five cartridges.

For years George had coveted this pistol. Twice he had been soundly thrashed when caught handling it. But nothing could discourage his desire to own it. As he grew up, the desire increased. As his imagination became more vivid and the roles he selected for himself to play in his mind-fantasies became more violent, so the desire to possess this exciting weapon became more unbearable.

When he heard that his foster father had been knocked down and killed by a speeding car, George had no feeling of shock, nor of loss. He received the news in silence, thinking that now, at last, the pistol would be his.

He vividly remembered the scene: the fat, red-faced police sergeant who was doing his best to break the news as gently as his clumsy tongue could manage, his foster mother's white, frightened face and his own feeling of pending calamity.

"Dead," the police sergeant had said. "Very painful business, Ma'am. Perhaps you'd come to the 'ospital...."

George was fourteen at the time. He knew what death meant. He knew that the man who had acted as his father would never again come into the little dark hall, hang up his hat and coat and call, as he always called, "Anyone in?" He would never again say, looking round the door, a frown on his fat, heavy face, "Put that damn pistol down. How many more times do I have to tell you not to touch it?" It meant that the pistol was now without an owner. His foster mother had never taken any interest in it. She probably would never think of it, never ask for it. So, while the police sergeant was still muttering and mumbling, George had slipped from the room and gone directly to the place where the pistol was concealed. He would never forget the ecstatic surge of emotion that had flowed through him as he carried the cardboard box from his foster father's room to his own. For thirteen years the pistol had remained George's most cherished possession.

Every day he found time to take the pistol from its box. He cleaned it, polished its black metal and removed and replaced its magazine. It gave George an immense feeling of superiority to hold this heavy weapon in his hand. He would imagine with satisfaction how those who had been rude to him during his evening's work would react if they were suddenly confronted with this pistol. He pictured Mr. Eccles' reaction if he had produced the Luger, and the horror and fear that would have come to the big, flat face with its ridiculous blonde moustache.

George's finger curled round the trigger, and his face became grim.

... *"Get a fistful of cloud," George Fraser snarled, ramming his rod into Eccles' back. "We want those names and we're going to have 'em."*

Sydney Brant, white-faced, his eyes wide with alarm, crouched against the wall.

"Don't shoot him, George," he gasped. "For God's sake, be careful with that gun."

"Take it easy, Syd," George Fraser returned with a confident smile. "I've stood enough from this rat." He jabbed Eccles again with the gun. "Come on, are you giving me the names or do I have to ventilate your hide?"

"I'll do anything," Eccles quavered. "Don't shoot—I'll do anything you say."

"Get on with it, then," George Fraser said impatiently, "and if you try to pull a fast one, I'll blast you!"

When the terrified man had left the room, George Fraser wandered to the desk and sat on it, swinging his legs. He winked at Brant, who was gaping at him in open admiration....

George sighed. That was the way to treat swine like Eccles. He fondled the gun. Brant wouldn't be so keen to sneer and jeer if he thought George would stick this suddenly into his ribs. George had no time for cheap tricks. Look at the way Brant had got those names and addresses. Just a cheap trick. If that was the way he was going to cover the territory, Wembley would he useless for another World-Wide salesman to work. Of course, Brant wouldn't care. He was just a selfish, small-minded trickster. So long as he got what he wanted he didn't think of any-one else.

George pulled the magazine from the gun and turned it over absently between his fingers. Still, there was something about Brant. He was more powerful, more domineering than George. George knew that. But George with the Luger was more than a match for anyone, including Brant.

George picked up the oily rag at the bottom of the box and wiped the gun over carefully. Then he picked up the wooden box of cartridges and slid off the lid. The cartridges were packed in rows of five, tight and shiny. He had never put a cartridge into the magazine. He always made a point of keeping the cartridges away from the pistol. Having cleaned the weapon, he would return it to its cardboard box before taking out each cartridge and polishing the brass cases. He had never wished to fire the gun, and the idea of feeding these small, shiny cartridges into the mag-azine alarmed him. He had read so much about gun accidents that he was acutely conscious how easily something tragic might happen. In spite of his violent imagination, he would have been horrified if, through his own carelessness, anyone was hurt.

Time was getting on. It still rained, but rain never bothered George. He put the cartridges back in the box, and carried it to its hiding place among his shirts. Then he went to the cupboard over his washstand and took from it a bottle of milk and an opened tin of sardines.

"Come on, Leo," he called, holding up the tin for the cat to see.

Leo was at his side in a bound, and began twining his great, heavy body round his legs.

George put the tin down on a sheet of newspaper and filled his soap dish with milk.

"There you are, old son," he said, his face softening with pleasure. "Now I'll go out and get my supper."

Out in the street, the rain was cold on his face and the wind beat against him. As he hurried along, he felt the urge to sing or shout for no reason at all except that driving rain and a boisterous wind gave him a feeling of freedom.

The saloon bar of the "King's Arms" was almost deserted. It was early yet—not quite a quarter to seven—and only three of the usual *habitués* had braved the weather. George hung up his hat and mack, and went to his favourite corner.

"Hello," Gladys said, smiling. "'Ere we are again."

"That's right," George said, sitting on a stool and looking at the cold meats, pickles and bowls of salad and beet root with a hungry eye. "Nasty night, isn't it?"

"Wretched," Gladys agreed. "I've got some nice cold pork if you fancy it, or some beef."

George said he thought he'd try the pork.

"That was the bloke with the scar you were talking about, wasn't it?" he asked as she cut him a liberal helping.

"That's 'im," Gladys said darkly. "I was sorry to see you going off with 'im. Mark my words, 'e's a bad 'un. I know a bad 'un when I see 'im."

"He's working for Robinson," George said, feeling that he should excuse himself. "Can't say I like him myself."

"I should think not indeed," Gladys said firmly. "You watch out. A fellow like that could get you into trouble quicker than wink."

"Oh, I don't know about that," George said a little crossly. Did she take him for a child? "I can look after myself all right."

"I'm glad to hear it," Gladys returned, as if she didn't believe him. She set the plate before him, gave him a roll and butter and a pint of mild and bitter, and then hurried off to serve another customer.

George was quite content to keep in his corner, away from the main bar, and eat his supper, read the evening paper and watch Gladys cope with the bustling activity. The bar was filling up now, and the atmosphere became damp and steamy.

No one paid George any attention. Mr. Henry came in and nodded absently to him, but immediately looked away, as if he were nervous that George would wish to join him. Other *habitués* came in. They also nodded to George, but it was a disinterested greeting more from habit than anything else.

His meal finished, George lit a cigarette, pushed his tankard forward so that Gladys, when she had a moment, could see that he wanted it filled, and settled down to the crossword puzzle. The warm, damp atmosphere, the buzz of conversation, the click of billiard balls in the next room, soothed him. It was, he thought, the nicest, most homely atmosphere a man could wish to be in.

At nine-thirty he called for his last pint. One for the road, he told himself. He was pleasantly sleepy, and he looked forward to stretching out in bed. Perhaps Leo would keep him company. Tomorrow still seemed a long way off, and George decided that perhaps, after all, life wasn't so bad.

A hand reached out and touched his arm. George started, and peered at Sydney Brant, at first in blank surprise, then in embarrassed confusion. He felt blood rising to his face, and he nearly upset his beer.

Brant wore no overcoat; his threadbare jacket and worn trousers were black with rain.

"Hello," George said awkwardly. "You gave me quite a start. What are you doing here?"

Brant leaned up against the counter.

"I'm looking for you," he said. "I thought you'd be here."

"Well, you only just caught me," George said lamely. "I—I was just going to bed."

Brant eyed him contemptuously. Then he looked at Gladys and snapped his fingers impatiently.

"A lemonade," he said, and then turned back to George. "What was your racket?" he asked.

George blinked. "Racket? What racket?"

"You said you worked with Frank Kelly. What did you do?"

George's brain crawled with alarm. This would never do, he told himself, flustered. He wasn't going to admit anything to Brant. It was all very well to tell Ella tall stories, but Brant was quite a different kettle of fish.

"That's my business," he said, looking away. "I don't talk about it."

"Don't be wet," Brant said. "I'm in the game myself."

George was startled: he turned and stared into Brant's hard, grey-blue eyes. He flinched away from what he saw in them. "What game?" he repeated.

Brant smiled. "I don't talk about that either," he said. "Do you think I'd mess about touting books unless I had to? Would you?"

George had no idea what he was driving at. He said nothing.

"As soon as it's cooled off I'm going back to my racket," Brant said, and he touched the raw, livid scar, his eyes clouding and his face set in grim lines.

So Gladys was right. He was a wrong 'un, George thought, and, somehow, he felt envious. He knew he shouldn't feel like that, but he had always longed to live dangerously.

For something to say, George blurted out, "That's a nasty scar you've got there. Is it recent?"

An extraordinary change came over Brant's face. It seemed to grow dark and thin. It twisted out of shape so that it was moulded into a mask of terrifying hatred.

He leaned forward and spat on the floor.

"Come on," he said, speaking through stiff white lips. "We're going to see Robinson."

"Not tonight," George returned hastily. "It's raining. Besides, it's too late now. We'll see him tomorrow morning."

With an obvious effort Brant controlled himself. Once more his face became blank and indifferent.

"Do you keep a record of the orders you've taken?" he asked.

"Why, yes," George returned, wondering why he changed the subject so abruptly.

"Got it with you?"

George produced a tattered notebook, and Brant took it from him.

He examined the pages covered with George's neat writing and then he glanced up.

"This the lot? I mean from the time you started?"

George nodded blankly.

"Robinson owes you thirty quid. Do you realize that?"

"As much as that?" George was doubtful. "Well, it can't be helped. I shan't get it from him. He never has any money."

"We'll see about that," Brant said, slipping the notebook into his pocket. He finished his lemonade with a grimace, put a shilling on the counter and turned to the door. "Come on," he went on impatiently.

"It's no good tonight," George protested feebly. As he spoke the bar hand began to call, "Time, gents. Time if you please."

He followed Brant out, avoiding Gladys's eyes. It was dark in the street and rain fell heavily.

"I'm going home," he said, water dripping off his long nose. "We'll see Robo tomorrow."

"Come on," Brant said, jerking his words out as if they burned his mouth. "We're going to see him tonight."

"But I don't know where he lives," George returned. "Let's be sensible. We're both getting soaked."

Brant said an ugly word and walked on.

George went with him. He felt there was nothing else to do. Brant seemed to know where to go. He turned down a side street, lined with small, two-storey houses, and after a few minutes he stopped.

"That's it," he said, looking up at one of the houses. "He's got a room there." He pointed to a window on the top floor. Although the blind was drawn, they could see a light was still burning. "Come on," Brant went on, walking up the worn steps. He put his thumb on the bell and kept it there.

George stood at his side, feeling the rain against his face and his heart pounding uneasily.

There was a shuffling sound beyond the door, and a moment later a fat old woman peered inquisitively at them. "Ood'yer want?" she demanded, holding a dirty dressing gown across her ample bosom. "Ringing the bell like that. You'd think the 'ole blooming 'ouse was afire."

Brant advanced a step, his head thrust forward. "We're friends of Robinson," he said, steadily forcing the old woman back into the dark little hall. "He's waiting for us."

"'Ere, 'alf a mo," the old woman said, trying to block Brant's progress. "I didn't tell yer to come in, did I? You come back termorrer."

Brant kept moving forward, staring down at the old woman, flustering her. "It's all right," he said. "He's expecting us. Don't worry. We'll go up."

George had followed Brant into the hall, and was aware that rain from his hat and coat was making puddles on the coconut matting that covered the floor.

Brant suddenly sidestepped the old woman and began to mount the stairs. She stood watching him, uneasy, unsure of herself. She stared at George, who hunched his great shoulders, unconsciously making himself look sinister and frightening. He went up the stairs behind Brant.

"The old cow," Brant said, under his breath. "Who does she think she is?"

He walked along the short passage to a door under which they could see a light burning. He paused outside the door and put his ear against the panel. He stood there listening, intent, menacing, and George, standing a few feet behind him, suddenly saw him in an unexpected and frightening light. It was as if he could see evil and danger emanating from him like a thought-form. He was aware, too, that the old woman had come halfway up the stairs and was watching Brant with fear and curiosity.

Brant glanced over his shoulder at George, made a grimace, and jerked his head towards the door. George had no idea what he intended to convey. He had no time to ask, for Brant, turning the handle of the door, pushed it open and walked into the room.

Not wanting to be left in the dimly lit passage under the disconcerting gaze of the old woman, George took a few hesitating steps forward, which brought him to the door.

Brant was standing just inside the doorway, looking across the large room at Robinson. George peered past Brant, a sheepish, apologetic expression on his face.

Robinson stood before a dressing table in his trousers and vest. His feet were bare, and the circle of dirt round the ankles embarrassed George, as did the dirty, tattered vest that covered his pigeon chest. He had taken out his false teeth, and his lips were sunk in, giving his mouth an odd, puckered look that reminded George of a dried pippin.

Robinson stood gaping at Brant, terror in his eyes, his blotchy complexion gradually paling as blood drained from his face.

Across the room was a large bed, the head and foot of which were ornamented by brass knobs. A woman lay huddled up in the bed. George could not guess her age. He thought perhaps she was thirty-five to forty. She was big, blowzy and coarse. Her dyed hennaed hair, black at the roots, frizzed round her head like a soiled halo. She wore a pink nightdress which was creased and dirty and through which her great, bulging figure strained to escape.

"Shut the door," Brant said, watching Robinson intently.

Not quite knowing what he was doing, George obeyed. He thrust his trembling hands into his mackintosh pockets and stared down at the worn carpet, fearful of what was going to happen.

The woman in the bed was the first to recover from the shock.

"Who in hell are you?" she demanded in a strident, furious voice. "Get out! Chuck 'em out, Eddie...."

Robinson, still clutching his trousers, backed away from Brant's baleful eyes.

"Have you fellows gone crazy?" he finally mumbled. He looked round with despairing eagerness, picked up his teeth and slipped them between his trembling jaws. He seemed to draw courage from them, and when he spoke again the quaver had gone from his voice. "You can't come in here like this."

Brant thrust his head forward. "We didn't know you had company," he said softly, "but now we're here, George wants to talk to you, don't you, George?"

"If you don't get out," the woman screamed at them, "I'll call the cops!" She slid out of bed, a mass of jiggling flesh, snatched up her dressing gown and wrapped it round her. "Don't stand there like a wet week," she went on to Robinson. "Get 'em out of here."

Robinson tried to pull himself together. "You'll pay for this, you two," he said, working himself into a rage. "I've a mind to sack you on the spot. You must be drunk. Get out, and I'll see you in the morning."

George, wishing the ground would open and swallow him, groped for the door handle, but Brant's voice froze him.

"Talk to him, George. Tell him what we've come for."

Robinson turned to George. He felt that he could cope with him. "So you started this, did you?" he snarled. "I'm surprised at you! You'll be sorry for this, you see if you aren't. You wait until tomorrow."

George opened and shut his mouth, but no sound came.

The woman, afraid of Brant, swung round on George. "If you don't get out, you big, hulking rat, I'll scratch your eyes out!" she shouted at him.

"Tell this tart to lay off," Brant said in a soft, menacing voice to Robinson, "or you'll both be sorry."

The woman swung round on him with a squeal of rage: then she stepped back, her furious, blood-congested face paling. Robinson also took a step back, catching his breath with a sharp, whistling sound.

Brant was holding an odd-looking weapon in his hand. The harsh light of the unshaded overhead lamp made the blade glitter. The sight turned George's stomach.

"You'd better be careful," Brant said, addressing Robinson and the woman. "We don't want a scene, and you don't want me to get rough, do you?"

The woman sank down on the bed, fear and horror on her fat, flabby face. Robinson was so terrified that he looked as if he were going to have some kind of a fit. His face turned yellow-green, and his legs trembled so much that he had to sit on a chair.

George wasn't in much better state. He expected the woman to scream at any minute and for the police to come rushing in.

Brant seemed to know by instinct that George wasn't going to be much use. He dominated the scene.

"You've been cheating Fraser," he said to Robinson. "I've found out how much you should have paid him." He took the notebook from his pocket. "It's all here. You owe him thirty quid. We've come to collect."

Robinson stared stupidly at him. He opened and shut his mouth like a dying fish, but no sound came from him.

"Hurry up!" Brant said impatiently. "I'm wet, and I want to go to bed. You know you've been cheating, so come on and pay up!"

Robinson gulped. "I—I haven't got it," he said in a voice like the scratching of a slate pencil.

Brant suddenly leaned forward. His hand moved so quickly that George only caught a brief flash of the weapon. Then Robinson started back with a faint squeal. A long scratch now ran down his white, blotchy cheek from which a fine line of blood began to well.

The woman opened her mouth to scream, but the sound died in her throat as Brant looked at her.

"You'll get it too," he said softly, and he edged a little towards her. "Come on," he went on to Robinson. "Do you want any more?"

Robinson, blood on his dirty vest and neck, waved his hand in a frantic, despairing gesture to the dressing table.

Brant picked up a wallet that was half hidden under a grimy handkerchief. He counted out twenty-two pounds and held them in hand, looking at Robinson.

"Where's the rest?"

"That's all I've got," Robinson sobbed. "I swear that's all I've got."

Brant put the money in his pocket.

"You're through," he said. "From now on we're working this territory. Do you understand? Get out and stay out. If I see you again I'll fix you."

Listening to his words, George experienced a strange feeling that he was witnessing a scene from one of his own fantasies. Those words were the kind of words George Fraser, millionaire gangster, would have said to Al Capone or Charlie Lucky or any of the big shots. Somehow it took the horror from the situation: he half expected the door to open and Ella to come in with a cup of tea, interrupting this vivid, but surely unreal drama.

Brant was pushing him to the door. "Good night," he was saying. "You might be thinking of telling the cops about us, but I shouldn't if I were you. I don't carry this sticker around with me unless I've a job to do. They won't catch me as easily as that: but I'll come after you."

He stood in the doorway looking at Robinson and the woman, then, jerking his head at George, he walked out of the room.

CHAPTER FIVE

This is ridiculous, George thought, as he followed Brant down the stairs. He can't get away with this. Who does he think he is? He can't steal my thunder in this way and then calmly walk off as if, nothing had happened.

George had enacted the kind of interview they had just had so many times in his mind that Brant's flagrant trespassing on his preserves angered and humiliated him. Of course, he hadn't been particularly bright at the interview. He had to admit that. He had been scared of Robinson and the woman, but that was only because he had felt defenceless. How was he to know that Brant would produce a razor and commit violence? If he had known, he would have brought his gun. Then it would have been quite a different story. With the Luger in his hand, he would not only have dominated Robinson and that ghastly slut of a woman, but he would have also dominated Brant. What an opportunity to have missed! All because Brant hadn't taken him into his confidence. A sullen anger began to rise in him against Brant. It was like Brant to horn in, to push him aside and take all the credit.

Out in the darkness and the rain, George grabbed hold of Brant and jerked him round.

Anger and disappointment and a feeling of shame gave him courage.

"What are you playing at?" he asked roughly. "Why didn't you tell me what you were going to do? I could have handled it. I know how to handle a job like that—without messing or cutting people."

Brant stared at him: his gaunt, cold face startled. "What are you talking about?" he demanded, shaking off George's hand. "A fat lot of good you were...."

"So that's what you think?" George said furiously. "Well, it was your fault. I didn't want to go. I told you. If I had known what you were up to, it would have been different."

"How different?" Brant asked. "I've got the money and I've kicked him out of our territory. We're free to do what we like now. What more could you have done?"

George was a little taken aback, but he was so envious and angry that he blurted out, "It would have been different if I'd brought my gun."

"Gun?" Brant repeated. "What gun?"

George had never told anyone about the Luger. It was not the kind of thing you did tell anyone about. He had no licence for it. If the police heard about it, there would be trouble. They would most likely take it from him.

But he told Brant. There was nothing else he could do. It was either that, or loss of face.

"What do you think?" he said gruffly. "I've had a gun for years. Brought it back from the States; only it's not a thing I talk about. The police don't stand for that kind of thing."

"A gun," Brant said, making it sound tremendously important. "So you've got a gun?"

"Had it for years," George repeated, uneasy, yet pleased with the impression he had made. "It saves a lot of talking. I'm not much of a one to talk. I don't need to talk with a gun."

"I didn't know," Brant said, and his hardness and confidence somehow didn't seem to matter any more to George.

"I don't mess around with razors," George went on, his voice sounding strange even to him. "That's small-time stuff."

"You can't get guns here," Brant said mildly, almost apologetically. "But we scared the rat, didn't we?"

"We scared him all right," George returned, losing his ill-temper now that Brant was acknowledging his share in Robinson's defeat. "I'll never forget his face when you produced that sticker," he went on, feeling a generosity that compelled him to give the lion's share of the exploit to Brant.

"Pity you didn't bring the gun," Brant said, equally generous. "He'd 've had a heart attack."

George sniggered. Brant, he decided, wasn't such a bad sort after all. "I'll fix him if he tries anything funny," he went on grandly. "What with my gun and your sticker, we've got him where we want him."

"You're a pretty good shot, I suppose?" Brant said, his head down and his yellow hair plastered flat by the rain.

"Me?" George laughed, delighted with Brant's interest. "I was considered to be fair enough. I could split a playing-card edge on at twenty-five yards. Bit out of practice now, of course."

"That's good, isn't it?" Brant said, hunching his shoulders. "I bet you've bumped off a few guys in your day."

George opened his mouth, saw the trap just in time, and walked on without speaking. It would be stimulating to brag that he had been a killer, but not to Brant. It was safe enough to tell Ella. She wouldn't talk, but Brant might.

"What's it like, killing a guy?" Brant asked, after a moment's pause.

"That's something I don't talk about," George retuned, shortly.

Brant glanced at him. "Kelly killed a lot of men, didn't he?"

That was safer ground. "A good few," George said, shrugging his big shoulders carelessly. "It was us or them in those days."

"But you didn't, eh?"

Again George resisted the temptation. "That's something I keep to myself," he said, and after a moment's hesitation, he added gruffly, "Lay off, will you?"

"That's all right," Brant said quickly. "I guess that's something no one would talk about."

"Now you're smart," George returned, surprised at his own audacity.

At the street corner they paused.

"Well, you better take your money," Brant said. There was a note of reluctance in his voice, but he held out the crumpled roll of notes willingly enough.

George hesitated; at the back of his mind, although he was loath to admit it, he knew he would not have had the nerve to have taken the money. He knew that Brant expected him to share it with him, and after a mental tussle, he took the notes, hurriedly counted ten from the roll, and offered them to Brant.

"Here," he said, his face hot with embarrassment, "we'll share on this. After all, you helped get them."

"Fair enough," Brant said, and took the notes, putting them in his pocket.

George was rather taken aback by this cool acceptance of what was rightly his.

"Well, I'll be getting off," Brant said, before George could recover. "I don't think we'll have any further trouble with Robinson. We'll work the territory and send the orders direct to the Company. If Robinson starts trouble—well, we'll introduce him to your gun."

George nodded. "That's the idea," he said eagerly. "I'll put the wind up him all right."

Before Brant went, he put his hand on George's arm and actually smiled at him. "You're all right, George," he said, pinching George's massive muscles. "You're going to go places."

It took George some time before he could settle to sleep that night. Even the regular, soothing sound of Leo's purring failed to lull him. He felt that Brant no longer regarded him with contempt. He felt somehow that he had impressed Brant—a difficult, almost impossible person to impress. It was risky, of course, to have told Brant about the gun, but he just could not have let him get away with his homemade sticker.

George spent a long time reconstructing the scene with Robinson, only this time it was he who played the leading part. It was he who intimidated Robinson and made him hand over the money, and it was Brant who stood speechless, his grey-blue eyes alight with admiration.

The next evening George met Brant in a pub opposite Wembley underground station. It was quite startling how Brant's attitude towards George had changed. He now seemed to regard George as the leader, and although he still had the same cold, bored expression in his eyes, and the thin hardness about his mouth, he was diffident, almost ingratiating, in his manner. To George's relief, the gun was not mentioned.

"We'd better get to work," George remarked, after calling for a second pint. "Have another lemonade while I explain things to you."

Brant shook his head. "Not for me," he said, "but don't let that stop you."

"We can manage without Robo all right," George went on, after he had taken a pull from his tankard. "I had a word with Head Office. I told them we preferred to work together, and Robo was willing. They don't care one way or the other so long as they get the orders." He lit a cigarette, and for a moment enjoyed the feeling that he was now the head salesman, instructing a novice. "The first thing you have to do when you're canvassing is to get into the house. It's easy once you know how.

For instance, if you knock on the door and say 'Is Mr. Jones at home?' the old girl is bound to ask 'Who is it?' If he isn't in, then you have to tell her the whole story, and the old man is tipped off when he does come home. That means he's ready for you when next you call. Don't forget the surprise visit gets the business." George took another pull from his tankard, and then went on, "If, on the other hand, you knock on the door, and when the old girl comes you raise your hat and begin to move away, and at the same time you say, "I suppose Mr. Jones is not in?' then she'll answer nine times out of ten, 'No, he isn't.' You then say, 'I'll look in some other time,' and by that time you're halfway to the gate without telling her what you want."

Brant shifted restlessly. "I don't know if all that's so important," he said.

"But it is," George returned. "You try it and see. Robinson worked out all the angles, and they're worth studying. Now, if the old man is at home, your question, 'I suppose Mr. Jones isn't in?' gets the answer, 'Oh yes, he is,' and as like as not she starts yelling for him. When he turns up, you'll find he'll lean against the doorpost, blocking your entrance and ask what you want. You mustn't tell him until you're inside the house."

Brant had a far-away look in his eyes. He seemed hardly aware of George's droning voice at his elbow.

"You must get inside before you start your sale, so you say, 'I've come to talk to you about Johnny's education.' That usually gets you in," George went on. "If he still won't ask you in, you put it to him straight. 'I wonder if I might come in? I can't very well talk to you on the doorstep.' "

"You've certainly got it wrapped up haven't you?" Brant said. "Well, let's see it work. Come on, I'm sick of this pub."

George consulted his packet of names and addresses. "All right," he said. "Let's try Mr. Thomas. He's got two kids: Tommy and Jean. It's important to know the children's names. The old man thinks you're a school inspector if you mention the kids by name, and you're inside before he finds out you're not."

They walked along the wide arterial road, housed on either side by box-like Council dwellings. They were an odd-looking couple, and the women standing in the doorways, the men in their gardens and the children playing in the road, stared curiously at them.

"Here we are," George said, uneasy under the battery of inquisitive eyes. He paused outside a drab little house, pushed open the wooden gate, and together they walked up the path.

George rapped on the door. There was a rush of feet and the door jerked open. Two small children, a boy and a girl, stared up at them with intent, wondering eyes.

"Is your father in?" George asked, smiling down at them,

They did not move nor speak, but continued to gape at them.

Brant said, "Get someone, can't you? Don't stand there gaping at me." His voice snapped viciously, and the two children immediately turned and ran back down the passage.

"Ma ... Ma ... there're two men ..."

George and Brant exchanged glances.

"It's always the same," George said. "Damn kids ..."

A middle-aged, slatternly-looking woman came down the passage, drying her pink, soap-softened hands on a dirty towel. "'Oo is it?" she asked, eyeing them suspiciously.

"I suppose Mr. Thomas isn't in?" George asked, raising his hat and edging slowly away from the door.

"'E's in the garden." She raised her voice and shouted "Bert ... 'ere . . . come 'ere ..."

"That's all right," George said hastily. "We'll go round," and before the woman could protest, he left her and walked round to the back garden.

Mr. Thomas was resting after a bout of digging. He stood in the middle of a patch of newly turned ground, his cap at the back of his head, the spade thrust into the soil and the glow of sweat and health on his large, simple face.

He blinked when he saw George and Brant, and paused as he was about to light his pipe, uncertain, uneasy.

"Good evening, Mr. Thomas," George said, approaching with a cheerful smile and a wave of his hand. "Getting ready for planting, eh? That soil looks good. By Jove! I envy you this garden."

"'Evening," Mr. Thomas grunted, and took off his cap to scratch his head.

"I wonder if you can spare us a moment?" George went on. "We've come to have a little chat about Jean and Tommy. I hear they're doing very well at school."

Mr. Thomas brightened; embarrassed suspicion left his face. "From the school, are yer?" he said. He looked round the small garden a little helplessly, and then, raising his voice, he bawled, "'Ere, Emmie! Come 'ere, can't yer?"

Mrs. Thomas and the two children joined them.

"These two gents are from the school," Mr. Thomas said, wiping his hands on the seat of his trousers. He glared at the children. "Wot 'ave you two bin up to?"

"Oh, it's nothing like that," George put in hastily as the two children looked sheepish. "Your kiddies are a credit to you both. They're doing so well at school I thought you might consider helping them to do even better."

Mr. Thomas looked blankly at his wife. "I dunno about that ..." he began, and, getting no support from his wife, he lapsed into silence.

"Perhaps we could go inside for a moment?" George asked, moving towards the house. "I won't keep you long, but it's easier to talk inside than in the garden, isn't it?"

Rather reluctantly, Mr. Thomas led the way into the squalid little house. They all crowded into the small front parlour. Mr. Thomas dusted two chairs with his cap and pushed them forward, warned his children that if they didn't sit quiet he'd knock their blocks off, and sat down himself. Mrs. Thomas stood by the window.

George glanced round the room and cleared his throat. He was not nervous. He knew what he was going to do, he had an interested audience, and the result of what he had to say was his bread and butter. More important still, he wished to impress Brant with his salesmanship.

"Before I come to the point," he began, taking up his position behind the chair and grasping the back of it firmly in both hands, "let me put to you both a very important question. You will both agree with me that education today is the most vital factor in the life of any child?"

Mr. Thomas and his wife emphatically agreed that this was so, and Mr. Thomas began a rambling account of the lack of education in his time.

George hurriedly interrupted. "Fortunately, Mr. Thomas, times have changed. Now, education is so important you can't leave all the work to the school teachers. Many a time your kiddies have asked you questions which you're unable to answer. There're thousands of such questions, and they are very difficult to answer. I've had a lot to do with children, and I know how worrying it is not to be able to satisfy their craving for knowledge."

"That's right," Mr. Thomas returned, nodding his head. "Fair terrors these imps are. Always asking questions...."

"And what questions!" George went on, beaming at, the children. "I don't have to remind you of all the conundrums, do I? You know only too well. All the same, these questions should be answered."

Mr. Thomas nodded again. He had no idea what all this was about, but he felt that George did appreciate their difficulties and was trying to be helpful.

"Very well, then," George said, getting into his stride. "Children are thirsting for knowledge. Teachers haven't the time to explain everything children want to know. Parents haven't the knowledge. So what happens?" He leaned forward, suddenly looking stern. "Your children, Mr. Thomas, are being mentally starved. Make no mistake about that! You would be ashamed to starve their bodies, yet you are openly starving their minds. Knowledge is to the mind what food is to the body."

Mr. Thomas began to have doubts about George's good intentions. He scratched his head and glanced at his wife for support.

George paused until there was a long, awkward silence, and then he flashed on his old heartiness again. "Now, don't let that disturb you," he went on, beaming round on them. "I'm here to put all that right. I have a wonderful work that'll be the silent teacher in your home."

From his hidden poacher's pocket, he produced the specimen of the *Child's Self-Educator*.

"Let me show you."

He laid the book on the table. Mr. and Mrs. Thomas and the two children crowded round him. He began to turn the pages slowly, making a comment for every page.

"Look at these magnificent pictures. Here, children can slip over to Africa and roam about the jungle in perfect safety. They can see the wild animals, study their habits and learn how they live. The King of Beasts. Isn't that a wonderful picture? Look, Tommy, look at the tiny cubs. They're like ordinary kittens, aren't they? But they'd scratch if you met them in the jungle." He glanced at Mr. Thomas. "See how interested the boy is? Every page has been planned to attract children to look further. It's scientific teaching of the highest possible standard." He turned another page. "Now, what have we here? The story of the wireless, and more interesting still, how to construct many various kinds of sets. I'm sure you, Mr. Thomas, would be interested in this section. Have you ever thought of making your own wireless? These instructions are simple, and you don't have to have any previous knowledge." He made sure that Mr. Thomas was looking at the coloured plates a little wistfully before turning on to another section. "Here's something that's useful to everyone in the home: the Medical section. Your kiddie might scald himself— so many kiddies do—turn to page 155 and you learn how to deal with such an emergency. Your own doctor in your own home! Isn't that something worth having? No waiting, no bills, easy reference—possibly a life saved!" He noted the slow-rising interest, but decided that neither Mr. nor Mrs. Thomas was as yet quite convinced, so he turned on, delighted with the sound of his own voice, pleased with the set, worn phrases which now automatically came to his lips without the need of thought. "Tommy perhaps has to write an essay on ships: here it is, all ready for him. Tommy will soon be at the top of his class. Jean has a problem in arithmetic: she finds her answer here. You, Mr. Thomas, want to know what will best grow in your garden: here is the whole thing ready for you in the Gardening section. A few nights' reading and Mr. Thomas' garden is the envy of all his neighbours. Mrs. Thomas, although you're no doubt an excellent cook, you can get new ideas from the Cookery section." He stepped back and thumped his large fist on the back of the chair. "It's a great work! A work for every one of you. You will agree with me, I am sure, that it'd be useful to have a set of these magnificent books in your home? Can't you see how they'd help your kiddies get on and assure a sound future for them?"

Mrs. Thomas stared at her husband, her eyes bright. "Ain't that a wonderful turnout, Bert?" she said. "I've never seen anything like it. What say, shall we 'ave 'em?"

"Yes, dad," the children chimed in, "let's 'ave 'em. Coo, dad, look at all them pictures...."

"You shut up," Mr. Thomas growled. He scratched his head and fingered the specimen thoughtfully. "I'm not saying they ain't all right, but this sort of thing costs money...."

"Now let me explain about that," George said, with an expansive smile. "The *Child's Self-Educator* is in four handsome volumes. Although we're making every effort to put this work in all homes at cost price, it still needs a little effort on your part to secure it. Good things don't just fall from Heaven. I wish they did, but they don't. You have to make a small sacrifice for them." He shook his head solemnly. Then, lowering his voice, he said impressively, "It's going to cost you tuppence a day."

"Tuppence a day?" Mr. Thomas repeated blankly. "Wot yer mean?"

"Just that," George replied, knowing that he had reached the crucial part of the sale and moving with caution. "Consider what tuppence a day means. A shilling odd a week for your children's future success. Surely that isn't asking too much? We don't collect the money daily or weekly, of course, but monthly: five shillings a month.

"The whole work costs seven pounds, ten shillings. We're not asking you for that amount, we're asking for five shillings a month. The way to look at it is that you're going to pay tuppence a day to help your children and yourselves."

"Seven pahns ten!" Mr. Thomas gasped. "Not bloody likely! Not for me, chum. No, I can't afford that." He picked up the specimen and handed it to George. "Thank yer for calling, mister, but it ain't no good."

The two children immediately began an uproar, and Mrs. Thomas had to drive them from the room. The small house echoed with their disappointed yells, and George became slightly flustered.

"Now, one moment. Mr. Thomas," he began hurriedly, realizing that he had struck the worst kind of prospect—the man who can't afford it. "You've agreed the books are good and ..."

"The books're orl right, but the price ain't," Mr. Thomas said, a stubborn light in his eyes. "It's no use arguing. I can't afford it, so that's that."

George stared at him helplessly, aware that Brant was watching him with a sneering grin.

"Of course you can afford it," George said warmly. "You mean you can't afford to be without it. Tuppence a day! Why, anyone can afford *that*."

"Well, *I* can't, and I don't want a lot of talk," Mr. Thomas said irritably. "I've got to get back to my garden."

"Just a moment," Brant said quietly. "I can *prove* you can afford to pay tuppence a day for these books."

Both Mr. Thomas and George turned and stared at him. He was eyeing them with a hard, calculating expression in his eyes. Before they could speak he went on, "You're a sporting man, Mr. Thomas. I bet you half a dollar you can afford to pay tuppence a day. If I prove to your satisfaction that you wouldn't miss this small sum, will you buy the books?"

"You can't prove it," Mr. Thomas said, beginning to grin.

"In that case, you'll get the half-dollar," Brant said, putting a half a crown on the table. "Fair enough, isn't it?"

Mr. Thomas hesitated, then nodded his head. "Okay, cocky, prove it."

Brant produced a soiled ten-shilling note. "I'll have another bet with you," he said, his lips curling into a smile, but his eyes like granite. "I bet you don't know how much money you have in your trousers' pocket."

Mr. Thomas blinked at him. "Wot's that got ter do with it?"

"If you can tell me to the exact penny how much you have in your pocket, I'll give you this ten bob."

"I can do that orl right," Mr. Thomas returned, automatically moving his hands to his pockets.

"No ... don't do that. Tell me, without looking, exactly how much you have."

Mr. Thomas scratched his head, suddenly embarrassed. "Well," he said slowly, "I reckon I've got four bob."

Brant leaned forward. "To the exact penny, Mr. Thomas. What is it? Four and three or three and ten? Tell me the exact amount and the ten bob's yours."

Mr. Thomas scowled. "I dunno," he admitted. "Not to the exact penny.

But wot's all this got to do with it?"

"All right," Brant said briskly, putting his ten-shilling note away. "You don't know how much you have in your pocket, do you? So if I put tuppence into your pocket without you knowing it, you wouldn't know you were tuppence to the good? In the same way, if I took tuppence out of your pocket, you wouldn't miss it. It therefore follows that you can afford to pay tuppence a day for these very valuable books."

Mr. Thomas gaped for a moment, and then a wide grin spread over his face. "That's smart," he said, admiringly. "I never thought of it that way. Orl right, give us the order form. I'll sign it." George watched the signing of the order form with mixed feelings. He was angry that Brant had interfered with his sale. He was humiliated that Brant should have come to his rescue so successfully when *he* should have been the one to have shown Brant the dodges. Again it crept into his mind that Brant's success had been a cheap trick. Of course it was a cheap trick. A confidence trick!

But Brant seemed oblivious to George. He took the order form from Mr. Thomas, examined it carefully, smiled and folded it. Without looking at George, he put the form casually into his pocket.

There was an awkward pause. George felt blood rising to his face, but this was no time to protest. They both shook hands with Mr. Thomas, had a word to say to Mrs. Thomas and then walked down the path in silence.

Once out in the road, away from the house, George said, "Look here, old boy, that's my order, you know. I did all the selling, and besides, it was one of my addresses."

Brant smiled, "Don't be a fool," he said, bored and cold, his hard eyes on George's face. "You'd never've landed it: not in a hundred years. What do you think I am—a sucker?" He glanced up and down the road. "Well, I can manage now. I see how it's done. If you ask me, it's a mug's game. All that talking for thirty bob." He shrugged indifferently. "I'm not going to waste my time on this job for long."

George shifted his feet; a tiny spark of anger flared up and then went out. "I think we might split it, old boy," he said a little feebly.

"I thought you didn't go in for small-time stuff," Brant returned, jeering at him. "I got you twenty-two quid last night, and now you're haggling over fifteen bob." He began to move away. "I'll be seeing you. While we're on the ground, we may as well do some work. So long, George."

"But wait a minute ..." George began.

Brant shoved his hands deep into his pockets. "So long," he repeated, and slouched away, his head down, the long straw-colour lock of hair falling forward, hiding his scar.

CHAPTER SIX

It was Saturday afternoon, and George was alone in his room, alone also in the big, dingy house. The other boarders had gone away for the weekend. George had watched them go from his window. They looked, he thought, a little odd and somehow theatrical out of their drab City clothes: the plus fours, the flannel suits, the summer frocks gave them a festive air, not in keeping with George's depressed mood. Ella also had gone off immediately after lunch. It was her half-day, and George, peering round the curtain, had watched her hurry to the 'bus stop. A half an hour or so later Mr. and Mrs. Rhodes had strolled towards the local cinema. He was now alone in the house, which seemed still and oppressive to him.

Saturday afternoon depressed George: he had nothing to do, nowhere to go, and he usually sat in his armchair by the window with a book and Leo for company.

George found himself this afternoon more restless than usual. His book did not interest him, and he felt the loneliness of the big house weighing down on him. He had Brant on his mind, too. Brant, in two days, had become a star salesman. He had obtained six orders for the *Child's Self-Educator*: nine pounds in his first week! George had only managed to scrape up two orders that week, and he was vaguely resentful of Brant's success. He was sure that Brant was using a series of cheap tricks to obtain his orders. George tried to convince himself that he would rather not get an order unless the sale was a fair one, but he could not help envying Brant's success—tricks or no tricks.

George found the "King's Arms" lonely without Robinson for company. Brant seldom came to the pub. Although he was still friendly—if you could call his odd, cold manner friendly—he kept to himself, and George saw him to talk to only when they journeyed out to Wembley together. Even then Brant scarcely said a word.

George put his book down. He stared across at Leo, who blinked, stretched lazily and ducked his head at him.

It was strange how an animal could take the edge off loneliness, George thought. Without Leo, he would have gone out and wandered aimlessly about the streets.

He got up and crossed to the bed. For some minutes he stroked the cat's fur and talked to it, pleased with its ecstatic response. He rolled it gently onto its back, and the cat, its eyes half closed, encircled his hand with its front paws, its claws carefully sheathed. While he fondled Leo, George brooded about their relations. Leo was important to him: how empty his life would be without the cat! It came as a revelation that he was entirely alone, that no one bothered with him, and he had no friend he could trust. A wave of lonely emotion swept through him, and his eyes watered. He didn't care, he told himself, picking Leo up and holding the cat in his arms, its face against his face, its whiskers tickling his nose. He could get on all right alone so long as he kept his health and had Leo for company. All the same, it was a pretty dreary outlook. As he was beginning to pity himself, he heard the telephone ringing downstairs. The bell startled him. Somehow, it sounded creepy, coming up from the deserted basement. He put Leo down and went to the door. It wasn't much use going all the way downstairs. By the time he was down the bell would have stopped ringing. He opened his door and glanced along the dimly-lit passage. The bell was ringing insistently—a muffled, nagging note that disturbed him.

He shrugged his shoulders uneasily. Let it ring, he decided. It was certainly not for him. No one had ever bothered to ask for his telephone number. It was probably for one of the boarders, or for Mr. Rhodes. But he could not bring himself to shut the door. He had a guilty feeling that he ought to answer the telephone and see who was calling. Then, as he had almost made up his mind to go down, the bell ceased to ring.

He closed the door and went back to his armchair, but a moment later he was on his feet once more as the bell began to ring again.

This time he did not hesitate; he lumbered out of the room, along the passage and down the stairs. It seemed a long way down, and the bell nagged him. He descended the basement stairs with a rush, snatched up the receiver and said "Hello?" in a breathless voice.

"You've taken your time, haven't you?" a flat, metallic voice said in his ear.

"Who's that? Who do you want?"

"It's Brant," the voice said impatiently, as if he ought to have known. "I thought you'd be in. Look, George, I want you to do me a favour."

"Brant? Why, hello.... I didn't expect you...."

"Never mind that. Have you anything to do this afternoon?"

"Me?" Of course George had nothing to do. He never had on Saturday afternoons; but how did Brant know? Anyway, he wasn't going to admit it: at the same time, he didn't intend to miss anything. He spoke with caution. "Well, I don't know. I was reading...."

"You can read any time, can't you?" Brant's voice jeered at him. "I wouldn't ask you, only it's important. I want someone to go to Joe's and leave a message."

"Joe's?"

"It's a club in Mortimer Street, not far from you. They're not on the blower, otherwise I'd 've rung 'em."

"Mortimer Street—that's near Paddington Station, isn't it?"

Brant grunted. "I've taken the key of my flat by mistake, and I'll be back late. It's my sister. She doesn't know, and she won't able to get in. Will you leave a message for her at Joe's?"

"I didn't know you had a sister."

There was a moment's silence, then Brant said, "Well, I have. We share a flat, see? I should've left the key under the mat. She'll have to amuse herself as best she can until I get back. But I want her to know, otherwise she'll kick the door down. Will you do it, George? Just tell the barman I've taken the key and won't be back until after two. He'll tell Cora."

George thought for a moment. He felt a rising excitement. Why, if you like ... I'll tell her myself. I mean I'll wait for her and tell her."

"You don't have to do that. I don't know when she'll go to Joe's. All I know is she'll be there some time tonight." George had no idea why he should feel so excited and elated. Brant's sister! Not five minutes ago he didn't know that Brant had a sister, and now he was getting het-up about her, as if she were someone exciting, someone who'd be interested in him. It was extraordinary.

"Of course, I'll do it," he said. "You leave it to me, old boy. I'll tell 'em. You don't think I ought to wait and explain it to her myself? They might forget to tell her ..."

"They'll tell her," Brant said, his voice a ghostly murmur in George's ear. "You don't have to worry about that."

"All right," George said happily. "You leave it to me. You won't be back until after two, is that it?"

"Something like that. Well, thanks. If you do see her ... she's dark, doesn't wear a hat and has a red bone bangle. You can't mistake her. The bangle's about three inches wide."

"Well, maybe I will see her...."

A faint, sneering laugh came over the wire.

"What was that?" George asked, not believing that Brant had laughed.

"Nothing. I've got to get off. So long, George."

"Good-bye," George said, and the line went dead.

George ran up the three flights of stairs to his bedroom. His violent entrance startled Leo, who sat up with pricked ears and wide eyes. George didn't even notice the cat. He stood before the long mirror, and saw, not without satisfaction, that his face was flushed and his eyes bright. This was going to be exciting, he told himself. Organized properly, he would be able to extend the excitement until bedtime. He glanced at his watch. It was still early: a few minutes to three. He must make himself smart. Perhaps a shave. He ran his fingers over his chin. Yes, he could do with a shave. Then a clean shirt, his best suit.

He took a towel and shaving outfit to the bathroom. The geyser lit with a little plop, and while he waited for the water to heat up he stood looking out of the window, across the grey roofs and, beyond, at the blue sky and the sunshine.

Cora! An exciting name. She wouldn't be like Brant. He was sure of that. She was dark, didn't wear a hat and had a red bone bangle: an exciting description! George took off his collar and tie, and filled the basin with hot water. He would spot her all right, he assured himself. Even if he didn't speak to her, it would be interesting to look at her. But, of course, he was going to speak to her. Alone in the steamy little bathroom, George felt very confident. He forgot that he was shy with women. Somehow, Brant's sister would be different. He was quite sure of that. It was odd how stupid he had been about women in the past. He stared at himself in the mirror. There was no sense in working himself into a fright because of what had happened years ago. He had been fifteen then, and big for his age. That always seemed to be the trouble. He was always too big for his age. Schoolmasters expected too much from him. During the war, when he was fourteen, people expected him to be in the army. Even at fifteen he had been backward and, of course, innocent. He had been in the park by himself when the woman began talking to him. She was an impressive-looking woman, rich, well dressed, refined. She said she was lonely, and George had felt sorry for her. He was lonely himself. They stood talking beside the duck pond; at least, she did the talking, while George listened politely. He was really more interested in watching the herons; but she was lonely, so he listened. She talked about people being nice to each other, about being lonely and what a fine, strong fellow he was. It was talk that George could understand. So when she suggested he might come to her house because it was chilly standing by the pond, he was flattered, and he did not see anything wrong in going with her.

He thought it odd that she should take him straight up to her bedroom. He had never seen such a beautiful room. But before he could appreciate it, the refined lady seemed to take leave of her senses. George never quite knew how he got out of the house. It was like a nightmare, and he dreamed for many years about running down long passages and opening and shutting many doors with someone screaming names after him as he ran.

That experience kept cropping up at the back of his mind when he had anything to do with women. He never quite got over it. It made him shy and suspicious of women. Of course, sometimes he needed a woman, but his need was not as strong as his nervousness, so he never did anything about it. Once or twice, when he had been a little tight, he had ventured as far as Maddox Street. But the waiting women he found there seemed so unlike any other women he had seen that he had abruptly turned back and caught a bus home.

Now, in the solitude of the bathroom, he only felt the excitement and not the fright that women raised in him.

It was after four o'clock before he left the house. In high spirits he walked briskly down the street. It was a grand afternoon, and he found a secret pleasure in mingling with the crowds moving along the Edgware Road. He was now one of the crowd; he had somewhere to go, someone to meet. It gave him a feeling of security and confidence. He must do this more often, he told himself. It was absurd to bury himself away in his bedroom as he had been doing.

Mortimer Street consisted of a row of small shops, three or four hawkers' barrows and a public house. George had to walk the length of the street before he discovered "Joe's Club". It was over a second-hand bookshop. The open door revealed a flight of uncarpeted stairs that rose steeply into darkness, and through the doorway came the smell of stale scent, spirits and tobacco smoke.

He hesitated for several minutes before climbing the stairs. Finally he went up, his hand on the rickety banister, his feet treading cautiously, the stairs creaking under his weight.

There was a dimly lit passage at the top of the stairs, and at the end of the passage there was a door on which was a dirty card with "Joe's Club" printed in uneven, illiterate letters.

George turned the doorknob and pushed open the door. He found himself in a long, narrow room, which, he guessed, must stretch the width of the two shops below. At the far end of the room was a bar. Rows of bottles stood on shelves within reach of the bartender's hands. All round the room stood tables on which chairs were stacked, their legs pointing to the dirty, grey-white ceiling. Opposite the bar, at the other end of the room, was a dais containing a piano, three battered music stands and a drummer's outfit. The walls of the room were covered with large reproductions of nudes from *La Vie Parisienne* and *Esquire*. A public telephone box stood just inside the door.

"The joint's closed," a man's voice said at his elbow.

George jumped. He looked round, took a step back and stared at the little man who had come silently into the room. His flat, broad face was unpleasant; his complexion was shiny white, the texture of a slug's body. Reddish hair like steel wool grew far back on his head and gave him a great deal of domed white forehead. His small, bitter, green eyes probed at George inquisitively.

"Besides, you're not a member," the little man went on. His voice seemed to come from the back of his throat, like that of a ventriloquist. His bloodless lips hung open, but did not move as he spoke.

"Yes," George said. "I know." He fingered his tie uneasily. "I really came to leave a message...."

"Why should I bother with messages?" the little man asked curtly. "Do you think I've got nothing better to do?"

That settled it, George thought, delighted. He would have to wait for Brant's sister. You couldn't rely on this nasty little specimen to pass on any message.

"All right," he said, shrugging. "Perhaps you can tell me when Miss Brant will be here? I'll tell her myself."

"Who?" asked the little man. "Miss Brant? Never 'eard of 'er

"Never mind," George said firmly. "It doesn't matter. I'll come back later."

The green eyes probed his face.

"Do you mean Cora?"

George was startled. "Yes," he said. "Miss Cora Brant." A sly, sneering smile came into his green eyes.

"Gawd Almighty! We're putting on side, ain't we?" the little man said. "Okay, palsy, leave your message. I'll take care of it."

George's growing dislike for the little man suddenly turned to suspicion. He looked a real bad lot: a shady character, a gangster. He could have been anything—a racing tout with a razor, a pimp with a knife.

Abruptly he turned to the door. "I'll see her," he said shortly. "Don't you bother."

He went downstairs. The little man watched him all the way down. As he reached the street door, the little man called after him, "Now wait. Don't be so 'asty," but George did not stop. He walked rapidly away, his face hot and red.

At the end of the street he paused and tried to make up his mind what he was to do. Obviously the club wouldn't open until the evening. But what time in the evening? He'd have to find that out. He crossed the road and entered a shabby little tobacconist's. He bought a packet of Player's, and as he was waiting for his change he asked, "When does "Joe's Club" open?"

The old woman who had served him shook her head. "You want to keep away from that place," she said. "No good's ever come out of it."

George opened the packet of cigarettes and lit one. "Oh?" he said, feeling a stab of excitement. "What do you know about it?"

"Enough," the old woman answered shortly, and put the odd coppers on the counter.

George lowered his voice. "I'm interested," he said. "Perhaps you can help me."

"A den of thieves," the old woman said, her thin, yellow face creasing in disgust. "The police ought to 'ave closed it down long ago. I wish I was the mother of some of those little sluts 'oo go there: I'd warm their backsides for 'em!"

"I'm supposed to meet someone there," George said, looking at her a little helplessly. "I don't want to get mixed up in anything. Who's the little bloke with the red hair?"

"You'll get mixed up all right," the old woman said contemptuously. "You keep away from that 'ole."

"Thanks for the tip," George returned, smiling at her. "But who is the little bloke with the red hair?"

"That's Little Ernie; everyone knows 'im and his women."

"What time does the club open?" George asked again.

"Seven, and take my advice, keep clear of the place. They might take you for a copper, like I nearly did." The old woman smiled secretly. "It ain't healthy being taken for a copper in "Joe's Club"."

George raised his hat and went out into the sunshine. Dark with a red bone bangle; a den of thieves; Little Ernie and his women. What a wonderful Saturday afternoon!

He caught a bus at the corner of the street and travelled to Hyde Park. There he lost himself in the crowds, listening to the speakers, walking along the Serpentine, sitting on the grass. He didn't mind waiting, because the evening was so full of promise. This was the world that fascinated him: the world he had read about and dreamed about.

At half-past six he walked back to Mortimer Street. It had a forlorn, deserted appearance now that the hawkers' barrows had gone and the shops were shut. He went into the public-house which was opposite "Joe's Club" and ordered a pint of bitter. He took his glass to the window, where he could see the club entrance. From the window he had an uninterrupted view of the street. He lit a cigarette and waited.

It was a long wait, but he did not mind. The street was full of interest. After seven o'clock a couple of stout, flashily dressed Jews came along, paused outside the Club, talked for a minute or so and then entered. Almost immediately a blonde woman wearing fox furs came down the street with a coarse, elderly man who was talking excitedly, gesticulating with his hands, an ugly look of rage on his badly shaven face. The woman walked along indifferently. She swayed her hips, and George recognised her for what she was. They, too, disappeared up the stairs to "Joe's Club". A little later three young girls—the eldest could not have been more than seventeen—all blonde, all wearing cheap, tight little frocks, all talking in high-pitched, nasal voices, disappeared, giggling and yapping, through the shabby doorway.

George ordered another pint and continued to watch. From what he had seen, "Joe's Club" seemed to attract the most odd type of man and woman from the shadowy night life of London. They were out of place in the sunlit street, like slugs you reveal when you turn over a log that has been lying in thick grass for a long time. Sunshine was not for them. Dark streets, dimly lit pavements, tobacco-laden air, the clink of glasses, the sound of liquor running from a bottle—that was their background. They were the "wide" boys and girls of London—the prostitutes, the thieves, the pimps, the touts, the pickpockets, the cat burglars, the hangers-on, the playboys and the good-time girls all moving in a steady stream, like a river of rottenness, into "Joe's Club".

As George watched them, summed them up, recognised them, he began to think about Brant's sister. Would she turn out to be a brassy, hard little piece like these other girls who had gone up the stairs to "Joe's Club"? He hated that type of girl. He had no personality to cope with them. He knew what kind of man they liked. He had listened to them in the park often enough. They and their boy friends: young men with spotty complexions, padded shoulders, snappy felt hats and cigarettes dangling from their loose mouths. Wise-cracking: every remark had a double meaning. The girls would scream with shrill laughter, vying with each other in appreciation. You were not wanted if you couldn't make them laugh; if you didn't know all the off-coloured jokes. Would Cora be like that?

George didn't think so. He felt certain that she would mean something to him when they met. He didn't know what their relations would be, but he was sure that meeting her was the most important thing in his life. The longer he waited the more excited he became.

Then as he was about to call for another pint, as the hands of the clock above the bar shifted to eight o'clock, he saw her. She was around twenty and dark. She had on a pale blue sweater and dark slacks and she didn't wear a hat. There was a three inch-wide red bangle on her wrist. But even without these clues he was quite sure he would have known her. It was as if the finger of destiny had pointed her out to him.

He crossed the bar in two strides, jerked open the door and stepped into the street. He crossed the street, removing his hat, as Cora reached the club door. She stopped when she saw him and stared at him. Her eyes were slate-grey, and had almost no expression when they looked at him.

"Are you Miss Brant?" he asked, colour flooding his face. He tried, unsuccessfully, not to look at her breasts. She was flaunting her figure; with every move of her slim body, her breasts jiggled under the soft wool covering. She ought to wear something, he thought.

"Yes," she said.

"I'm George Fraser," he went on, aware that his heart was thumping wildly. "I don't know if Syd ever mentioned me. He asked me to tell you that he'd be late. He's taken the key!"

Her eyes travelled over him. He had never experienced such intense scrutiny. He felt that she was even peering into his pockets.

"Of course," she said, "I know all about you. But come into the club. We don't have to stand out here, do we?"

Without waiting for his reply, she turned abruptly and walked out of the sunshine and the clean-smelling air into the darkness of the building.

Following her, a helpless victim to the raven hair and slim, jaunty hips that preceded him up the stairs, George went towards his doom.

CHAPTER SEVEN

George knew the exact moment when he fell in love with Cora Brant. It happened suddenly, and, to him, as dramatically as a blow in the face. He found it was extraordinary that he could fall in love with Cora in this way. It wasn't George's idea of love at all. He had always imagined that two people fell in love only after they had probed each other's minds, learned each other's habits and outlook and came to know each other so well that the obvious thing for them to do was to live together. That was George's idea of falling in love. He often thought about marriage, and how he would behave when the right girl came along. He had assured himself over and over again that he wouldn't do anything hasty. He had always imagined a leisurely, satisfying courtship that would give him an opportunity of offering his affection slowly, but with increasing warmth, until the girl he had chosen gladly accepted him.

But when it happened with this unexpected, extraordinary suddenness he was dismayed to find that he had no control over the situation nor over his feelings. At one moment Cora was just someone—admittedly exciting and unusual—to talk to and to look at and with whom he hoped to alleviate an hour of lonely boredom; at the next she was someone he was physically and mentally aware of in a most overpowering way. For some unexplained reason he was tremendously moved, wanting to cry: an absurd emotion, which, again, he had never experienced before, and which made him feel tremendously happy and light-headed.

He had only a hazy recollection of what had happened in the club. The room had been thick with tobacco smoke, noisy with jive and strident voices. But he had eyes only for Cora Brant. The people around him and the noise were incidental: a background out of focus. He had been so excited that he still was unable to remember what she had said to him. He had only been aware of her presence and his own triumph, and he nursed this triumph with secret and delighted pleasure.

He had bought drinks, and he had been startled that she tackled a pint of beer. The large glass seemed grotesque in her thin, white hand: a claw. He had absently noticed that her nails were scarlet, and her knuckles were a little grubby. And when he looked more closely at her, he realized she was not immaculate in the accepted sense of the word. She was slatternly: her black hair was lustreless, her pale blue sweater was no longer fresh, and there was face powder on her slacks.

But George was not critical. Any woman was a novelty to him, and a girl like Cora Brant was far more than a novelty—she was an exciting experience. Because of the noise of the music and the voices around them, they hadn't said much to each other. George had been content to admire her. He had, of course, explained about Sydney. To make himself heard, he had to lean across the table and shout at her. He found that embarrassing: it was like carrying on an intimate conversation in a crowded tube train. Cora had listened, her eyes on his face, her perfume in his nostrils. She had nodded and shrugged her shoulders, waving to the band as if to say it was no use talking at present.

"We'll go somewhere quieter in a little while," she had said, and had turned to watch the band.

After that it would not have mattered to George if she had not spoken again during the whole evening. She had actually said that they were going to be together, and he relaxed, rather astonished, but so grateful that he could have wept.

Then later, when the band had left the dais for a short interval, she looked at him and raised her eyebrows.

"Shall we go'?" she said, pushing back her chair.

Obediently George followed her down the stairs to the street. The sudden decision to leave, the complete indifference to his own plans, and her take-it-for-granted attitude that he wanted to go with her reminded him of Sydney Brant. That was how he behaved. Both of them knew what they wanted. They led: others followed.

Neither of them spoke as they walked along the pavement together. Cora's small head, level with George's shoulder, moved along smoothly before him, as if she were being drawn along on wheels. She left behind her the faintest smell of sandalwood.

The evening light was beginning to fade. Storm clouds crept across the sky. The air in the streets had become stale, like the breath of a sick man, and sudden gusts of hot wind sent dust and scraps of paper swirling around the feet of the crowd moving sullenly along the hot pavements.

At the corner of Orchard and Oxford Streets, Cora paused. She glanced along the street towards Marble Arch: a street thronged with people all making a leisurely way to the Park.

"I'm hungry," she said. "Let's get something to eat."

"That's an idea," George said eagerly, conscious of Robinson's eleven pounds in his wallet. "Where would you like to go? The Dorchester?" He was quite willing to spend his last penny on her if it would help to create a good impression. He had never been to the Dorchester, but he had heard about it. It was the smartest place he could think of that was close at hand.

"The what?" she asked, staring at him blankly. "Do you mean the Dorchester Hotel?"

He felt himself flushing. "Yes," he said. "Why not?"

"What, in those clothes?" she asked, eyeing him up and down. "My dear man! They wouldn't let you past the door."

He looked at his worn shoes, his face burning. If she had struck him with a whip she couldn't have succeeded in hurting him more.

"And what about me?" she went on, apparently unaware that she had so completely crushed him. "The Dorchester in these rags?"

"I—I'm sorry," George said, not looking at her. "I just wanted to give you a good time. I—I didn't think it mattered what you wore."

"Well, it does," she said coldly.

There was a long, awkward pause. George was too flustered to suggest anywhere else. She'll go in a moment, he thought feverishly. I'm sure she'll go. Why am I standing like this, doing nothing? I can't expect her to suggest anything—it's my place to make the arrangements.

But the more he tried to think where he could take her, the more panic-stricken he became.

She was eyeing him curiously now. He could feel her eyes on his face.

"Perhaps you have something else to do …" she said suddenly.

"Me? Of course not," George said, overeager and almost shouting. "I—I've got nowhere to go. I just don't go anywhere, that's all. I—I don't know where you'd like to go. Perhaps you'll suggest something."

"Where do you live?"

Astonished, George told her.

"Let's go to your place," she said. "I'm tired of the heat and the crowds."

George could scarcely believe his ears.

"My place?" he repeated blankly. "Oh, you wouldn't like that. I mean it's only a room. It—it isn't much. It's not very comfortable."

"It's somewhere to sit, isn't it?" she said, staring a little impatiently at him. "Or can't you take women there?"

He hadn't the faintest idea. It was something he had never contemplated doing. He had visions of Mrs. Rhodes' disapproving face, and he flinched away from the thought. Then he remembered once seeing one of the other boarders bring a lady visitor to his room. Of course, the visitor hadn't been like Cora; but if one boarder could do it, why couldn't he? Besides, if they went at once, Mrs. Rhodes would be in the basement having supper. She wouldn't even see him…

"Oh, that's all right," he said eagerly. "Nothing like that. We can go if you would like to. It's only the room isn't much…"

She was beginning to move towards Edgware Road. Now that that was settled, she seemed to have lost interest in him. She walked on as if he weren't with her.

George tagged along behind. Of course he was excited. To have a girl like Cora in his room! He thought at least she would want to dance, or go to the pictures, or do something extravagant.

She suddenly stopped outside a snack bar.

"Let's take something in with us," she said, looking at the appetising show in the window. Without waiting for him agree, she entered the shop.

"Two chicken sandwiches, two cheese sandwiches and two apples," she said to the white-coated attendant behind the counter.

George planked down a ten-shilling note while the attendant packed the sandwiches and apples in a cardboard container.

"How much?" Cora asked, ignoring George's money.

"That'll be two and six, miss," the attendant said, looking first at her and then at George.

"Here you are," George said, pushing the note towards the attendant.

Cora put down one shilling and threepence. "That's my share," she said shortly, and picked up the cardboard container.

"I say!" George protested. "This is my show." And he tried to give her back her money.

"Keep it," she said, turning towards the door. "I always pay myself."

"You can't do that ..." George said feebly, but she was already moving away, and by now had left the shop.

"The sort of girl I'd like to go out with," the attendant said wistfully. "Most of 'em take the linings from your pockets." George, his face burning, snatched up his change and ran after Cora.

When he caught up with her, he said, "You really must let me pay...."

"Now shut up!" Cora said. "I never accept anything from any man. I'm independent, and if I'm going to see you again, the sooner you understand that the better."

If she was going to see him again! George stared at her hopefully. Did that mean ... ? He blinked. It must mean that. People just didn't say things like that if they didn't intend seeing you again.

"Well, if you really want to ..." he said, not quite sure how he should react to such an ultimatum.

"I do!" she returned emphatically. "Now come on, don't stand there blocking the way."

"We'll want some, beer," George said, falling in step beside her. "I suppose you want to pay for your bottle, too?" He said it half jokingly, and then looked at her quickly to see if he had caused offence.

She glanced at him.

"I'm certainly going to pay for my own beer," she said. "Does that amuse you?"

And as he looked down at her, arrogant, small but durable, it happened. He found himself suddenly, utterly and completely in love with her. It was an overpowering feeling that stupefied him, made him water at the eyes, made him weak in the legs.

They looked at each other. Whether she saw the change in him, he wasn't sure. He felt she must be able to read his thoughts. She couldn't fail to see how completely crazy he was about her. If she did, she made no sign, but went on, her head a little higher, her chest arched.

They bought two bottles of beer at the off-licence at the corner of George's street. Then they went on to the boarding house.

"I'm afraid it isn't much," George muttered apologetically as he opened the front door. "But if you think you'll like it ..." His voice died away as he glanced uneasily round the hall.

There was no one about. The sound of dishes clattering in the basement reassured him.

Cora went straight upstairs. She wasn't a fool, George thought. She knows I'm nervous about her being here. She's going straight up. There's no nonsense about her.

He eyed her slim hips as she went on ahead of him. She was beautiful. There was absolutely no doubt about it. Most women looked awful in trousers. They stuck out and they wobbled, but not Cora. She was hard, slim, neat.

So he was in love with her. And he was lucky, too. Not many men would be as fortunate as he. She wasn't going to run him into any expense. He knew what girls were like. Spend—spend—spend, all the time. They didn't think you loved them unless you continually spent money on them. But Cora wasn't like that. She was independent. "If I'm going to see you again ..." It was the most wonderful evening of his life!

"Just one more flight," he said, as she glanced back over her shoulder. "And you turn to the right when you get to the top."

She stopped on the landing.

"In here," he said, passing her and opening the door. He stood aside to let her in.

"It's not much," he said again, seeing the room suddenly in a new light. It did somehow seem small and sordid. The wallpaper seemed more faded and the furniture shabbier. He wished that he had a bright, well-furnished room to offer her.

He saw Leo curled up on the bed.

"That's my cat ..." he began.

Then Leo opened its eyes, took one scared look at Cora and was gone, streaking through the open doorway, sending a mat flying. They heard it rushing madly down the stairs.

George sighed. That hadn't happened for months.

"He's awfully scared of strangers," he said, apologetically, and closed the door, "I had quite a time with him at first, but we're great friends now. Do you like cats?"

"Cats?" She seemed far away. "They're all right, I suppose." She put the cardboard container on his dressing table and moved further into the room.

George took off his hat and hung it in the cupboard. Now that he was alone with her in this little room he felt shy, uneasy. The bed seemed horribly conspicuous. In fact, the bed embarrassed him: the room seemed all bed.

"Do sit down," he said, fussing around her. "I'll get some glasses. I've got one here, and there's another in the bathroom. I'm afraid they're only toothglasses, but it doesn't matter does it?"

Without waiting for her to reply, he left the room and hurried to the bathroom on the next floor. He was glad to be away from her for a moment. In fact, he would have been pleased if she had suddenly changed her mind about spending the evening with him. He was finding her a little overpowering. The experience of falling in love with her like this was a bit shattering. He needed quiet to think about it.

He was nervous of her too. There was something cynical and cold and cross about her. He felt that if he said the wrong thing she would be unkind to him. He wanted to avoid that at all costs. So far, apart from the *faux pas* about the Dorchester—that had been a dumb, brainless suggestion—he had managed fairly well up to now. But he was losing his nerve. It was like walking a tightrope. He had had one narrow escape, and now, out on the rope with a sheer drop below, he was rapidly getting into a panic. What was he to talk about? How could he hope to amuse her for the next hour or so? If only she had asked to be taken to a movie! How simple that would have been! All he would have had to do was to buy the tickets—and anyway, she would probably have insisted on paying for herself—and the film would have taken care of the rest of the evening.

He mustn't keep her waiting, he thought, as he took the glass from the metal holder. He hurried back, hesitated outside the door and then went in.

She was sitting on the bed, her hands on her knees, her legs crossed.

"There we are," George said, with false heartiness. "Let's have a drink. I'm hungry, too, aren't you?"

"A bit," she said, looking at him as she might look at some strange animal at the Zoo.

"Have the armchair," George went on, busying himself with the drinks. "It's jolly comfortable, although it looks a bit of mess."

"It's all right," she said. "I like beds."

He felt his face burn. He was angry with himself for being self-conscious about the bed, also conscious of the double meaning. He was sure she didn't mean it in that way. It was just his mind.

"Well, so long as you're comfortable," he said, handing her a glass of beer. "I'll unpack the sandwiches."

He kept his back turned to her so that she should not see the furious blush on his face. It took him a minute or so to recover, and when he turned, she was lying on her side, propped up by her arm, one trousered leg hanging over the side of the bed, the other stretched out.

"Take my shoes off," she said. "Or I'll make the cover dirty."

He did so, with clumsy, trembling fingers. But he enjoyed doing it, and he put the shoes on the floor under the bed, feeling an absurd tenderness towards them.

Although the window was wide open, it was hot in the little room. The storm clouds had now blotted out the sun, and it was dark.

"Shall I put the light on?" he asked. "I think we're going to have some rain."

"All right. I wish you'd sit down. You're too big for this room, anyway."

He put the sandwiches on a piece of paper within reach of her hand, turned on the light, and sat down by the window. He was secretly delighted to hear her refer to his size. George was proud of his height and strength.

"Why don't you do something better than selling those silly books?" she said abruptly.

"It suits me for the moment," George returned, startled by this unexpected reproach; and feeling he ought to offer a better explanation, added, "It gives me a lot of free time to make plans."

"There's no money in it, is there?" Cora went on.

"Well, your brother made nine pounds this week," George said, munching with enjoyment.

"As much as that?" There was a sharp note in her voice.

George studied her. The blue smudges under her eyes, her whitish-grey complexion, her thin, scarlet mouth fascinated him.

"Oh yes. It isn't bad, is it?"

She sipped her beer.

"He never tells me anything," she said in a cold, tight voice. "We haven't had any money for ages. I don't know how we live. Nine pounds! And he's gone off for the evening." Her hand closed into a small, cruel fist.

"Of course, he mayn't be so lucky next week," George went on hurriedly, alarmed that he might have said something wrong. "You can never tell. There's a lot of luck in the game, you know."

"I could kill him!" she said viciously. "Look at me! I've been in this stinking outfit for months. That's all I've got!"

"You look marvellous," George said, and meant it. "It suits you."

"You're all alike," she returned. "Do you really think a girl ought to live in a get-up like this?" Her lips twisted. "I haven't another rag to my name."

Pity stirred in him. "I say—I'm awfully sorry ..."

She finished her sandwich, her eyes brooding and bitter.

"So long as Sydney gets what he wants," she said after a pause, "he doesn't care a damn about me. He doesn't care what I'll do tonight." She suddenly shrugged. "Well, never mind. It's early to worry about that now." She pushed a wave of hair back from her cheek and then rubbed her temple with one finger. "Tell me about Frank Kelly."

"Who?" George flinched away from her.

She bit her knuckle and looked at him over her hand.

"Sydney told me. You and Frank Kelly. At first I didn't believe it, but now I've seen you ..."

George emptied his glass and got up to refill it. There was a glint in her slate-grey eyes that could have meant anything: curiosity, admiration, desire....

"Seen me? I don't understand."

"You don't have to pretend with me. I'm sick of men without spine. At least, you're a man."

George slopped a little of the beer on the carpet. A surge of emotion crawled up his back.

"What do you mean?" he asked, putting the glass on the mantelpiece. He tried to control the huskiness in his voice without success.

"You've lived dangerously. You've killed men, haven't you? That means something to me."

George faced her. There was nothing in her eyes now. They were like drawn curtains. He stared at her, suddenly afraid.

"Who told you?"

"I don't have to be told. I'm not a fool. I know men. When Sydney told me about you, I thought you were one of those ghastly little miscarriages who boast about what they have done: who lie, cheat, and brag because they haven't the guts to live like men. But Sydney told me I was wrong. Even then I wouldn't believe him. He told me you had a gun, and I said you were lying."

George found perspiration was running down his face. He took out his handkerchief and mopped himself. He realized that if he wanted her admiration—and he wanted that more than anything else in the world—he could not admit that he had been lying to Brant. He was caught in his own trap; but, oddly enough, he didn't care. What possible harm could it do if he did pretend that he was a big-shot gangster? She wouldn't tell the police about him. And just suppose she did? He could always say that he had been pulling her leg, and he could prove that he had never been out of the country. All right, if she thought he had lived dangerously, if she thought he had killed men, and if, knowing that, she admired him, he would give her the opportunity to admire him even more.

"I don't talk about that side of my life," he said, picking up his glass. "It only sounds like bragging; but if you really want to know ... well, I suppose I've had as exciting a life as most men."

"Men are such liars," she said calmly, leaning down to put her glass on the floor. "I still think you could be lying ..."

George bit his lip. What was she up to now?

"Show me your gun," she said. "I'll believe you if you really have a gun."

He hesitated. Some instinct warned him not to show her the gun. He had never shown it to anyone. It was his secret. He had never intended sharing it with anyone.

She was watching him now, her eyes cold and cynical.

"Bluffing?" she asked, in a contemptuous, amused tone.

He went to his drawer and took out the cardboard box. "You mustn't tell anyone," he said, putting the box on the bed.

She pushed his hand away and took off the lid. She had the gun now. It was odd, but it looked right in her hands. It looked as right in her hands as a scalpel looks right in the hands of a surgeon. She sat up and examined the gun. Her face was expressionless, but there was an intent concentration in her eyes that worried him.

"Is it loaded?" she asked, at last.

"Oh no," George said. "Now let me put it away. I don't know why you should be interested in it."

"Show me how to load it," she urged. "Where are the cartridges?"

Without waiting for him to show her, she slid off the bed, went to the drawer and found the little wooden box.

"No," he said, surprised at his own firmness. "You leave those alone. Put them back."

She was looking at the shiny brass cylinders.

"Why?"

"I don't want any accidents. Please put them back."

She shrugged impatiently; but she put the box back and sat on the bed again. She picked up the Luger and pressed the trigger.

"Why doesn't it work?" she asked, frowning.

"It's stiff," George said. "You have to pull very hard." She tried again, but she still couldn't pull back the trigger. "Here, I'll show you," George said, taking the gun from her.

"Like this."

He exerted his great strength, and the hammer snapped down.

"It wants adjusting really, only I haven't bothered. I'll never use it here. At one time it had a hair-trigger, it would fire at the slightest touch; but it's a little out of order now."

"How do you adjust it?" she asked, taking the gun from him and curling her slim finger round the trigger. By holding the gun in both hands and pressing very hard, she managed to raise the hammer an inch or so. "Phew; it is stiff! How do you adjust it?"

George sat on the bed by her side and explained the trigger mechanism to her.

"It's simple; only I prefer to keep the trigger stiff, just in case of accidents."

"You're scared of accidents, aren't you?" There was a mocking note in her voice. "Even when the gun isn't loaded, you're scared."

"It's better to be safe than sorry," he returned, and took the Luger from her. His hand touched hers, and for one brief moment he felt a flame shoot through him: a burning desire to take her in his arms.

He got up at once and put the gun away.

"Now perhaps you believe me," he said, with an embarrassed laugh.

"I believe you," she returned, stretching out on the bed. "Give me an apple, will you?"

He gave her an apple, and took the other himself. He went back to the window, feeling that it was too disturbing to be so close to her.

"I say!" he said, looking into the street. "It's beginning to rain."

"Oh, hell!" She raised her head. "Hard?"

"I'm afraid so." He leaned out of the window, feeling the rain on his face. "It looks as if it's set in for the night. I can lend you my mack, of course, but I'm afraid you'll get wet."

As she didn't say anything, he glanced over his shoulder. She was lying flat on her back, staring up at the ceiling.

"This bed's comfortable," she said, as if speaking to herself. "I think I'll spend the night here. It doesn't seem much sense going out in the rain, especially as Sydney won't be back until late. Besides, I'm tired."

George realized that his breath was whistling through his nostrils. He felt his blood moving through his veins: it was a most odd sensation.

"You'll sleep here—?"

She seemed to become aware of him.

"Would you mind?"

"You mean—sleep in my bed?"

"Where else do you suggest ... on the floor?"

"Well, no. I didn't mean that. I don't know what they'd say ..." He floundered; excited, frightened and acutely conscious of wanting her in an overpowering way.

"Oh, I'd go early," she said indifferently. "They needn't know unless you tell them."

"No ... I suppose not."

This was fantastic, he thought. She's offering to sleep with me, and I'm behaving like an idiot. He was suddenly stricken by tremendous shyness. This wasn't the way he had imagined it at all. In his imagination he had slept with many lovely women, but it was only after a long and arduous courtship. That really was the most exciting thing about love. Now that she was being so cold-blooded about it, he felt frightened, although his desire was at fever heat.

"Then you don't mind?" she said impatiently. "Make up your mind. Can I stay?"

He moved slowly towards the bed.

"Of course," he said, standing over her. "I—I'd love you to, Cora."

This was the first time he had used her name. It gave him great pleasure. Cora! It was a lovely name.

She looked up at him and yawned.

"And you don't mind sleeping in the chair?"

He stood very still.

"The chair?"

"Perhaps you've got another bed somewhere," she said, and then, seeing the expression on his face, she sat up abruptly. "Oh, God!" she went on. "Did you think you were going to sleep with me?"

George could only stare at her, dumb, embarrassed misery in his eyes. She swung her legs off the bed.

"I'm going," she said. "I was forgetting you don't know me very well." George shook his head.

"No, don't. It was my fault. Please stay. The chair's all right."

He crossed to the window and stood looking out, trying to recover from the shock and disappointment.

Of course she was right. He was glad in a way that she hadn't meant it. Only it was such an odd way of putting it. He couldn't be blamed for misunderstanding. She was really quite fantastic. What confidence she had in herself!

And how like Sydney! Taking his bed, making him sleep in a chair, no thought for his comfort. Had she managed to guess that he was easily scared, that he was timid and uneasy with women? Was that the reason why she was pushing him out of his bed—because she knew very well he wouldn't have the nerve to force his attention on her? He didn't think so. How could any girl be sure of that?

She was standing at his side.

"I'll go if you want me to," she said. "You mustn't let me impose on you. I'm selfish. If you don't want to sleep in the chair, turn me out."

As if he would.

"Of course not," he said eagerly. "I'm awfully pleased to have you here. I mean that. I'm sorry I was so stupid. I'm really ashamed of myself ..."

She looked at him. Was that odd expression contempt? He looked again, but her eyes had become expressionless.

"All my friends know about me," she said. "I'd forgotten that you don't. Still, you don't want me, do you? You must have dozens of women."

"But I haven't ..."

"I don't sleep with men," she went on, ignoring his interruption. "It's part of my independence. I'm very independent. I never take and I never give."

He didn't say anything. What was there to say?

"You'll probably think I'm lying, but I'm not. My bed life is very exclusive. I hate being mauled. It's inconvenient sometimes. I suppose I shouldn't be so damned poor if I wasn't so damned fussy."

George flinched.

There didn't seem to be anything further to say about the subject. They stood side by side looking out of the window at the street lights, the rain and the wet pavements. They remained like that for a long time.

CHAPTER EIGHT

George was asleep when Ella brought him his morning tea. He raised his head as she drew the curtains, and blinked round the room.

"'Ave you been using scent, Mr. George?" she asked, her shiny little face tilted up as she sniffed the air. "It's ever so nice."

Scent? What did she mean? George gaped at her.

"No," he said, yawning. "Of course not." Then he remembered Cora, and a guilty flush rose to his face.

Ella was watching him.

"Well, I am surprised at you, Mr. George," she said, her eyes wide. "'Oo was she?"

It was no use lying to Ella. She could see his embarrassment too clearly.

"Oh, a friend," George returned, sinking back on the pillow. "She only looked in for a moment last night. I must say her perfume was pretty strong."

Ella wasn't so easily fooled.

"Well, I never!" she ejaculated. "Fancy you bringing a young lady..."

"Now, look, Ella," George said a little shortly. "I want to rest. I didn't sleep very well. Be a good girl and run away."

"All right, Mr. George," Ella returned. "But I'm surprised at you all the same."

George closed his eyes, and after a moment's hesitation Ella went away. George knew that he hadn't heard the last of it, but at the moment he didn't care.

As soon as she had gone he slipped out of bed and opened the door for Leo. He still felt stiff, and his neck ached after the night in the armchair, but he didn't mind. It had been a wonderful evening and a wonderful night.

He got back into bed and drank his tea.

It really seemed like a dream. Looking round the small, sordid room, he could scarcely believe that Cora had been there. He could smell her perfume on the pillow. Her hair had rested there. It had been all very exciting and marvellous, and he was mad about her.

Just then Leo stalked into the room.

"Come on, old boy," George called, snapping his fingers.

But the cat was suspicious, sniffing the air and looking at George with big, uneasy eyes. Obviously it didn't like the smell of Cora's perfume.

"Puss! Puss!" George called. "Come on. Up you come."

Silently Leo turned and slid out of the room. George called, but the cat had gone.

A little distressed, he settled down once more. Well, if Leo wanted to be stupid, then he would have to go his own way, George thought. There were other things to think about besides Leo. He had been longing for the time when he could think back on last night and savour all its excitements, brood over what Cora had said, and dwell on Cora herself.

It had been a wonderful night, in spite of the bad beginning. George hadn't talked so much in his life. It was extraordinary how easy it was to talk to Cora. She led him on. Not that she said much herself, but she knew how to listen. And he had thought that he wouldn't have been able to amuse her! Even now he found it difficult to believe that he had been such a success.

She had wanted to know about his life in the States. That was after she had got into bed. Her getting into bed was exciting. She hadn't been a scrap self-conscious. It was he who had been embarrassed.

"What can I sleep in?" she had asked. "Or do I have to sleep in my skin?"

He had given her a pair of his pyjamas. Of course, they had been ridiculously big, but she didn't seem to mind.

"And now I want to spend a penny," she had said, and he couldn't help going as red as a beet root. He had to show her where the bathroom was, and he had to hang about outside in case someone spotted her coming out. Although he was shy about it, he secretly enjoyed the intimacy between them.

Then he stayed outside the door until she was in bed. He thought she looked absolutely smashing in bed. She had rolled up the sleeves of the pyjamas, and somehow they seemed to fit her quite well. There she lay, her hair like spilt ink on the pillow, the sheet adjusted above her breasts, and her red-nailed hands folded on her tummy.

George had sat by the window with his overcoat over his legs and his feet up on a chair. They finished the beer and had talked. She had asked him to tell her about his adventures in the States. George was too happy to be cautious. So he began to talk. Everything he had read about the gang wars of America was marshalled and trotted out as his own adventures. Never had he been so inspired. He had described how he had been one of the first to arrive at the little cabin in the hills where Ma Barker and her son had made their last stand.

"I'll never forget that day," he said, looking out of the window as he tried to remember what he had read of Ma Barker's death. "We arrived early one morning. There was a ground mist, and we got right up to the cabin without being seen. I was with a bunch of G-men, and they were jittery. I didn't blame them, because hell was likely to break loose any minute.

"I'd had some experience working on both sides of the fence, and I had been in some pretty tough spots. If Fred Barker hadn't played me a dirty trick, I wouldn't have been hunting him with the Feds. At that time I was out for excitement, and I didn't care which side I was on, so long as I got into a scrap.

"The Feds didn't want a battle, but they hadn't the nerve to call on Ma to give up. So I offered to do it. I wanted to show them I had more guts than they.

"I walked to the door of the cabin. I don't mind telling you my knees were knocking.

"I hammered on the door. Ma Barker, a tommy gun half hidden behind her back, appeared at the window. I could see her wrinkles, her narrowed eyes and the wattles on her sagging neck.

"'Come on, Ma,' I said. 'You know me. You're caught, and you might just as well come quietly.'

"'To hell with you!' she yelled and ducked out of sight.

"Then Fred opened up with a machine gun. I thought I was a goner. Slugs nipped at my clothes and splattered my shoes with dust. It was a pretty tough moment. One of the Feds started grinding his machine gun, and that put Fred off. I got under cover with slugs still chasing me.

"We fought it out for over an hour, but they didn't stand a chance. A burst of automatic rifle fire caught Ma as she was peering through the window. When we found Fred, he had fourteen slugs in his carcass."

So he had gone on. He paraded them all before her—Baby Face Nelson, Frank Nash, Roger Touhy, Jake Fleagle; violence, shooting, racing cars, police sirens. He had never done better.

"And they took me for a ride," he went on, scowling at the ceiling. "Me! They took me in a wood, and they said I was washed up. There were three of them. There was a guy called Wineinger. I can see him now. A pot-bellied little runt, with a scar where someone had bashed him with a bottle. There was Clyde Barrow, thin and mean, with ears like a bat. And Gustave Banghart. They were a dangerous, tough mob, and it didn't look so good. I hadn't anything to lose, so I jumped Wineinger and got his rod. It was the fastest thing I've ever done in my life. I came out of that wood on my feet, and I came out alone."

Oh yes, he had never been better, and she had listened without moving, absorbed, excited. Her intent interest had been a spur to his imagination.

"I'm glad you told me," she had said, when he finally stopped talking. "It was what I expected of you."

Then he had edged the conversation round to Sydney. He wanted to know more about Sydney—what he did, where he lived, how Cora and he got on together.

But she didn't tell him much. She suddenly became guarded. She said she didn't know much about Sydney herself. He didn't tell her things. Look at that nine pounds! He hadn't told her about that. Didn't that show how secretive he was? They never had any money—at least, that was what Sydney always told her. He was supposed to be the bread-winner. She didn't do anything except keep the flat. Yes, they had a flat off Russell Square. George must see it one day. Sydney didn't welcome visitors. He wasn't sociable, but when he was away, George must come.

George had a vague feeling that Cora was frightened of Sydney. "He's very domineering," she said, "and we fight."

But when he pressed her for details, she rather pointedly changed the subject.

"I think I'll go to sleep now," she said, settling further down in the bed. "I was late last night."

George eased himself in his chair. It wasn't a bit comfortable now he was trying to make a bed of it.

"I hope you sleep well," he said. "What time do you want to be called in the morning?"

"Oh, I'll wake up. I always do," she returned.

"I say ..." George said, after a moment's silence, "won't Sydney worry where you are?"

"He doesn't worry about me. He doesn't worry about anyone," Cora said. "He's a bit touched, if you must know."

"Oh, I wouldn't say that," George protested.

"Well, I would."

"How did he get that scar?" George asked, at last screwing up courage to ask something that had been worrying him for days. "He's very sensitive about it, isn't he?"

"He had an accident," Cora said shortly.

"I thought it was something like that," George said, still curious. "It was pretty recent, wasn't it?"

Cora didn't say anything.

After a moment's hesitation, George went on, "How did it happen?"

"He's got enemies," Cora said.

George looked up, startled. "Enemies?" he repeated blankly.

"Look here, I want to go to sleep," Cora said sharply. "I wish you'd turn out the light."

George got up from his chair and crossed the room to the light switch. He paused as he passed her bed. "Comfortable?" he asked, thinking how lovely she looked.

"Yes. Now please put out the light."

George sighed. How much nicer it would have been if she wasn't quite so matter of fact. It was as if she was used to sleeping in strange men's rooms. George didn't want to go to sleep. It was all too exciting. He wanted to sit on her bed and watch her, even if she didn't wish to talk.

But he put out the light and groped his way back to his chair. "I don't suppose this means anything to you," he blurted out after a long silence.

"Oh, God!" she said impatiently. "Can't you sleep? What means nothing to me?"

"Being here ..." George was glad it was dark. He felt the irritating flush mounting to his face. "I've never had a girl in my room before."

"You're a simple soul, aren't you?" she said. "Are you getting a kick out of this?"

George warmed to her immediately. So she could be kind in a rather patronizing way!

"Of course I am," he said, and encouraged by the darkness, he went on, a little haltingly. "This has been a marvellous evening for me. I don't suppose you realize what it means to me."

"Why not?"

"Well, perhaps you do; but you're not lonely like I am. I spend most of my time on my own. I don't know why, but I just don't seem to make friends. I haven't met anyone I wanted to make my friend—until now." He coughed nervously, alarmed at his own rashness. Well, he had said it now. He almost cringed while waiting for her to reply. Was she going to be kind?

She didn't say anything.

George waited anxiously, and then realized, with a sense of frustration, that she wasn't going to reply.

"I expect you think I'm a bit of a fool," he said, a little bitterly. "I suppose I am really. I suppose most people would think I'm a bit soft being so fond of Leo—he's my cat. It's funny about Leo. I used to think people were a bit soft myself, being fond of animals; but somehow Leo's different." He stared into the darkness, trying to see her. "It's when you're lonely, you know. Animals seem to understand. They don't demand anything from you. If you don't feel like talking, they just sit with you. If you want to go out, they don't mind. Leo's jolly good company, but of course it isn't the same as having someone you can really talk to. Is it?"

She still didn't reply.

He waited a moment and repeated a little louder, "Is it?"

"Is what?" she asked sleepily.

"Oh, nothing; you're nearly asleep, aren't you? I'm sorry. But it's not often I get anyone to talk to."

"That's pretty obvious," she said tartly, turning on her side. "You'd talk a donkey's hind leg off."

But he couldn't let her go to sleep just yet. It was only eleven o'clock, and it seemed such a wicked waste of a marvellous opportunity, just to sleep.

"I say, Cora," he said, lighting a cigarette.

"Hmmm?"

"Shall I see you again after this?"

He could just make out her head lifting off the pillow. "If you're going to smoke I may as well have one, too," she said. "Then I am going to sleep, and if you disturb me again I'll throw you out of the room."

He hurried across the room and gave her a cigarette. The flickering flame of the match lit up her face. She looked up at him, her eyes dark and tired, expressionless.

"You don't mind me calling you Cora, do you?" George went on, bending over her.

"Call me what you like," she said, lying back on the pillow.

The tip of the cigarette glowed red, and he could just see her straight, small Roman nose.

He sat on the edge of the bed. "Shall I see you again after this?" he repeated, because it was something important, something that was preying on his mind. He couldn't bear the thought of not seeing her again.

"I suppose so," she returned indifferently; "only Sydney doesn't like people hanging around."

"Doesn't he?" George was startled. "Why not?"

"You'd better ask him."

"But that needn't mean we won't see each other again, will it?"

"What's the matter with you?" she asked. "Surely a fellow like you has got dozens of girls."

"I haven't," George said, too anxious to keep in character. "I don't like women as a rule. But you're different."

"Am I?" There was a slight note of interest in her voice. "What do you mean?"

George hesitated. What exactly did he mean? He wasn't sure himself. She was beautiful, of course. But was that all that mattered so much to him? He didn't think so. There was something else. There was something strong about her, independent; she was someone he could rely on.

"I think you're wonderful," he said slowly. "You're the most astonishing person I have ever met."

"Don't be a fool," she said, almost gently. "Of course I'm not."

Encouraged by her tone, George said, "But you are. You're lovely. You're so independent and headstrong. You know your own mind. You—you're interesting."

She lay silent for a long time. George wondered uneasily if he had offended her. Then she said, "You're not falling in love with me, are you?"

George clenched his fists. In love with her? He was mad about her!

"Oh yes," he said. "I'm in love with you. The moment I saw you..."

"Men are fools, aren't they?" she said in a confidential tone, as if she was speaking to another woman. "The men who have said that to me! Hundreds of them!"

"I'm sure of that," George said, sighing. "But it needn't matter to you, need it? I mean a girl like you wouldn't be bothered with anyone like me."

"You're a bit spineless, aren't you?" Cora said, flicking ash on the floor. There was contempt in her voice.

"I suppose I am," George said, crushed. "You see, I'm not used to women. I don't understand them."

"Well, at the rate you're going on, you never will," she returned. "What makes you think I wouldn't be bothered with you?"

George shrugged. "Well, you won't, will you?"

"What does that mean? You won't, will you?"

"What's the good of talking about it? You asked me if I loved you, and I said I did. You don't love me, do you?"

"Of course I don't," she returned, "but that doesn't mean that I couldn't love you, does it?"

George stared at her. "What was that?"

"Don't be so dumb!" There was an impatient note in her voice. "I said that doesn't mean I couldn't love you, does it?"

"Could you?"

"Not if you behave like a stuffed bull. A girl likes a little action now and then."

George could scarcely believe his ears. "Action?" he repeated blankly.

"My God!" she exclaimed, and suddenly laughed. "I don't believe it's possible! You're nothing but a schoolboy! Why don't you grow up?"

He began to tremble. God! He was making a mess of this, he thought desperately. What a stupid fool he was! She was inviting him to make love to her, and all he could do was to sit and tremble!

"What's the matter?" she asked sharply. "Aren't you well?"

"I'm all right," he said, and suddenly reached out for her hand. It felt cool and slim in his burning great paw. "Cora! I say, Cora ..." and he pulled her upright and kissed her clumsily.

She made no move, leaning back against his arm, her face a white blur in the darkness. Her perfume intoxicated him, the touch of her smooth cheek against his lips sent blood pounding in his ears.

"I do love you so," he said, and kissed her throat, holding her against him tightly.

They remained like that for a minute or two, then she pushed him away.

"All right, George," she said, "now back to your chair. That'll do for one night. It seems you can grow up when you want to." He didn't want to go, and took hold of her hand.

"Be nice to me, Cora," he pleaded. "Let me kiss you again."

"I said that's enough," she said sharply. "Here, put this somewhere," and she gave him her cigarette butt. He took it and crossed the room to the fireplace. His legs felt weak, and he was in a kind of stupor. When he had got rid of the cigarette butt he stood at the foot of the bed, looking into the darkness where she was.

"We will meet again, won't we?" he said, terrified now that this experience was going to slip through his fingers, like all the dreams he had ever had.

"We'll meet," she returned, yawning, "and now I'm going to sleep."

"But what about Sydney? What shall we do about him?"

"He needn't know."

This excited him almost as much as when she had said that she might come to love him. Having a secret between them—a secret from Sydney—seemed to seal the bond of their relationship.

"Are you on the 'phone?"

"Hmmm."

"Can I ring you sometimes? We might go out one night."

"All right."

"I'd better make a note of the number," George felt feverishly in his pocket for a pencil.

"It's in the book. Harris & Son, Greengrocer. We've got a place above the shop."

"That's wonderful. Harris & Son. That's easy to remember, isn't it?"

"Now for God's sake go to sleep," Cora said. "If you dare say another word I'll really be angry with you!"

"All right," George said, satisfied. "Good night."

"Good night," she returned shortly, and he heard her turn over in the bed.

He groped his way to the chair and settled down. He glanced out of the window. It had stopped raining, and a misty moon floated in the sky. The pavements looked black and shiny in the street lights. In the distance a clock struck the half-hour after eleven.

George shut his eyes. He was too excited to sleep. The whole of his cramped, lonely world had suddenly opened up like a gay sunshade. What an evening it had been! His life was going to be very different now. With Cora, he need never be lonely again. Whenever he wanted someone to talk to, he could ring her up. If he hadn't enough money to take her out, he could always have a few words with her on the 'phone. There was a telephone box at the corner of his street. There would be no need to stand in the passage in the basement, for everyone to hear what he had to say to her. Marvellous things, telephone boxes, he thought. Little houses of glass where you could talk to the one you loved, see the people passing, and knowing they could not overhear what you had to say.

You need never be lonely if there was a telephone box handy and a girl like Cora at the other end of the line.

He had been a bit of a fool with her. But he had been lucky. Or rather she had been pretty decent about it. "A girl likes a little action now and then." Fancy her saying that! Well, he wouldn't wait for such an invitation again. Not he! He'd take her in his arms and kiss her right off next time they met. What was it she called him ... a stuffed bull? Well, she wouldn't have to call him that again. She *was* marvellous! Simply smashing! And Sydney wasn't to know about it. Queer about Sydney. What did she mean about "enemies"? What enemies? "He's got enemies," she had said when he had asked how Sydney had got the scar. What an odd thing to say! He looked furtively across the room at the bed. He wanted to ask her to explain. Better not, he thought. She's got a temper all right, and it wouldn't do to provoke her again. No, that was something he would ask her the next time they met. He'd ring her tomorrow, just to show that he hadn't forgotten her ... as if he ever could! Yes, he'd ring her tomorrow.

Eventually he went to sleep, and when he woke at six o'clock the next morning, feeling stiff and cold, she had gone.

CHAPTER NINE

The next four or five days were, to George, exciting, confusing, exasperating and worrying. He had imagined that he would have been able to talk to Cora on the telephone at least once a day, and to see her within forty-eight hours of their first meeting. But it didn't work out like that at all. Cora, it seemed, was as elusive as a will-o'-the-wisp. Take Sunday, for instance. Now, Sunday was a good day for George's work. He usually began his calls immediately after lunch and worked through until dark. He was always sure of finding his prospects at home. He had arranged with Sydney to work this Sunday, and before getting up, he made elaborate plans for talking to Cora.

It was obvious that since the telephone was in the greengrocer's shop, he would have to make certain that Sydney wasn't in the flat when he telephoned. If the greengrocer had to call Cora to the 'phone, Sydney would want to know who was calling. So Sydney had to be out of the way. George found this added complication rather pleasing. It was much more exciting to have to plot and plan to talk to Cora than just to go to the telephone box and ring her in the usual way. The thing to do, he decided, was to 'phone from Wembley when he knew for certain that Sydney was actually working on the job. He knew Wembley pretty well now, and he remembered there was a public call box at a junction of four streets which they had still to canvass. He would make a canvass or two, and then, when he was sure that Sydney was safely inside a house, he would slip over to the call box and have a word with Cora.

He liked the idea immensely. Cora would be amused, too. He would give her a running commentary on Sydney's movements. "He's coming out of the house now. By the frown on his face, it doesn't look as if he got an order that time. He's looking up and down the road. I expect he's wondering where I've got to. He can't see me from where he's standing. There he goes now. He's opening another gate. There're three kids in the front garden; they're following him up the path. He's knocked on the door. He's waiting. I wish you could see how he looks at those kids. He'd like to bang their heads together. Hello, that's a bit of luck for him. The old man himself has come to the door. They're talking now. The old boy doesn't look too pleased. I expect his afternoon nap's been disturbed. But trust old Sydney. He keeps plugging away. Yes, I thought so; he's got into the house. The front door's shut now. Well, it looks like another *C.S.E.* is on its way from the factory...."

Oh yes, Cora would be tickled to death. And then he would tell her how much he loved her and make plans to take her out the following evening.

George was finishing his lunch at the "King's Arms" when Sydney appeared. The moment he caught sight of the hard, white face with its disfiguring scar, he felt a qualm of uneasiness. Sydney nodded to him and ordered his inevitable lemonade.

"Hello," George said; the beef and pickles he was chewing suddenly tasted of sawdust.

Sydney grunted. He came straight to the point. "Did you see Cora last night?"

George felt his face grow red. "Cora?" he repeated, wondering in panic whether she had told Sydney that they had met.

"Deaf?" Sydney said rudely, eyeing him. "What's the matter? You're going puce in the face."

George gulped. What a hateful, arrogant brat this Sydney was! he thought furiously. He put his hand to his cheek. "Got an exposed nerve," he muttered, looking away. "It gives me jip sometimes."

Sydney helped himself to a sardine on toast. "Did you see Cora last night?" he repeated.

"I—I left the message," George said. "Didn't she get it?"

"Oh, she got it; but the little bitch stayed out all night." George flinched. He thought sadly that George Fraser, millionaire gangster, would have knocked Sydney's teeth out for calling her that.

"That's not a nice way to talk about your sister," he protested; "perhaps she stayed with friends. It was a pretty poisonous night, wasn't it?"

"Friends?" Sydney repeated, his blank, hard eyes still probing George's face. "What makes you think she's got friends?"

"How do I know? Hasn't she?"

"No. I haven't any friends either. We don't want friends." Was Sydney threatening him in a subtle way? George wondered uneasily.

"If I knew who she was sleeping with, I'd mark him for life," Sydney said viciously.

George suddenly felt sick. He remembered the razor blade set in the cork handle and how Sydney had slashed Robinson's face. He remembered particularly the lightning movement that Sydney had made: a movement impossible to avoid.

"Well, I delivered the message," he said, cutting up his beef with exaggerated interest. "That's all you wanted me to do, wasn't it? I don't know anything about anything else."

"Yes, George," Sydney said softly. "That's all I wanted you to do—deliver the message."

"Well, that's what I did," George said shortly.

"She won't stay out again in a hurry," Sydney muttered, half to himself.

Immediately George became alarmed. Had he done anything to her? He suddenly lost his nervousness of Sydney. The thought that this vicious thug might have hurt her enraged him.

"What do you mean?" he asked, turning on Sydney.

"Just that," Sydney returned; "she knows what she'll get the next time she stays out all night."

Perhaps, after all, he had only threatened her, George thought, his unexpected surge of anger dying down. Well, that showed how careful they had to be. This confirmed his belief that Cora was frightened of Sydney. And no wonder. "A bit touched," she had said. Looking at him now, George thought he might really be a bit touched. There was something vicious about those eyes: not only vicious, but fanatical.

He thought it safer to change the subject, and began to talk about their afternoon calls.

He was now most anxious to speak to Cora. He wanted to hear her side of what had happened. If she wanted protection, she only had to ask him. If Sydney really had ill-treated her, he'd make him sorry. Just how he would do this he didn't know, but the details could be worked out later.

Once on the territory, George found it much harder to get to the telephone box than he had imagined. For one thing, all his calls were at the wrong end of the long street. Then Sydney seemed to be doing most of his canvassing in the front gardens. George was so anxious to talk to Cora, so worried that Sydney would spot him sneaking into the telephone box, that he spoilt four calls, where he was pretty sure, if he had been in the right mental attitude, he would have got orders.

This is ridiculous, he thought. I'm throwing away money I can't go on like this. I'll go to the call box right now. I won't wait for Sydney to get out of sight. I'll tell him I'm making a date with a friend, or something like that.

He hurried down the street towards the telephone box. As he passed one of the little houses, Sydney appeared at the front door. George kept on, feeling himself grown hot.

"Where you going?" Sydney called.

George glanced over his shoulder. "I've got a 'phone call to make," he said, without stopping. "It won't take me a minute.'

He caught a glimpse of Sydney's sneering smile, and then he looked quickly away. Did Sydney suspect who he was going to call? No, he didn't think so, but it couldn't be helped if he did. George just could not wait any longer.

It took him some time to find Harris & Son in the telephone book. There were twenty-seven columns of Harrises to wade through. The telephone box was hot and stuffy, and George kept looking down the street, worried in case Sydney suddenly decided to find out whom he was calling. When eventually he found the number, he was dismayed and exasperated to find that he had no coppers. He decided recklessly to use sixpence, but the sixpence persisted in falling right through the box and coming back to him: it was as if it was endowed with human feelings and resented his extravagant mood. Thoroughly irritated, George left the 'phone box and looked up and down the road. Sydney had disappeared, but a policeman was coming along. George got some coppers off the policeman—coppers from a copper! he thought foolishly—and returned to the telephone box. He dialled the number and waited. *Brr-brr! ... Brr-brr!* In a moment or so he would be listening to her cold, tight, exciting voice. What a marvellous invention the telephone was! he thought. They were taking their time about answering. He shifted impatiently. Phew! It was hot in this booth. *Brr-brr! ... Brr-brr!* The bell went on and on. No one answered. George stood there, obstinate, sweating, irritated. What were they playing at? he asked himself. Why didn't they answer? Then he remembered. What a fool! Sunday! Of course, the shop would be shut! Oh hell! Now he would have to wait until tomorrow. He hung up and pressed button "B". Coming out into the sunshine, he felt suddenly deflated. Twenty-four hours ... how absolutely sickening! he thought. Why did she have to have a telephone in a shop? That meant he would never be able to talk to her on a Sunday. That meant that from now on Sunday was going to be the worst day of the week, instead of being the best day. It was a day he looked forward to because he had something to do in the afternoon as well as in the evening: it was also the best day for business. Now it would be the day when he was cut off entirely from Cora.

As it happened, it turned out to be the worst day he had had for a long time. People were ruder to him, more people were out, more people wouldn't come to the front door, although he could see them peeping at him through the curtains. When he did get inside, he found he wasn't concentrating, and he did not succeed in getting anyone sufficiently enthusiastic to sign an order form. Those who showed a slight inclination to buy put him off by asking him to call again. "I want to think about it," they said. "I don't want to rush into anything."

Of course, to make matters worse, Sydney got three orders. At the end of the evening, when they decided to go home, Sydney joined him at the corner.

"How many?" he said, looking at George with a jeering expression in his eyes.

George was tempted to lie, but he knew Sydney would demand to see the completed order forms, so he just shrugged and admitted he hadn't had any luck.

"Well, I got three," Sydney said in triumph. "What's the matter with you? Got something on your mind?"

Of course he had something on his mind, but he couldn't tell Sydney about that.

"It's just the luck of the game," he said, envious and disappointed. "I've worked through a lot of dead calls, and I'll get a batch of orders tomorrow."

"You hope," Sydney said, and laughed.

Monday wasn't much better. He was in a fever of excitement all the morning and afternoon. When Sydney and he reached Wembley at four o'clock, and as soon as Sydney was safely out of the way in one of the little houses, George rushed to the telephone box.

"'Ullo?" said a man's voice in George's ear.

"Could I speak to Miss Brant?" George asked, trying to imagine what the man looked like from the sound of his voice.

"Oo?"

"Miss Brant," George repeated, raising his voice.

"Not now, yer can't. I got no one to send."

"But I must speak to Miss Brant," George said firmly.

"Well, I dunno. I can't leave the shop, now can I? It means going hup the stairs. I ain't good at stairs, either ... not at my age, I ain't. Can't you ring later? The missus'll be back then."

"No, I can't," George said, thoroughly irritated. "I understood that Miss Brant could use your 'phone. I want to speak to her."

"Orl right, orl right," the voice said crossly. "I'll give 'er a yell. 'Ang on, will yer?"

George waited. It was insufferably hot in the telephone box, and he pushed the door open. He could hear voices faintly over the line. Once he heard the voice that had spoken to him shout, "Two pahnds of greens, six pahnds of spuds and a pahnd of onions...." And he swore under his breath. The old devil wasn't getting Cora at all, he thought savagely. He was serving his rotten customers! But there was nothing else to do but wait. Time was going. He really ought to be on the job. Well, he wasn't going to hang up now he'd got so far. He would have to work a bit longer to make up for losing time like this. Oh, come on! Come on! he thought furiously. Why don't you hurry!

He waited nearly five minutes, then he heard the voice bawl, "Emmie Emmie ... someone wants that Brant girl on the blower...."

"That Brant girl!" How dare a greengrocer talk like that! Well, anyway, it wouldn't be long now. Any second he would be hearing her voice.

"You doing your selling by 'phone?" Sydney asked.

George nearly jumped out of his skin. He whirled round, his face turning crimson, to find Sydney lolling against the telephone booth, watching him with suspicious, calculating eyes.

"I shan't be a minute," George spluttered, not knowing which way to look. "I'll be right out," and he tried to pull the door to, but Sydney had wedged it back with his foot.

"What's all this telephoning about?" Sydney asked. "Yesterday and now today. I thought you were a keen salesman."

"Hello?" Cora said in George's ear.

George looked from Sydney to the telephone mouthpiece. Sweat was running down his face. He didn't know what to do.

"Hello? Who's there?" Cora asked, her voice snappy and impatient.

He daren't speak to her with Sydney listening. Damn the rotter! George thought desperately. Why can't he go away!

"'Phoning your best girl?" Sydney asked, a sneering grin on his face. "I wish you could see your mug! You look like a pickpocket caught in the act. Well, I won't embarrass you; only time's getting on, you know."

"Hello? Hello? Hello?" Cora was saying.

George waved Sydney away: an imploring, frantic gesture. Shrugging, Sydney slouched off, and as the booth door closed, a sharp click sounded in George's ear. Cora had hung up!

Sydney was still hanging about a few yards away, watching George through the glass panels. It was no good! He didn't dare risk dialling the number again. He was sick with disappointment and frustrated rage. Damn Sydney! Damn the greengrocer! Oh, damn everything!

Tuesday and Wednesday were as bad. Both times when George rang he was told that Cora was out. In desperation, he risked calling her on Thursday morning before he went to the "King's Arms," and after some delay Sydney's voice floated over the line. Hurriedly, as if he had trodden on a snake, George hung up. Five days now and he hadn't spoken to her or seen her. And he had thought he was never going to be lonely again! It was worse now: far worse. Before, he didn't have this clamouring for the flesh, wasn't tormented by thoughts of loving Cora, holding her in his arms, feeling her smooth cheek against his lips.

He had to do something! This couldn't go on. His work was suffering. He had only earned thirty bob in five days, while Sydney had made himself seven quid. It infuriated George to hear the way Sydney sneered at seven pounds.

"Chick feed," he said, when George handed him the money order received from Head Office. "It's almost time I slung this job in. Seven nicker for slogging my guts out every evening. In the old days I'd do a job that'd take me an hour or so, and pick up twenty quid as easy as kiss your hand."

"What job?" George asked curiously.

Sydney brooded. "When things cool off a bit," he said at last, "maybe I'll let you in my racket. But right now I've got to keep out of sight," and then, for no apparent reason, he flew into a vicious rage and went off, looking almost murderous.

The more George saw of Sydney the more uneasy he became. The fellow was unbalanced. Perhaps he really was cracked. These sudden vicious tempers, the vicious, fanatical look in his eyes, the mysterious hinting about "his racket" worried George. The thought of Sydney's razor worried George even more.

Well, he certainly wasn't going to mix himself up in Sydney's racket. He knew instinctively that it was crooked. Sydney was the kind of fellow who'd land up in jail. Jail-bait, that's what he was!

In spite of his instinctive fear of Sydney, George was determined to speak to Cora the next day, Friday. Even if it meant doing no work at all and staying in a telephone box all the evening, he was going to talk to her! He wanted her to spend Saturday evening with him. He planned to take her to a movie and then to dinner somewhere. He had put away the eleven pounds that Sydney had got from Robinson, earmarked for this outing. He was determined to stand treat: he wasn't going to have any nonsense from Cora about paying for herself. And what was more, when they met he would kiss her: he'd show her he was a man of action.

To be certain of speaking to Cora, he decided not to work that evening. He told Sydney he wasn't feeling too well. He said he'd drunk some bad beer: it had upset his stomach.

"I think I'll stay at home," he said, avoiding Sydney's probing eyes. "I don't feel like going out on the job tonight."

"Please yourself," Sydney said, shrugging; "it's your loss. You'd better pull up your socks. You've only taken one order this week."

George didn't need to be reminded of this unpleasant fact, but he assured himself that once he had seen Cora he would be able to settle down to work again. Selling books demanded all your attention. How could he concentrate when he was longing so much to hear Cora's voice?

As soon as he was sure that Sydney had taken himself off to Wembley, he left his room and hurried to the call box at the end of his street. At first the line was engaged, then he dialled a wrong number, then he found he hadn't any more pennies, and he had to go to the newspaper shop across the street to change a shilling. When he got back there was a woman in the box, and she kept him waiting nearly ten minutes. He had ceased to be impatient. He was now obstinately dogged: determined, whatever happened, to speak to Cora. If it took him a hundred years to speak to her, he wouldn't mind, so long as he succeeded.

At last the woman left the call box, and George took her place. There was a ghastly smell of cheap scent and stale perspiration in the box: it was like an oven, too. But George didn't care. He dialled the greengrocer's number and waited.

"'Ullo?" asked the irritatingly familiar voice.

They went through the same dreary performance: the greengrocer wanting to know "'ow I can leave the bloomin' shop?" and George coldly determined that the greengrocer should call Cora to the telephone.

"She's in 'er bawth," the greengrocer said after a wait of nearly a quarter of an hour, and he hung up before George could leave a message.

There were three people waiting outside the telephone box by now. They were all glaring at George, and when he came out one of the women muttered, "And about time, too. Some people think public telephones are private property!"

George didn't care what they said or thought. He walked over to the "King's Arms," had a pint, avoided conversation with Gladys—by this time he was almost hysterical with frustrated temper—and returned to the telephone box half an hour later.

Again he had to wait while a man finished his conversation. Watching him through the glass, George guessed he was talking to his girl. There was a fatuous, smug expression on his face, and he talked for a good ten minutes.

When George finally got through to the greengrocer's again, the rough voice nearly snapped his head off.

"Look 'ere," it said violently. "I got better things to do than answer bloomin' telephones like this. I'll 'ave to complain if this goes on much more. You've been ringing hup every day this week!"

Complain! That'd mean Sydney would hear about it! He might even guess that it was George making the call. It might give him a clue that it was George who had spent the night with Cora. The memory of the gleaming razor blade became vividly unpleasant.

"But I haven't even spoken to her," George protested. "I can't help it if she's always out, can I?"

"'Ere, miss, 'ere," the greengrocer suddenly bawled. "This ere bloke's on the blower again. Every day 'e's been on ... it's got to stop."

"Hullo," Cora said. "Yes?"

George knew she was in a temper all right, but it was so marvellous to hear her voice—even if it did sound snappy—that he didn't care.

"This is George," he said, aware that he had begun to tremble violently.

"Have you been ringing every day?" she barked at him.

"I'm afraid I have," he returned in studiedly gentle tones, quite sick with fear that she was going to be unkind.

"Well, couldn't you have been a bit brighter?" she demanded. "You've caused a lot of bother as it is."

"I'm terribly sorry," George said, "but I did want to speak to you."

"What do you want?"

In that kind of temper it was quite likely she would refuse to go out with him. But it had to be now or never. Now he had at last caught her. He couldn't just fawn and cringe and go away.

"I—I was wondering ... if you haven't anything to do tomorrow ... I mean, would you like to come out with me? ... that is, if you're not busy or something."

"What do you mean ... or something?" The waspish note was still in her voice.

"Well, you know ... if you're not going out with anyone else."

"Oh, I see."

There was a long pause while he waited for her to add anything to this, but she didn't, so he screwed up his courage, and, knowing that he was inviting a direct snub and refusal, said, "Well, do you think you could?"

She still tried to make him pay for causing a bother on the telephone by appearing to be dense. "Could I ... what?"

"Could you come out with me? I—I thought we might do a movie and have dinner somewhere."

"I can't waste my money on movies," she said shortly.

"But this is my treat. I—I'm inviting you ..."

"Oh."

There was another long pause, then he said, "What would you like to see? There's a good movie at the Empire ... Spencer Tracy."

"I don't think I can go to a movie," she said, a gentler note in her voice. "I'm busy tomorrow."

It was his turn to say "Oh" now.

"I could come to dinner."

He brightened at once.

"Oh, good! That's fine. Where shall we go?"

"I know a place."

"All right. Then when shall we meet?"

"Eight o'clock at the pub opposite Joe's." Now that she had made up her mind to go out with him she was taking charge of the outing. George didn't care. He had won his point about paying for the outing—or at least he thought it was going to be all right—and if she wanted to say where they were to meet and where they were to dine, it was all right with him.

"That's fine," he said. "I say, Cora—I'm looking forward ..." but the telephone was dead. She had hung up.

Even that didn't detract from his happiness. At last! After all those beastly hours, trying ... trying ... trying to get her, he had finally succeeded, and she was coming out with him again!

He drew a deep breath and came out into the fresh air, feeling fine.

CHAPTER TEN

Cora, with George tagging along a step behind, turned off the main road into a narrow street, lined on one side by backs of shops, and on the other side by a brick wall, along the top of which bristled pieces of broken glass, set in cement. At the end of this street she turned the corner and walked down an even more sordid street of small, shabby shops. A group of dark-skinned, bare-headed men stood at the corner; they glanced at George, and then concentrated on Cora. They stopped talking and eyed her, their faces expressionless, their eyes hot and intent. Cora went on her way, her small head held high, unaware of their interest.

They came to a double-fronted shop, the big windows hung with yellow muslin curtains. The glass panel of the door was painted green. Gilt letters, "Restaurant," crawled diagonally across the green expanse.

Without pausing, Cora pushed open the door and went in. George followed her.

The room in which they found themselves was long and narrow. Tables lined each side of it, and vast mirrors, fly-blown and yellowing with age, hung from the walls. Red-shaded lamps stood on each table.

A big woman, her hair straggling and untidy, as if someone had upset custard over her head, sat at the cash desk. Behind the bar near the door was a tall, elderly Hebrew in a dirty white coat. Two waiters stood idly at the end of the room. There were only a few people at the tables: bright-eyed women, hatless and bold; dark-skinned men, immaculately dressed, middle-aged and wooden.

Cora sat down at a table with her back to the wall. George, following her, felt the woman in the cash desk examining him closely. Somehow, he didn't quite know why, the atmosphere in this dimly lit, gaudy room made him uneasy.

He was aware, too, that the men at the tables paused in their eating and watched Cora furtively, under lowered eyelids; their eyes on her slim hips and the shameless movement under her woollen sweater.

She was wearing the same outfit, and the red bone bangle, as she had worn when they first met. Their meeting tonight wasn't at all how George had planned it to be. He had arrived at the pub at a few minutes to eight to find Cora already there. She was drinking a whisky and water, and she seemed peevish. Of course, he hadn't kissed her. Even if they had been in the bar on their own, he wouldn't have had the courage, now that he was once more face to face with her. He really marvelled that he had kissed her the other night. That had, of course, only happened because it had been dark.

As soon as Cora saw him she finished her whisky and came to meet him.

"Come on," she said shortly, without even a smile of greeting, "I'm hungry," and she walked right out of the pub without giving him even a second glance, and went off down the street.

George, bewildered and a little hurt, hurried after her. She kept on, a scowl on her face, and George followed her. He decided not to speak to her. He could not think of anything to say, anyway, that wouldn't irritate her, so he kept behind her until they reached this little Soho restaurant.

He had an uneasy presentiment that the evening wasn't going to be a success.

He sat down opposite her, his back to the room. She looked past him at the waiter, a bent, elderly man who came over to them with a bored, tired look in his eyes.

George was about to ask her what she would like, but, still ignoring him, she said to the waiter, "Oysters, grilled steaks, salad and ice cream. Two bottles of vin rouge: and let's have some service."

The waiter went away without saying anything, but by the way he flicked his soiled napkin, he managed to express his contempt for them.

Two bottles of wine! Oysters! My word! George thought, she knows what she wants all right.

Well, he couldn't just sit there and say nothing. He hadn't said a word since they met in the pub.

"It's lovely to see you again, Cora ..." he began, wondering if he was going to set her off.

She seemed suddenly to realize that he was in the room. "I'm bad-tempered," she said, resting her chin on the back of her hand. "I'll be all right in a moment."

That's better, George thought. As if I didn't know she was in a temper. Well, so long as she admits it, she may get over it soon.

Feeling that he must add something to the meal—Cora ordering everything had rather deflated him—he beckoned a waiter and ordered two large dry martinis.

"Nothing like a cocktail to cheer you up," he said, smiling. "I've been in the dumps myself today."

She didn't say anything. He noticed she was staring across the room at a table in the far corner. There was an intent look of spite in her eyes.

Puzzled, George glanced at the man sitting at the table. He was a slender blonde with a complexion like peaches and cream, and big, soft eyes like a deer. He was wearing apple-green trousers, very neat, with pleats at the waist; and his coat was fawn colour.

George turned to Cora. She wasn't looking at the blonde man in the corner any longer, but at him. There was that odd expression in her eyes that made George feel like a strange exhibit in a Zoo.

The waiter brought the two martinis.

"Here's how," George said. "I've been looking forward to this no end."

She glanced at him, and her lips smiled, but her eyes still remained sulky. They drank. George was surprised at the "kick" the martini had.

"These are jolly good, aren't they?" he went on, still too nervous to begin a real conversation.

"They're all right," she said, and again her eyes strayed to the blonde man across the room.

This won't do at all, George thought. Why does she keep looking at that horror over the way? She couldn't be interested in that type, surely? Why, anyone with half an eye could see he was a cissy. Perhaps she was just bored. Anyway, he couldn't let her attention wander like this.

"I've been worrying about you," he said, leaning towards her. "Did you get into trouble for staying out all night?"

"Trouble?" Her eyebrows went up. "You talk as if I'm a child. I can stay out all night if I want to."

Baffled, George sipped his martini. Not quite the same idea that Sydney had conveyed. He glanced at her thoughtfully. "From what Sydney said ..."

"Oh, don't listen to him. He's always bragging about how he treats me. I go my way, and he goes his."

George was sure she was lying, but there was no point in telling her so.

"Well, I worried because I wondered if I should have kept 'phoning. I didn't want to get you into trouble."

"I wish you wouldn't keep 'phoning," she said shortly. "Old Harris doesn't like it."

Before he could say anything further, the waiter brought the oysters. When he had gone, George muttered, "I wanted to speak to you. You said it was all right to 'phone."

"Oh, don't nag!" she said sharply, and forked an oyster into her mouth.

There was no doubt she was in a foul temper. Or was she nervous about something? George studied her. She did look tired and jumpy. There was also an uneasy expression in her eyes.

"What are you staring at?" she demanded, looking up and catching his eyes on her face.

"You," George said simply. He felt an overwhelming love for her suddenly well up inside him. "What's wrong, Cora? Is there anything I can do to help?"

"Wrong, what should be wrong?"

"You look nervous ..."

"Do I?" she suddenly laughed. "I'm in a foul temper, that's all."

He could see the tremendous effort she was making to sound natural. It began to worry him. There was something on her mind: something she was anxious that he should know nothing about.

"I got up late," she went on, "Everything's gone wrong today." She finished her cocktail just as the waiter came with the two bottles of wine. He drew the corks and filled their glasses. "I feel like getting tight tonight," she went on.

George was still not satisfied. "Are you sure there isn't something else?"

"Of course not!" she said, the waspish note back in her voice. "It's just that it's been a hell of a day, and I'm tired."

"Well, never mind," George said, certain now that there was something on her mind. "The wine will make you feel better."

And he began to talk to her about the only subject he was really competent to talk about—crime in America. He didn't want to talk to her about that. He would much rather have talked of his love for her, and even to confide in her that all his stories of violence and adventure were figments of his imagination, and that he was only a simple type of fellow, but very much in love with her. But she was so unsympathetic and hard and nervous that he knew it would be inviting disaster to be sentimental. So he told her more fictitious stories of his adventures in America. He had been reading a lot lately, and was well primed with material. She seemed to welcome these stories, probably because she didn't wish to talk herself. While he talked, she smoked incessantly. The ash tray was piled high with cigarette butts, smeared with lipstick. She had scarcely touched her meal, but she had drunk a good deal of the sour red wine. When George asked her if she felt all right, as she had made such a poor dinner, she said abruptly that it was too hot to eat. Remembering that the first words she had greeted him with were, "Come on, I'm hungry," George shrugged hopelessly. Her moods defeated him.

But she listened to his tales of crime, sitting still, with her chin in her cupped hands, her eyes expressionless.

George soon became engrossed in his own stories, and when the lights in the restaurant began to go out, he realized with a start of surprise that it was half-past eleven and he was a little drunk. The restaurant was empty now, except for the blonde man at the table opposite, the Hebrew barman, the fat woman at the desk and the waiter who had looked after them.

"We'd better be going, I suppose," he said regretfully. "I'm afraid I've been doing all the talking again. I hope I haven't bored you."

Cora shook her head. Her face was flushed by the wine, and when she spoke, the sickly smell of the wine was on her breath. "I wanted you to talk," she said. Then she looked again at the blonde man at the table across the room. George suddenly realized that all the time he had been talking to her she had been casting glances in this man's direction.

He couldn't resist saying, "Do you know that man?"

She looked through him, her eyes drawn curtains, "That isn't rain, is it?"

George frowned. "I hope not." He glanced over his shoulder. Rain marks showed on the windows. "It is, I'm afraid. Aren't we unlucky? It always rains for us."

"Oh, damn! I hope we can get a cab."

George signalled to the waiter, who brought the bill. It was for twenty-five shillings. Cheap, and jolly good, George thought. We must come here again. Only perhaps she'll be less worried and jumpy next time. He had to admit that the evening hadn't been a success. Cora had behaved—was behaving now—like someone awaiting a major operation. She had not been concentrating, and George was prepared to swear that she couldn't have repeated to him anything of what he had said to her during the whole evening. Her eyes were never still, and she continually moistened her lips with her tongue. She had all the symptoms of acute nervousness.

George waved away the change which the waiter brought him. "Shall we go, or shall we wait a bit?" he asked Cora.

"We're closed now," the waiter said as he moved away.

"Oh, well," George said, pushing back his chair, "I suppose we'd better go, then."

Cora drew a deep breath and got to her feet. George was surprised to see that she swayed unsteadily. It dawned on him that he was feeling comfortably tight. The martinis and the two bottles of wine had found their way to his head. He grinned a little foolishly. They certainly seemed to have found their way to Cora's legs.

"Steady," he said, taking her arm; "careful how you go."

She pushed him away. "Shut up, you fool!" she said in a low, furious whisper. Her eyes blazed, and George was so astounded by her vehemence that he gaped at her. She lurched unsteadily down the aisle between the tables, and he heard her muttering furiously to herself. The sudden change in her mood stupefied him. She had seemed sober enough while she had been at the table, but now she seemed as tight as a tick.

What was she up to now? What was she doing at the blonde man's table? George stood watching her, unable to make up his mind to follow her. She had paused, her arms folded across her breasts, facing the blonde man, who looked at her with curious, bored eyes.

"Well?" she said loudly. "You'll know me again, won't you?" The blonde man eyed her up and down and looked away, a sneering little smile on his face.

"You heard what I said, you cheap masher," Cora went on, her voice high pitched. "You've been trying to make me all the evening!"

George wanted to sink through the floor. How could she behave like this? Had she suddenly gone mad?

The blonde man flicked his cigarette ash on the carpet. He continued to smile, but he was regarding Cora now with a frozen look in his eyes.

"Run away, little girl," he said, "or I shall get annoyed with you."

"Keep your filthy eyes off me in the future!" Cora suddenly screamed, and, leaning forward, she spat a stream of obscene vituperation at him.

Although George was shocked into a stupefied immobility, he was aware that the woman with the blonde hair, the Hebrew behind the bar and the waiter were standing tense and angry, looking at Cora.

The blonde man ceased to smile. "You're drunk," he said. "Get out before I have you thrown out!"

Cora snatched up a glass of wine that the blonde man had scarcely touched, and with one swift movement threw the wine in his face.

Somewhere in the building a bell began to ring. George was conscious of the bell more than he was conscious of the stillness of the blonde woman, the Hebrew and the waiter, although they were menacing enough. He was more scared of the bell than he was of the blonde man, who sat staring at Cora, wine running down his face into his shirt and coat.

Then a concealed door halfway down the room opened, and two men came into the restaurant. They looked like Greeks—hard little men with flat, squashed features, dressed in black, with black cloth caps on their bullet heads.

The blonde man said in a drawling voice, "Well, you'll certainly pay for that, you drunken bitch."

George rushed to Cora's side. He was sick with fright, but he wasn't going to let anything happen to her.

"Cora!" he said, taking her arm. "My God! Cora!"

He could feel her trembling, and he realized that she was as terrified as he was.

"Don't let them do anything to me!" she said wildly, clinging to him. "George! Get me out of here. Don't let them touch me!"

This frantic appeal stiffened George's courage. He pushed her behind him and faced the two Greeks.

"Now, don't get excited," he said, his voice sounding as if he had a pebble in his mouth. "I'm sorry about this ... she didn't know what she was doing ..."

The blonde man got to his feet. His face was white now with vicious rage. "Take care of this lout, Nick," he said. "Get the girl away from him."

George thought, desperately, furiously, They won't have her! They'll have to kill me first. If I'd only got my gun! He put his hand behind him and pushed Cora against the wall; he stood in front of her, crouching a little, his left fist extended, his right slightly across his body. Vaguely he remembered seeing James Cagney stand like this, protecting his girl. Cagney had faced a room full of thugs and he'd licked the lot! George eyed the two hard little men, who kept just out of his reach, like two terriers waiting for an opening to jump in. The blonde man was still behind his table: he was wiping his face with a napkin.

"You'd better be careful," George said. "I don't want to hurt anyone!"

The blonde man suddenly laughed. "Fix the fat fool," he said sharply. "Go for him!"

The Greek called Nick edged closer, and George swung wildly at him. His great fist smashed into empty air, as the Greek shifted his head.

Cora screamed and clutched at George, hampering him.

Then suddenly long, thin blades flashed in the shaded light. The sight of the glittering steel shocked George's courage into a frozen ball of terror.

Something flashed, and pain seared him.

They'll kill me! he thought, and like a wounded, terrified bull, he lashed out frantically.

A red curtain of terror hung before George's eyes. He heard Cora scream. Then he found himself on the floor, a rattling, groaning noise in his ears, and he realized that he was making the noise himself.

A solid weight dropped on his shoulders, pushing him flat on the dusty, smelly carpet. Nick knelt on his back.

"Don't move," the Greek said. "She'll be back in a little while."

George lay still.

Then a sound came from somewhere in the building—a violent scream, which was immediately stifled, as if by a ruthless hand. Every nerve in George's body stiffened.

"Still!" Nick said, breathing garlic and wine fumes in George's face.

Slowly and cautiously George raised his head and looked round the room. The woman at the cash desk, the Hebrew behind the bar and the waiter were all staring at him.

George thought he heard another muffled scream, but he could not be sure. He looked at the others, but they showed no sign that they had heard anything. The woman at the cash desk curled a straggling lock of dyed hair round her fat finger. Her eyes were stony, blank.

What were they doing to Cora? George made a convulsive movement.

"Still!" the Greek warned, pressing a sharp knee into George's back.

The silence in the room and in the building terrified George. Minutes ticked by slowly. It seemed to him that he had been lying on the dirty, evil-smelling carpet for hours.

Then suddenly the Greek got up. "Right," he said, and kicked George hard in the ribs. "Get up, you."

Somehow George crawled to his feet. Without quite knowing what he was doing, he took out his handkerchief and wrapped it round his bleeding left hand: He swayed unsteadily as the other Greek appeared, pushing Cora through the concealed doorway.

Then somehow they were in the street together, in the darkness and the rain.

George stood gulping in the hot, damp air, unnerved, his limbs trembling.

"What happened?" he said. "What did they do to you?"

Cora, her arms tightly crossed, doubled herself up. Her long wave of hair fell forward, concealing her face. She stood like that for several minutes, and the rain poured down on her.

"Can't I do anything?" George said, forgetting about his own wounds, frightened to touch her, terrified by her behaviour. Her ragged, laboured breathing made a dreadful sound in the rain and the darkness.

She began to walk up and down the street, still doubled up, still holding onto herself.

"Cora! Tell me!" he said, following her. "What is it?"

They were near a street lamp now, and she suddenly straightened. Her hair was plastered to her head by the rain. She looked wild. A hissing sound came from her lips, and he could see she was grinding her teeth.

"They crammed a pillow over my face," she gasped, "and then they flogged me with a cane!" She drew her saliva into a ball of fury and spat into the darkness. "They did that to me! I'll make them pay! I'll make *him* pay, too! The treacherous swine! *He* knew what they'd do! I'll kill them all for this! All of them!" And she began to cry with rage and pain, wriggling her body and stamping her feet.

George stood in the rain, helpless, watching her with dismayed, bewildered pity, the handkerchief round his hand growing soggy with blood.

Suddenly she grabbed his arm, her fingers biting into his muscles. "Don't look at me," she panted, standing first on one leg and then on the other. She contorted her body, arched her back, straightened and bent double again. "Damn you!" She broke away from him and went down the street, only to stop a yard or so farther on. She held her head between her hands and began to walk round in small circles. Then she came back to him and gripped his arm again. He could feel the fever in her, burning through his coat sleeve.

"Take me home," she cried, pulling at him. "For God's sake, take me home. I'm hurt! I'm on fire! Don't stand there doing nothing, you stupid, stupid fool! Take me home!"

CHAPTER ELEVEN

George never quite knew how they reached the little flat above the greengrocer's shop. He vaguely remembered stopping a taxi, but had no recollection of the actual drive. He remembered the long, painful climb up some stairs, and Cora hammering wildly on a door. He remembered, too, hearing Sydney shout, "All right, all right. I'm coming! Stop banging on that bloody door."

Then he had a dim recollection of Sydney, in a dirty white dressing gown, staring at him in blank astonishment.

He took a step forward, and his knees gave under him. He fell heavily. Before he blacked out he heard Cora scream: "You swine! You said he wouldn't touch me! Oh, I hate you! I hate you!" and then he lost consciousness.

He had no idea how long he remained unconscious. He must have drifted into a heavy sleep before coming round. But when he opened his eyes it was morning and he was lying on the floor, a pillow under his head and a blanket over him. He sat up slowly and looked round, not quite remembering where he was.

He was aware of pain, and found his hand had been expertly bandaged and sticking plaster covered the cuts on his face. He pushed the blanket aside and stood up. He didn't feel too bad. A little weak, perhaps, but otherwise not bad. He looked round the room with blank astonishment. It was a perfect pigsty of a room. The mantelpiece was thick with dust. The fireplace was full of cigarette ash and butts. A table, pushed against the wall, was piled with old newspapers, unwashed crockery and empty bottles. A dish containing some evil-smelling meat was under an armchair. On all the flat surfaces of the furniture were sticky circles made by wet tumblers. Two bluebottles buzzed angrily against the dirty windows.

"Hello," Sydney said quietly. "How's the bold warrior?"

George blinked at him. Sydney was standing in the doorway, dressed in a dirty white dressing gown, his lean, hard face cold and expressionless.

"I must have fainted," George said, moving over to an armchair and sitting down. He examined his hand uneasily. "Did you do this?"

Sydney grunted. "Don't worry about that," he said casually. "I shoved a few stitches in it. It'll be all right."

"Stitches? You put stitches in it?"

"Why not? In my racket you get used to razor cuts. Did you see what they did to Cora?"

"They beat her ... didn't they?" George went cold.

"They certainly did. Nice mob. They'll pay for this, George."

George held his head in his hands. "I don't understand," he said. "Why did she do it? She threw wine in his face."

"Never mind why she did it," Sydney said. "You're in love with her, aren't you?"

"Yes," George said, no longer caring what Sydney would say or do.

"That's fine," Sydney said, his eyes glowing like live coals. "I'm glad about that. You and me are going to fix Mr. bloody Crispin."

"Crispin?"

"The nice-looking lad who beat Cora. She told me what happened. She was tight, but that doesn't matter. No one's going to touch her without getting into trouble. I'd handle him myself, only you and me can do it better."

"Do what better?" George asked. He remembered the two Greeks and their razors, and he felt a little sick.

"We'll see him tonight. You and me. He's got a bungalow at a place called Copthorne. It's not far. He'll be down there today. Well, we'll go down, too, and we'll take a cane. It's a lonely place, and we won't be disturbed. We'll see how he likes a beating. That's what we'll do."

"Wouldn't it be better to complain to the police?" George asked, in sudden fright. "They're dangerous. Look what they did to me."

"When you were in the States," Sydney said, cold cruelty in his eyes, "did you go to the police?"

George waved his hands nervously. "That was different," he said. "No one went to the cops in those days. It's different now."

"No, it isn't," Sydney said. "This is something personal. We'll be dangerous too. We'll take your gun."

George stiffened. "No, we won't!" he said. "I'm not doing a thing like that. That's how accidents happen."

"Oh yes, you are, George," Sydney said, wandering across the room. "You don't have to load it. Crispin will fall apart just to see the gun. I'm not suggesting you kill him. I don't like murder myself. Feel like getting the gun now?"

Again George was going to refuse, when he suddenly thought of the blonde man's sneering smile. He thought of the two Greeks creeping towards him with their razors. With the Luger in his hands, they would have been terrified. A smouldering anger—something he had never before experienced—urged him to seek revenge. Cora's shrieks still rang in his ears.

He got to his feet. "All right," he said, "but I'm not loading the gun."

"I'll come with you," Sydney said. "Come and talk to me while I dress."

George followed him into a tiny bedroom.

"Who is this Crispin?" he asked, leaning against the wall.

"I used to fool around with him," Sydney returned, slipping his blue shirt over his head. "Keep this under your hat. He knocks off cars in a big way. There's bags of money in that game." He glanced quickly at George and went on, "I chucked it after a bit. Got too hot for me. Cora hates the guy. He doesn't know she's my sister. He'll have a surprise when he sees me—and you." He was dressed now. "You'd better have a wash. Those cuts on your face aren't deep, but you look a bit of a mess. Those Greeks know how to use a razor all right."

He took George into the grubby little bathroom. George stared at himself in the mirror. A long strip of plaster ran down the side of his face, and another strip was above his ear. He rinsed his face, getting rid of the blood smears. There was blood, too, on his coat and collar.

"I look a sight," he said, suddenly secretly proud of himself. He looked tough and frightening: a real gangster.

"I'll find you a scarf," Sydney said. "You can change when you get to your place."

"Where's Cora?" George asked, drying his face on a grimy towel.

"Asleep," Sydney said indifferently. "She's got weals on her back as thick as my finger."

George flinched. His anger blazed up.

"Let's go," he said.

It was only seven-thirty by the time they reached George's place, off the Edgware Road. The house was silent: no one was up. George took Sydney to his room and closed the door. While Sydney sat on the bed, whistling softly, George changed his shirt, put on another suit and had a hurried shave.

In the familiar surroundings of his room his anger died down. He was now beginning to realize what it meant to live dangerously. He had read so much about it in the past; had constructed scenes in which he had experienced breathless adventures, fought and killed men, and had gloried in it all. But this was different. This was something out of his control. He knew that if in one of his fantasies he were trapped by desperate men, he would not be killed. He would be able to create a situation that would save him at the last moment. But this business was different. If that Greek, Nick, had wanted to kill him, he could have done so. It was just sheer luck that he hadn't cut George's throat.

George suddenly hated the thought of what was going to happen that night. He had been angry, but now, back in his room, the thought of fresh danger gave him a sick, nervous feeling in his stomach. To beat this man Crispin was primitive justice, but it was bound to lead to trouble. If they did succeed in catching Crispin alone, did Sydney really think that Crispin wouldn't get his own back on them later?

As he rinsed his razor, he considered whether he should refuse to go with them, but immediately saw the impossibility of this. If he wished to keep Cora's regard—and there was no question about that—he would have to go through with it. All he had to do was to threaten Crispin with the gun. Well, that was all right. He could do that. There would be no danger in that, as the gun wasn't loaded. He was confident that Crispin would obey him if he had the gun in his hand. It was an ugly-looking weapon. It would scare him stiff. Besides, Sydney would be there.

"Getting cold feet?" Sydney asked in a sneering voice.

George started. He had forgotten that Sydney was in the room. He had been so busy with his thoughts that Sydney had gone completely out of his mind. He turned.

"Of course not," he said. "I've been in tighter spots ..." and then he stopped.

Sydney was holding the Luger carelessly in his hand.

"Where did you get that from?" George said, suddenly angry. "I'll trouble you not to go to my drawers without asking me."

Sydney smiled. "Keep your wool on," he said, examining the Luger with interest. "I only wanted to satisfy my curiosity."

"Well, give it here, then," George demanded, crossing the room. "I suppose Cora told you where I kept it." He decided that he would hide the gun in another place in the future.

"She did," Sydney returned, his finger curling round the trigger. "What's the matter with it? Is it jammed?"

"No," George said shortly. "It's stiff, that's all. The trigger wants adjusting. Here, let me have it."

Sydney pulled at the trigger, and with an effort managed to snap down the hammer.

"With an action like that," he said, tossing the Luger on the bed, "you don't have to worry about accidents."

"That's why I keep it that way," George said, picking up the gun and slipping out the magazine. He made sure there was no cartridge in the breech, grunted, and shoved the gun in his hip pocket. It felt bulky and heavy, but it gave him a secret thrill to have it against his hip.

"Well, are you ready?" Sydney asked, getting up.

George nodded.

"Let's go, then," Sydney said, and they left the room and began to walk downstairs.

George suddenly remembered Leo.

"Just a tick," he said. "I've got to feed my cat."

"Forget it," Sydney said shortly. "There are other things to think about besides cats."

George ignored Sydney's impatience, ran back to his room, put a saucer of milk and the remains of the sardines on the floor where Leo could find it, and then hurried after Sydney, who was waiting for him in the street.

"Go back and keep Cora company," Sydney said. "I've got things to do." He looked at George with a jeering grin. "She thinks you're quite a hero."

George went a dull red. "Does she?" he asked eagerly. "Well, I don't know about that. I couldn't do much against those razors." He nursed his aching hand. "If it had been a fair fight ..."

"I know, I know," Sydney said, moving away. "You tell her about it. I've got things to do."

George was delighted that Sydney wasn't returning to the flat. He hurried to Russell Square, eager to be alone with Cora. He passed a chemist's shop, and remembering what Sydney had said about the weals on Cora's back, he retraced his steps, went in and asked for a bottle of witch hazel.

It was after nine o'clock when he entered the little flat. Cora was in the bathroom. She shouted through the door that she wouldn't be long, and he wandered into the sitting room.

He put the Luger on the mantelpiece, and after looking round the room, he decided that he might as well tidy up a bit. The decision gave him some pleasure. He had nothing to do, and he liked messing in a house.

He went back to the bathroom and told Cora through the panels of the door what he intended to do.

"Come in," she shouted. "I can't hear you."

He opened the door and looked into the tiny, steam-filled room. Cora was lying in the bath; only the back of her head and white shoulders were visible from where he stood. She glanced over her shoulder. A damp cigarette hung from her mouth.

"What is it?" she asked, a little sharply.

"How—how are you, Cora?"

"I'm all right," she returned. "God! You look a sight." George grinned happily. "I know," he said. "It's my hand that's bad. These are only scratches."

"You've got guts," she said. "I didn't think you had it in you."

It was worth the pain and the terror to hear that.

"This'll take the smarting away," George said, putting the bottle of witch hazel on the wooden bath surround. "You just rub it in ..."

She regarded the bottle, reached out a wet hand and picked it up. She read the label, frowning.

"Thank you, George. You're thoughtful. Now run away and tidy up, as you put it. I won't be long."

George worked happily until Cora joined him. She was wearing Sydney's dirty white dressing gown.

"You are a busy little bee, aren't you?" she jeered, looking round the room, her eyebrows making question marks.

He had put the old newspapers and empty beer bottles in one corner. He had wiped off all the sticky circles on the furniture and cleared up the mess in the fireplace. The dirty dishes he had taken into the kitchen. Already the room looked cleaner and brighter.

George grinned sheepishly. "I like doing this," he said. "I'd like a place of my own."

She sat in the armchair, lowering herself cautiously and with a little grimace. She lit a cigarette. "You're a bit of a dope, aren't you?" There was an unexpected note of kindness in her voice that George hadn't heard before. He looked at her quickly, but she was regarding him with faraway, bored eyes, as if she were only half aware of his presence.

"I say, Cora ..." he began, and then hesitated.

She glanced up sharply. "If you're going to talk about last night, you'd better skip it. I'm in no mood to go over that business now."

George scratched his head, embarrassed. "Well, all right," he said; "but hang it all, Cora, I think you ought to explain. I mean I—well, look at me. And then, you've been hurt, too. I think I ought to be told. What I mean to say is—"

"Oh, shut up!" Cora said, shifting her body in the chair. "We'll talk about that later. Suppose I was tight? No one's going to leer at me all the evening without a come-back. And no one's getting tough with me without damn well paying for it! Now, shut up, George!"

Baffled, George's gaze wandered round the room. Then he had an idea. "Where are your clothes, Cora?"

"In the bedroom. Why?"

"I'll wash them for you. They'd look quite smart. I'm a bit of a dab at that kind of thing."

She lifted her shoulders helplessly, closed her eyes and didn't say anything.

He went into the bedroom and collected the sweater and slacks. He found an unopened packet of Lux in the kitchen and he shut himself in the bathroom.

When he had hung the garments out of the back window to dry in the sun, he returned to the sitting room. She was still there, a cigarette dangling from her lips, her eyes brooding.

"I've got some hot water ready," he said. "I'd like to wash your hair."

She giggled suddenly, explosively. "You're crazy," she said.

George shook his head. "No, I'm not," he said stubbornly. "I want you to look nice."

She studied him for a long moment. "You really are in love with me, aren't you, George?"

"Of course. You didn't doubt that, did you?"

She got to her feet and crossed over to him.

"All right: wash my hair if you want to."

They went into the tiny bathroom together, and Cora sat on a stool before the wash basin.

"Have you ever washed any other girl's head?" she asked, watching George with a thoughtful expression in her eyes.

George wrapped a bath towel round her shoulders. "No," he said. "I've never wanted to before."

"So there were other girls?"

He hesitated. "Well, no, there were no other girls," he said. "You see, until you came along ..."

"I think you're a bit potty," she said, holding her head down. "Aren't you, George? Just a little potty?"

He poured water over her hair, then the shampoo. His hands felt her hard little skull. The water turned a muddy brown.

"Dirty slut, aren't I?" Cora said, with a sudden embarrassed laugh. "Does it put you off?"

"Keep still," George said. "I've nearly finished." He experienced an overwhelming feeling of love and pity for her: a feeling that he imagined a mother must have for her child. "There. Now you can sit up. Come into the other room and sit in the sun. It'll dry quickly in the sun."

When Cora was sitting by the window, George turned his attention to the room.

"Maybe I could sell these newspapers for you," he said.

"You're the giddy limit," Cora returned, laughing. "Try if you want to. I've been too lazy to bother with them. There's a sheeney across the way who buys junk. He keeps open on Sundays."

George nodded. "I'll try him. There's such a lot of rubbish here. You can hardly move for falling over it. And the bottles, too. Can I clear them all out?"

"Go ahead, if it amuses you," she said, regarding him with a puzzled expression in her eyes.

It took George a long time to shift the rubbish, but it pleased him to do so. He made four journeys to the junk shop, and finally, hot and a little exhausted, he presented her with five shillings.

"There!" he said. "A clear flat and five bob. It's funny, isn't it, that even rubbish is worth money?"

She nodded. "You're an awful dope, George," she said. "Why don't you think big? Look at the effort you've just made to get five bob. With that effort you could have made five pounds."

He thought about this seriously. "I don't think so," he said at last. "You see, no one can make five pounds quickly unless he has specialized knowledge. Even if it's only backing a horse, you have to know the right horse to back. You can't make money unless you've been properly trained." He shrugged uneasily. "Perhaps that's why I've never had any real money."

She flicked the cigarette butt into the empty fireplace. "If I liked to go on the streets," she said, "I could earn a hundred pounds a week. I don't have to have specialized knowledge to do that."

"Why don't you?" George asked, interested to hear what she would say.

She smiled secretly. "Because it's too easy."

"I wonder."

"All right. Because I'm too proud. I've got other ideas."

"I don't understand how you two live. Does Sydney keep you?"

"You're curious, aren't you?"

George nodded. "I suppose I am. Well, perhaps I shouldn't ask."

"We get along. We've been getting along like this for a hell of a time … getting nowhere."

George stood over her. "You can't go on like this, Cora," he said. "I can't go on the way I'm going on now much longer. Couldn't we get together? You and me might do well if we stuck together."

"Think so?" she said, looking out of the window. "Well, there're things to do first. I've got other things on my mind … important things," and her hands closed into tight little fists.

She's thinking about tonight, George decided uneasily. In his burst of activity he had forgotten about Crispin and the two Greeks. Instantly his old fears returned.

"I say, Cora," he said, moving over to the fireplace, "shouldn't we leave bad alone? I mean there might be more trouble." He glanced in the mirror at the plaster strips on his face. "They're a pretty rough crowd."

"If you expect us to stick together," Cora said slowly, "you'll have to show a little more guts. I don't like men without spine." She stood up and, turning her back, she pulled her dressing gown aside. "Take a look, George."

He had one momentary glimpse of the red and black marks on her white flesh before she jerked the dressing gown into place: a sight that sickened him, angered him and embarrassed him.

She faced him, her eyes probing and cold. "Well?"

"Oh, Cora," he said, going to her. He put his arms round her, but she was hard and resisting. She pushed him away.

"Not now, George," she said impatiently. "All that can come when this business is over." She glanced up at him. "If you really care for me, you're not going to let Crispin get away with this. You've talked a lot about what you did in the States. I want to see what you can do here. When I've seen that, I could be very nice to you." Her eyes came alive for a moment. "Very nice to you," she repeated.

This was too important to George for any misunderstanding. He clutched her hands.

"I'll do anything for you, Cora," he said, looking wildly into her eyes for her assurance. "If I do that, you will be nice to me? You will be really nice?" He wanted to say, "You're promising to give yourself to me?" but he hadn't the courage to come out with it as bluntly as that.

She seemed to know what was in his mind, because she gave him an unmistakable look of promise.

"You won't be disappointed, George," she said. "I don't like men messing me about, but you're different. You'll get your reward."

Later, they went out for a snack. George wanted to take the gun, but Cora wouldn't let him. "Leave it there," she said, a little sharply. "It won't run away."

He walked a step behind her, and glanced from time to time at her with secret pride. The pale blue sweater had shrunk a trifle, but it looked bright. The slacks had a knife-edge crease which he had put in with great care, using an old-fashioned flatiron he had found in the kitchen. Her hair was sleek and glossy. She had taken pains to put her lipstick on neatly. He thought she looked lovely.

Although she did not complain, she walked stiffly, but she held her head high, and she had lost none of her arrogance.

They went to the pub at the corner of the street and leaned up against the bar. They ordered pints of bitter and sausage rolls.

"This is fun, isn't it?" George said, in seventh heaven.

She flicked a flake of pastry from her mouth and grimaced. "Think so?" she said, biting into the sausage roll again.

"I suppose it's nothing to you," he said, hurt; "only I've been lonely for a long time. Having a girl like you for company means a lot to me."

She raised the beer glass and drank, gazing at him with thoughtful eyes over the top of it. She put the glass down and drew a deep breath.

"You're a sentimental fool, aren't you?"

He looked to see if she was jeering at him, but she was serious in an unexpectedly kind way.

"I suppose I am." He brooded, looking down at his shoes. "But there's nothing wrong in that. I know people sneer at sentimentality, but they're usually pretty unhappy themselves."

She wasn't listening to him. Her attention was centred on a short man who had just come in. George followed her gaze. He recognized the man. It was Little Ernie.

Little Ernie joined them. "My word!" he said, staring at George, "has she been making love to you?"

George didn't say anything.

"For Gawd's sake," Little Ernie went on to Cora, "what's 'appened to the bloke? Saw 'im a week ago, and 'e was as lovely as an oil painting. Look at 'im now."

"Dry up, Ernie," Cora said. "He's been in the wars."

"I'll say 'e 'as," Little Ernie said, undisguised admiration in his eyes. "Well, well. What'll you 'ave?" He rubbed a dirty finger under his nose and then wiped his finger on his trouser leg.

"We've got drinks, thank you," George said, a little stiffly. He didn't like this man. He didn't like the way he was eyeing Cora, a lewd look in his small green eyes.

Little Ernie rapped on the bar with a coin. "Hurry up," he shouted. "I ain't got all day. Gimme a double Scotch." He turned to Cora. "Sure you won't 'ave one?"

"All right," she said, leaning her back against the counter. She propped herself on her elbows and thrust her chest at him. "Give George one, too. You're lousy with money, aren't you?"

Little Ernie winked. "I get by," he said, and raising his voice he shouted, "Make it three doubles, Clara, and out of the boss's bottle!" He looked at Cora again, then he glanced at George. "Fine gel, ain't she?" he said. "What a dairy! You could make pounds outta 'er if you knew 'ow to 'andle 'er."

"Shut your dirty trap," Cora said, her eyes bright with suppressed laughter. "George's not like you." She reached round and picked up her glass. "How's Eva? Still buying your suits?"

Little Ernie's cruel face darkened. "You don't 'ave to shout all over the shop, do you?" he said, glancing uneasily over his shoulder. "Old Crockett was down the street not five minutes ago. She's all right. She's a good girl. Work! Gawd love me, I've never known a girl to work like it!"

Cora sneered. "That's her trouble, Ernie. She does like it."

George was listening to this conversation and not understanding a word of it. He wished Little Ernie would go away. He was so repulsive that he embarrassed George.

"Believe she does," Little Ernie agreed thoughtfully. "You're a smart gel, Cora. Pity you don't get wise. I could fix you up in no time. Think of it! A flat of your own, 'undred smackers a week, and a dawg if you wanted one."

The barmaid planked down the three double whiskies, and Little Ernie parted with a pound.

"Gimme twenty Player's and keep the change, ducks," he said. He turned back to Cora. "Well, I suppose you know what's good for you," he went on. "Only if you ever change your mind, give us a ring." He picked up his whisky. "Well, 'ere's to better days." He drank half the whisky, sighed and rested his small foot on the brass rail. "What 'ave you been doing to yourself?" he said, eyeing Cora. "You look orl right; a proper knock-out."

"My new valet," Cora said, nodding at George. "He washed my pretty clothes and gave me a shampoo."

Little Ernie stared at George blankly.

George turned scarlet under the bitter, green eyes.

"Well, well," Little Ernie said. "Fancy that." He picked his nose and moved restlessly. "Hmm, well, well." He seemed at a loss for words.

"He's not a cissy," Cora said, glancing at George as if he were a stranger. "He's a tough guy, and when I say tough, I mean tough. He was Frank Kelly's gunman."

Little Ernie put down his glass. "Is that so?" He stared at George with interest.

George wished that Cora hadn't brought that up again. He shuffled his feet and fiddled with his tie. "Have another Scotch?" he said, in a desperate attempt to be at his ease.

"'Ave one yourself," Little Ernie said. "It's on me." He snapped his fingers at the barmaid. "Same again, Clara, and don't drown 'em." He looked at Cora questioningly, but she only gave him back a jeering smile. "Kelly's gunman, eh? Hmm, what are you doing over 'ere?"

"Mind your own business," Cora snapped, before George could think of anything to say. "He's one of us now." The green eyes narrowed. "Is that so?"

"That's right. Three thugs once took him in a wood. They had ideas about him. He walked out on his feet and alone," Cora said, her eyes, cold and hard, on George's bewildered face. "But he's modest. He doesn't talk about it." She fished a crumpled packet of cigarettes from her hip pocket. "He's quite a guy."

Little Ernie lit her cigarette and then produced two cigars. He offered one to George, who took it, not because he wanted it, but because he was so embarrassed that he wasn't quite certain what he was doing.

"Seems a quiet type of bloke, doesn't he?" Little Ernie went on regarding George.

"He's quiet all right," Cora returned. "Aren't you, George?"

George mumbled something. He didn't know what all this was about, but he did feel a sense of pride at the respectful way Little Ernie was regarding him.

"Syd said you'd be here. I thought he was joining us. What's he up to?" Little Ernie asked suddenly.

"He's busy," Cora said.

Little Ernie handed round the whiskies again. "Oh, well," he said, "I expect 'e is, but 'e said 'e'd be 'ere. Seen Crispin lately?" he went on casually, after a pause: too casually.

George started, slopping his whisky. He felt Little Ernie's eyes on him.

Cora nodded. Her expression didn't change. There was a jeering, confident expression in her eyes that obviously impressed Little Ernie.

"I saw him last night: so did George."

Little Ernie glanced at the sticking plaster and at George's bandaged hand and whistled. "Impulsive bloke, our Crispin," he said. "Shouldn't be surprised if 'e didn't get 'imself into a spot of trouble one of these days."

Cora smiled again, her face frozen. "Neither should I."

The two eyed each other. George, watching them uneasily, had a feeling that a drama was being enacted before his eyes, yet he could not understand what it was all about.

"Funny stories one 'ears," Little Ernie went on, watching Cora like a hawk. "Gawd knows who puts 'em in circulation. I did 'ear you and Crispin 'ad a little fun together last night."

Cora sipped her whisky. Her eyebrows lifted.

"I had a little fun," she said quietly. "Crispin's share is on ice at the moment, isn't it, George?"

George grunted. He had no idea why she was talking like this. To him it seemed dangerous. If they were going to get their own back on Crispin, why tell this sordid little man about it? Suppose he warned Crispin?

"Well, well." Little Ernie studied George, who was scowling down at the floor. He thought George looked a pretty *tough hombre.*

"He put me over a table and flogged me with a cane," Cora said calmly. "It hurt like hell ... it still hurts like hell."

Little Ernie's eyes bulged. "Gawd!" he exclaimed. "'E must 'ave been barmy to do a thing like that to you."

Cora nodded. "George thinks so, too. In fact, George got quite annoyed about it. The Greeks had to cool him with razors. Now, of course, George is really mad. Aren't you, George!"

"Yes," George said uncomfortably.

He tried to show how angry he was by scowling at Little Ernie and tightening his mouth. He had no idea how menacing he looked. He never took into account his great bulk, nor the fact that when he frowned his big, fleshy face was misleadingly hard and coarse. The strips of plaster also added to the effect. It was impressive enough to make Little Ernie whistle again.

"Well, for crying out loud," he said, "what's going to 'appen?"

Cora's eyes went blank. "You want to know a lot, don't you?" she said, stretching out her leg and looking at her shoe that George had cleaned so industriously. "It mightn't be healthy to know too much, Ernie."

He nodded. His eyes, quick as a ferret's, showed he was startled. "That's right," he said. "I don't want to know. I don't want to know anything about you three. 'Ave another drink?"

Cora shook her head. "You're not staying, are you, Ernie? Because we've got things to talk about."

"Who, me? No, I'm not staying. I've got to get along. You know me, Cora, always on the move. Well, so long." He grinned at George. "So long, palsy. Glad to 'ave met you," and he left them.

George finished his beer. The whiskies and the beer gave him rather a pleasant floating feeling. He knew he was just a little tight.

"You told him a lot, didn't you?" he said, looking at Cora questioningly.

"Ernie's all right," she said shortly. "He hates Crispin as much as we do. Besides, it's as well to let them know we're a mob now, not just a boy and a girl."

This continual hinting worried George. What did she mean when she kept saying he was one of them? Now she was talking about a mob.

"I may be a bit dense," he said slowly, "but I wish you'd explain. What mob? What do you mean by mob?"

She regarded him steadily. He again experienced the disconcerting feeling that she was looking inside his skull, even inside his pockets.

"I shan't be a moment," she said, fishing out her little purse from her pocket. "I want to spend a penny."

He understood then that these hints did mean something, but she had no intention of telling him.

He watched her walk across the room, jaunty and arrogant, to the door marked "Ladies."

CHAPTER TWELVE

It was a good film, and George gave it all his attention. The atmosphere of the cinema soothed him. The darkness, the bright screen, the drama which he could watch as an interested onlooker gave him a feeling that he had escaped into another, more pleasant world. He knew, at the back of his mind, that outside in the hot sunshine his world waited impatiently for his return; but for the next two hours here was escape.

He had been disappointed that Cora had wished to see a movie. The whiskies had made him amorous, and as soon as they left the pub he began a clumsy manoeuvre to persuade Cora to return to the flat.

He was careful, of course, not to let her know what he had in mind, but his eyes, his flushed face and his incoherent speech gave him away. Not that she let on that she had spotted his little game; she didn't. She said she felt like a movie, and although he had protested, and even said that it would be nicer if they went back to the flat together, imploring her with his eyes, she remained adamant.

He was hurt and angry that she could be so hard. What was the sense in wasting the afternoon in a cinema, when they could have been together alone and undisturbed in the flat?

He had sulked, and was determined that when she asked him which of the three cinemas they should choose, he would pointedly show his indifference.

But she didn't ask him. She walked down the street a step ahead of him, passed the first cinema and went straight to the box office of the second one, a few hundred yards farther down the road.

"Get circle seats," she said abruptly, and went on towards the stairs.

He got the tickets and followed her, seething with frustration and disappointment. And when she pushed one-and-sixpence into his hand, he snatched the money from her and pocketed it without a word.

But once he had settled down in his seat, the magic of the darkness, the music and the drama on the screen overcame his ill-temper.

It was a good picture: the kind of picture he liked. There were beautiful women, tough, well-dressed men, and music. There were long sequences of dimly lit streets and shadowy figures, guns in hand, moving silently from doorway to doorway. There were gun battles in the dark. There was a bedroom scene that titillated his desire for Cora, so that he fumbled for her hand and held it moistly, until she impatiently withdrew it.

As the drama progressed, he became so engrossed that he even forgot Cora was with him, and when the film came to an end he was sorry.

Moving down the stairs, a little dazed by the bright sunlight, he realized that he was a few hours closer to pending danger. Perhaps, after all, he could persuade them not to go; but his courage failed when he saw the cold, distant expression on Cora's face.

She, too, seemed to realize that time was running out. He could tell that she was uneasy. There was a subtle tension about her which hinted at taut nerves. When he made a comment about the film, she did not seem to hear him. She walked on, moving through the crowds almost as if she were sleepwalking.

It was six o'clock, and George wanted a cup of tea. He suggested they might have one, but she paid no attention. She kept on inexorably, alone in a crowd of people, deep in her secret thoughts.

He felt she was going to a definite place, and as he followed her, he had a premonition of danger. It was so acute that he stopped and caught at her arm.

"Where are we going?" he asked sharply. "Why are you so quiet? Is there something wrong?"

They stood in the middle of the pavement. The crowd broke up, passed them and joined up again. They received angry glances.

"Come on," she said with equal sharpness. "It's only round the corner."

She went on. His uneasiness growing, George followed her. In a few minutes they were in a quiet side street, and this time it was Cora who stopped.

"There's a shop down there," she said, pointing and looking at him with a curious intentness. "Go and buy a whip. A horsewhip will do. Something you can hide under your coat." She thrust a pound note into his hand.

In spite of the sun and the hot pavement, George suddenly went cold. His instinct warned him to have nothing to do with this. It was as if he were being asked to cross a piece of ground which he knew was not solid and into which he was certain he would sink, and then suffocate.

"It's Sunday," he said, drawing away from her. "You can't buy anything today."

"Why do you think I came here?" she said impatiently. "They are all Jews down here. They closed yesterday."

His mind darted like a startled mouse for a way of escape.

"I'm not buying it," he said obstinately. "If you want it, you'll have to get it yourself. I'm not having anything to do with it. I—I don't believe in that sort of thing."

She looked at his set, obstinate face and she suddenly smiled. "You're quite right, George," she said softly; "it's stupid to wait. When two people are in love...." She pushed the pound note again into his hand. "Get the whip and let's go back. We've still time before he returns."

George stared at her, seeing in her eyes a fainting desire: an unmistakable invitation of receptive, expectant femininity.

"Cora!" he said, his fingers clutching the pound note, "you mean— now? You really mean *now?*"

"I said I'd be nice to you, didn't I? Well, why should we wait? ... Only you'll have to hurry."

He went down the street with an unsteady, shambling gait, a feverish, incoherent puppet, without a will, without regard to danger, without a thought for anything except what she was offering him.

He blundered into the shop she had indicated. Saddles, rolls of leather, horse blankets, dog collars, trunks, bags and whips overflowed on the counter, the floor and the shelves behind the counter.

An elderly man with a great hooked nose came out of an office at the back of the shop. He looked curiously at George.

"Good afternoon," he said. "Is there something I can show you?"

George looked round the shop, his eyes bloodshot and wild. He saw a whip, a riding switch, whalebone bound in red leather, with an ivory handle. He picked it up with a shudder.

"I'll have it," he said, thrusting it at the Jew, and threw down the pound note.

The Jew shook his head. "I think it's a little more than a pound," he said, picking up the whip with long, caressing fingers. He turned the price ticket and glanced at it. "It's a fine piece of workmanship." He smiled. "It's fifty-five shillings."

George gulped. "Give me something for a pound, something like this, only for a pound."

"Certainly." The Jew did not move, but continued to touch the riding-switch with caressing fingers. "I should like to point out, sir, that it would be more economical to buy a better whip while you are about it. Now, this is something that will last a lifetime. It is beautifully made and impossible to wear out. The extra money will be saved over and over again."

What was the matter with this fool? George thought, feverishly. Didn't he know he was wasting precious time?

"I don't want it," he said violently. "Give me what I want, and for God's sake stop talking!"

He was not aware of the sudden alarm that jumped into the Jew's eyes, nor his curious stare at George's congested face.

George was only aware of the passing time, and when the Jew offered him another whip, saying in a grieved voice that it was a guinea, George threw down a shilling on top of the pound note, snatched up the whip without looking at it, and rushed from the shop.

Cora was waiting at the corner, serene and arrogant. Her hands were thrust deep into her pockets and her eyes watchful.

"I've got it," George said thickly, falling into step beside her. "Let's go back."

She allowed herself to be hurried through the streets. They did not speak. George was only conscious of a pounding in his ears and a suffocating desire for her. He almost pushed her up the stairs to the flat, and when she had to search through her pockets and purse for the key, he stood trembling, in an agony of suspense.

Finally she opened the door and they entered the flat. He threw the whip into the armchair and caught hold of her.

"Hello, George," Sydney said from the door.

George didn't look round. His arms dropped to his sides, and he stood staring down at Cora with glazed eyes. The hateful sound of Sydney's voice crushed him.

Sydney wandered into the room and regarded him sharply.

"I say, what a state you're in!" he said in his sneering voice.

George turned away. He caught a cold, jeering look from Cora that sent a stab into his heart. He was sick with disappointment and frustration.

"What have you been up to, Cora?" Sydney went on, flopping into the armchair. "What's this?" he continued, picking up the whip. "Oh, something for Crispin, eh? That's wonderful." A quick, cautious note crept into his voice. "Did George buy it?"

"He bought it," Cora said, wandering across the room and opening a cupboard. "He didn't want to at first, but I persuaded him; didn't I, George?" She took from the cupboard a bottle of whisky and two glasses.

George sat down limply and wiped his face and hands on his handkerchief. He didn't say anything. He had a feeling that they had, between them, tricked him in some way. He felt that ever since Sydney had telephoned him, asking him to take the message to "Joe's Club", a series of carefully planned manoeuvres had taken place to trap him.

Cora came over to him with a glass half full of whisky. "Have a drink, George," she said, putting the glass in his hand. "You look as if you needed it."

Then she sat on his lap and slipped an arm round his neck. His suspicions were immediately lulled, and in their place came an overwhelming tenderness and love for her. She rested her head against his shoulder and gently swung her legs. She, too, had a stiff whisky in her hand.

Sydney was eyeing them with thoughtful interest.

"It seems I came back a bit too early," he said, settling more comfortably in his armchair.

"You did," Cora returned, tormenting George by rubbing her face against his. "George and I had made plans, hadn't we, George?"

He gripped her tightly, but didn't say anything. His hand trembled so that he slopped a little whisky on her slacks.

"Careful, George," she said, and suddenly laughed. "You know, our George is quite a lad," she went on to Sydney. "I believe he'd make one of the world's greatest lovers."

"Never mind about George," Sydney said. "We've got other things to think about."

Cora slipped off George's lap. She crossed the room and picked up the whip.

George, feeling suddenly deflated, watched her. She swished the whip once or twice, her face spiteful. Then she laughed. "I'll bet he'll yell the place down," she said.

"It's all fixed," Sydney said. "He'll be alone. I've got a car. We leave at eight-thirty. It'll take us about an hour. By that time it'll be getting dark."

Cora raised her glass. "To our new member," she said, looking at George, and she tilted her head and emptied her glass.

George felt hot. Whisky burned in his stomach. He was a little light-headed, but uneasy, nervous.

The past hour had been difficult. As the hands of the clock crept forward, all of them showed signs of strain. Even Sydney, for all his sneering coldness, began to fidget and look at the clock.

Cora drank steadily. She showed no sign that the whisky was affecting her, except that her face became paler and her eyes brightened.

When, at last, Sydney got to his feet, there was an immediate tightening of the tension. George looked from one to the other.

"Perhaps we ought not to go ..." he began, facing them.

They stood side by side, brother and sister, their eyes cold and cautious, oddly alike. They stared at him as if he were a stranger.

"Don't talk wet," Sydney said.

"Go on," Cora said. "We're coming."

Sydney shrugged and moved to the door. He opened it and began to walk down the stairs.

Cora went to George.

"You're coming back here tonight," she said, putting her hand on his arm. "I don't cheat. I meant what I said, only I didn't think Sydney would be back so soon." Her eyes were inviting. Then she added, "I'll be nice to you tonight—promise."

After that it didn't seem to matter. When he turned to pick up the gun, she was before him. She took it up very carefully by the barrel.

"I'm your gun moll," she said, her mouth smiling. "I want to carry it." She slipped it into a leather bag she had slung from her shoulder. Then she went up to him. "Kiss me," she said.

They left the flat a few minutes before eight-thirty. It was a sultry night; the sky was cloudless, but there was the smell of rain in the air.

They joined Sydney in the street a few moments later. There was a smear of lipstick on George's mouth and he seemed bemused.

None of them spoke. Cora walked stiffly because of the whip she had thrust down the leg of her slacks. George was between the two of them, and it seemed to him that they were his jailers.

They turned down an alley and into a little courtyard. A dark green Ford coupe was standing round the corner, out of sight from the mouth of the alley.

Sydney unlocked the door and slid under the wheel. Cora got in at the back.

"Come on," she said to George, who was hesitating. He got into the car beside her and slammed the door. "I didn't know you had a car," he said blankly.

"He thinks this is our car," Cora called to Sydney.

Sydney laughed. It had a mirthless sound. He started the engine and drove the car slowly down the alley.

"Well, isn't it your car?" George asked.

"We borrowed it," Sydney said. "Now shut up. I want to think."

They drove out of London in silence. As Big Ben, coming over a wireless set, struck nine, they passed through Wimbledon. Later they got on to the Reigate Road.

George sat hunched up, alone and lost. He thought of his room in the dull boarding house and Leo. That part of his life seemed remote now: he wasn't even sure that it had ever happened. But Cora—he could feel her thigh against his—was real enough, so was the back of Sydney's head, and the swift passage of the car through the darkening streets: all frighteningly real.

He lost count of time. He didn't want to think about it. He felt that the car was taking him towards a destiny from which there was no escape.

Sydney leaned forward and switched on the headlights.

"We turn off just about here," he said shortly: there was a nervous hesitation in his voice.

They peered through the windows. They were over-anxious, as if it were the most important thing in the world not to miss the turning.

They saw it at last, and they both exclaimed.

"All right," Sydney said, braking sharply. "I'm not blind."

They turned into a country lane and stopped. The headlights made the grass banks and hedges on either side of the lane look startlingly fresh and green.

"It's just at the end of the lane," Sydney said, cutting the engine. "We'll leave the car here."

He twisted round in his seat so that he could look at them. The white moonlight lighted his face. It frightened George. The ghastly scar burned red, and there was a look of animal viciousness and hatred in Sydney's eyes.

"We'll go in together," Sydney went on. His voice trembled in a breathless kind of way. "If he shows fight, give George the gun. Now listen, George, this is important. Go up to him and ram the gun in his stomach. Do you understand? Wind him. Look tough. You don't have to say anything; I'll do the talking. When Cora gives you the gun, walk up to him and slam it in his guts. That'll take the starch out of the rat. You wait: it'll do you good to see the way he'll curl up. Then we'll go for him."

George licked his dry lips. "Listen, just a minute ..."

Cora put her hand on his knee. Her touch sent the blood pounding in his head. Words of caution died in his mouth.

"What is it?" Sydney asked.

"Nothing," Cora said. "He's fine, aren't you, George?"

"Well, don't mess about," Sydney said. "This is serious. Now come on; let's get it over."

He got out of the car.

"We're coming," Cora said.

As Sydney moved away down the lane she fell against George, her hands pulling his head down to her open mouth. A suffocating desire engulfed him. They remained like that for some time, their mouths crushed together, and then Cora pushed him away and slid out of the car.

"Come," she said.

As if hypnotized, George followed her. His heart hammered against his ribs and blood sang in his ears. He couldn't think about Crispin. He couldn't think of anything.

Cora held his arm. She was pulling him along. He couldn't see, and his feet stumbled. Sweat dripped down his face. The air had gone dead. There was no movement in the trees; no wind, only a hot stillness that oppressed him. In the distance, thunder rumbled. A line of black clouds began to edge above the horizon.

"Quiet," she said softly, and he could feel her trembling.

Sydney moved towards them out of the darkness.

"It's all right," he whispered. "He's there, and alone."

He went on ahead. Cora followed, seemingly able to see in the dark. She steered George through a gateway and up an overgrown path. Then suddenly they came on a small bungalow. One window was open, and light streamed from it into the garden.

The three of them stopped abruptly. Thunder crashed not far away, startling George, so that he clutched Cora's arm. Her muscles felt hard under his hand, as if she were keyed up, her nerves at breaking point.

They edged forward so that they could look into the room. Crispin, in a blue-and-white-flowered dressing gown, was sitting at a table. A cigarette dangled from his lips; he was writing on a pad of notepaper. A lawyer's briefcase lay half-open at his elbow. It appeared to be bulging with pound notes.

George shivered. The sight of all that money frightened him even more than the thought of bursting in and assaulting this strange-looking man. He glanced at Sydney. He could just make out his features in the light from the window. He was hissing between his teeth, a frightening look of pent-up hatred in his eyes.

A spear thrust of blue-white lightning split the sky, was followed in a few seconds by a tremendous clap of thunder. George ducked instinctively. A drop of ice-cold water fell on his hot face. It began to rain.

Cora jerked at his arm. Sydney was already creeping towards the front door. In a kind of dream, George followed him. As before, when they had burst into Robinson's room, he suddenly felt extraordinarily at ease. This was, of course, just another of his fantasies. George Fraser, millionaire gangster, was again on the job. It couldn't really be happening to poor old George, the lonely, cat-loving book tout. Not this: this was too fantastic. It would be all right. In a few minutes Leo would come in and jump up on his bed. Ella would come in with his tea. There was no need to get alarmed, or for his heart to pound like this. He might just as well enjoy this fantasy. What the devil was this little runt of a Sydney doing, leading the way? George Fraser always led the way. It was too late now. Sydney had opened the front door. They were all in the room now, looking at Crispin.

This was exciting! Crispin was behaving just as George imagined he would behave. He had turned green with terror.

George flexed his great muscles and scowled at him.

"Hello, Crispin," Sydney said.

Crispin put a hand on the leather briefcase. He didn't move his body and he didn't say anything.

"Get up, Crispin," Sydney said. "I've had to wait a long time to get even with you. We have you now where we want you."

Slowly Crispin rose to his feet; even then he couldn't find his voice.

"I've brought a whip," Cora said, polite as a tailor at a fitting. She pulled the whip from her trouser leg and laid it on the table.

"We'll start with that," Sydney said.

Cora zipped open her bag casually and took out the Luger. A faint click sounded through the room. It was immediately lost in a clap of thunder.

"Here, George," she said, and pushed the gun into his hand.

George looked at Crispin. Crispin looked at him and then at the gun. His face seemed to fall to pieces. He began to back slowly away.

Oddly enough, the heavy Luger felt good in George's hands. He felt extraordinarily elated to see the terror in Crispin's face.

Crispin, white, his mouth working, backed against the wall. He looked lonely.

George bore down on him.

"Don't ..." Crispin said, and squirmed against the wall like a beetle pinned alive to a board.

"Get your hands up," George said, and rammed the gun hard into Crispin's chest.

A zigzag of brilliant lightning streaked through the window. Thunder sounded like a trunk being moved in an attic. Above the crash of the thunder came another sound—a sharp crack, like the breaking of dry wood magnified many times. A wisp of smoke rose in the air: it smelt of gunpowder.

In that moment of sound George felt the gun in his hand kick like a live thing, and it jumped out of his hand onto the floor. He became conscious of two things: a tight, deep-throated scream from Cora, and a curious red mess on the wall where Crispin had been standing.

Slowly, his eyes travelled from the red stain down the wall, past the sideboard, to the floor. Crispin lay huddled up, as if the bones in his legs had been broken. There was a red stain on the front of his white-and-blue dressing gown.

A voice came to George, as if someone were shouting in a tunnel. He heard the voice, but the words meant nothing to him.

It's all right, he said to himself. This has happened to you hundreds of times before. All you've got to do is to hang on and wait. You'll wake up in a moment.

Someone was shaking him. A strident voice was shrieking at him.

"You fool! You fool! You stupid, bloody fool!"

Something hard hit him in the face, and he shivered. Something inside his head exploded into fire and darkness, and just before the darkness he felt a sharp flash of nausea. He staggered, clutched at nothing, recovered his balance and groped with blind fingers.

The shock left him after a while.

Cora was speaking again. She was speaking softly.

"You did it," she was saying. "We don't touch murder. That's something we don't stand for. We didn't tell you to shoot him. We only wanted you to frighten him."

He could see her eyes, slate-grey, hard, frightened. Her face was misty. He looked at Sydney. He wavered before George like weeds in a fast-moving river.

Then—*snap!*—everything became sharp and clear. Cora and Sydney seemed to spring to life, sharp-etched, like a film that has been suddenly correctly focused.

He stared down at Crispin, caught his breath and shied away.

"No!" he said huskily. "The gun wasn't loaded! I didn't do it! I didn't do it!"

They watched him, cold, pitiless and accusing.

"It's your mess," Sydney said, his voice flat and metallic. "Keep away from us. We don't want you. We don't touch murder."

George wasn't listening to him. He was looking at Cora. She wouldn't desert him: "I don't cheat," she had said. "I'll be very nice to you tonight—promise." She'd promised, hadn't she? She couldn't desert him now. She must know that this had nothing to do with him.

He went to her.

"Cora!" he said. "I didn't do it! You know I didn't. The gun wasn't loaded. I can prove it. The cartridges are at home. There's twenty-five of them. That's all I had. They haven't been touched! Don't you understand? They haven't been touched!"

Her mouth curled in loathing.

"You stupid, creeping fool!" she cried. "I hate you! Look what you've done! Don't ever dare come near me again!" And she struck him across the face with her clenched fist.

Then they went out and left him.

He stood looking at Crispin; he was numbed with horror. Slowly he bent and picked up the Luger. It smelt strongly of gunpowder. He examined it. The safety catch had been moved. He pressed it down. There came a faint click. His memory moved, groped, floundered. There had been the same clicking sound when Cora had given him the gun. He remembered now. Had she deliberately released the safety catch? He didn't think it likely. He didn't know. His finger curled round the trigger. The hammer instantly snapped down. He snapped the hammer down three times before it dawned on him that someone had fixed the trigger mechanism so that the gun would fire at the slightest touch. Even then he was too terrified to think much of the discovery.

Rain beat in through the open window, and the curtains ballooned into the room as waves of hot air disturbed them. Thunder crackled.

George stood still, listening. He heard a motor car start up. It seemed to be moving at a great speed, and its sound quickly died away.

He found himself looking at the table and noting with stupefied fascination that the briefcase full of money was no longer there.

CHAPTER THIRTEEN

George opened his eyes. The room was shadowy, but comfortingly familiar. The faint dawn light edged round the blind. It was early.

Although his body ached, and there was a feeling of lassitude in his limbs, his brain was clear and awake. He raised his head and glanced at his wristwatch. It was half-past five. He lay back again and stared up at the ceiling, his mind crawling with alarm. He must avoid panic. He must relax and go over the whole business carefully and calmly. If he thought enough about it, got it into its right perspective, there must be a way out. The trouble was that he wasn't very good at thinking, nor was he very good at keeping calm, nor, of course, had he killed a man before.

He sat up in bed and deliberately turned the pillow, patted it and lay down again. By this simple act—something that anyone would do—he hoped that he would recapture a feeling of security. He adjusted the sheet under his chin and moved his legs. The bed felt warm and comfortable. The little black cloud of panic that had begun to edge over his brain receded. It would be all right, he told himself, if he kept calm.

He closed his eyes, and immediately Crispin's crumpled body in the bloodstained dressing gown swam into his mind. He started up, his fists gripping the sheet. This wouldn't do, he thought, and forced himself to lie down again.

It took some time before he could trust himself to think. But he knew that he could not for long avoid facing the facts. He had killed a man. Now he must make plans. He had no idea what plans he had to make, but he couldn't lie in bed for the rest of his days. He had to decide what he was going to do. The easiest way, of course, would be to go to the police and tell them everything. That would shift the responsibility from him to them. They couldn't do anything to him. It had been an accident. He could prove that it had been an accident. The cartridge must have been in the breech for a long time. George frowned. No, that couldn't be right, because he had pulled the trigger many times, liking the sound of the sharp snap of the hammer. If the cartridge had been in the breech it would have been fired long ago. Then how did the cartridge get into the breech? He had twenty-five cartridges, but he had never put one of them into the magazine. He had been most careful about that. He was so sure about this that he began to consider whether it was his gun that had fired the fatal shot. Perhaps someone lurking outside had fired through the open window. Then he remembered how the gun had smelt of gunpowder, and his mind again began to crawl with alarm.

Someone must have put a cartridge into the gun. That could be the only explanation. Someone had also fixed the trigger mechanism. He would tell the police. It wasn't his business to say who did it. All he had to do was to show them the box of cartridges, and they could see at a glance that none of them was missing. Surely that would prove his innocence?

He looked at the dressing table across the room and then got out of bed. He opened the drawer and took out the small wooden box of cartridges; then he got back into bed again, holding the box tightly in his hand. He mustn't lose this box, he told himself. His life depended on it. That seemed an exaggerated statement to make, but it was true. His life did depend on it.

He'd go to the police and explain. He would open the box and show them the tight-fitting cartridges. He took the lid off the box. One cartridge was missing. He looked at the empty space for a long time and then he put the box very carefully on the table by his bed.

He lay back on his pillow and began to weep, weak with hysterical fear. He had known all along that a cartridge would be missing. It was all part of this ghastly nightmare: this web that was inexorably creeping round him, but he had tried to make himself believe that there was still a loophole of escape.

It was some time before he began to think again. Now his brain moved in quick darts, snatching at anything that could sustain hope.

He didn't arrive at any conclusion, and he knew he wouldn't arrive at any conclusion until he had controlled the panic that was gripping his heart and his mind.

Somehow one of the cartridges that belonged to him had got into the gun. How? Who did it?

His mind darted to Sydney.

Sydney.... Well, yes, he could have taken a cartridge from the box when he had sneaked the Luger from George's drawer while George had been shaving. It was just the sort of sly thing that Sydney would do. Then, while Cora and he had been at the movies, Sydney could have fixed the trigger mechanism and put the cartridge in the breech. Cora knew, of course. It was obvious. That was why she had insisted that George should leave the gun on the mantelpiece when they went to the movies. It was there for Sydney, who was waiting for them to go. It also explained why Cora had insisted on carrying the gun when they set off for Copthorne.

"I'm your gun moll," she had said, and she had kissed him. He thought of Judas, and remembered how shocked he had been when, as a child, he had read of the betrayal. The same sense of shock returned.

Well, he was getting on. He now knew how the cartridge had been put in the gun and how the trigger mechanism had been fixed. Cora had put the finishing touch to the trap. Just before she had given him the gun she had deliberately slipped back the safety catch. He remembered distinctly hearing the soft little click as the catch snapped back. It was almost as if she and Sydney had planned the murder of Crispin.

His mind shied away from this idea. He remembered Cora's look of loathing.

"We don't touch murder. That's something we don't stand for. We didn't tell you to shoot him. We only wanted you to frighten him."

Then why had they fixed the gun like that?

George rubbed his sweating face with his hand. There was something wrong. He had had a feeling all along that there was something wrong, but he had been so besotted with Cora that he had not heeded his own uneasiness.

Begin at the beginning, he said to himself. The telephone booth at Joe's. That started it.

"It's a club in Mortimer Street, not far from you. They're not on the blower, otherwise I'd 've rung 'em," Sydney had said.

But they had been on the blower. He had seen for himself the telephone booth in the Club.

Sydney must have known that. But if he hadn't lied about the telephone, there would have been no reason for George to go to Joe's and leave a message for Cora. And that would have meant that he would never have met her, never have fallen in love with her, never have been a besotted fool and never have allowed himself to be persuaded to commit murder.

The more he thought about it, the plainer it became. The story about the key and Cora not being able to get into the flat had been part of the plot. It was so simple that it had never crossed his mind that he was walking into a trap.

What devils these two were! The trouble they had taken to trap him into murder. He remembered the briefcase full of money. There must have been five or six hundred pounds in that case. That was the motive, of course! They had trapped him into killing Crispin so that they could steal the money! He sat up in bed, his eyes wild. Then the scene in the restaurant had been part of the plot. Cora had deliberately staged that business to fool him into believing they had no other motive in visiting Crispin but for revenge. And they had fooled him. Was it possible that she had allowed herself to be flogged like that just to fool him? There was no doubt that she had been flogged. He had heard her shrieks and had seen the marks. The red, bruised, broken skin was something you couldn't fake. Had she really accepted such a beating in order to provide a false motive just to fool him?

He floundered in a pit of doubt, turning the facts over in his mind. Then he remembered something she had said to Sydney when they had returned to the flat, just before he had fainted, "You said he wouldn't touch me!" He remembered, too, how nervous she had been, and that after she had thrown the wine in Crispin's face she had begged him not to let Crispin touch her. It looked as if Sydney had also double-crossed Cora. He had trapped *her* into picking a fight with Crispin, assuring her that she would come to no harm.

The more George thought about it, the calmer he became. It was an utterly fantastic story, but he felt confident that if he kept his head and explained everything very carefully, and in its proper sequence, the police would believe him.

The face of Little Ernie suddenly swam into his mind, blotting out the vision of hope he had so carefully constructed.

Cora had practically told Little Ernie that George was going to get even with Crispin.

"I had a little fun," she had said. "Crispin's share is on ice at the moment, isn't it, George?"

And Little Ernie had looked uneasy. He would remember the conversation, and when he heard about Crispin's death, he would go to the police.

George began to sweat again. What would the police say after they had listened to Little Ernie? And then he thought of the whip. What had happened to the whip? Cora had been diabolically clever in the way she had persuaded him to buy the whip. So much for her promises. Well, he would know another time—if there was another time. If the police found the whip, they would trace it to him. The old Jew would remember him. He had been so anxious to get Cora back to the flat that he had behaved like a madman. He put his hand to the strips of plaster on his face. The Jew would remember those strips. How easy it would be for the police to spot him! The Jew would give the police a full description of him. It would tally with the description that Little Ernie would give them. No one had seen Cora. She had kept away from the shop. The whip had been left in the bungalow. It was an obvious clue. He hadn't even removed the price ticket. It wouldn't take them more than a few hours to trace it, and then his description would be in the newspapers.

He lay back in bed, his throat dry and his heart pounding. He felt he could explain everything except the whip. It proved that he was planning revenge. Without the whip it would be Little Ernie's word against his.

What a fool he had been! Why hadn't he taken the whip with him? Why had he run out of the bungalow and pounded down the lane without making sure that he had left no fingerprints or anything that could incriminate him?

He stumbled out of bed and stood trembling on the cold linoleum. This wouldn't do, he thought, wringing his hands, and he crushed down his fear. It was twenty minutes to seven. Ella would be in with his tea in a little while. He mustn't let her suspect that there was anything wrong. She must find him as she always found him, sleepy and in bed. When she had gone he would get dressed and take a train to Three Bridges, which was the nearest station to Copthorne. It wasn't likely that anyone would discover Crispin's body for some time. With luck, no one ever went to the bungalow except Crispin. He would have to be very careful, of course. He thought of the *Child's Self-Educator.* He could pretend that he thought there was a child in the bungalow, and he would go up to the door and ring the bell. If no one answered, he would break in and get the whip.

He became calm again. It was all right so long as you kept your head and used your brain. Once he had the whip he could go to the police and explain everything, but it wouldn't be safe until he had it.

A soft scratching at the door startled him; then his face softened. He opened the door and let Leo in. He got back into bed, and the cat jumped up and settled down close to him. It began to purr.

George stroked its long hair. "You're all I've got, Leo," he said softly. "There's no one else, and even you can't help me."

The regular, contented noise the cat made soothed him. Very gently, he stroked the top of its head, and it stretched out a paw and touched his face, as if understanding that he was alone, in need of affection and sympathy.

Later, Ella came in. She put down the cup of tea and walked across the room to pull up the blind.

When she saw his face, she gave a little scream. "Why, Mr. George," she said in horror. "What have you done to your poor face?"

"I got into a razor fight," George said after a moment's hesitation. "That's why I stayed out last night. They're only scratches, Ella. Don't look so frightened."

She continued to gape at him. "A razor fight?" she repeated. "Oh, Mr. George!"

Just to see the admiration and awe in her eyes was like a tonic to George's crushed, frightened ego.

"It's nothing," he said carelessly. "I've been in tighter jams before. Mark you, I did have an anxious moment, but I taught the fellow a lesson."

"How did it happen?" Ella asked. "Who was he?"

"Be a good girl and don't ask questions," George returned, suddenly cautious. "Promise me you won't tell anyone. The fellow got hurt, and I don't want to get into trouble. Mind you, he started it, but I did give him a terrific hiding. Now don't ask any more questions, and if anyone asks if I was in last night, will you say I was?"

Ella, her eyes like marbles, promised.

"You're a good sort, Ella," George said. "I think I'll go out and get something for my head. It aches like mad. The chemist will be open by the time I get dressed."

Obviously Ella wanted to hear more details, but George seemed so ill and worried that she felt a sudden pity for him.

"Shall I put on your bath, Mr. George?" she asked.

"No, I won't wait," he said quickly. "I want to fix this head."

As soon as she had gone, he got up and had a quick, uncertain shave. It was difficult, with the plaster in the way, but he managed somehow. He dressed and gave Leo some milk.

"I'll have to get you some food tonight, old chap," he said, rubbing the cat's head. "I've been pretty busy, but I'll bring you something nice tonight."

He picked up his book specimens, slipped them into his pocket, and was ready to go.

He reached Victoria Station a few minutes past eight-thirty. There was a local train that stopped at Three Bridges, due out at eight-forty. He had just time to buy a paper and his ticket before the train left.

He got a corner seat facing the engine, lit a cigarette, and glanced quickly at the other two occupants of the carriage. They did not even glance at him as they settled in their corners.

He searched the newspaper for any hint that Crispin's body had been found, but he found nothing to alarm him. A tiny paragraph tucked away at the back of the paper gave him pause. A green Ford coupe had been stolen from outside a doctor's house the previous afternoon and so far had not been traced.

So the car had been stolen. Was there no end to the wickedness of these two? They were so callous and calm about everything. Why, driving down to Copthorne, they might easily have been arrested for being in possession of a stolen car, and the loaded gun would have been found. George gritted his teeth. They would all have gone to prison.

He folded the newspaper and put it in his pocket. As he did so, he wondered what Sydney and Cora were doing at this precise moment. They were probably in bed and asleep, secure in mind that they had safely fastened the murder on to him. Or perhaps they had decided to pack up and leave London. With all that money they could go anywhere. Whatever happened to him, George thought grimly, they wouldn't get away with this. If they were still at the flat, he would go and see them. He would have it out with them: threaten them with the police.

The train began to slow down, and finally pulled into Three Bridges station. He began the long walk to Copthorne. It was a perfect summer morning, the sun was not too hot, the country looked fresh and green.

One or two cars passed him, but he was nervous of asking for a lift. He didn't want anyone to remember him. He had been careful to put on a pair of flannel slacks, a sports shirt and an old tweed jacket. He looked like a City clerk on holiday.

Eventually he arrived at the turning that led to the bungalow. He paused at the top of the lane, listening and watching. Nothing aroused his suspicions. Taking out his book specimens and holding them in his hand, he walked down the lane.

As he approached the bungalow he became nervous and on edge. It was lonely in this country lane. The bungalow seemed to be the only building within sight. The only sounds that came to him were the rustling of leaves in the wind and the twittering of the birds. It was not an atmosphere that should have created fear, but by the time he had reached the wooden gate that led to the bungalow he was terrified.

He paused outside the gate and looked up and down the lane, screwing up his courage to go on.

Suppose the police were waiting for him? Suppose this silent, overgrown garden concealed a trap?

He struggled with his fears. He had to get the whip. It was worth any risk. He would be all right if he kept his head and showed them his book specimens. He would say that he had wanted a day in the country and was canvassing to make his expenses. That was a straightforward story.

They would believe him. It wasn't as if he looked like a murderer.

He drew a deep breath and pushed open the gate. It squeaked sharply, setting his teeth on edge. Again he had a powerful urge to turn back, but he forced himself on.

Cautiously, he moved up the overgrown path. In the shelter of the trees and high hedges, the garden was silent and close. The scent of clover and wallflowers was heavy in the still air.

He reached the bungalow and rapped on the door. Sweat ran down his face as he stood in the hot, sheltered porch, listening, his nerves slowly tightening.

And as he stood there, a thought crept into his mind that drove the blood from his heart. Suppose Crispin answered the door? Suppose he got up from the floor and opened the door and stood before George with blood on his dressing gown?

George backed away, his mouth open in an idiotic grimace of terror.

He couldn't even run away. He stood paralysed, waiting.

Nothing happened.

He fought down the panic that had seized him, conquered it and returned to the door. He rapped again.

There was no one in the bungalow except Crispin: and Crispin was dead.

George put an unsteady hand on the door latch, lifted it and pushed upon the door. He braced himself and peered into the room. Then breath whistled between his clenched teeth, and blackness dropped like a curtain before his eyes. He clung to the doorpost and waited. Evil-tasting bile rose in his mouth; he wanted to be sick.

Except for the furniture, the room was empty.

George's heart began slowly to pump blood back to his brain. It was some minutes before he could move again. Then he stepped into the room and stared with unbelieving eyes at the carpet where Crispin had fallen. There was no sign of murder in the room. Fearfully, George looked for the red mess on the wall. That was not there either.

Was he going out of his mind? Had all the fantasies of violence that he had created in the past brought him to this? Were Sydney, Cora, Crispin and all the other nightmare people mere figments of a deranged imagination? Was it possible that the murder had happened only in his mind?

He looked wildly round the room, and then he stiffened.

On the sideboard lay the whip.

There was no question about it. It was there, leather and whalebone, and the little white price ticket on the handle.

He edged forward and picked it up. He stood for several minutes gazing at it, aware that it was the symbol of his sanity.

Then, in the hush of the lonely room, above the drone of the bees and the rustle of the hollyhocks against the window, he heard voices.

Still grasping the whip, he stepped to the door and listened. A man was speaking some way off in the garden behind the bungalow.

Moving silently, in blind panic, George slipped out of the house, crossed the path and sank down on his knees under the overhanging hedge. He found a dry ditch that ran along the side of the garden, and cautiously lowered himself into it. He adjusted the leaves of the hedge so that they formed a screen over him.

He found that he had a good view of the bungalow, and he was confident that he could not be seen. He waited, his hand gripping the whip, his heart fluttering against his side.

He heard the sound of feet moving through the long grass. Then round the corner of the bungalow came four people: the Hebrew barman, the two Greeks and the woman with the blonde greasy hair.

They looked odd and somehow sinister against the background of the peace and fertility of the garden.

The Hebrew wore a double-breasted, navy-blue suit, shiny at the elbows and the knees; on his head was a bowler hat. The woman had on a shapeless cotton dress; its pattern of flowers had faded with constant washing. Her thick legs were bare, and blue-black veins crawled up the backs of her calves. Her feet were squeezed into a pair of high-heeled court shoes. The two Greeks were in dark suits and cloth caps. They carried spades on their shoulders, and their boots were heavy with yellow clay.

A cigarette dangled from the blonde woman's lips. Her fat, loose face was expressionless, but the Hebrew was weeping. He did not make a fuss about his grief. Tears welled out of his eyes and ran down the wrinkles in his leathery skin. He made no attempt to wipe them away.

The woman looked at the bungalow, her eyes bleak. "Was he expecting anyone?" she asked.

The Hebrew lifted his shoulders in despair. "I know nothing," he said. "He didn't confide in me. I told him it was dangerous to have a lonely place like this. I told him many times."

The woman sat down abruptly on the grass. She was only a few yards from where George was hiding. She plucked a long piece of coarse grass and began to chew it.

"Sit down. The sun will do you good."

The Hebrew and the two Greeks sat down near her. They looked self-conscious, worried. The Hebrew still wept.

"The way you go on!" the woman said impatiently. "I'm his mother. Shouldn't I be the one to weep?"

The Hebrew took out a handkerchief and wiped his eyes. "You're hard, Emily," he said. "What a burial to give a son!"

The woman, Emily, snapped her thick fingers. "He wouldn't mind. He didn't believe in God. If that what's worrying you." She brooded, tearing the blade of grass with her sharp teeth. "What did you expect me to do? Leave him there for the police to find? They would be crawling over us like flies on bad meat in no time. Haven't they done enough harm?"

When he didn't say anything, she went on. "Who do you think did it?"

"Vengeance is mine, saith the Lord," the Hebrew said, pulling at his long, straggly moustache.

"You don't fool me," Emily said. "I know what you're thinking, don't I, Max?"

"Do you?"

The two Greeks had lit cigarettes. They were not listening to this conversation. They lolled back on their elbows, their dark faces raised to the sun, their eyes closed.

But Max listened. He sat bolt upright, his long, thin legs crossed like a working tailor, his bowler hat very straight on his pear-shaped head.

"We don't have to worry about the police," Emily went on. "He wouldn't have liked it. We can find out who did it, and we can settle the score, can't we?"

Max looked across the garden. "There's the money," he said. "He should never have brought it here. Seven hundred pounds!"

"Stop worrying about the money," Emily said sharply. "Is that what you're crying about?"

"The gun worries me," Max said, not listening to her. "A razor, yes, but a gun! ... It's someone we don't know."

"Well, we can find out, can't we?" Emily persisted. "Does the whip mean anything?"

"It must do. It's new. Crispin wouldn't buy a thing like that."

There was a long pause. A bee droned across the hot garden and lighted on a hollyhock.

"Who was that girl? The one Crispin thrashed?" Emily said, plucking another blade of grass and chewing it.

"I was thinking about her, too," Max said. "The whip might tie up with her. Do you mean that?"

"It could do. And the big man. Who was he?"

Max shook his head. "I don't know. I've never seen either before. There was something odd about the way that girl behaved. She wasn't drunk. She was faking."

"Crispin was a fool to have touched her. She might have complained to the police."

"Why didn't she?"

"Yes, why?"

There was another long pause while they brooded.

"Maybe they came down here for revenge, found the money and killed Crispin to steal it," Emily said at last.

"How could they know Crispin had this place? No one knew that he came here."

"Sydney Brant knew," Emily said thoughtfully.

"Brant? He hasn't been around for months. Besides, after Crispin burnt him, he was too scared to come near the place. This is nothing to do with him; but the girl and the big man ... maybe, I don't know ..."

"Well, we can't waste time. We must settle this business. Whoever did it will have to pay."

"They'll pay all right." Max's harsh voice floated on the still air, and George shivered. These people, so calculating, so ordinary to look at, plotting revenge in the hot sunshine, had a nightmare quality that made his flesh creep. "We'll have to find out about the big man. We'll have to find out where the whip came from. Once we know that, it'll be easy!"

Emily brooded, "Well, trace it. The price ticket will help," She looked across at the Greek, Nick. "Get the whip," she went on. "I want to examine it."

With his blood freezing in his heart, George watched the Greek get up and wander into the bungalow. He was away a few minutes and then he came to the door.

"It is not there," he called.

"The whip," Emily said, snapping her fingers impatiently. "Don't keep me waiting. Bring me the whip."

"It is not there, I tell you," Nick said indifferently. Emily and Max exchanged glances.

"Find it for the fool," she said.

Max got up and walked stiffly into the bungalow.

Nick shrugged. He came back and sat down, a frown of irritation on his flat, ugly face.

"He will not find it," he said sullenly. "It is gone."

Emily said nothing, but her fat hands squeezed into fists.

Max called from the window. There was an urgent note in his voice. "Emily!"

The woman got up and stared at the gesticulating figure at the window.

"I told you," Nick said. "It is gone," and he lolled back on his elbows and closed his eyes.

CHAPTER FOURTEEN

A week went by. As each day gave way to night, and night gave way to another day, George's fears receded. He was not, after all, going to be hunted by the police. The murder was to remain a secret shared only by Cora, Sydney and himself, and Emily, Max and the two Greeks. The vast police organization, trained and equipped to track down a murderer, was not going to swing into action against him. He had read so often about police methods, and knew that once the hunt was on, the fugitive seldom escaped. It was the thought of this efficiency and the vast man-hunting machine that had frightened him.

As long as no one discovered Crispin's body, he would be safe. He had only to keep away from Russell Square and the Soho district to avoid being discovered by Emily and her mob. How could they possibly find him, unless he was stupid enough to visit their territory? They had no organization to trace him. They did not have thousands of uniformed, highly trained men to keep a constant watch for him. They could not circulate his photograph or his description in every newspaper in the country. How, then, could they hope to find him—so long as he was careful?

Although, as the days went by, he began to settle down to his ordinary routine life, the murder continued to prey on his mind. He no longer thought in terms of violence, nor did he read his American pulp magazines. The pictures of the bruised faces of the gangsters after the third degree, the bloodstained, bullet-riddled corpses, the gang battles, which before had thrilled him, now made him feel sick. He had been purged of violence. He had seen a man die violently, and now he had no further interest in reading about murder.

He had bad dreams, too. Continuous nightmares, that began as soon as he fell asleep, drained his vitality. One dream constantly recurred. It was a dream of terrible intensity. He dreamed that Cora came into his room, and he thought she leaned over him with the fainting desire in her eyes that inflamed his blood. And as he reached out to seize her, she seemed to waver before his eyes and slowly transform into the tall, elegant figure of Crispin—Crispin in all his horror: the twisted grimace of terror and blood welling thickly from a great hole in his chest.

George found also that he had to make a tremendous effort to go out each evening to work. He had lost his hearty manner with his prospective buyers, and they now seemed suspicious of his strained, white face and his brooding eyes. He had to make twice as many calls, and even then he sold fewer sets of books.

Saturday afternoon found him restless and uneasy. He was sitting alone in his room by the window, and his mind kept dwelling on that fateful, yet marvellous Saturday afternoon when he had first met Cora. It was about this time that Sydney had telephoned. Even now the house was empty except for Leo, who was somewhere in the basement. George thought of Cora, and his body cried out for her. Somehow, the murder now seemed trivial beside the clamouring desire that was torturing him, had been torturing him for the past days. At this moment he did not care how badly she had treated him. If she came into the room now and offered to be nice to him, he would have forgiven her everything.

Thinking of her, remembering her, brooding on that exquisite moment of fear and excitement when she had kissed him so passionately in the stolen car, he began to make excuses for her behaviour. Perhaps it wasn't her fault. Perhaps she had been in the power of her brother, and had been forced to betray George against her will.

Was it possible that she had really loved him all the time, and that Sydney was at the bottom of the whole business?

George got to his feet and began to pace up and down. He must see her again. It was no good torturing himself like this. He must see her, and have it out. She might be longing for him, too, wanting to see him, but afraid of what Sydney would say.

His physical need for her was so overpowering that it swamped all caution and reason. He knew at the back of his mind that she had trapped him into murder, that she was as bad as Sydney, but he wanted her too badly to care.

He didn't believe really that she could ever love him. In his present mood of frustrated desire, he did not mind, just so long as she would be "very nice to him:" even just once. If he could only have his moment with her, a brief spell of bliss, he would be content, even if she were a beast to him afterwards.

He sat still, gnawing his under lip. If he wanted her so badly, he'd have to do something about it. He would have to see her. Then why was he hesitating? He would go to her flat now—this very minute. As soon as he had made the decision, a great weight rolled from his mind. The decision was something he had been longing to make for the past few days.

He picked up his hat, and as he crossed the room he looked at himself in the mirror. He stared at his white, drawn face in astonishment. It was as if he had only just become aware of himself, and the change shocked him. He had aged; there were streaks of white in his hair at the temples. He had lost weight, his eyes were feverish and deep set, and the thin red scars from the razor cuts gave him a look of menace. He continued to stare at himself for some minutes, then left the room, uneasy, worried.

When he reached Southampton Row, he got off the 'bus and walked towards Russell Square. He glanced at his watch. It was a few minutes after four. He wondered if she would be in. What was he going to say to her? Suppose Sydney came to the door? He became more and more undecided as to what he was going to do. But he kept on, refusing to heed the warning note that was sounding at the back of his mind, determined, if he did nothing else, to look at her flat once again.

He turned the corner of her street. People busied themselves with their weekend shopping. The pavement before the row of small shops was crowded with women, small children and perambulators. He could see the greengrocer's shop over which was her flat. The greengrocer, elderly, bald, and fat, was outside the shop. He was shovelling potatoes onto the scales while a tired-looking woman waited, a string bag ready to receive them.

George stood for some time at the corner, unconsciously assuring himself that it would be safe to cross the street.

Finally, he made up his mind and walked towards the greengrocer's shop with mounting excitement. As he drew near, he looked up at the window of her flat. The drab muslin curtain told him nothing. For all he knew, she might be watching him, and the thought sent his blood racing through his veins.

He slowed down as he reached the shop. A smell of potatoes, fruit and onions hung in the air. He glanced at the door that led to her flat, and then he paused. There was a notice stuck on one of the glass panels of the door, and a sudden feeling of dread came to him.

The greengrocer had gone into the shop: there was a momentary lull in trade.

George stepped quickly to the door. He read the sprawling handwriting on the notice:

FURNISHED FLAT TO LET
Two bedrooms, sitting room, kitchen, bath.
42/-weekly.
Apply: Harris & Son. Greengrocer. (Next door.)

So they had gone. They had packed up and bolted. In a way, he wasn't surprised. It was the obvious thing to do. They were making sure that no one would get on to them; that Emily and Max and the two Greeks wouldn't get the money from them.

He wondered how long they had been gone. It crossed his mind that they might have left a clue which would lead him to them.

While he was hesitating, the greengrocer came out and glanced at him inquiringly.

Without stopping to think, George blurted out, "I'm interested in this flat."

"Flat?" the greengrocer repeated. "Yes, it's still in the market. It's a nice little place. 'Ave it meself if it weren't for the stairs. Can't manage the stairs now. Not as young as I was."

"Can I see it?" George asked.

"I'll get the keys."

There was a short delay. Then the old man returned.

"It'll be a month in advance," he said, a bitter, injured note in his voice. "I've 'ad enough of fly-by-nights. If yer want the place, it'll be a month in advance."

"Had trouble with the previous tenants?" George asked, taking the keys.

"Done a flit," the old man said, and spat in the road. "Might 'ave known no good would 'ave come from those two. Wot 'e did for a living I never did find out, and she ... my missus said she took men up there, but seeing's believing. If I'd caught 'er at it, I'd 'ye 'ad 'er out, but I never did. I wish I'd got rid of 'em before."

George nodded, and turned to the door. "Don't bother to come up," he said. "I'll have a look round and then talk it over with you."

The old man grunted. "I ain't coming up," he assured him. "Can't manage them stairs. You'll find the place in a mess. The missus's been cleaning it up, but it ain't quite finished. The way those two lived ... like pigs."

George's heart was thumping as he sank the key into the lock. He pushed open the front door and entered the tiny hall. The flat had obviously been cleaned, but there was still a faint smell of sandalwood in the air. It affected George. He felt alone, miserable.

He went into the sitting room. Now that the curtains had been washed, the carpet swept and surrounds scrubbed, it looked quite a homely little place. He went through the drawers, looked into the empty wastepaper basket, and the cupboard, but he found nothing. He went into Sydney's bedroom. He found nothing there, nor did the kitchen reveal anything. He purposely left Cora's room to the last. When he opened the door, a vein in his temple began to pound. The room had not been touched. He could tell that by the dust on the mantelpiece, the rubbish piled in the grate, and the soiled towel with a trace of lipstick that hung over the back of the chair.

He entered the room and closed the door. He remained still for a few minutes, trying to sort out the various odours that hung in the stale, stuffy atmosphere. There was sandalwood and tobacco smoke, stale perspiration and dirt. There was an elusive smell which, although scarcely perceptible, excited him. It was Cora's own intimate smell—a heady, slight smell, feminine, yet fleshly.

He pulled open the drawers of the dressing table. They were filled with empty jars, sticky tubes, cigarette cartons, and bottles. Eyeblack mingled with a spilt box of face powder. A tube of toothpaste oozed over a pair of sun-glasses. A bottle of witch hazel—the bottle he had given her—had leaked, filling the drawer with a layer of white grease. He had never seen such a disgusting mess.

The second drawer was empty except for a soiled handkerchief. He closed the drawer with a grimace. Then he went to the fireplace and examined the scraps of paper, newspapers, a sheet of greasy brown paper that smelt strongly of decaying fish.

He was very patient, and at last he found what he was looking for: a business card of an estate agent in Maida Vale.

He stood up, his eyes bright and excited. Maida Vale! Yes, they would fit in in Maida Vale. It had either to be Russell Square, or Soho, or Maida Vale. He slipped the card into his waistcoat pocket, pleased with himself.

Then he locked the door and went downstairs.

"I'll think it over," he said to the greengrocer. "I'd like my wife to see it."

His wife! He thought of Cora, and there was a bitter taste in his mouth.

From the top of the 'bus he watched the crowded street. Then suddenly his heart gave a lurch. At the corner of Southampton Row and High Holborn he saw Nick, the Greek. He was standing on the curb, a cigarette hanging from his thin lips, reading a newspaper. George shrank back.

He remained uneasy and alarmed until the 'bus began to crawl up Baker Street, and then his fears quieted. The Greek hadn't seen him. It was a near thing, of course, but he hadn't seen him.

He got off the 'bus at Maida Vale and went immediately to the estate agent. It was a small office, and a fat little man, behind a shabby desk, was the only occupant.

He seemed startled when George opened the door and entered, as if he seldom had callers.

"Good afternoon," he said, fingering a heavy silver watch chain. "Is there something ...?"

"I don't know," George said, and smiled. He was anxious for the little man to like him. "I don't want to waste your time, but I believe you can help me." He took out the card and studied it. "It's Mr. Hibbert, isn't it?"

The little man nodded. "You're lucky to find me here," he said. "Most places close on Saturday afternoon, but I thought I'd hang on a little longer ..."

"I'm looking for a couple of friends," George explained. "It's important I should find them." He smiled again. "You see, I owe them money."

Mr. Hibbert scratched his head. "I don't know," he said. "Perhaps you'll tell me how I can help...."

"Oh yes," George said eagerly, taking out a crushed packet of Player's. "Will you smoke?"

Mr. Hibbert took a cigarette rather doubtfully. "I don't usually smoke in office hours," he explained. "But seeing it's Saturday ..." He had a trick of not finishing his sentences.

They lit up.

"You see," George went on, "they were looking for a place. I've been away for some time. As a matter of fact, I've been in the States. I traced them to a flat near Russell Square, and now I learn they've moved to Maida Vale. I think they came to you for a place."

"The States?" Mr. Hibbert's eyes grew dreamy. "Often thought I'd go there myself. Wonderful place, I believe."

George nodded. "It's all right," he said with assumed indifference. "But I suppose I've seen too much of it. Give me England any day." He dropped ash carefully into the tobacco tin lid that served as an ashtray. "These two," he went on, anxious not to stray from his purpose. "They were young—brother and sister. Brant is the name. The fellow had a bad scar: a burn."

Mr. Hibbert's face darkened. "Oh yes," he said, frowning. "I remember them. Hmm, yes, I remember them quite well." He conveyed that he did not approve of them, and that because George knew them, he wasn't sure whether he should approve of him.

"It's just that I owe them money," George said apologetically. "They did me a good turn once." What was he saying? A good turn? But he went on, "They're not friends of mine, you understand; but one must honour one's debts."

Mr. Hibbert nodded. He looked at George with sudden warmth. "Those sentiments do you credit. I like to hear a man talk like that. Wouldn't think *they'd* honour anything."

George shook his head. "A wild pair," he said. "Did you fix them up?" He waited, his heart thumping dully against his side.

"Against my will," Mr. Hibbert told him sadly. "Business is not what it was. A year ago I'd 've sent them packing. As it happened, I had a place. A couple of rooms over a garage. There were rats in the place; no one seemed to want it, so I let them have it. They can be as wild as they like there. They'll have no neighbours." A sly, lewd look came into his faded eyes. "The girl's remarkable, isn't she? No better than she makes out to be, I shouldn't wonder. Her figure ..." He shook his head. "Wants a mother, I shouldn't doubt ... brazen ..."

A hot flame of desire flickered in the pit of George's stomach. He knew what Mr. Hibbert meant.

"I'm most grateful," he said, after a pause. "Could you write the address down for me?" He stubbed out his cigarette and added bitterly, "It'll be a surprise for them."

Mr. Hibbert wrote the address on the back of his card.

"It's a turning off Kilburn High Street, a mews. It's easy enough to find."

They parted warmly.

While George waited for a 'bus to take him down the long, straight road to Kilburn, a man with a bundle of evening papers passed, and George bought one. He glanced down the columns, scarcely concentrating. An item of news caught his attention for a second. An unknown man had fallen on the live wire at Belsize Park Station. A train had entered the station a moment later, and the hold-up had caused a considerable delay on the line. George was glad he hadn't been there: a beastly, messy death. He looked down the road impatiently. A 'bus was in sight, but it was taking its time. Then George stiffened, spider's legs ran down his spine. He looked at the newspaper again. The small print swam before his eyes. The unknown man, the reporter wrote, was about twenty-two. He had a scar—a bad burn—on the right side of his face, a shock of straw-coloured hair. He wore a dark blue shirt, a red tie, grey flannel trousers and a tweed coat. The police were anxious to identify him. There was nothing in his pockets nor on his clothes to say who he was and where he had come from.

The 'bus passed George. He made no attempt to signal to it. He stood reading the notice over and over again. Could it be Sydney? The description was exact. Were there other men with scars, straw-coloured hair, who wore dark blue shirts and red ties? It seemed unlikely.

He had to find out. The trip to Kilburn could wait. He had to find out whether Cora was now on her own. It might make a tremendous difference.

He began to walk towards Kilburn, not knowing where he was going, but anxious to think. What a death! How unlike Sydney to fall in front of a train! Was it suicide? He thought of the cold, ruthless face, and decided that Sydney most certainly would not have taken his own life. An accident, then? But how did people fall in front of trains unless they deliberately jumped or were pushed? Pushed? His mind began to crawl with alarm. Was he pushed? Suppose Emily and Max and the two Greeks . . .? He gritted his teeth. Was this the beginning of their revenge? He looked furtively over his shoulder, and quickened his pace. It was the kind of clever, ruthless trick they would stage: a murder that looked like an accident. Of course, the dead man might not be Sydney, and in that case he was getting alarmed over nothing. But he wouldn't rest until he knew for certain. He supposed the body would be in some mortuary, but he hadn't the vaguest idea which one. He was scared to go to a police station. The memory of Crispin now filled him with nervous dread.

Farther up the road he saw a policeman coming towards him. He forced down his natural fear of the uniform and with misgivings planted himself in the policeman's path.

"I think I know this man," he blurted out, pushing the newspaper at the policeman. "I believe he's a friend of mine."

The policeman gave him a quick, inquisitive glance, and then looked down at the newspaper. He frowned, chewing his moustache.

"What man's that, sir?" he asked patiently.

George pointed to the paragraph. His finger danced on the page.

The policeman ponderously read the item, then he glanced at George. "You think you know 'im, do you, sir?"

George nodded. "I suppose I ought to do something," he said helplessly. "I thought you could advise me."

The policeman brooded. "If you think you know 'im," he said at last, "it'd be your duty to—er—view the remains." He shook his head sympathetically. "Unpleasant job, sir, at the best of times, but seeing as 'ow you might identify 'im ..."

"Where should I go?" George asked. The word "remains" made him feel sick.

"Well, the accident 'appened at Belsize Park Station," the policeman said. "'E'd be at the 'Ampstead mortuary as like as not. If you come with me, sir, I'll 'phone. There's a police box just round the corner."

A few minutes later George was on his way to the Hampstead mortuary. It took him some time to screw up enough courage to ring the bell outside the double gates. After what seemed to him an interminable wait, a small door in the gate opened and a white-coated attendant looked at him inquiringly.

"I think I know this man," George said, offering the newspaper. "The man who fell under the train this morning."

"Then you'll 'ave come to identify 'im," the attendant said cheerfully. "This way, if you please, sir."

George ducked through the doorway, and found himself in a small yard. A low brick building faced him, and with a tight feeling in his stomach he followed the attendant across the yard into the building.

"If you'll wait 'ere a moment, sir," the attendant said, "I'll get P.C. White."

Left alone in the white-tiled passage, George looked round uneasily. There was a door at the end of the passage through which the attendant had disappeared. Near where George was standing he noticed a small window covered by a yellowing blind. He thought the place looked exactly like a public convenience, and because of the familiar association, his fears began to subside.

The door at the end of the passage opened, and the attendant beckoned. George entered a box-like room which served as an office. A police constable rose from behind a desk as George came in.

"Good morning, sir," the police constable said. He had a kind, understanding face, and he was obviously anxious to set George at ease. "Sit down, will you? You think you can identify the unfortunate gentleman who died this morning?"

George nodded. He was glad to sit down. He took off his hat and began to twirl it round between his sweating fingers.

"Distressing business, sir," P.C. White said, settling down in his chair again. "But you've nothing to worry about, sir. There won't be anything unpleasant. Perhaps you'd give me a little information; just to keep our records straight." He drew a sheet of paper towards him. "Your name, sir?"

George's mind went blank with fright. He hadn't thought they'd ask questions about himself. It would be madness to let them know that he had anything to do with Sydney. If they ever found Crispin ...

A name jumped into his confused mind. "Thomas Grant," he blurted out, and then, tightening his control over himself, he volunteered, "247, North Circular Road, Finchley." He had once stayed at the address, a boarding house, when he first came to London.

P.C. White wrote for a moment, his head on one side, taking pride in his neat, copper-plate handwriting.

"And what makes you think you know the deceased?"

"It's the description," George said, slowly recovering from his first fright. "The burn. I had a friend once who was fair and had a burn on the right of his face. I haven't seen him for some months. He used to live at my address—it's a guest house. Timson was his name. Fred Timson."

P.C. White did a little more writing. "You haven't seen 'im for some time?" he repeated.

"Well, no, Of course, I may be mistaken. But, I thought ... "

"Very good of you, I'm sure. We're grateful for any help. The gentleman had no papers nor anything to tell us who he is." He got slowly to his feet. "Well, sir, if you'll come along with me."

George suddenly felt that he couldn't go through with this ghastly business. P.C. White noticed how pale he had gone.

"Now, don't worry, sir," he said. "We try to make this sad business as pleasant as circumstances allow. You'll only need to take a quick look at 'is face. You won't see anything unpleasant."

George did not trust his legs. He sat still, gripping the arms of his chair, uneasy, frightened that he was going to be sick.

"All right, sir," P.C. White said, sitting down again. "Take your time. It takes people like that sometimes. Of course, we're used to it. I've been on this job now for fourteen years. You'd be surprised 'ow some people react. Some of 'em are as callous as can be; others get unnecessarily upset. It depends on their temperament, I always say. Why, only an hour ago we 'ad a young lady in to see the same gentleman wot you're going to see. She was a cool card all right. I knew I wasn't going to 'ave trouble with her, soon as I sets eyes on her. Cool as a cucumber; in her trousers and sweater. Don't 'old with that get-up for a girl myself, but, then, I suppose I'm old-fashioned. A bit too immodest, if you takes me meaning. Well, this young lady comes in, looks at the remains, and although she didn't know 'im, I had difficulty in getting her away. She stood there staring and staring, and she made me and Joe feel a bit uncomfortable: don't mind admitting it. But, for all that, she never turned a 'air—not one blessed 'air."

George licked his dry lips. "Did she say who she was?" he asked in a low, tight voice.

P.C. White hesitated. "Well, it don't matter to you, does it, sir?" he said. "I mean we don't.... You see, it wasn't as if she knew him."

So Cora had already been here. If she didn't know the dead man, then he wasn't Sydney. George's nausea went away.

"I'm all right now," he said, getting slowly to his feet. "I'm sorry, but this business has upset me."

"Don't you worry about that, sir," P.C. White assured him. "Take your time. Now if you feel like it, just step out into the passage. I'll be right with you."

George moved slowly into the white-tiled passage. P.C. White took his arm and led him to the blind-covered window that George had noticed when he had been waiting to go into the office.

"All right, Joe," White called. "Now, sir, just a quick look. It'll be over in a few seconds."

George braced himself as the white-coated attendant, from behind a partition, pulled up the yellowing blind. A light clicked on. Close against the window, on the other side of the partition, stood a cheap, brown-stained pine coffin on trestles. The lid was drawn back a foot from the head of the coffin. George started back with a shudder of horror as he recognized Sydney Brant.

A comforting hand gripped his arm, but he was scarcely aware of it. He stared down at the waxen face. There was a sneering half smile hovering on the bitter mouth. The eyes were closed. A lock of straw-coloured hair lay across the scarred cheek. Even in death, Sydney Brant seemed to jeer at him.

Almost in a state of collapse, George turned shudderingly away.

"It's a mistake," he said in a strangled voice. "I don't know this man. I've never seen him before in my life."

And out of the corner of his eye, he saw the blind come down in silence, slowly, almost regretfully, like the curtain of the final act of an unsuccessful play.

CHAPTER FIFTEEN

It was growing dusk when George left the Heath. From the mortuary he had walked along the Spaniards Road and had cut across the Heath to Parliament Hill. His mind was blank during the walk, and it wasn't until he reached the deserted bandstand perched on Parliament Hill, with its magnificent view of the City of London, that he realized that he had been wandering to no purpose, with no idea where he was going. He sat down on the grass under the shade of a big oak tree and lit a cigarette.

He had sat there brooding for nearly two hours. Sydney was dead. There was no doubt about that. How he met his end was a mystery.

George was sure that he hadn't killed himself. And another thing, why was Sydney in Belsize Park Station? Where had he been going when he met his death? No one seemed to have seen him die. At that time in the morning—George had discovered that Sydney had died at ten-thirty—few if any people used the station. It was a convenient place for murder.

George shuddered. If it had been murder, then Cora and he were in danger. Would Emily and Max and the two Greeks be content with one life? He doubted it.

The obvious thing to do would be to leave London, but he had no intention of doing so, even if they were really hunting for him. He would not bring himself to believe that they were. It was all too fantastic. Anyway, he was not going to leave Cora. She might need him.

He thought about her, his mind confused by fear and desire. What was she going to do without Sydney? How was she going to live? He had to see her. Pity stirred in him. He might save her from herself. Without Sydney, surely she would wish to get away from the evil life they had led? George would be only too happy to leave London if she would go with him. All this beastliness could be forgotten in a year or so.

It worried him that she had not identified her brother. What strange, sinister motive prompted her to do that? Didn't that point to murder?

He went on thinking and brooding for a long time along these lines. Each train of thought always finished at the same place. He must see Cora. If he didn't see her soon, it might be too late. She might again move somewhere where it would be impossible to find her.

He left the Heath, walking quickly past the Hampstead ponds, and cut through into Haverstock Hill. It was eight-thirty by the time he reached Belsize Park Station. He bought a tuppenny ticket, and only half certain what he had in mind, descended to the platform.

The platform was deserted except for a porter, who glanced at him without interest.

The urge to know the truth forced George forward. He rattled his loose change in his pocket suggestively. The sound caught the porter's attention.

"Excuse me," George said. "Perhaps you can help me. It's about the man who was killed here this morning. He was a friend of mine. I'm trying to find out how it happened." He took out two half-crowns and let the porter see them. "Was there anyone on the platform at the time?"

"There wasn't anyone on the platform when my mate found 'im," the porter said, eyeing the half-crowns with interest.

"You don't know if anyone bought a ticket about the time he did? I mean someone might have seen what had happened and dodged across to the other platform. They might have done that, mightn't they?"

The porter turned this idea over thoughtfully. "They could an' all," he said, nodding his head. "Never thought of it like that. Might not want to get themselves mixed up with the inquest, like."

"That's what I thought. I wonder who could tell me."

"I was on duty upstairs," the porter said. "I remember some people. S'matter of fact, I remember the bloke what did 'imself in. I saw 'im come into the booking-'all and buy a ticket. I noticed 'im because 'e seemed a bit upset like."

"How do you mean—upset?" George asked sharply.

"Well, I dunno," the porter said, scowling in an attempt to concentrate. "Sort of worried, kept looking over 'is shoulder like 'e expected someone to meet 'im."

George went cold. "You say you remember some other people?"

"That's right. Two foreign-looking blokes came into the station and bought tickets a few minutes before your friend arrived. I particularly noticed them. Little blokes in black, wearing cloth caps."

"Go on," George said in a husky whisper.

"Well, your friend came in, and about a couple of minutes after—by the time 'e'd got down on the platform, I should say—a big woman arrived. She 'ad a lot of yellow 'air, and I noticed 'er because she was a bit like my old woman, fair busting out of 'er dress she was."

"I see." So it had been murder, after all. "And none of these people were on the platform when he was found?"

"That's right, but of course they could 'ave taken the up train on the other platform. It don't mean because they were down 'ere they saw anyfing."

A sudden thought dropped into George's mind for no apparent reason. "Was my—my friend carrying anything?" he asked.

The porter scratched his head. "Carrying anyfing?" he repeated. "Well, now you comes to mention it, 'e was. 'E 'ad a black leather case under 'is arm. Now, that's funny, I don't believe they found it. Now I come to fink of it, 'e 'ad it with 'im when 'e was getting 'is ticket. I remember that distinctly although it'd gone clean out of me 'ead until you mentioned it."

"Oh, I expect the police have got it all right," George said hurriedly. "Don't worry about it. I'll ask them."

He gave the porter the two half-crowns and left the station. He was frightened now. For all he knew, they might have got onto him and were planning *his* death. He thought of his gun. There wasn't a moment to lose. He must never be without the gun again. He must get it immediately.

Back in his room, he took the gun from under his shirts. It still smelt of gunpowder. What a careless fool he had been! That alone could have hanged him. He spent ten feverish minutes cleaning the gun, and then, without hesitation, he pulled out the magazine and filled it from the box of cartridges. He was careful not to jack a bullet into the breech, and he was careful also to make sure that the safety catch was down. He put the gun into his hip pocket and picked up his hat. All right, he thought, if they start being funny with me, they'll find they've bitten off more than they can chew. They weren't going to scare George Fraser! And they'd better not get ideas about Cora either. Cora was his girl now; she was under his protection.

He paused, frowning. This is extraordinary, he thought. I don't feel frightened any more. He looked at himself in the mirror. He saw a great, bulky figure; the scarred face looked tough and hard, the eyes were cold and steady. It was the gun, of course. It had given him a sudden, quite mysterious confidence in himself. He wasn't poor old George, the cat-loving lonely book tout any longer. He was George Fraser, millionaire gunman. He had killed a man, hadn't he? At this moment they were hunting for him, seeking revenge. Why, he was every bit as good as the gangsters he had read and dreamed about. He was better, in fact: he wasn't frightened; the *Front Page Detective* had always described the gangsters as frightened, yellow rats.

Deliberately he took out his battered cigarette case and selected a cigarette. Then he found a match in his pocket and flicked it with his nail. It flared up. That was a trick he had seen on the movies, and which he had tried again and again to imitate, but had never succeeded. He stared at the match, his face lighting up, then he lit the cigarette and tossed the match away.

All right, he thought, buttoning up his coat, I'm ready for them. They'll be damn sorry they started anything with me. Now for Cora; and he wasn't going to stand any nonsense from her in the future. She was going to be his girl. "I'm your gun moll," she had said. Well, that's just what she was going to be!

It was almost dark by the time he reached the garage mews off Kilburn High Street. He moved cautiously, aware of a feeling of excitement, and that his nerves were steady. As he stepped through the gateway and crossed the builder's yard, he drew the Luger, holding it down by his side.

The mews was in darkness. It was an ideal place for murder, he thought. The noise of the traffic in the High Street would drown any cry for help. It might even drown the sound of a shot.

He paused outside the flat. At first it seemed in darkness, but a second glance revealed a chink of light coming round the curtain of the front room.

There was no bell nor knocker, so he rapped sharply on the door with his knuckles. He waited, his ears pricked, his breathing deep and steady.

No one answered. He waited, and then rapped again. Perhaps she was out. It would be like her to leave the light on: typical of her indifferent carelessness.

He stepped back so that he could look up at the window. The hair on the nape of his neck bristled. The light had gone out.

He stood hesitating. So she was in there. Why had she turned off the light? Why wasn't she answering the door?

He flicked his fingers impatiently. Of course; she was taking precautions. She would have been insane to have come down and opened the door in such a lonely alley, not knowing who it was who was knocking.

He returned to the door and rapped again, then he pushed open the letter box and called.

"Cora! It's George. Let me in."

Almost instantly, as if she had been waiting for this assurance, she jerked the door open.

"You frightened me," she said. "Come in quickly."

The sound of her voice, the smell of the sandalwood and the nearness of her presence had an overpowering effect on him. He stumbled forward into the darkness, and the front door closed behind him. He heard her shoot a bolt home.

"Can you find your way up?" she asked. "I don't want to show a light. They're watching this place." Her small, warm hand took his, and she drew him up a steep flight of stairs.

A moment later a light sprang up. He blinked round. The room was large and poorly furnished. A big divan bed stood in one corner. A table and armchair and a cupboard made up the rest of the furniture. A worn carpet covered only the centre of the floor.

He turned and looked at her.

She was still wearing the blue sweater and slacks. They looked as if they could have done with another wash. Her hair was untidy, and her lipstick put on anyhow. The blue smudges under her eyes had now turned to purple. She somehow looked older, more worn, more shop-soiled.

"Good old George," she said in a low voice. "I was beginning to wonder what I was going to do."

"Do?" he repeated. "What do you mean?"

She giggled. It was a grating sound that made George's nerves recoil.

"They're out there waiting for me," she said, jerking her head towards the window. "And then you turn up."

He suddenly realized that she was terrified, but her pride, her arrogance were holding her terror in check.

"Cora?" he asked, a little startled. "They killed him. You know that, don't you?"

She wandered across the room, pounding her clenched fists together.

"Clever George," she said. "How did you find that out? No one was supposed to know."

Her jeering voice stung him. "Sydney planned Crispin's death, didn't he?" he said, standing over her. "Sydney and you. You wanted to push it on to me."

She looked up at him.

"We have pushed it on to you," she said, and giggled again. Had he any understanding, he would have seen she was close to complete nervous collapse. "But they want us, too."

He took hold of her by her shoulders and shook her, snapping her head back, startling her.

"Sit down," he said, pushing her onto the divan. "It's nothing to giggle about. You're going to talk. You're going to tell me everything."

"Don't do that!" she said, suddenly angry. Her eyes flashed and she shifted away from him. "Keep your paws to yourself."

"Shut up!" he said, possessive and determined. "You've played around with me long enough. Now you're going to explain."

She stared at him. "My poor George," she said, "have you gone mad?"

"I'm not your poor George," he said angrily, and giving way to a blind instinct, he smacked her face. As his hand connected with her cheek, he pulled back, so that the blow was a light one, but even at that, her head jerked back.

She was instantly on her feet.

"How dare you!" she stormed at him. "You cheap rotten—"

He smacked her again. This time he hit her hard, knocking her onto the divan.

He stood over her. "I don't like doing this, Cora," he said, breathing heavily, "but it's the only way I can show you I've changed. From now on I'm master, do you understand?" She leaned back on her elbows, one side of her face red, the other side like wax. Then she giggled.

"You?" she sneered. "You haven't the guts of a rabbit."

Confident in his new-found courage and strength, George merely shrugged. He took out a cigarette, found a match, flicked it alight with his thumbnail. He lit the cigarette and forced a stream of smoke down his nostrils.

"Killing a man makes a lot of difference," he said shortly. "You may as well get used to the idea, Cora."

"We'll see," she said, twisting her hands in her lap. "We'll see how brave you are, George my pet. You're big enough to knock me about, but we'll see what you're like against them."

"Yes," George said, and he crossed the room and sat down in the arm-chair.

"I wonder why they let you come here," she went on, looking towards the window. "I should've thought it'd 've been easier for them to have killed you in the darkness."

George stiffened. "Kill me?" he said. "You mean they're out there in the alley?"

"Nick is. I saw him not half an hour ago. Poncho, his brother, is round the back." She ran her fingers through her hair, and he knew at once why it looked so untidy. She must have been doing that for the past half-hour.

"It's silly, isn't it? But I'm scared stiff," she went on. Her flash of temper had been short-lived. He could see she was sick with panic. "When I get frightened my tummy turns to water."

"Here, have a cigarette," George said, going over to her. "I won't let them hurt you."

She lit the cigarette. "I don't fancy going out there," she said, trying to control herself. "Nick's hot stuff with a razor." She shivered.

"Can they get in?" George asked.

She looked up sharply. "I suppose so. They could break a window if they really wanted to get in, couldn't they?" Her inside rumbled loudly and she giggled. "Collywobbles," she said. "I'm a yellow little bitch, aren't I?" And she squeezed her stomach with her crossed arms and scowled down at her feet. "I saw him this afternoon, all tucked up in a coffin. He looked filthy. I hope I don't look like that when I'm dead." A sob jerked in her throat. "I was terribly, terribly fond of him, George, although he was such a rotten bastard."

"I saw him, too," George said, not looking at her.

She sat for a little while as if she hadn't heard, then she said, "You're not such a fool, are you, George? They must have pushed him in front of the train. He was running away from me." She flicked ash onto the carpet and rubbed it in with her foot. "And I loved him so. I never thought he'd do that to me. He wouldn't let me touch the money. And I had helped him. If I hadn't 've helped him he'd 've never got the money. He never gave me a penny of it: not a damn penny. And as soon as he was sure they weren't after him, he skipped. He took the money and left me without even a word." She beat her clenched fists together. "After all I've done for him!"

George crushed out his cigarette and immediately lit another. He felt a little sick.

A cheap clock ticked excitedly on the mantelpiece. The distant traffic rumbled up the High Street.

"I told him he was playing with fire," she went on, after a pause, "but he wouldn't listen. He thought he was smart. Over and over again I told him they wouldn't stand for it. He never did think they had any brains. He was so pleased with his plan—his stupid, silly little plan. What a fool I've been! I should never have listened to him. But he was mad, I know he was mad. After Crispin burnt him, he was never the same. He brooded all day and half the night; looking at himself in the mirror, his hand to his face, planning revenge. I warned him! I told him it wouldn't succeed. But he wouldn't listen. And now he's dead." She got up and wandered round the room. "And I'll be dead, too, before very long. They won't rest until they've killed me, and they won't rest until they've killed you."

While she had been talking, George had been looking round the sordid little room, his mind listening to her words, his eyes unconsciously seeing the various articles in the room. He found himself looking at a cheap fabric suitcase; from it was hanging a luggage tag, and on the tag, printed in bold letters, was the name *Cora Nichols*.

It only wanted that to confirm his suspicions. Very quietly, suppressing the sick dismay that rose inside him, he said, "Then you're not his sister?"

"Sister?" she said bitterly. "Do I look like anyone's sister? I wasn't even his wife."

George shivered. So all the time he had been dreaming about Cora, all the time she had promised to be very nice to him, she had been sleeping with Sydney.

"I see," he said, clenching his fists. "Well, that accounts for it, I suppose."

"I loved him!" Cora exclaimed, "and he treated me like a dog. I love him still. If he came back to me this very moment, I'd forgive him. I'd forgive him taking the money; I'd forgive him leaving me without a word, if only he'd come back." She sat down, holding her head in her hands, her eyes like holes cut in a sheet.

"Who was he?" George asked, after a long pause.

"Sydney?" Cora said. "Who was he? A cheap thief. That's who he was.

He stole cars for Crispin. Then one day he found a car with a case of jewellery in the back. He turned the car over to Crispin, but kept the jewellery. He thought he was being smart. The things he promised me when he had sold the jewellery! And then he was stupid enough to try to sell them to the fence who worked for Crispin. That's how smart he was! And the Greeks came after him. They got him in the end, and they took him down to Copthorne, and Crispin put a mark on his face. He said if he ever saw him again, he'd mark him again." She went back to the divan and sat down. "They didn't know about me, so I was the one to watch them. Sydney kept out of the way. That's why he took up selling those silly books. He had to earn money somehow, and he had to keep out of the West End. I fooled them all right. I found out that the fence was going down to Copthorne with seven hundred pounds to buy a collection of stuff from the various cars Crispin had stolen. So Sydney made his plans."

George listened grimly to all this. "Well, go on," he said bitterly. "When he met me he decided I was to be the stooge?"

"Yes," Cora said listlessly. "He saw his chance to kill Crispin and pin it onto you. I believed in him because I loved him, but I knew it wouldn't come off. I knew they'd be too smart for him. But he wouldn't listen."

"It meant nothing to you that I should be trapped into killing a man? You didn't care what happened to me, did you?"

She frowned. "Why should I? You meant nothing to me."

George flinched; then, stung to anger by her brutal callousness, he said furiously, "Well, I'm going to mean something to you now! And the sooner you realize it the better!"

But she wasn't listening. "Did you hear?" she said, a white ring suddenly appearing round her lips.

Somewhere in the building came the faint tinkle of breaking glass.

"They're getting impatient," she said, and ran her fingers through her hair. "I hope I don't start screaming, George. I'm in an awful funk."

George sprang to his feet. "Barricade the door," he said, his voice quivering with excitement. "We ought to have thought of that before. Help me with the cupboard."

She did not move.

Without waiting for her, he pulled the cupboard towards him and began to drag it across the room. It was heavy, but with a tremendous effort he managed to wedge it against the door.

"They can't get in that way," he said, panting from his exertions. "Can they get in through the window?"

She giggled. "Not unless they've got wings," she said. "You are a scream, George. Why don't you go down and kill them, like you killed Wineinger, Barrow and Banghart?"

He stared at her, not understanding for a moment what she was saying. Then he flinched. He had forgotten about Wineinger, Clyde Barrow and Gustave Banghart. It seemed a long time, another age, since Cora and he had sat in that restaurant together and he had told her all those stupid lies.

"I thought you liked tough spots," she went on, watching him with frightened, jeering eyes. "I thought you were out for excitement, and you didn't care which side you were on, so long as you got into a scrap." Her inside rumbled again. "Well, there's a juicy scrap waiting for you downstairs. Why don't you get into it? You're not scared of two little Greeks and a fat old woman, are you?"

"Stop it!" George said, sharply. "I was lying. You may as well know now. I've never been to the States. I've never seen a gangster. I was a fool. A vain, stupid fool."

She beat her fists together. "Poor old George: as if we didn't know. It was easy, George: easy as falling off a log. As soon as you started bragging, Sydney saw how he could use you. Pretend you love him, he said to me, and he's ours."

George couldn't look at her. He wanted to hate her, but shame and desire seemed to be his only emotions.

She was listening again. Her eyes darted like those of a frightened animal.

The stairs creaked outside as someone moved cautiously up them.

"It's Poncho," she whispered, bending forward. "He's got in from the back."

George started up. The heavy Luger bumped against his hip. He had forgotten the gun. Instantly he had it in his hand, and thumbed back the safety catch.

"I'll kill him if he tries to get in here," he muttered.

"They'll be sure of you if they know you have a gun," she said, watching him intently. "They'll know for certain you killed—"

"Shut up!" he said. "I don't care. They know enough as it is," he faced the door, waiting.

There was a long pause, then they heard the handle of the door turn. The door opened an inch or so and then stopped, blocked by the cupboard.

George raised the Luger. His hand was steady. He pressed the trigger, lifting the cartridge from the magazine into the breech. Then he waited, tense, sweating.

There was another long, ghastly pause. Cora was holding her head between her hands, her mouth was open, and her smeared lips formed a soundless scream. Someone outside was breathing softly, making a faint, whistling sound. Then footsteps went away. The stairs creaked. Once more there was silence except for the hum of distant traffic along the High Street and the excited ticking of the clock.

"He's gone," George whispered, lowering the gun.

Cora lit another cigarette. "Not far. They're used to waiting."

"Let them wait," George said. "We'll see who gets sick of waiting."

She lay back across the divan. "I didn't think you had the nerve," she said, a new note in her voice. "You looked fine standing up to him."

George scarcely heard her. He was staring up at the ceiling. "We could get out that way," he said. "You can't live here any more, Cora. We'll have to find some place where they'll never find us."

"We?" she said, rolling over on her stomach and looking at him. "So you're not going to desert me?"

"Did you think I would? I may be a fool, but I love you. I don't know why, because you've always been rotten to me. But I love you, and I'm going to look after you."

She held up her hand. "What's that?" she asked, her eyes dilating,

He listened. A murmur of voices floated up from the alley: whispering, hushed voices of people in church. He went over to the window, and without moving the blind, he listened. He heard a woman's voice and then a mutter of men's voices.

"Turn out the light," he said. "It's Emily."

Cora stiffened; she remained where she was. She beat on the pillow with her clenched fists.

George crossed the room and snapped off the light. Then he returned to the window and cautiously lifted the curtain.

The moon was rising above the roofs of the buildings, and part of the alley was no longer in darkness. Immediately below him he could see Emily, Max and Nick. They were standing before the front door. As he watched them he heard a bolt slam back and heard the front door open. Emily said something, and then they all entered and the front door closed.

As George put on the light again, they could hear footsteps moving about in the garage below. They made no attempt to conceal their presence now. They talked. They opened and shut doors. Once Nick laughed. The noise they made was more menacing than their previous stealth. They were confident that they would be undisturbed, and that they had George and Cora in a trap.

"We've got to get out," George said. "They're up to something. We can't stay here any longer."

Cora sat up. She was shivering, and she chewed her knuckles until one of them bled.

George went over to the window and opened it. He leaned out. The gutter above him was out of reach; the ground below was too far away. There was no escape through the window. He turned and looked up at the ceiling.

Footsteps came up the stairs and along the passage. The door handle turned and the door was opened until it was stopped by the cupboard. There was a fumbling sound at the door that sent a cold shiver of excitement down George's spine. He sprang across to the fireplace and snatched up a poker. Then he climbed up on the table and began to hack at the plaster of the ceiling.

"Turn it on," Nick's voice called.

A hissing sound filled the room.

Cora screamed.

The sharp point of the poker sank into the plaster, and a large part of the ceiling came down with a crash. George was choked with fine white dust, and almost blinded. He went on hacking at the ceiling, tearing at the wooden laths with his hands.

A strong smell of gas filled the room. So that was what they were up to, he thought, not pausing in his efforts to make a hole in the ceiling. Well, they were too late. The window was open, and it would not be possible to build up a strong enough concentration of gas to suffocate them. But suppose they set the place on fire? It'd go up like a powder barrel!

He worked for a few seconds like a madman. Voices sounded in the alley. They had left the garage. Any moment they might set fire to the place. The hole was big enough to get through now. He shouted to Cora, but she just sat on the divan, coughing and wringing her hands.

He jumped off the table and grabbed hold of her. She resisted weakly, but somehow he got her on the table.

"Through the hole," he gasped, "it's our only chance."

He caught hold of the back of her slacks and hoisted her up. She clutched at the torn edges of the hole and he bundled her through. Then he hoisted himself up.

They crouched between the plaster and the tiles. He smashed at the tiles with the poker, and a moment later he saw, through the hole he had made, the cloudless sky and the bright moon floating serenely above them.

"Up," he panted, grabbing Cora round the waist, and he shoved her onto the roof which sloped gently to the flat roof of the next building. He followed, and together they slithered down the warm tiles, ran across the flat roof, dodged round a chimney stack and paused at the foot of the next sloping roof. Then suddenly a huge yellow flame shot into the air, followed by a violent rush of air and a tremendous bang. The blast tossed them against the roof. A great wave of black smoke engulfed them: the sound of flames and crackling wood roared up in the night.

CHAPTER SIXTEEN

They came out of a little shabby pub into the darkness. Away to their right, the sky glowed red where the fire still raged, burning the row of garages, flaring up every now and then as the flames reached a reserve of petrol.

They stood for a moment in the shadows watching the glow in the sky, the whisky they had swallowed steadying their nerves, bolstering their courage.

"When they hear we weren't found," Cora said, pushing her hands deep into her trouser pockets, "they'll begin looking for us again."

George glanced up and down the dark, deserted street. It was just after ten o'clock. His legs ached and his body sagged. The exertion of breaking out of the flat, the wild scramble over the roofs with the flames pursuing them, the nightmare climb down a water pipe had exhausted him. Dust and grit scraped his skin every time he moved. His clothes were white with plaster, his face streaked with smuts. Cora was no better off. She had a triangular tear in the knee of her slacks, and her elbows had burst through the woollen sleeves of her sweater. The smell of smoke still clung to her hair.

But she had recovered her nerve. She had swallowed three double whiskies in rapid succession, and George had seen the terror drain out of her like dirty water out of a sink.

"Plans," she said, and took out a crumpled packet of cigarettes from her pocket, stuck a cigarette between her lips and lit it. She drew hard on the cigarette, and then forced a stream of smoke down her nostrils. "We've got to go somewhere tonight." She cocked her head at him. "Got any money, George?"

He pulled out a handful of loose change. He had twelve shillings and a few coppers.

She grimaced. "That's no use," she said. "Any money at home?"

He shook his head.

"I don't think it'd be safe to go to your place. We've got to duck out of sight, and keep out of sight."

He thought in dismay of his clothes, his books, his personal belongings.

"I'll have to go back," he said.

She shrugged. "Go, if you want your throat cut, but you'd better wait until the morning."

"We've got to go somewhere," he said helplessly. "Look at the mess we're in. If the police spot us, they may ask questions."

She brooded into the darkness. The red glow of her cigarette bobbed up and down.

"Little Ernie," she said, at last. "'He'll put us up."

Immediately George became uneasy. "He knows too much," he said. "I don't think we should go to him."

"You don't know anything about him," Cora returned shortly. "Ernie's all right. He'll help us." She began to move down the road. "He's had his eye on me for some time."

George fell into step beside her. "I don't like him," he growled. "He'd better keep his hands off you."

Cora didn't say anything.

They walked on in silence until they reached a 'bus stop. While they waited, George watched her out of the corners of his eyes.

Her grey-white face was hard and expressionless, but she held her head high, and she moved with a jaunty swagger.

The 'bus took them along Piccadilly, and they got off at Old Bond Street. The passengers on the 'bus gaped at them in undisguised astonishment. George, embarrassed, kept his eyes fixed on his dusty, cut shoes. Cora looked round with arrogant indifference, staring with jeering contempt at anyone who looked at her.

They walked up Old Bond Street towards Burlington Street: an odd couple in one of the richest streets in the world. Four prostitutes waited at the corner of Old Bond Street and Burlington Street. Their harsh voices chattered excitedly in broken English. Their French accents reminded George somehow of the Parrot House at the Zoo.

Cora paused, gave them a quick glance, and said, "Eva about?"

The four women stopped talking and stared at her. One of them, tall, hideous, fox furs hanging from her gaunt frame, seemed to recognize her.

"What a mess you're in, darling," she said, with a harsh laugh. "What have you been doing with yourself?"

"Seen Eva?" Cora repeated, her hard little face tightening.

"She went back with a client about ten minutes ago."

Cora nodded and walked on.

George hadn't stopped. He crossed the road and waited on the opposite corner.

"Come on," Cora said impatiently. "I hope Ernie's at home."

They paused outside a tall building in Clifford Street.

"This is it," Cora said, pushing upon the front door. They began to walk upstairs. On every landing was a front door with a card set in a brass frame. George read the lettering on the cards as they passed. "Frances," "Suzette," "Marie," "José."

As they turned to mount the last flight of stairs, they heard a door open, and a moment later, an elderly, well-dressed man came down the stairs, whistling softly. When he saw them, alarm jumped into his eyes and he stopped whistling. He paused, uncertain, and gripped his stick.

"Well, make up your mind," Cora said contemptuously. "Either come down or go back. We want to come up."

He came scuttling down, his mouth working with fear. He shot past them like a startled rabbit.

"I bet we put the fear of God into him," Cora said, and laughed.

George sympathized with the man. He knew how startled he would have been to see two such filthy, wild-looking people if he were coming from such a place.

They reached the top landing. The card on the door read "Eva." Cora banged on the door with the little brass knocker.

There was a pause, then the door opened and a young woman in a smart grey tailored coat and skirt gaped at them. She had a mass of red hair, and her face was a mask of makeup.

"Ernie in?" Cora asked shortly.

"Well, my dear!" the young woman exclaimed. "Whatever have you been up to? What a surprise! Who's your boyfriend?"

They stepped into a well-furnished hall. The floorboards gleamed, the big brass tray on ebony trestles glittered, and the thick rug on which they stood tickled their ankles.

"This is George," Cora said, waving her hand carelessly in George's direction. "I want Ernie."

The young woman smiled at George. She had big, strong white teeth. "I'm Eva," she said. "I've heard so much about you. And what a mess you're in! But don't stand there, come in, come in."

She took them down a passage and threw open a door. "Look, my precious, what's blown in," she called.

Little Ernie glanced up. He was lying in a big armchair, his small feet up on a padded stool. He looked completely out of place in the lavishly furnished room.

George had never seen such a room. It was too big, the ceiling was too high, and the white carpet that went from wall to wall looked like a fresh fall of snow. The ivory furniture had chromium on it, and the enormous scarlet drapes hung from the tops of the high windows and tumbled on to the white carpet. Four big white suede armchairs stood about the room. A vast cocktail cabinet, filled with dozens of bottles of every conceivable drink, stood by the window.

If he had been told that he had strayed into Buckingham Palace, he would have believed it. The room was exactly his idea of a Queen's boudoir.

Little Ernie scrambled to his feet. His eyes gleamed with sudden excitement and eagerness.

"For cryin' out loud!" he exclaimed. "Cora, my ducks, and me old pal, George. Well, well, fancy you coming 'ere." He turned to Eva. "'Ere, get 'er cleaned up, and then we'll 'ave a nice little chat. Come on, palsy," he went on to George, "you come along with me. You two've been in trouble, I can see that."

He took George out of the room and down the passage. He pushed open another door and led George into a small bedroom. It was elegant and well furnished.

"There you are," Little Ernie said. "The bathroom's just through there. Make yourself at 'ome. Sorry I can't give you a suit, but you and me ain't quite in the same class, are we? Featherweight and 'eavyweight, eh?" He smirked. "You 'ave a clean up, and I'll get a drink for you. Could you do with a bite to eat?"

George suddenly realized that he was famished. "It's good of you," he muttered, embarrassed, worried. "If it's not putting you out ..."

Little Ernie winked. "Leave it to me," he said, and moved to the door. He could not resist saying, "Posh place, ain't it? D'yer like it?"

George nodded. "I've never seen anything to touch it," he said frankly envious.

Little Ernie jerked his thumb to the door. "She works like a nigger," he said, lowering his voice. "Never no trouble. Takes a pride in the place. A gold mine," and, nodding, he left the room.

Twenty minutes later George returned to the big sitting room. He had made himself as tidy as he could and brushed his suit. He had had a bath, and his big face was shiny and red from the hot water and soap.

He found Little Ernie busying himself before the cocktail cabinet. A small table was laid with a snowy white cloth and glistening silver. Eva was perched on the arm of a chair, a cigarette in her full red lips, her eyes expectant and curious.

"What'll you have?" she asked George as he came into the room. "A dry martini?"

"'Ave a whisky, chum," Little Ernie said. "You don't want cissy drinks like them French cocktails." He came across the room with a tumbler a third full of whisky and clinking ice. "Ain't Cora ready yet? You women ... you'll be the death of me."

While he was talking, George noticed that Eva did not once take her eyes off his face. She looked at him with open admiration and expectancy. He suddenly realized that Little Ernie had probably told her he was a killer. It gave him an exciting feeling of power.

"Come and sit down," Eva said, patting the chair next to hers. "I've been dying to meet you ever since Ernie told me about you."

"That's right," Little Ernie said, grinning. "Meet Frank Kelly's gunman. He's tough, but 'e don't like talking about it."

George sat down. The gun dug into him, and deliberately he pulled it from his hip pocket, and then glanced at the other two, tightening his mouth and scowling.

They both froze at the sight of the gun. Eva's eyes dilated and her lips parted. Little Ernie stiffened, his face expressionless.

"Do you mind if I put it on the mantelpiece?" George said, carelessly, getting to his feet. "It's a bit in my way."

"That's all right, chum," Little Ernie said, his voice a trifle husky. "You make yourself at 'ome."

As George put the Luger on the mantelpiece, the door opened and Cora came in. George looked at her; a shiver of pleasure and desire ran through him. She had washed her hair, which was now soft and fluffy; she was cleaner than he had ever seen her before, and she was wearing a scarlet wrap which enhanced her strange beauty. Her feet and legs were bare. George suspected that she wasn't wearing anything under the wrap, and the thought sent his blood racing through his veins.

Nor was he the only one. Little Ernie, too, looked at her with frank admiration and lechery.

"Come on in," he said, turning to the cocktail cabinet. "What'll you 'ave? Doesn't she look a beauty, Eva?"

"Wonderful," Eva said, without any sign of jealousy. She reached forward and rang a bell. "I've got to leave you now," she went on, gathering up her hat and bag. "Ernie'll look after you. And keep your voices down, won't you? My gentlemen friends are ever so nervous. They like to think they're all alone with me, the poor darlings." She waved her hand and went off, blowing a kiss to Ernie on her way out.

"What a gal!" Little Ernie said, sitting down. "See what I mean? It's work all the time with 'er."

The door opened and a thin sad-faced woman in black came in pushing a small trolley. She manoeuvred the trolley near the table, and went out without even a glance at any of them.

"There you are. Just 'elp yourself," Little Ernie said, beaming on them. "Eat as much as you like."

There were bowls of jellied soup and lobster salad, a pile of chicken sandwiches, and a plate of finely cut, lean ham. A silver bucket containing a bottle of champagne on ice completed the meal.

While they ate, Little Ernie took charge of the champagne. "Only the best," he said, smirking at George. "That's Eva all over. Beats me 'ow she picks everything up. Must be 'er posh friends. You wouldn't believe it, but I found 'er in a smelly little restaurant in Pimlico washing dishes. I took one look at 'er shape and took a chance on 'er. Like a monkey, she is. Picks up everything. Talks posh even. Best day's work I ever done."

He kept up a ceaseless chatter during the meal, and when the woman had taken the trolley and table away, he poured fresh drinks and sat down.

"Well," he said, stretching out his short legs, "don't tell me if you don't want to, but you two certainly were in a state when you came in."

Cora looked at him mockingly. Now that she had eaten and rested, she was once more her old self.

"That's our secret," she said, with a short, hard laugh. "If you really want to know, Ernie, we had a fire."

Little Ernie picked his nose. "I 'eard the fire engines going," he said. "So you 'ad a fire, did you?"

Cora nodded.

"Burnt your 'ouse and 'ome, eh?"

"Everything went up in a gorgeous bonfire."

"Hmm."

There was a long pause.

"'Ow's Syd?" Little Ernie asked, looking at Cora sharply.

She looked away, her mouth tightening. "Didn't you see in the newspapers?"

Little Ernie's eyes narrowed. "Was that 'im? I wondered. Gawd love me ... what a death! 'Ere, Cora. I'm sorry. You know that, don't you? I'm sorry. I liked Syd. 'E'd got guts."

Cora moved restlessly. The wrap slipped, and both men caught a glimpse of her naked thigh. She adjusted the wrap impatiently.

"I didn't identify him," she said tonelessly. "They may as well bury him.

I haven't any money."

George shivered. It sounded so brutal, and yet he realized that it was only the sensible thing to have done.

"'Ow did it 'appen?"

"He slipped," Cora said, looking Ernie straight in the eyes.

"Wasn't pushed?"

"He slipped."

There was another long pause. George felt that these two had forgotten him.

"Ain't seen Crispin about for some time," Little Ernie said thoughtfully. "'Ave you?"

"I can't be bothered with him," Cora returned, her eyes watchful. "He's around, I suppose."

"I wonder." Little Ernie lit a cigarette and tossed the match into the fireplace. "I did 'ear that 'e'd come to a sticky end. Marvellous, ain't it, the way I 'ear things?"

Cora continued to stare at him watchfully.

"Listen, Ernie," she said. "I want a place for a week."

"Do you now? What makes you think I've got a place for you?"

"Come off it, Ernie. You must have dozens of flats in the West End."

"And they cost me a packet, too," Little Ernie said darkly.

"I only want it for a week."

"'Ow much can you pay?"

"Nothing."

"'Ave a 'eart."

She looked at him. He seemed to read something in that look, because his ferrety eyes lit up.

"Why don't you get wise, ducks?" he said. "You ain't got any dough. Why don't you get in the game?"

While this conversation had been going on, George sat listening, a dull, brooding expression on his face. He was trying to imagine how Frank Kelly or any of the other big-shot gangsters would have handled Little Ernie. He was sure they wouldn't have stood a rotten little pimp like him for five seconds. All the same, Little Ernie knew too much: he might also be useful. It wouldn't do to get too tough with him. But it wouldn't do, either, for him to think that George was a stooge who sat and listened and was not consulted.

His contempt for the little man was so great that he felt no diffidence in handling him.

He surprised them both by barking, "Cut that out!"

When they jerked round to stare at him, he went on, sitting forward, his heavy face congested with blood, "She's not going on the game, and you can keep off that subject if you know what's good for you!"

Little Ernie's eyes opened. "That's all right, palsy," he said hastily. "I was only having a bit of fun," but he glanced at Cora uneasily and looked away.

Cora's mouth tightened. "Don't get excited," she said, giving George a long, cold stare. "Ernie's only trying to be helpful." She looked at Little Ernie. "Don't worry about him. He's a bit jumpy. Now, be nice, Ernie. How about a flat?"

Little Ernie opened his mouth to say something, but caught the look in Cora's eyes. He hesitated and then said, "For a week, eh? Well, per'aps. I'll think about it."

George bunched his great shoulder-muscles. "You'd better do more than that," he said. "We want a place. You'll get your money all right. I've got plans."

Little Ernie scratched his head. He was suddenly not quite sure of George. The gun, which continually caught his eye, lying on the mantelpiece, disturbed him. This big, hulking fellow could be dangerous. It might be wise to get in with him, rather than antagonize him.

"You leave it to me," he said. "I'll fix you up tomorrow." He got up and went over to the cocktail cabinet. "'Ave another drink?"

George shook his head, "No," he said shortly. "I've had all I want."

Cora was watching George with a puzzled expression in her eyes. "Can we sleep here tonight, Ernie?" she asked.

Little Ernie nodded. "Sure," he said. "'E can 'ave my room and you can 'ave the spare room, unless you and 'im want to kip together."

George felt the blood rush to his face. He got up and walked over to the mantelpiece and picked up his gun, keeping his back turned to them so they should not see his embarrassment. He wanted to say that Cora and he would share a room, but his nerve failed.

"I want a bed to myself," Cora said in a cold, tight voice.

George drew in a quick breath. What else had he expected? he thought angrily. There was time for that when they got a place of their own.

"That's settled, then," Little Ernie said. "Well, I've got to shoot off. Must 'ave a word with the girls before turning in, you know. Gotta encourage 'em, bless their sweet 'earts. I'll be seeing you. Make yourself at 'ome," he went on, looking at George. "I'll see you tomorrow." He nodded, gave Cora a quick, searching glance, and went off, moving softly, like a ghost.

George and Cora stood silent until they heard the front door click shut, and then Cora said sharply, "You dotty or something? Ernie can help us.

What do you want to bark at him for?"

"He's a filthy little rat," George said, clenching his fists. "I saw the way he kept looking at you."

"So what?" Cora said, sitting on the settee. "Why should you care, if I don't?"

George stood over her. This was the time. It was now or never. One of them had to be master, and if he were to have any peace in his life, it must not be Cora.

"Because you're my girl," he said. "I love you, Cora. You're on your own, and you need someone to look after you. Well, I'm going to be that someone."

She leaned back and crossed her legs. "You?" she said. "Don't make me laugh. What have you got to offer me? Why, you can't even look after yourself."

"We'll see about that," George said grimly. "If Ernie tries any funny stuff, he'll be sorry!"

Cora's jeering expression suddenly changed to blazing rage.

"If you interfere with me," she exclaimed, jumping up, "I'll make you sorry! I'm going to do what I like! I'm in the market. The man who offers most gets me."

Again George's slow mind groped for inspiration from Frank Kelly. Kelly always kept his women. He treated them tough and loaded them with jewels. But how could he do that? Now he had got Sydney out of the way, he wasn't going to lose her. Little Ernie could give her the world. He had just got to compete with Little Ernie.

"What do you want?" he asked abruptly, struggling to conceal his doubts and fears.

"What do you mean?" she demanded.

"You're in the market, aren't you?" he said, clenching his fists. "Well, then, what's the price?"

"I think you must be drunk or mad," she said angrily, and turned away. "What can you give me? Leave me alone and peddle your silly books!"

George sat down. He took out a cigarette and lit it. His hands were steady, his mind coldly determined.

"I've got nothing now," he said, "but I can get it. You don't want to throw yourself away on a little rat like Ernie. Name something and you shall have it."

"Oh, shut up!" Cora snapped. "You're nothing but a cheap bluffer. You live in dreams. I want more than dreams, and I'm going to have more than dreams."

The Luger dug into George's hip. It gave him extraordinary confidence in himself. Thoughts crowded into his desperate frustrated mind. He had killed a man! Nothing else that he could do could be worse than that. Even if he killed another man, it wouldn't be worse than the first killing. *Once a gangster kills there is no stopping him.* He had read that somewhere, and it was true. Sooner or later Crispin's body would be found. Bodies were always found. Then the hunt would be on. If the police didn't get him, then Emily and Max and the two Greeks would. Well, until then he was going to live his life to the full. He was going to have Cora. He wasn't enduring this black, ghastly frustration any longer. If he had to buy her, then he'd buy her, no matter what the cost.

He reached out suddenly and caught hold of Cora's arm. He jerked her down beside him on the settee. The silk wrap parted, and he had a momentary glimpse of her that tipped the scales of his sanity. He caught her to him and held her, his great strength crushing her, frightening her.

"What do you want?" he said, her hair against his face. "I mean it. There's nothing I can't get for you."

"Let me go!" she said. "Will you let me go!"

He released her and sat back.

"Well?" he said. "What do you want?"

Cora could scarcely believe this was the same man. The hard face, the wild, desperate eyes, chilled her. But she was quick to see that she must call this ridiculous bluff. In his present state of mind, she felt he was dangerous. He might do anything unless she provided an outlet for his pent-up, violent repression.

"I want a complete outfit," she said. "And I want it now. Give me that, if you can, you cheap bluffer."

George looked at her steadily. "You mean clothes?"

"Of course, I mean clothes. I want something to wear when I go out tomorrow morning. I want a complete outfit. And don't think I can't get it. I've only to ask Little Ernie."

"I'll get you the money," George said slowly.

"I don't want the money, I want the clothes. I want something decent to put on when I get up tomorrow morning."

George hesitated. She had purposely asked for the impossible. There were no shops open at this time, but, of course, Little Ernie could get an outfit from one of his girls. It would be the simplest thing in the world for him to do. But George had no girl to borrow anything from. She had laid the trap and he had walked into it.

Cora, studying his face, saw doubt and dismay there, and she got up with a laugh.

"Now shut up, you bluffer," she said. "I've had quite enough from you for one night. I'm going to bed." She went to the door, and looked back over her shoulder. "I don't think you and I have much in common, do you, George?" she went on. "I think you'd better go back to your cat and your bookselling."

George sat brooding for some little time after she had gone. She was slipping through his fingers. He had to do something. Tomorrow would be too late. She had asked for a complete outfit of clothes: well, she must have it.

He got to his feet, picked up his hat and stood staring down at the thick white carpet. Getting an outfit of women's clothes at eleven-thirty at night might set even Frank Kelly back on his heels. He must prove to himself that he was a better man even than Frank Kelly.

He crossed the room and quietly let himself out of the hateful little flat.

CHAPTER SEVENTEEN

In the network of narrow streets that lie behind Shaftesbury Avenue there is one particular street where taxi drivers leave their cabs while they have a meal after the theatre rush.

It was to this street that George made his way. He moved along Piccadilly, past the Piccadilly Hotel, threading his way through the crowd of men and women lingering outside the hotel for a final word before dispersing to their homes. He stood on the curb, his back turned to the darkened windows of Swan & Edgar, while he waited impatiently for the traffic lights to stop the flow of traffic towards Regent Street. There was an apprehensive feeling, like a lead weight, in his stomach. He had conceived a desperate, reckless plan. It depended for success on one thing: the strength of his own nerves. A week ago he would have shied away from such an idea as any person in their right mind would have shied away from touching a red-hot stove. It was the kind of thing he had read about, the kind of desperate act that, at one time, American thugs used to commit in the wild, dangerous days of prohibition. It was a plan conceived by desperation, the only possible solution of Cora's demand.

At first he had thought of breaking into one of the big stores, like Selfridge's or Swan & Edgar. Here, he knew, he would be able to steal some women's clothes. But even if he succeeded in breaking into the store, he had still to select the right clothes, the right size, the right match. Cora had said she wanted a complete outfit. It was no use making a mess of it. She must have something that she could put on, complete to the last button, and that went for hat, shoes, stockings and bag as well as the clothes. He couldn't possibly go from counter to counter picking the right things. That was out of the question.

There was only one thing to do. He had to find a girl of Cora's size and take from her her clothes and everything that went with her outfit. Only in that way would he be sure that he had forgotten nothing, that everything fitted, that everything matched.

His great shoulders hunched, his head down, he walked across the Circus, pausing for a moment under the statue of Eros, before gaining a foothold on the crowded pavement of Shaftesbury Avenue. He went on past the Windmill Theatre into Archer Street, where chorus girls in their street clothes were coming out of the stage door.

The next street brought him to a long line of taxis. He slowed his pace, looking sharply at each taxi as he passed. They were all empty, and through the lighted door of an eating place a few yards farther on came the sound of men talking and laughing. Without stopping he glanced through the glass door. A crowd of drivers sat over their food at long, wooden tables in a room hazy with tobacco smoke.

He stopped before the eating house, turned and began to wander back again. He continued on to where the first taxi headed the long row of deserted vehicles.

Once more he paused. He fished out a cigarette and lit it. As he did so, he glanced up and down the street, his eyes watchful, his face expressionless.

Satisfied that there was no one coming, he got quickly into the driver's seat. It was some time since he had driven a car. His feet fumbled, feeling for the accelerator, the footbrake and the clutch. His hand grasped the gear lever, and pushing out the clutch, he manoeuvred the lever through the gate. It worked smoothly, and he was surprised and pleased that he made no mistake.

This begins it, he thought, his heart thumping against his side, and he pressed the starter. The engine growled, but nothing else happened. He caught his breath sharply, and stabbed at the starter again. The whirring, frustrated sound of the engine trying to start made a tremendous racket in the silent street.

His nerve wilted. In a few seconds they would be out after him. He cursed the engine feverishly as he stabbed at the starter again. Then he cursed himself. He hadn't switched on! What a damn, stupid, frightened clod he was! He turned on the ignition with fumbling fingers, pressed the starter and immediately the engine sprang to life.

Somehow he got the cab moving, and turned the corner. He was now in such a fever that he clamped down on the accelerator, yet the cab moved slowly, making a terrific din. He clung to the wheel, his eyes bolting out of his head, terrified, wild. Then, as no one shouted after him, he gained control of his nerves and managed to change into second and then into top.

The cab went on. Ahead was Oxford Street. George swung blindly into the busy thoroughfare. He nearly collided with a 'bus, and he realized with alarm that he had crossed against the red traffic light. The 'bus driver shouted at him, but he accelerated and left the 'bus behind.

He was coming to Oxford Circus now. The lights changed to red when he was a few yards away, and he pulled up so sharply that he stalled the engine.

He sat in a heap, sweat running down his face, his ears pricked. He felt he was experiencing some horrible nightmare.

He became aware that cars behind him were blaring with their horns and klaxons. Without his noticing it, the traffic light had changed to green. Hurriedly he started the engine, forgetting he was still in gear. The taxi jumped forward and went bounding down the street like a startled frog.

People were staring at him from the pavement. Another taxi overtook him, and the driver leaned out: "Make it waltz, mate," he pleaded as he passed. "You've done everything else."

Gritting his teeth, George changed down. He turned right and drove on, past the B.B.C., up Portland Place and into Regent's Park.

There was scarcely any traffic in the Park, and he became calmer. He must get used to this cab, he thought, before he ventured again into the wilderness of traffic lights and heavy traffic. He drove round the inner circle several times, stopping and starting, changing up and down, until he had regained some of his confidence. Then he stopped and lit a cigarette and tried to make a plan. He decided that he would go down Park lane, along Piccadilly to Berkeley Square, up the square to Bruton Street, into New Bond Street and down into Piccadilly again. It was getting late, and his best chance was to catch some girl coming from a night club.

He would have to be quick, because the theft of the cab would be reported very soon and the police would be looking for it. He had, at the best, a half an hour in which to find the girl and get her out of the West End.

He started the cab again and headed for Park Lane. A number of people hailed him, as he drove along, hugging the curb, but after a quick glance in their direction and seeing that they were all in parties, he kept on.

Without stopping, he drove along the route he had planned. His nerves began to ease as he went on. There seemed to be no unescorted girls waiting for a taxi, and he began to hope that the plan would fizzle out.

But as he drove down New Bond Street for a second time, he saw a girl standing on the curb, and she waved to him.

One look was enough. She was about Cora's build, and she was wearing a dark coat and skirt; a smart little hat was perched on her head, and as she waved at George a gold bangle glittered in the street light.

George pulled up, eyeing the girl, his mouth suddenly dry, his nerves tingling.

The girl was a typical Mayfair deb—the kind of girl whose picture appeared regularly in the *Bystander* and *Tatler*, and who seemed to spend their lives either smiling vacantly at some sleek young man in tails and white tie at Lady Someone or other's ball, or resting their hard little sterns on shooting sticks while attending a shoot in Scotland.

"Chunks!" she shouted excitedly. "I've got one. Chunks, do come on!"

Oh, hell! George thought in a fever, she's not alone! He wanted to engage gear and drive away, but the girl had already jerked open the cab door, and was standing looking over her shoulder at the open door of a building, partly obscured by the darkness.

"Do come on, Chunks," she called again. She turned to George, "He won't be a minute. I want to go to Highgate Village."

At this moment a tall young man came running down the steps. "You *are* marvellous, Babs," he said. "I don't know how you do it. You're just too nauseatingly efficient. Why couldn't you let the porter find you a taxi?"

"I like doing things for myself," the girl said.

"Are you *sure* you don't want me to come?" the young man asked. "I don't mind. I don't mind a bit."

George stiffened. He looked quickly at the girl, willing her to refuse.

"Of course, I don't," she returned. "Besides, you always get a bit hectic in taxis, Chunks, and it's too hot to wrestle with you all the way to Highgate."

The young man giggled. "All right, darling," he said. "Have it your own way. I'll see you tomorrow."

"Thanks for a terrific evening," she returned, climbing into the taxi.

The young man slammed the door.

"Manor House, Parkway," he said to George. "Do you know it?"

George nodded, keeping his face in the shadow. He was shivering with excitement, and he let his clutch in with a jerk and roared away towards Hyde Park Corner. What a bit of luck! he thought. She's just right. I'm sure she's just right. Now, what's the next step? Highgate Village lay beyond Hampstead Heath. That was a good spot to do what he had to do. At this hour it would be unlikely that anyone would be about. He gripped the steering wheel tightly. He had perfect faith and confidence in his gun. He felt positive that all he had to do was to point the gun at this girl and she would obey him. There was nothing the Luger couldn't get for him—and for Cora.

He turned up Park Lane and slid to a standstill as the traffic lights changed. As he sat waiting, he noticed a policeman at the corner, watching him, and his heart lurched. Were they looking for him already? The light turned to amber, and he hurriedly drove on.

He heard the girl singing to herself. She seemed a pretty lively type, he thought. Rich, and spoilt, without a care in the world. What a different world Cora lived in! He went on up Orchard Street, past Baker Street station and on towards Swiss Cottage.

It wouldn't be long now. A distant clock chimed the quarter past midnight. He'd have to look slippy. Any moment now the police might be looking for him. He sent the cab whizzing up Fitzjohn's Avenue, and in a few moments he was on the Heath.

A bright moon hung in the sky, lighting the trees and the scrub, throwing heavy black shadows. The place seemed completely deserted. He kept on until he saw a large clump of trees standing by the roadside, then he reached forward and cut the ignition. The engine died with a splutter and the cab coasted towards the trees, finally coining to a standstill in the deepest shadows.

George sat for a moment, screwing up his nerve, then he climbed down stiffly onto the road.

The girl poked her head out of the window.

"Why are you stopping?" she asked. "Is there anything wrong?" She seemed quite calm and mildly interested.

George pulled his hat farther down over his eyes.

"Petrol," he grunted. "I'm sorry, miss; I thought I'd filled up."

"What a bore!" she exclaimed, opening the cab door. "Now, I suppose I'll have to walk. Well, it's not so far. What are you going to do?"

George was startled that she should think of him. It was not what he expected from the upper classes.

"I'll manage," he said, his hand on the cold butt of the gun.

"If you like to walk along with me," she said, "I'll give you a tin of petrol. You've got miles to go back."

He wished feverishly that she hadn't been like this. He wished she had flown into a temper and had upbraided him, it would have been so much easier. Now she was making him feel like a rat. His mind flew to Cora. He had to go through with it. He couldn't return to the flat empty-handed. He eyed the girl's clothes furtively. They were expensive and well cut. He was sure they would fit Cora. He could imagine her face when she saw them: that thought decided him.

"Would you like to do that?" the girl was saying. She had opened her bag and was lighting a cigarette. "You can leave the cab...."

"Don't be frightened," George said, pulling the Luger from his hip pocket, and pointing it at her. "This is a—a hold-up."

She stood staring at him, the match burning in her finger: Her eyes went to the gun and then back at him. She flicked the match away.

"Oh," she said, and stood very still.

George kept the muzzle of the gun pointing at her. He looked at her for signs of fear, a change of expression, any reaction which would give him courage to complete this beastly business.

But her expression didn't change. She seemed very calm, and she took the cigarette from her lips as if she were in a drawing room full of her own kind.

"I'm not going to hurt you, if you do what you're told," George went on, making his voice gruff.

"Well, that's a blessing," she said quietly. "I most certainly don't want to get hurt. What do you want?"

George gulped. This was going all wrong. She ought to be frightened, she ought to be grovelling before the menacing threat of the gun.

"I want your clothes," he said.

A look of complete astonishment crossed her face. "My clothes?" she repeated. "Oh, come. How can you have my clothes? I want them my-self; and besides, what in the world would you do with them? You can have my money—not that I've got much—but I really can't let you have my clothes. Do be reasonable."

"I see," George heard himself say feebly. He stood baffled. The calm tone of her voice, her obvious disregard for the Luger, the quiet reason-ing of her argument, flummoxed him.

She opened her bag and took out several pound notes. "That's all I've got. Four pounds. I suppose I'll have to give it to you, but it'll make me beastly short. You've no idea how close Daddy is. He won't give me a penny more than twenty pounds a month. That's not much, is it?"

"Well, no," George said, gaping at her. "I suppose it isn't."

"Of course it isn't," the girl went on, holding out the money, "but I suppose you want it more than I do, otherwise you wouldn't be taking such a risk. I do think you're being awfully silly, you know. You could get six months' hard for this."

This was quite fantastic, George thought. I must control this situation. But he made no move to take the money. The girl was so reasonable, so unafraid. He wondered wildly what Frank Kelly would have done in such a situation. He would probably have shot the girl, but George couldn't do that. Besides, he admired her. She'd got more guts than he had. He had the gun, but he was flustered, near panic, while she was cool and at ease.

"Look here," he said desperately. "I'm sorry about this, but I've got to have your clothes. I don't want to hurt you, but if you don't give them to me, I'll have to ..."

She looked at him intently. "You're not a sex maniac, or something, are you?" she asked, then, before he could say anything she answered her own question. "No, I'm sure you're not. Would you like to tell me why you want my clothes so badly. It sounds interesting."

George stared at her helplessly.

"Do tell me," she went on. "Let's sit down." She went over and sat on the running board of the car. "I might be able to help you. Don't look so worried. I'm not going to run away."

Slowly, bemused, George lowered the gun. It was going all wrong. He knew now that he would never be able to attack this girl, he knew that he was not going to get her clothes, and the reaction of the excitement and strain made him feel giddy. He came over and sat limply down by her side.

"You've never done this kind of thing before, have you?" the girl went on. "Not that you're bad at it. You fooled me completely, but I think you're a bit too kind really to make a success of it, aren't you?"

George nodded miserably. "I suppose so," he said. "No, I've never done this kind of thing before. But I was desperate. I'd better drive you home now. I—I'm sorry if I frightened you."

"Well, you did give me a bit of a turn," the girl admitted, "but now you're being nice, I don't mind. But do tell me why you wanted my clothes. I can understand you wanting my money, but why my clothes?"

George hesitated. Then he blurted out, "They were for my girl," he said. "She's got nothing to wear...."

"Your girl?"

George nodded. "I promised her I'd get her anything she wanted, and she thought I was bluffing. She said I could get her a complete outfit. She wanted it tomorrow morning."

"How romantic!" the girl exclaimed. "Why, if I asked Chunks to get me a complete outfit in the middle of the night, the poor lamb would commit suicide. He'd do anything for me. I think I must really try this one on him."

George clenched his fists. She didn't understand! And he was so hoping that she would.

She noticed the change of his expression. "I say, I am sorry," she said quickly. "I didn't mean to be funny, I suppose you're pretty badly in love?"

Instantly George warmed to her. "Yes," he said.

"Is she very lovely?"

George nodded. "She's marvellous," he said, looking across the limitless expanse of the Heath. "You see, she doesn't think I've got any guts. She—she won't have much to do with me. She deliberately laid this trap, knowing that I couldn't do anything about it. That's why I tried." He drew in a deep breath. "I—I stole that taxi."

"Are you quite sure she's the right one for you?" the girl asked, looking at him curiously. "She doesn't sound your type at all."

"She isn't really," George admitted, "but sometimes one can't help that. A girl like that gets in one's blood and there's not much one can do about it. I can't, anyway."

The girl thought about this for a moment, then she nodded. "Yes, I can understand that," she said; "but you ought to be careful. A girl like that could get you into a lot of trouble."

Trouble? George thought bitterly. She had done that all right, if you could use such a word for murder.

"Well, I can't help it," he returned tonelessly. "I can't do without her."

The girl stood up. "All right," she said. "I'll help you. Take me home and I'll give you an outfit. I'd like to surprise your girlfriend. I only wish I could be there to see her face when you give it to her."

George stared at her, scarcely believing his ears.

"You'll give me an outfit?" he repeated stupidly.

"Yes, I'd much sooner give you one than have to go home without a stitch." She suddenly laughed. "I have to think of Daddy. It would give the poor darling a stroke; and think what the servants would say!"

Was this a trap? George wondered, suddenly suspicious. Was she going to get him to the house and then send for the police? Why should she give him the clothes? She had never seen him before. What was behind this?

She seemed to read his thoughts.

"It's all right," she said, looking down at him. "I'm not going to trap you into anything. It's just that I have a lot of clothes and it pleases me to help you. What do you say?"

Still George hesitated. The suggestion was preposterous. He had set out as a desperate bandit, and now the girl he had planned to rob was actually going to give him what he wanted.

"Do make up your mind," she said, throwing away her cigarette. "It's getting late, and I ought to be home."

He got slowly to his feet. "I don't know what to say," he muttered, looking at her uneasily. "It's fantastic."

"No, it isn't. You're nervous I'll send for the police, aren't you? I won't. I promise."

He remembered Cora's promise. Women made promises lightly, he warned himself, but looking at her he was inclined to believe her. Anyway, if he became suspicious he had his gun ... and he'd use it, too!

"Well, thanks," he said. "I think it's awfully decent of you," and he opened the cab door for her.

"Has she my colouring?" the girl asked, sitting on the little turn-up seat so that she could talk to George as he drove.

Cora had her colouring all right, but that was as far as the resemblance went. She had a better figure, more character in her face than this girl—not that this girl wasn't nice-looking. In a way, George preferred her to Cora. She hadn't Cora's sulky expression, nor the lines near her mouth. She had a better skin than Cora's, and her hair was more beautiful. But that didn't mean she was more exciting than Cora: she wasn't. There was something about Cora which tortured George. He knew this girl would never torture him.

"Yes," he said. "She's about your size, and she's got hair like yours."

"What do you think she'd like?" the girl asked. "Would she like a frock, or a costume, or a coat and skirt?"

Was she pulling his leg? George wondered. Had she got so many things to give away?

"Well, I don't know," he said. "I thought something like you're wearing."

She laughed. "Of course, that's why you picked on me, wasn't it? I think I've got something that'll do. I don't mind parting with clothes. It's money I hate parting with. You see, Daddy pays for my clothes, and gives me pocket money for extras. He doesn't seem to mind how many clothes I have, but he just won't part with any more cash."

George drove on, bewildered.

"We're just here," she called after a few minutes. "The gate's on the right."

George hesitated. Should he drive in? Should he risk a trap? Before he could make up his mind, he had reached the gates and had turned into a long, winding drive. But when he sighted a vast house through the trees, he slowed down and stopped the cab.

She jumped out.

"Stay here," she said. "I won't be long."

"All right," he said uneasily, and watched her walk swiftly towards the house.

As soon as she was out of sight, George left the cab and moved off the drive into the garden. He couldn't afford to trust her. He would give her ten minutes, and then he'd go. From where he stood, in the shadow of a big magnolia tree, he could see the house. He could see her run up the broad, white steps, open the door and go in. The ground floor was in darkness, but the windows of both the wings on the two upper floors showed lights.

He stood still, watching the house, his hand on the butt of his gun. A moment or so later a light sprang up in one of the centre windows, and he caught a glimpse of the girl as she passed to and fro before the window.

He relaxed slightly. Anyway, she wasn't telephoning, he thought. How astounding! He was sure if anyone had tried to hold *him* up, he would have given them over to the police at the first possible opportunity.

Scarcely ten minutes had gone by before he saw her coming down the steps again. She held a bundle under her arm, and George, convinced of her sincerity at last, went to meet her.

"I bet you had a bad ten minutes," she said, smiling at him. "I hope I haven't been too long. You'll find everything there. I duplicated the underclothes. The hat's the only thing I wasn't sure about. Does she wear hats?"

George blinked. "No," he said. "How did you know?"

"I somehow felt she didn't." She pressed the bundle into his arms.

George stood gaping at her, a prickly sensation behind his eyes. "I—I don't know how to thank you. I don't really."

"I've got to get in now. Good night, and please don't hold up any more girls. You know, we don't really like it."

He watched her go, then he turned and stumbled back to the taxi. People were kind! he thought. He would never have believed it. Never! To think that a girl like that, so rich, who had everything, should have been so damned decent, especially after the fright he had given her. It was terrific of her! It really was marvellous.

Driving back across the Heath, George had this girl Babs more in his mind than Cora. Cora had never been kind to him. She had always jeered at him. Babs was the only girl who had ever been decent to him—except, of course, Gladys; but Gladys didn't count. It was her job to be decent to everyone. But Babs—why, she could have called the police. She could have trapped him easily enough; but instead, she had given him the impossible. She had done more for him—a complete stranger—than Cora would ever do for him, even though Cora knew he loved her.

He wouldn't wait for the morning, he decided. He would go into her bedroom and wake her up and lay the clothes on the bed for her to admire. He would stand over her and grin. It was something to grin about, wasn't it? "You cheap bluffer!" she had called him. Well, this would show her whether he was a bluffer or not.

A sudden stab of desire caught him. She might be so pleased that—well, it was no good thinking along those lines just yet. But she might feel that she could be nice to him. She might be very nice to him. After all, few people would have done what he had done. He wouldn't tell her about Babs. He'd just say he kidnapped a girl and stripped her of her clothes. That'd startle her. That'd show her he had guts!

He was so excited at the thought of bursting into Cora's room that he threw caution to the wind and drove right through the West End to Hanover Square. There was no difficulty in leaving the cab on the cab rank there. It was nearly one o'clock and the Square was deserted.

He hurried down George Street, across Conduit Street and into Clifford Street. He ran up the stairs to the top flat.

There was a light on in the hall, and he could hear Eva's voice coming from the sitting room. A moment later, Little Ernie answered. He wondered if Cora was with them; then he remembered she said she was going to bed. Well, he'd look in her bedroom first. He went down the passage very quietly, and opened the door.

The room was in darkness, but the heady, exciting smell of sandalwood greeted him.

"Cora?" he called softly. "Are you awake?"

"Who is it?" Cora's voice asked sleepily, then she said more sharply, "What is it?"

"It's me, George."

"What do *you* want?" She sounded irritable, and a moment later she snapped on a light over her bed.

George looked at her, feeling a great rush of love and tenderness to his heart.

She's wonderful, he thought, looking at her. She was wearing a pair of satin, peach-coloured pyjamas he guessed she must have borrowed from Eva.

"What is it?" she repeated, looking at her wristwatch. "Why, it's after one. Haven't you been to bed?"

"May I come in?" George asked, still standing awkwardly in the doorway. "I've got a surprise for you."

Instantly a quick, calculating expression jumped into her eyes. "A surprise? What is it?"

"I've got you some clothes," George said, showing her the bundle. Now he was in the light he saw that Babs had put the clothes in a pillowcase.

"Are you mad?" she said blankly. "What clothes?"

"You wanted an outfit," George said patiently. "I—I've got you one."

Cora sat up in bed. "You've got me one?" she repeated.

It was just as George had hoped it would be. He had staggered her. She was excited. She had never looked at him like this before.

He nodded. "I said you had only to ask and I'd get it for you."

"But how?" Cora demanded. "Don't stand there like a dummy. Come in, shut the door." She slid out of bed, now thoroughly awake and excited. "How did you do it?"

This was George's moment. This was the sweetest moment in George's life.

"Well, it wanted a bit of thinking out," he said, coming into the room and shutting the door. "I couldn't rob a store. I hadn't any money. So I decided to take the clothes off someone about your size."

Cora gaped at him—actually gaped at him! "You didn't!" she exclaimed.

George nodded. Tears of elation pricked his eyes. "I had to pinch a taxi. That wasn't too easy, and then I cruised around the West End until I spotted a well-dressed girl. I offered her a lift. She lived in Hampstead somewhere and—and I took her up on the Heath and made her take her clothes off and—well, here I am.

"George!" Cora gasped. "I don't believe it."

But she believed it all right; he could see the look of startled admiration in her eyes.

"You did that for me?" she said, jumping up. "Why, George! Why, it's wonderful!"

For a moment he thought she was going to throw her arms round his neck, but instead, she ran past him to the door and threw it open.

"Eva! Ernie! Come here! Come here at once!"

He didn't want the other two. He wanted to hear Cora say over and over again that he was wonderful. He wanted her to be very nice to him in that lovely peach-coloured suit. He wanted to be able to hold her in his arms and feel her hair against his face.

Eva and Little Ernie appeared in the doorway. They looked startled.

"Wot's hup?" Little Ernie asked, looking from Cora to George.

"You must hear this," Cora exclaimed, excitedly. "I asked George to get me a complete outfit of clothes. Of course, I was fooling. I knew he couldn't get them at this time of the night, but I wanted to pull his leg. I pretended to be dead set on having some clothes for tomorrow...."

"Well, I could have fixed you up," Little Ernie said, leering at her. "I've got tons of clothes. It's me job to keep my girls smart, ain't it, Eva?"

This was a triumph for George. Well, he'd beaten the little rat! In the morning Cora would have gone to him, and George would have had the humiliation of seeing her wear clothes from a pimp.

"Shut up, Ernie," Cora said sharply. "George has actually done it! It's the most fantastic story I've ever heard. He pinched a taxi, picked up a girl, took her on the Heath and pinched her clothes."

George could feel Eva's admiring gaze. Even Little Ernie's mouth fell open.

"For Gawd's sake!" Little Ernie said. "The old Chicago stuff! Wot 'appened to the girl? Cor luv me! I'd given me eyes to 'ave seen 'er. She must 'ave been 'opping mad."

George smirked uneasily. "I didn't bother my head about her," he said, shrugging his shoulders. "I told her to scram, and she scrammed!"

"I bet she did," Little Ernie giggled. "And pinching a taxi! Wot an idea! That's brains! Lolly Cheese! I wouldn't 'ave thought of that one meself."

"Let's look at the clothes," Eva said. "What has he got you?"

"Of course!" Cora cried, snatching the bundle from George. "Let's see if his taste is good."

George giggled with excitement. He couldn't help it. Suddenly it seemed he was one of them. They were smiling at him, nodding at him. They said he had brains. Cora was like a kid in her excitement.

The two girls took the pillowcase over to the bed, while Little Ernie sidled up to George.

"Wot was she like, palsy?" he whispered. "Orl right?"

George winked. He suddenly quite liked this redheaded little man, and when Little Ernie nudged him in the ribs and put the obvious question, George shoved him off playfully and said, "That's telling."

There was a sudden silence that made him turn his head. Cora and Eva were looking at him. They were no longer smiling. There was a look of suppressed rage and disappointment in Cora's eyes that startled him.

"Do you like them?" he asked, with a catch in his voice.

Little Ernie moved forward. "Wot's hup?"

"Nothing," Cora said viciously. "I might have known the fool was pulling my leg. What are you trying to do. George? Get even?"

George suddenly went cold.

"What do you mean?" he said, feeling the blood leave his face.

"What I say," she said, pointing to the bundle on the bed. He pushed past her and turned the things over. At first he couldn't believe what he saw. He held up one garment and stared at it stupidly. It looked like a pair of black combinations, only it had a long tail. He dropped it as if it had bitten him and stared down at the rest of the stuff.

"It's a Mickey Mouse outfit," Eva cried suddenly. "My God! It's Mickey Mouse!"

Little Ernie started to laugh. Eva joined him. Together they shrieked at George and Cora.

"Wot a card!" Little Ernie spluttered. "In the middle of the night! Stone me! 'Ad our Cora properly. Oh dear, oh dear, this'll kill me!" He collapsed howling in an armchair.

George turned away. He wanted to be sick. He wanted to die.

He heard Cora say in a voice hoarse with frustrated rage, "Get out! Do you hear! Get out, both of you!"

And when Little Ernie and Eva, roaring with hysterical mirth, had stumbled out of the room, Cora turned on George.

"You rotten rat!" she said. "Do you think that's funny'? Do you think you can make a fool out of me?"

George wasn't listening. He picked up a scrap of notepaper that he had just noticed lying on the bed. It seemed to be a letter written in small, neat handwriting:

Dear Dick Turpin,
You really shouldn't trust a woman, and you should never threaten if you can't go through with it. I hope the girlfriend likes the costume. From the sound of her, I shouldn't trust her either. It's not April 1st yet, but remember this when it comes round. You did frighten me, you know. And I don't like people frightening me.

He became aware that Cora was standing at his elbow, reading over his shoulder. He screwed up the note and turned away, crushed and dazed.

Cora suddenly burst out: "So you weren't lying! You did it! And she made a fool out of you! God! What a sucker you are! What a damn, stupid, dim-witted fool!" And she suddenly went into peal after peal of jeering laughter. "Go away, you chump," she cried, throwing herself on the bed and rolling backwards and forwards, holding her sides. "Oh, it's the funniest thing I've ever heard. You sucker! You big tough, stupid sucker!"

George opened the door and went slowly down the passage to his room.

CHAPTER EIGHTEEN

The following night the first of three robberies took place at a garage on the Kingston Bypass. The police stated that the robberies were the work of one man, described by the three garage attendants as a big, powerful fellow with shoulders like an ox. They could give no better description than this, since the man had masked his face with a white handkerchief.

This fellow had walked into the Kingston Garage just after midnight. He seemed to know exactly what he was doing. He threatened the attendant with a Luger revolver, and before the attendant could gather his startled wits together, the man had given him a crushing punch on the jaw. When the attendant recovered consciousness, he found the till had been rifled and nearly twenty pounds were missing.

The following night a similar crime was committed at a garage on the Watford Bypass. The big man again succeeded in getting away, this time with thirty pounds.

Another attendant was attacked the next night in a garage on the Great West Road by the same man, and forty-five pounds were taken.

Then, as abruptly as they had begun, the garage robberies ceased.

George, with a net gain of nearly a hundred pounds, decided for the time being, not to tempt Providence further.

He had told no one what he had done; but Cora, reading of the robberies, knowing that the man who had been responsible for them was big and had carried a Luger, looked at George questioningly.

She was uneasy about George. Since the night she and the other two had laughed at him there had come over him a subtle change. He was hard now, and his temper inclined to fly up. There was a cold, bitter, brooding look in his eyes that Cora didn't like.

He had left Eva's flat before anyone was up on the morning following the scene with the Mickey Mouse costume. Cora, awakening to find him gone, hoped that she had seen the last of him, but he returned in the afternoon just as she was going out.

She was wearing a silk frock, silk stockings and high-heeled shoes borrowed from Little Ernie's wardrobe. Little Ernie and Eva had gone off to the dog racing at Wembley, and she was alone in the flat.

George came in and stood looking at her, the brooding expression in his eyes.

"What do you want?" she snapped, uneasy, and wondering why he had come back.

"Here," he said, thrusting an envelope at her, "buy yourself some clothes."

She took the envelope, and found inside five ten-pound notes. She knew the wise thing to do was to throw the money at him and tell him to go to hell, but fifty pounds impressed her, and she could not give up such a sum, no matter what the consequences might be.

"Where did you get this from?" she asked.

"I've had that sum by me," he returned, watching her. "I got it out of the post office for you. There's more where that came from."

"Well, thank you," she said, wondering just how much there was. Perhaps it would be as well, she thought, to wait a little while before getting rid of him.

"Now, come on," he said; "you're going to get yourself some clothes."

They went together, and when they returned, having spent all the money except for a pound or two, George pointed to the bedroom.

"Get out of that outfit," he said grimly. "You're not wearing clothes from a pimp."

She showed a flash to temper. "Who do you think you are?" she snapped. "I'll wear what I like."

Before she could stop him, he had reached out and had laid hold of the front of her dress in his thick fingers. He jerked her forward, and with a twisting movement he ripped the dress right down.

"Get out of those things or I'll tear them off you," he said, white as clay.

"You must be cracked," she gasped, startled out of her temper, but she went into the bedroom and changed into the clothes he had bought her.

When Little Ernie returned, he told them that he had a flat for them.

"How much?" George asked, staring with hot, intent eyes at the little man.

"Don't worry about that," Ernie said, shooting a quick glance at Cora. "You're my pal ..."

George walked over to him and caught him by his coat front.

"I ask no favours from you," he said between his teeth. "And listen, I don't like the way you look at Cora. She's my girl. If you try anything with her, I'll kill you. I shan't warn you again."

And Little Ernie, looking into the brooding eyes, suddenly went cold.

The flat that Little Ernie rented them was on the top floor of a block of offices in Holles Street, off Oxford Street. It was secluded and, after business hours, as lonely as a shepherd's hut on a Welsh mountain. It was vacant only because it was some distance from the usual haunts of the street prowlers.

George liked the place. It was his first proper home, and he took pride in it. He did everything in the house, including the cooking.

Cora, still in two minds as to whether she should stay or not, was influenced by the money that George had so suddenly acquired. She could ask him for anything and she got it. At first, it was clothes, and then it was jewellery. She was already brooding about a car; but she hadn't quite made up her mind what kind of a car to have.

She wasn't giving him anything in return. When he came to her room one night, a look of pleading hope in his eyes, she played a card which she was certain would keep him out of her room in the future.

She invited him to sit down; she even took his hand. Then speaking in a quiet voice, a sad expression on her face, she explained about Sydney. He was, she said, the only man she had ever loved. If George wanted payment, then she wouldn't resist him. But he would be making a prostitute of her, because, at the moment, she had no feelings for him. But if George were patient, if he let her recover from the shock of losing Sydney, then she might grow to love him. She was quite clever about this, and the look she managed to get into her eyes—a look of promise of wonderful things to come—completely fooled George.

He was crazy about her, and the thought of forcing his attentions on her was unthinkable. So it was agreed that she should have her own room, George should do the housekeeping and pay for everything, and Cora—well, they didn't come to any decisions about Cora. It seemed rather obvious that Cora wasn't to do anything.

And Cora did nothing. She stayed in bed most of the morning, reading the books George got for her from a twopenny library. She spent a long time before her mirror preparing herself for the day. They lunched together and loafed away the afternoon. In the evenings they either went to a movie or a theatre and had dinner out.

This kind of existence dragged on for a few days, and then George discovered his money was running out again. It was frightening how quickly money went, living in the West End with Cora as a companion.

He decided that he would have to stage another robbery. He viewed the prospects quite calmly. He had a lot of confidence in himself now. It seemed as if he were living a charmed life. He had killed a man, and no one had arrested him. He had attacked three garage attendants, and the police were still floundering. It would be all right, he decided, after some thought. He would leave garages alone this time and pick on a bank. That was dangerous, of course, but there was a lot of money to be found in banks: the prize was worth the risk.

He was sitting by the open window. It was eight o'clock in the morning, and Cora was still asleep. He sat there, making his plans, his hands caressing Leo's thick fur.

It was odd how he had brought Leo to the flat. The morning he had left Eva's place, after going to the post office to draw out the fifty pounds, he had returned to his room off the Edgware Road. He had hastily packed his things, paid his rent and told Mrs. Rhodes that he had been unexpectedly called out of town. He had said good-bye to Ella. She had known that something was wrong, and she had asked him outright.

"You're in trouble, ain't you, Mr. George?" she said. "Is it that gang you was telling me about?"

George nodded. He wished he could tell her the gang that was troubling him was a girl—far more dangerous than any make-believe gang he had bragged about in the past.

"I'll keep in touch, Ella," he said. "If anyone asks for me, tell 'em I've gone to Scotland on business. It's important that no one should know where I really am."

Leaving Ella thrilling with intrigue, he had picked up his bag, slung his mackintosh and overcoat over his arm and ran down the steps. It was while he was waiting for a taxi that Leo suddenly appeared. George put down his bag and stroked the cat. He suddenly realized that he was going to miss Leo. Leo meant so much to him: understanding, companionship, love even—odd things like that.

A taxi drew up, and George opened the door, put his bag and overcoat on the seat and gave the driver Eva's address. Then, without stopping to think, he picked Leo up, and got into the taxi.

He was glad now that Leo was with him. He had hoped that Cora would have filled the hollow loneliness of his life, but somehow, although they were together so much, she seemed like a stranger. She talked, but her talk meant nothing. There was no love nor understanding in her look. She might really not be there.

Leo did not like Cora, and whenever she was in the room the cat would creep under the settee; but alone with George it would reveal an affection for him which did much to comfort the big, wretched man.

Sitting in the armchair, Leo on his knee, George made plans to rob a bank. It would have to be a village bank, he decided. There was only one way to discover the right kind of bank. He would have to hire a car, and he would also have to leave Cora for a few days. He must never incriminate her. He guessed she knew that he was the mysterious robber who masked his face with a white handkerchief. But they had reached a silent understanding that they should not mention the fact. If he were caught, she must know nothing about the robberies.

So it was arranged. George explained to Cora that he had to go off on business. She gave him a quick look, read his expression correctly, and agreed without protest. He hired a car, and after putting Leo in a cat's home for a few days—he did not trust Cora to feed the cat—he set off for Brighton.

It took him three days to find the bank he was looking for. It was a tiny place in a village a few miles from Brighton. The staff consisted of only a branch manager who opened the bank twice a week. It did not take George long to obtain the information he needed. It was extraordinary how easy it was to rob the place. Of course, he had thought out a plan and had spent a lot of time on the ground, but somehow he felt it shouldn't have been quite so easy. He entered the bank at a few minutes to three, just as the branch manager was closing the door. There was no one else in the bank, and the manager, a red-faced, cheerful man of about sixty, shut the door and bolted it before attending to George.

"You're the last customer, sir," he said, rubbing his hands. "I want some golf this afternoon."

George hit him with his clenched fist in exactly the spot where he had hit the garage attendants. The manager slumped to the floor, and that was all there was to it.

George helped himself to two hundred pounds. If there had been more he would have taken it, but two hundred pounds wasn't to be sneezed at. He left by the back way, drove to London without incident and handed the car back to the garage where he had hired it.

He returned to the flat after four o'clock. It was pretty obvious that the place hadn't been touched since he had been away. It was in a complete mess, and George felt suddenly depressed and a little irritated. He put Leo on the settee. He had collected the cat on his way back to the flat, and set to work to tidy up. Cora wasn't in. Her bedroom was dirty, and hopelessly untidy, and there was cigarette ash over everything.

It took him until almost six o'clock before he had straightened the flat, then he made himself a cup of tea and sat down. Leo got onto his lap.

George wondered where Cora had got to. He wondered hopefully if she had missed him. Perhaps tonight she would decide that it was time to be nice to him. Somehow he didn't think he could go on indefinitely like this. The strain was beginning to tell on him. He could understand her feelings for Sydney. Though how she could have loved a fellow like that defeated him. Sydney had been very firm with her. Perhaps he had better be firm, too. Perhaps ... he clenched his fists. It was no good think now. He would see her tonight.

Cora returned at half-past six. George heard her come in and go to her bedroom. Almost immediately she came into the sitting room.

"So you're back," she said, looking at him curiously.

He looked at her, aware of a tightening in his throat. She was wearing wine-coloured slacks and a white silk-and-wool sweater. Her long black hair curled to her shoulders and partly hid her right eye.

George drew in a quick, deep breath. The sweater and slacks set off her sensual little figure. The sight of her in these new clothes fired his blood. He pushed Leo off his lap and went to her.

"Cora!" he said, taking her in his arms. "Can't you be kind to me now? Do I have to wait much longer, Cora? Look!" He pushed her away and took out the roll of notes. "Two hundred pounds! Think what we can do with that! I can get more. But can't you give me just a little ...?"

She studied him, a strange expression in her eyes. "I think so, George," she said at last. "Yes, I think so. I think you've waited long enough."

He took her in his arms again and kissed her. She stood quite still, her eyes closed, cold, indifferent. He tried to move her by his kisses, but her mouth was a hard line. He let her go at last, and sat down.

"I've got to get used to the idea," she said gently. "It's no good rushing me. George, will you do something for me?"

He stared up at her, his face congested. "Aren't I always doing something for you?" he said hoarsely.

"This is such a little thing," she said, smiling. "Will you leave me for an hour? I want to think. I want to get used to the idea. I have a feeling that when you come back ..." She turned away. "Well, you'll be surprised, George. I promise you that."

He had gone at once, and he had spent the next hour tramping the back streets, continually looking at his watch, his hunger for her deadening him to any other feeling.

When he returned to the flat, she had gone. She had packed her clothes, taken her jewellery and gone. There was no personal thing of hers left in her room except the faint smell of sandalwood.

He stood looking round the room for a long time, and then he wandered into the sitting room. He glanced almost indifferently at the mantelpiece where he had left the two hundred pounds. That had gone too.

He was angry. This was the last time a woman would make a fool of him! He didn't blame her in a way. He should have guessed that she still loved Sydney too much to have any feeling for him. It wasn't that that made him angry. It was the knowledge that she had deliberately thrown dust in his eyes, sure of her ability to fool him as she had fooled him before, as Babs had fooled him. What kind of a man was he, that women could fool him so easily? He clenched his fists, cursing himself for being such a simple, trusting weakling.

No doubt she hadn't expected him to return so soon. She had probably been getting ready to leave when he had returned. So she had got rid of him with a promise, and instead of keeping the promise, she had packed and gone.

He lit a cigarette and, taking Leo on his lap, he stared out of the window. He remained like that until it grew dark. While he sat there, he decided that he would wash his hands of her. He would pack and go. He would go to Eastbourne. He had always wanted to go to Eastbourne, and now he would see what the town had to offer him. He would put all this behind him and go back to his bookselling. It wasn't much of a life, but anything was better than this ghastly, reckless existence.

He was still sitting there in misery, trying to bolster up his spirits, when he heard someone rapping on the door. At first he wasn't going to answer, but the rapping went on and on, so he got up finally and jerked open the door.

Eva was standing there.

He stared at her blankly, wondering what she wanted. "Yes?" he said, blocking the way. "What do you want?"

"Is Cora here?" Eva asked. There was a cold, spiteful look in her eyes.

He shook his head.

"Where is she?" Eva asked.

"I don't know."

"You mean she's left you?"

He nodded. "Please go away," he said, and began to close the door.

"Perhaps you don't know she's been sleeping with Ernie for the past four days," Eva said.

George looked at her. "I don't know why you've come here," he said. "But I don't intend to listen to your lies."

"Lies?" Her voice shot up. "Why, you dumb fool, why should I lie about a thing like that! I want you to do something about it. Do you think I want a bitch like that to steal my man?"

George went cold. "I don't believe you," he said. "She's in love with Sydney. She wouldn't ..." And he stopped. Was this another of Cora's little tricks? Was all that talk about being in love with Sydney just an excuse to fob him off?

"She's been after Ernie for months," Eva said. "I've watched her. But until now Ernie hasn't been having any. But she's got money now. She's giving him things. She promised to give him a car! He's not satisfied with the car I gave him. Oh no, he wants another! She's been working for him all this week. Making money ... big money! Well, you've got to stop her! Do you hear? You've got to stop her!"

George clenched his fists. A red curtain hung before his eyes. So that's what she had been doing with his money. Giving it to Ernie, winning Ernie's attention.

"Working?" he said. "What do you mean?"

"He's given her a beat," Eva returned, her voice hoarse with suppressed fury. "And a flat in Old Burlington Street."

"Where's her beat?" George heard himself ask.

"Sackville Street," Eva returned, suddenly frightened by the ruthless, hard face before her.

"All right," George said, and closed the door in her face.

Fifteen minutes later he left the flat and walked across Hanover Square towards Sackville Street. Streetwalkers moved slowly along the back streets, paused to talk among themselves, looked at George hopefully and went on.

George walked down Sackville Street, along Vigo Street into Bond Street. He turned and retraced his steps. He had been doing this for over half an hour when he suddenly saw Cora. She was walking just ahead of a tall, well-dressed man in his middle fifties. She was loitering, a contemptuous expression on her hard little face.

George stepped into a shop doorway where he could watch, without being seen.

The well-dressed man overtook Cora, glanced at her and went on. She did not increase her pace, but kept on, swinging her hips, her head in the air.

The man walked as far as the street corner, and then stopped. He looked round furtively, noted that Cora was still coming towards him, and then looked up and down, as if to assure himself that no one was watching him.

Cora came on. She looked at him enquiringly as she paused before crossing the street.

The man raised his hat and said something. Cora smiled. She waved her hand towards Old Burlington Street. From the doorway, George could see the man eyeing her figure. He said something, and then looked away.

Cora turned and began to walk casually towards Old Burlington

Street, her hands in her pockets, her hips swinging. After giving her a start, the man followed her.

George came out of the doorway and followed them. They entered a tall building halfway down the street, and when he was sure that they were safely out of the way he went up to the front door. There were three bell pushes on the door. One of them had a little card: "Miss Nichols."

George stood looking at the card for several minutes, then he crossed the street and waited. He waited until the well-dressed man had left the building, and then he approached the place himself. As he was crossing the street again, he saw a man coming towards him. He thought it looked like Little Ernie, and he darted into a doorway, his hand flying to his gun.

It was Little Ernie.

George watched him coming down the street. Ernie called out cheerfully to a woman who was walking in the opposite direction. "'Ullo, ducks; don't loiter. There's still an 'our before bye-byes."

George gritted his teeth. The little rat had made Cora into one of these women! All right, he'd fix him. The world would be well rid of a filthy little brute like Ernie.

He stepped out of his doorway as Little Ernie turned into Cora's building. A few quick steps, and George was on him, as he was opening the front door with a key.

"Hello, Ernie," George said softly.

Little Ernie gave a squeal of terror. He spun round, throwing up his hands.

George rammed the gun into his side.

"I warned you, you rotten little rat. You won't get a car this time," and he pulled the trigger three times.

The noise of gunfire crashed down the empty street. The flash blinded George. But he wasn't nervous nor frightened. He watched Little Ernie flop on the steps of the house and then, bending over him, he shot him again.

A woman began to scream at the other end of the street.

George slipped the gun into his pocket and stepped from the shadow of the doorway. There was still no one about. Without hurrying, he walked to Clifford Street and stopped a passing taxi.

"Hyde Park Corner," he said, and got into the taxi.

He glanced through the little window at the back. People were appearing now. A policeman was running down Old Burlington Street. It was going to be all right. His luck was holding. In another few seconds he'd be out of danger. He sat back in the cab and closed his eyes.

He did not allow himself to think until he had paid off the taxi and was walking towards Knightsbridge. He had no horror at what he had done. It was as if he had stepped on a beetle, no more, no less.

What would Cora do? Would she tell the police? If she did that it would be the end of him; but he somehow didn't care. He was tired of this business, sick and tired of it. He wanted a little peace. Better keep away from the flat tonight, he thought. He wanted one more night of freedom. He'd go back the next morning. If the police were waiting for him, then he'd let them take him. But not tonight. He'd walk and walk, because he wanted to think. He wanted to make plans.

He woke the next morning in a Salvation Army hostel off the Cromwell Road. He remembered walking until he could walk no more, and had crawled into this place at three o'clock in the morning. Now it was just after seven o'clock, and he decided to return to his flat immediately.

On his way back he tried to think about Little Ernie, but what had happened the previous night had a dream quality about it, and he could not get his mind to believe that it had happened.

Even when climbing the stairs to the flat high above Holies Street, he could not believe that the police might be waiting for him. He was so tired, anyway, that he couldn't care one way or the other.

He pushed open the door, and for a moment hesitated, listening. There was no sound in the flat. He went into the sitting room. There was no one there, but there was a distinct smell of sandalwood in the room. He stood very still, trying to remember whether the scent had been there before Eva came to see him. He couldn't remember. Anyway, Cora wasn't likely to have returned. But the thought disturbed him, and he went quickly to his bedroom. Then he paused and looked blankly round the room. His cupboard and chest of drawers were open and empty. His clothes were scattered all over the room. One look at them was enough. They had been systematically ripped to pieces. His flannel trousers were in shreds. His tweed coat was armless and ripped down the back. His shirts were a mass of holes. Even his shoes were cut with a knife. Everything he owned was torn to pieces, as if it had been set upon by a wild animal.

Cora! Of course! She had come back to revenge Little Ernie.

Then he remembered Leo, and he felt so sick and faint that he had to sit on the bed. As he did so, he became aware of something in the corner, half hidden by the dressing table. He saw red streaks on the wall. He peered forward fearfully. In the shadowy light he could make out fur, blood, and then a squashed paw, and he closed his eyes.

He sat there shivering. After a while, he began to cry.

CHAPTER NINETEEN

Light rain began to fall, and islands of sullen grey clouds knitted together to form a depressing curtain of mist that blotted out the watery moon.

George stood in a shop doorway, his collar turned up and his hat well down on his ears. He carried Leo, wrapped in a bath towel; the bundle felt hard, a wood carving, against his side. He remained in the shelter of the doorway for some time, a lonely motionless figure, merged into the darkness, unseen.

One by one the lights behind the big window opposite, screened by the yellow muslin curtains, went out like the eyes of a robot figure closing in sleep. Several times the green-painted glass-panelled door with the gilt letters "Restaurant" on it, opened, and men and women, in pairs or singly, came out. George watched them disperse, their heads down, some arm-in-arm, moving rapidly to another more distant shelter.

There was only one light burning now. He could see the shadowy outlines of the big blonde woman, Emily, and the white-coated Hebrew, Max, through the curtain. The woman sat at the cash desk. He guessed she was emptying the till. The Hebrew seemed to be clearing up at the bar, washing glasses, drying them and putting them away.

It was time to talk to them. George crossed the street, pushed open the green-panelled door and entered the restaurant. The long room was stuffy, and smelt of food, cigars and coffee. The shaded light above the cash desk threw off an isolated yellow pool in the dim, smoky room.

"We're closed," Max said, continuing to put the glasses under the counter.

George looked first at the Hebrew and then at the woman, Emily. He closed the door and moved further into the light. Emily recognized him.

"Max ..." There was a quick, urgent note in her voice. She put her hand under the desk, and a bell began to ring somewhere in the building.

Max was bending down behind the counter, arranging the glasses in an orderly row. As he heard the bell and caught the sharp note in Emily's voice, he clashed the glasses together. One of them slipped from his fingers and dropped with a little thump on the carpet. He raised his head and peered at George, his pebbly eyes blank with alarm.

George waited. It was no use talking to them until they were ready to listen. At the moment their attention was concentrated in keeping him there, in trapping him.

"It's all right," he said, wanting to reassure them. "I've come to explain."

The two Greeks, black shadows, threatening, slid out of the darkness and stood between him and the door. The shaded light glittered on their razors.

"You mustn't let them touch me before I explain," George said quickly, not liking the expressions on the Greeks' faces. "That's why I've come."

Max straightened slowly. He put his veined hands on the counter, and his pale tongue touched the corners of his lips.

"Leave him be," he said to the Greeks.

There was a long pause. They did not seem to know what to expect or what to do with him now that they had got him.

George looked uncertainly at the Hebrew, and then at the woman. It seemed to him that since she was in charge of the cash, she should be the one he should address.

"May I tell you about it?" he said, looking at her anxiously.

Again there was a long pause, then Emily leaned forward. "You know what will happen to you, don't you?"

George nodded.

"Then why have you come here?"

He offered her the bundle. Immediately she drew back, suspicious, alarmed. The two Greeks made a slight movement: two blades of light danced on the ceiling as they lifted their razors.

The Hebrew said, "Wait." George's white face, the sharp etched lines of misery, his despairing eyes puzzled him. "What is that?" he asked, nodding at the bundle.

George put the bundle on the counter. "It's my cat," he said unevenly.

The woman looked at the bundle and then at George. "What's he talking about?" she asked impatiently.

Max touched the bundle with two bony fingers. He felt the hard body and he grimaced.

"Is this a trick?" he said, not believing it was a trick, but bewildered.

"Would you mind looking?" George said. "Could you look so that I don't have to see him again?" His mouth tightened. "I'm sorry to be so upset, but he was really the only thing that meant anything to me."

"Perhaps he's mad," Emily said, half to herself.

Reluctantly, the Hebrew lifted the corner of the towel. His face revealed an impersonal disgust, but he turned the bundle so that the woman could see.

"She did that," George said.

Both Emily and Max seemed to know whom he meant.

"Ah," Max said, dropping the towel. "It was your cat?"

George nodded. "I didn't think she'd do such a thing. I knew she might do anything to me, but I didn't think she would touch Leo. I suppose I ought to have thought of it, because there was nothing else she could have done which would have hurt as much as this."

"Is that what brought you here?" Emily asked abruptly.

"Oh yes," George said. "She can't be allowed to go on and on. She might hurt too many people. That's why I've come to you."

"You killed Crispin, didn't you?" Emily said, in a flat, cold voice.

"That's what I mean," George returned steadily. "I've come to explain. Then you must decide what to do."

"You were foolish to come," Max said softly. "You know what happened to Sydney?"

Again George nodded. "It doesn't matter about me," he said. "I don't care what happens to me. I just want to be sure that she won't escape."

Max glanced over at Emily.

"I think we should hear what he has to say," he said. "It might save a lot of time."

Emily nodded and walked round the cash desk. She crossed to a table and turned on the lamp. She sat down and pointed to a chair opposite her.

"Sit down and talk," she said.

George sat down. The two Greeks moved nearer so that they were immediately behind him. The Hebrew left the bar and joined them at the table.

"Perhaps one of you would take the gun," George said. "It's in my pocket. I don't suppose you would like me to take it out. Be careful how you handle it, it's loaded."

He felt the gun being lifted from his pocket. Nick slid it across the table towards Max, who put his hand on it.

"I want to tell you exactly how it happened," George said. "It'll take a little time, but it's important."

Emily shrugged. "Take as long as you like," she said indifferently. "It'll probably be the last time you'll talk to anyone."

George considered this. He found it strange that he was unmoved. He knew they were killers, but he was so tired and sad that nothing really mattered any more.

It was a relief to tell them about it. It was extraordinary how easy it was to tell once he started. He began by explaining about his parents.

"You see," he said, folding his hands on the table and looking at the woman's hard, fat face, "no one ever bothered with me when I was a kid. My parents were on the stage. They didn't want a child. I used to envy them. They had their names in the newspapers and on hoardings. I wonder if you can understand why I pretended to be someone quite different from what I really am? It was foolish, but I wanted so badly to be someone ... to impress people."

The woman nodded, understanding. She thought sadly of her son, Crispin. He also had wanted to impress people. "Go on," she said, "I understand that part of it."

"When I told Sydney about the gun he changed towards me. I know why now. I was just the fool he was looking for, but I didn't know then. It wasn't until after I shot Crispin that I knew."

They all stiffened when he said that. Nick reached forward and seized him by the back of his neck, but Max struck his hand away.

"Wait," he said.

"So you did shoot him?" Emily said, her eyes snapping.

"Oh yes," George returned, "it was an accident, but I shot him all right. It's something I'll never forgive myself for."

He told them about Cora.

"I don't understand women," he explained. "I've never had anything to do with them. It all happened so quickly. She rather swept me off my feet. I've been very stupid, I'm afraid."

He went on, explaining every detail, showing them the gun. He explained how Sydney had fixed the trigger and had stolen the cartridge. He pulled out the magazine and demonstrated how easily the gun fired. He told them how careful he had always been never to put a cartridge into the breech.

"I was afraid of accidents," he said, "but they loaded the gun without telling me. You see, they were determined to make me a murderer."

The woman and the Hebrew sat listening, their faces intent. The two Greeks wanted to have done with it. George could feel their restlessness. He knew they were not interested in what he had to say. He sensed that they were planning how to get rid of his body when they had finished him.

He told them about the whip and the visit to the cottage.

"I don't really know how it happened. She gave me the gun. I heard her slip back the safety catch, but it all happened so quickly that I had no chance to do anything. As soon as I touched the trigger, the gun went off."

Max blew his nose.

"I don't think there's anything else to tell you," George went on, leaning back in his chair, suddenly tired. "A lot has happened to me since then, but I won't bother you with that. I don't know what you want to do with me, but I know what I want you to do with her."

They looked at him.

"What do you want us to do with her?" Emily asked softly.

"I want justice," George said simply.

"Sydney's gone," Max said, looking down at his veined hands. "No one can touch one of us without paying the price. Crispin was one of us, you know."

Emily touched his arm. Her eyes reached George's face. "Where is she?"

George told her.

She got to her feet. "We'll go and see her."

"What about him?" Nick said, speaking for the first time.

"He'll come with us."

"It would be better ..." Nick began, but Emily shook her head.

"He'll come with us," she repeated.

She went over to the desk and put on a light coat.

"Get a taxi," she said.

Max changed his white coat for a black one, put on his bowler hat and picked up an umbrella.

"It's raining," he said gloomily.

While Poncho went for a taxi, Nick stood over George, threatening him with the razor. Somehow George felt no fear. He was hollow, without feeling, disinterested.

They waited, while the rain fell outside, and the sound of distant traffic vibrated the big windows.

A taxi drew up outside.

"All right," Emily said, picking up the Luger and putting it into her bag.

George stood up. "If you please ..." he began and stopped.

They looked at him.

"It's my cat," he said. "Could he be buried?"

Max nodded. "We'll bury him," he said, almost kindly.

George touched the bundle. He didn't want to leave Leo like this, wrapped in a soiled bath towel on a bar counter. Leo deserved something better than this, but there were other things to do. Besides, George was tired. He had no idea where to bury Leo. Cora must have felt the same way about Sydney. It was better, perhaps, to leave the cat in the hands of strangers.

A clock was striking eleven as they got into the taxi. Max and Emily sat on the turn-up seats. George, between the two Greeks, sat opposite them.

It did not take them long to reach Old Burlington Street.

"Shall I tell him to wait?" Max asked.

"We'll be some time." Emily said, "better not."

They watched the taxi drive away, and then they walked into the building and up the stairs.

George went first, then Nick, then Emily, then Max, clutching his umbrella, and finally Poncho. They were quiet. The soft scraping of their shoes on the coconut matting sounded like the scamper of rats.

George paused outside the flat door.

"This is it," he said. "Shall I ring the bell?"

Nick pushed him aside, looked at the lock, took something from his pocket, and a moment later there was a soft click as the door opened.

The light was on in the lobby, and a door opposite was ajar. There was a light on in the room.

Emily touched George's arm and motioned him forward. He shook his head, but again she pushed him. So he went into the room, leaving the others outside in the lobby.

The room was large and well furnished. Cora was sitting in an armchair. A cigarette dangled from her thin mouth. She was still wearing the white silk-and-wool sweater and wine-coloured slacks. There was a scraped-bone look on her face, but her lips were twisted in a humourless smile. She was holding a packet of pound notes in her hand, counting them with rapt concentration.

George stopped just inside the doorway, looking at her.

Her fingers ceased moving and she raised her head, fear jumping into her eyes. When she saw who it was, her mouth tightened.

"Get out!" she said, folding the notes quickly and slipping them into her pocket.

George continued to stare at her.

"Get out!" she repeated, her eyes wary. "We're quits, aren't we? Don't stand there looking at me. I'm not frightened of you."

What's the matter with me? George asked himself. Why am I feeling like this? I'm not still in love with her. I hate her.

"I wouldn't have done this if you'd let Leo alone," he said in a small voice. "Animals are so helpless. I suppose that's why I like them."

She got to her feet, an ugly expression in her slate-grey eyes. "What are you drivelling about?"

"I want you to know why I've done this."

"Done what?" she asked sharply.

"You see, you might do an awful lot of harm if you were allowed to go on and on. It's got to stop, Cora. I can't trust you any more," and he turned to the door and threw it open. "Will you come in, please?"

Emily and Max walked in. The two Greeks followed them. Nick slid across the room to the window, while Poncho closed the door and set his back against it.

Cora's hand flew to her mouth. "No!" she screamed, and her eyes rolled up, so that only the whites showed.

Emily marched over to the armchair and sat down. She opened her coat and fluffed up her untidy hair.

"Before we get down to business," she said, ignoring Cora, "I'd like a cup of tea. Can you make tea?" She looked at George.

"Oh yes," he said blankly, "but don't you think ...?"

"I don't," Emily snapped. "Get me a cup of tea, there's a good fellow."

George turned and looked helplessly at Poncho, who stared back at him with menacingly dark eyes.

"Let him make some tea," Emily said, watching them.

"He'll run away," Poncho argued, a little angrily.

"I don't think he will," Emily returned, taking out a packet of Woodbines from her bag and lighting one. "If he does, it won't matter."

Poncho shrugged and stood away from the door. George went out through the lobby into the little kitchen across the way. Not quite knowing what he was doing, he put on the kettle and laid a tray. He was glad to have something to do. Every now and then a tiny spark of horror flared up in his mind, but instantly it sparked out. He knew now that Emily was going to let him go free. By telling him to make the tea, she had shown that she had believed his story and she wasn't holding him responsible. It was justice. He had no pity for Cora. There would be nothing to worry about, not the way Emily would do it. Although he did not know how she would do it, he was sure that it would be as efficient and undetectable as Sydney's death.

He made the tea and carried the tray into the sitting room.

Max had sat down. His bowler hat and umbrella lay at his feet. He was glancing through a notebook, absorbed. Emily sat in a heap, her fat little feet stretched out before her, the cigarette dangling limply from her lips. She was looking round the room with a blank look in her eyes, her mind far away.

Cora still stood against the wall, her face twisted in a mask of frozen terror. She did not look up as George entered. The room was silent, and he distinctly heard the rumbling of her inside. She coughed nervously, as if to hide the sound, but George knew how frightened she was.

Poncho closed the door after George. He seemed startled to see him again.

George put the tray on the table. He was surprised to find how indifferent he was to all this. He felt cold, pitiless, and he realized then what real hatred meant. The discovery shocked him.

"Will you have some?" he asked vaguely, looking round. No one said anything, and he looked helplessly at Emily for guidance.

"I want a cup," she said. "Never mind about anyone else."

He poured out the tea and handed the cup to her.

"I think ... perhaps ... I'll have a cup myself," he said apologetically.

Emily stirred her tea, added sugar and sipped. Then she nodded to George. "It's good tea."

"Don't you think ...?" Max said, glancing at Cora.

Emily's hard little eyes snapped. "We don't have to talk to her," she said. "It's a question of how it's to be done."

Cora pointed to George. "He did it," she said breathlessly. "You can't blame me. He did it. He shot Crispin."

Emily smiled. "We know all about that," she said. "He told us." She looked Cora up and down. "No one can harm us without paying. You were in it as deep as Sydney. You must go too." She glanced at Poncho. "Arrange it, and be quick. An accident with an electric iron ... if there is one here."

Poncho came back after a few minutes with a portable ironing board, an electric iron and some underwear he had found in Cora's bedroom.

"Everything," he said, with a triumphal grin.

He worked quickly and methodically, setting up the ironing board and plugging in the iron. Then he produced a penknife and began working on the flex.

Emily noticed George's blank gaze.

"He's clever," she said, smiling. "In a moment that iron won't be safe to touch." She leaned forward. "They'll find her some time, and they'll think she died because of a faulty flex. The joke is, it will be because of a faulty flex."

Cora crossed the room slowly and stood before George. Her eyes were dark with terror.

"You're not going to let them do this to me, are you?" she said. "You can't do it." Then her voice suddenly rose to a scream. "George! You can't let them. Don't you understand what they're doing? They're going to kill me. Save me! I'll do anything! I swear I'll do anything if you'll only stop them! You can do it! You're big enough! Save me, George!" And she rushed forward, putting her arms round his neck, her face against his. "I'll never leave you, George," she went on wildly. "Forgive me! Don't let them touch me."

The feel of her slight body against his, the smell of her perfume, her hair against his face suddenly weakened him. He felt sick and faint.

Nick snatched her away from him, twisting her arms behind her.

"Have you forgotten your cat so soon?" Emily said, looking at him thoughtfully. "You'd better go. You needn't bother with her or us any more. You're lucky. You tell a good story, and I think it's true. I'm sorry about your cat. You mightn't think it, but I like animals myself."

"George!" Cora screamed. "Don't go! Don't leave me!"

Nick put his hand across her mouth. His fingers dug into her cheek.

"Go now," Emily said.

George walked unsteadily to the door. He hesitated, then went on out of the flat to the stairs. As he began to walk down the stairs a dreadful cry of terror and despair tore through the door past him into the dimly lit confines of the building. He shivered, the bleakness in his heart frightening him; but he kept on. Then there was a bright flash of blue light from the fuse box at the bottom of the stairs, and the lights went out. He knew that Cora would never worry him again.

For a moment he stood still, trying to see in the suffocating darkness. Thoughts flashed through his mind. Where was he going? What was he going to do? He would be lonely. There was no Leo now. There was no Cora either. He would have nothing. The future loomed before him: dark, empty, ageless.

He reached the front door, opened it and stepped into the rain. Men appeared from out of the darkness and crowded round him. He saw the glistening capes and the police helmets.

"What ...?" he began, weak with fear.

"I'm Detective-Inspector Tuck," a voice said, and George could just make out a tall man wearing a bowler hat pushing his way through the little crowd of policemen. "I think you are George Fraser. It's my duty to arrest you and charge you with the robbery of a garage near Kingston."

George blinked at the detective, then his fear went away and he sighed with relief. In his bones he had felt all along that they would get him in the end. Well, now they had him. It was a good thing that all this ghastly business was ended.

"Oh yes ..." he muttered, aware that two policemen were running their hands over his clothes.

"Stop," the detective said quickly. "I have also to caution you that any-thing you say will be written down and may be used in evidence at your trial."

"I understand," George said. "Thank you, but I want to tell you everything. You want me for murder too." He drew himself up feeling a sudden sense of pride. "I killed Crispin and Little Ernie."

They took hold of his arms, but they were quite gentle with him, and when the detective spoke again he sounded kind.

"Little Ernie? You did that? Hmmm, well, all right; it's a good thing to get everything off your chest. You come along with me. Who's this fellow Crispin you're talking about?"

"Oh, it's a long story," George said, suddenly feeling tired. "But the others are up there. They've just killed Cora. You'll find them all up there: Emily, Max and the two Greeks. You mustn't let them get away."

Four of the policemen pushed past him and entered the building. He could hear them running up the stairs.

"I don't know how you found me ..." George said, moving towards the car. "I've always read how clever you are. I thought somehow ..."

"You were identified," the detective said, getting into the car and sitting beside him. "The fellow at Kingston saw you about an hour ago. He telephoned the Yard, and here we are. We've had our eye on you for some time. We didn't like the company you kept. Here, have a cigarette." He offered a crumpled carton.

"I don't think I'll smoke," George said slowly. "I didn't drink my tea. Do you think I could get a cup where we are going? My mouth is very dry."

"That's all right," the detective assured him. "That's all we do—drink tea. There'll be a cup for you all right."

George nodded. "I suppose they'll hang me," he said. "You know, I'm not afraid. I've been awfully lonely all my life."

"Now don't talk like that," the detective returned, looking at him sharply. "While there's life there's hope, you know. You don't have to get depressed."

"Oh, I'm not depressed," George returned. "I'm really quite happy now."

A moment later the car took him away to meet his destiny.

THE END

JAMES HADLEY CHASE BIBLIOGRAPHY
(1906-1985)

No Orchids for Miss Blandish (1939; reprinted as The Villain and the Virgin, 1948)

The Dead Stay Dumb (1940; reprinted as Kiss My Fist!, 1952)

Twelve Chinks and a Woman (1940; reprinted as 12 Chinamen and a Woman, 1950, and as The Doll's Bad News, 1974)

Miss Callaghan Comes to Grief (1941)

Get a Load of This (1941; stories)

Miss Shumway Waves a Wand (1944)

Eve (1945)

I'll Get You for This (1947)

Last Page (1947; play, filmed as Man Bait)

The Flesh of the Orchid (1948)

You Never Know With Women (1948)

You're Lonely When You're Dead (1949)

Lay Her Among the Lilies (1950; reprinted as Too Dangerous to be Free, 1951)

Figure It Out for Yourself (1950; reprinted as The Marijuana Mob, 1952)

Strictly for Cash (1951)

The Double Shuffle (1952)

The Fast Buck (1952)

I'll Bury My Dead (1953)

This Way for a Shroud (1953)

Tiger by the Tail (1954)

Safer Dead (1954; reprinted as Dead Ringer, 1955)

You've Got it Coming (1955)

There's Always a Price Tag (1956)

The Guilty are Afraid (1957)

Not Safe to be Free (1958; reprinted as The Case of the Strangled Starlet, 1958)

Shock Treatment (1959)

The World in My Pocket (1959)

What's Better Than Money (1960)

Come Easy Go Easy (1960)

A Lotus for Miss Quon (1961)

Just Another Sucker (1961)

I Would Rather Stay Poor (1962)

A Coffin from Hong Kong (1962)

Tell it to the Birds (1963)

One Bright Summer Morning (1963)

The Soft Centre (1964)

This is for Real (1965)

The Way the Cookie Crumbles (1965)

You Have Yourself a Deal (1966)

Cade (1966)

Have This One on Me (1967)

Well Now, My Pretty (1967)

An Ear to the Ground (1968)

Believed Violent (1968)

The Whiff of Money (1969)

The Vulture is a Patient Bird (1969)

There's a Hippie on the Highway (1970)

Like a Hole in the Head (1970)

An Ace Up My Sleeve (1971)

Want to Say Alive? (1971)
You're Dead Without Money (1972)
Just a Matter of Time (1972)
Knock, Knock! Who's There? (1973)
Have a Change of Scene (1973)
So What Happens to Me? (1974)
Goldfish Have No Hiding Place (1974)
Believe This, You'll Believe Anything (1975)
The Joker in the Pack (1975)
Do Me a Favour Drop Dead (1976)
My Laugh Comes Last (1977)
I Hold the Four Aces (1977)
Consider Yourself Dead (1978)
Can of Worms (1979)
You Must be Kidding (1979)
Try This One for Size (1980)
You Can Say That Again (1980)
Hand Me a Fig Leaf (1981)
Have a Nice Night (1982)
We'll Share a Double Funeral (1982)
Not My Thing (1983)
Hit Them Where it Hurts (1984)

Omnibus Editions

Three of Spades (1974; includes The Double Shuffle, Shock Treatment and Tell It to the Birds)
Meet Mark Girland (1977; includes This is for Real, You Have Yourself a Deal and Have This One on Me)
Meet Helga Rolfe (1984; includes An Ace Up My Sleeve, A Joker in the Pack and I Hold Four Aces)

As Raymond Marshall
(reprinted as by Chase except *)

Lady Here's Your Wreath (1940)
Just the Way It Is (1944)
Blonde's Requiem (1945)*
Make the Corpse Walk (1946)
No Business of Mine (1947)*
Trusted Like a Fox (1948; reprinted as Ruthless, 1955)
The Paw in the Bottle (1949)
Mallory (1950)
In a Vain Shadow (1951; reprinted as by Marshall as Never Trust a Woman, 1957)
But a Short Time to Live (1951; reprinted as The Pick-Up, 1955)
Why Pick on Me? (1951)
The Wary Transgressor (1952)
The Things Men Do (1953)
The Sucker Punch (1954)
Mission to Venice (1954)
Mission to Siena (1955)
You Find Him—I'll Fix Him (1956)
Hit and Run (1958)

As James L. Docherty
(reprinted as by Chase)

He Won't Need it Now (1939)

As Ambrose Grant
(reprinted as by Chase)

More Deadly Than the Male (1946)

As René Raymond
(reprinted as by Chase)

The Mirror in Room 22 (1946; story, appeared in Slipstream: A Royal Airforce Anthology edited by René Raymond and David Langdon)

For further info on the works of James Hadley Chase, visit www.hadleychase.co.nr, compiled by Dr. P. C. Sarkar. This is the definitive Chase website.

"The king of all thriller writers!"

James Hadley Chase

978-1-933586-38-0
Come Easy—Go Easy /
In a Vain Shadow
$19.95
Two hardboiled thrillers from the master of the plot twist, originally published in 1960 and 1951. Includes a new introduction by Rick Ollerman.

978-1-944520-06-9
No Orchids for Miss Blandish /
Three Chinamen and a Woman
$19.95
Chase's first and most famous gangster kidnapping novel, paired with a second early detective thriller, available in their unabridged and unexpurgated versions for the first time in 75 years!

978-1-944520-07-6
He Won't Need It Now /
The Dead Stay Dumb
$19.95
Originally published in 1939 and 1940, two novels of gangsterism, corruption and greed, with a new introduction by Rick Ollerman.

978-1-944520-08-3
Lady—Here's Your Wreath /
Miss Callaghan Comes to Grief
$19.95
Two unexpurgated thrillers from the early 1940s featuring hardcase molls and hard-headed gunmen, white slavery and cold-blooded revenge. "Moves at a breathless speed." —*Manchester Evening News.*

978-1-944520-26-7
Just the Way It Is /
Blonde's Requiem
$19.95
"These two novels aptly show why Chase is well worth rediscovering by all lovers of crime fiction." —Alan Cranis, *Bookgasm*

In trade paperback from:

Stark House Press
1315 H Street, Eureka, CA 95501
griffinskye3@sbcglobal.net
www.StarkHousePress.com

STARK HOUSE

Available from your local bookstore, or order direct with a check or via our website.